THE BORO
PHALLACY

THE BORO PHALLACY

MICK RICHARDSON

First published in paperback in 2016 by Sixth Element Publishing
on behalf of Mick Richardson

Sixth Element Publishing
Arthur Robinson House
13-14 The Green
Billingham
Stockton on Tees
TS23 1EU
Tel: 01642 360253
www.6epublishing.net

British Library Cataloguing in Publication Data. A catalogue record for this
book is available from the British Library.

This is a work of satirical fiction. Names, characters, businesses, places, events
and incidents are either the products of the author's imagination or used in a
fictitious manner. Any resemblance to actual persons, living or dead, or actual
events and places is purely coincidental.

Printed in Great Britain.

ETERNAL THANKS

This book would never have reached completion, had it not been for the love, support and words of encouragement from family and friends. To this end, I'd like to use this space to personally thank those people that made it happen.

The Disciples of Jesus

Mel Small
6e Publishing's Gillie & Graeme
Catherine Richardson
Dad
Chris Butterwick
Micky Conlon
Noorah Knowles
Tim Prettyman
Mandy Cowey
Craig Jenkinson
Mark Hunt
Dave Alton
Jon Curran
Dave Richardson
John O'Hare
Peter Frost
Ian Hugill
Mark Jackman
Alison Kirby
Ann-Louise Maddox
Jane 'Penelope' Stevenson
Andy Stevenson
Andy Wilson
Karl Lilley
Emma Fletcher
Gavin Rutter
Sarah Turner
Rachel Willey

VIEWING THE AUTHOR

Ladies and Gentlemen, thank you for taking the time to view this book. Hopefully you'll be intrigued enough to buy it, read it and digest it before unceremoniously throwing it on the fire whilst saying three hail Marys. Children, if you have picked it up, sniggering at the silly title that's emblazed across the front, then put it down now, it's not for your innocent eyes.

I was told a while back that writing a work of fiction allows people to look inside the head of the author. So with that in mind, I thought it best to pre-warn you all as to what you are about to read. I'd then like to offer a weak excuse, no defence because if I don't go to court over this book then surely a stint in the looney bin beckons.

This book contains approximately 252 swear words, is poorly written and will never ever win the Booker prize for literature. I'm no William Shakespeare, that will become apparent early on, and poetic licence is somewhat hidden in a creative injustice to which the Royal Society of Literature still mourn.

It is, however, very funny, rather crass, embarrassingly crude and makes 28 different references to the male sex organ. It also resides in the British Library alongside Wuthering Heights, Jane Eyre and The Lord of the Rings.

Ha! In your face Mr Plummer.

So before you cross the road when you see me or judge the weird neurons that spark inside my head, know this:

I was raised and still live in Middlesbrough. I'm a father, husband, uncle, brother, cousin and godparent. I drink lager and adore the Boro. I've survived an assassination attempt by my youngest sister, have been involved in seven car crashes, had two emergency landings in helicopters, almost capsized on a ferry, had one emergency brake applied on a plane during take-off and walked away from a 15 tonne, cyclohexane vapour cloud that didn't ignite. As a result, I try not to take life too seriously. I suggest when you read this book, you take the same philosophy. Enjoy!

ENDEARING THOUGHTS
OF LOVE AND GRATITUDE

For my long suffering wife Catherine
and my three adorable children, Alex, Matthew and Emily.

I pray you never read this.

RITUAL FOREWORD

As I understand it, the idea for this book came about in a pub. Purists may well say that a licensed premises is no place from which to grow a work of literature, but then maybe not. Maybe it's this great country's fondness of a lager shandy that has cast our influence across the globe. I'm quite sure that the poetic form of the sonnet would have extended beyond its now traditional fourteen lines had Shakespeare not fallen off his barstool, propelling his hardboiled egg across the spit and sawdust in his decline. An unfortunate loss for the Bard, but in the same instant a seminal moment for scotch egg lovers everywhere.

Anyway, about the book. It's actually difficult to describe in any fewer words than it's written in, but at the same time it can be summed up in one, funny. It's probably not for the easily offended, but then offence lives in the mind of the offended. If you spend your life searching for opportunities to be shocked and appalled, then put this book back on the shelf now. If you're open-minded and enjoy a good laugh, then take it to the till.

In an attempt to describe what you will be purchasing, I'm reminded of an often cited fact that Eskimos have fifty words for snow. What rarely gets a mention is the far greater number of words that the much-maligned and often ignored Teessiders, few of whom have ever clubbed to death a seal, have for the male appendage. This tragedy is addressed within these pages, and I'm quite certain Mick has added a few more to the vernacular.

I write these few words in a year that took from us the creative geniuses that were David Bowie and Prince. Both of these took risks and ignored constraints. Mick may not be up there with such icons, but he certainly knows how to skip over the established boundaries.

Read on, my mates, and/or be damned.

UTB

Mel Small
Writer of This and That
www.melsmall.com

CHAPTER 1

Young Rob woke with a feeling of contentment. But then, doesn't everybody in those first few seconds? He opened his eyes slowly and allowed information to pour in, reasoning that it must be sometime during late morning, judging by the strength of the sun that was shining bright through a crack in the curtains. He could also hear the neighbours' muffled chat outside from the pavement below, no doubt giving each other the latest gossip from the turbulent Teesside grapevine. It was tittle tattle, he was pleased to note, that didn't involve him or his family this time around as it often did. When that chat subsided, Rob lay in his bed and listened to the sound of migrating birds in full song, nature's seasonal symphony that left him feeling surprisingly relaxed. An inner peace that told him all was well within the world that morning, and more importantly, within himself too, which was surprising really, considering the heavy session he'd had the night before. Although, in reality, it had been a night on the tiles that he could barely recollect.

He rubbed his eyes slowly as if it would somehow kickstart his brain. Piece by piece, he attempted to join the clues together. Lifting his head in a slow, controlled manner, he noted his clothes strewn on the floor, neither folded neatly nor placed with precision. It was clear to him that he'd been in a rush to hit the mattress last night, but then wasn't everybody who'd overdone the alcohol intake on a night out? Try as you might, when a Sleepeezee, king-sized bed came calling, you ran drunkenly into its warm, comfy arms. The detective work continued, with Rob next noticing a half-eaten doner pizza hanging precariously over the edge of his bedside cabinet. No alarm bells rang here either. This was a standard, boy's night out item and he'd have been more worried had he not seen the Turkish culinary delight, although the smeared garlic dip, in the devouring aftermath often left him retching.

He dropped his head back down on his pillow and gently slapped his weary face. Still, lying on his back in the rear bedroom of his comfortable Thornaby house, he simply couldn't recall his journey home, and his last recollection of the night was leaving the Europa restaurant around one. He'd lost count of how many times during his life he'd taken that 'mysterious beer scooter' home. That magical transportation device that steers you from drunken oblivion to the safe haven of one's own bed, or should he be lucky enough, somebody else's? Although luck, in Rob's case, could be rewritten as wishful thinking because in reality, he was still a virgin who had never scored with a bird in his life.

Glancing at the satellite clock, lodged in the bottom right corner of his peripheral vision, Rob was quickly becoming subdued. Something was starting to niggle at him. It was like a dark shroud cloaking his conscience. A familiar, yet unknown guilt in the pit of his stomach. The more he thought about it, the more the storm clouds in his mind gathered. He scanned the room once more, offering a more detailed search that the great Sherlock Holmes would have been proud of. Wall to wall and ceiling to floor, his eyes swept methodically, and it wasn't long before another clue presented itself. A black, three-point plug, placed in an electrical socket with the electric cable running across to the other side of the room. And upon that discovery, his heart plummeted into despair. Rob sat up to face the inevitable, if only to confirm his own self-doubt and, in doing so, set eyes upon the object he was hoping he wouldn't see. For sat there, staring at him with big admiring eyes of satisfaction, was the black and red face of Herbert the Hoover. It was at this point, he knew, with embarrassing realisation, it had happened again...

Rob was a robot, or rather a cybernetic organism built by Jesus to save the human race. Not Jesus Christ, the Saviour and Son of God, but Jesus Jones, an ex-instrumentation instructor from Middlesbrough's TTE College who had a dark art for all things electrical.

Rob and Jesus lived happily together in a father/son relationship, sharing a comfortable three up, two down home in Thornaby-on-Tees, a royal charter town within the borough of Stockton. It was a unique relationship that suited the two lonely characters but it was never without its dramas or problems. This was mainly due to the fact that not many people knew Rob was a robot and greeted his lack of emotional intelligence with contempt. Sure, his six-foot-four appearance was sharp, his movement slick and his voice carried a broad Teesside twang but at the end of the day, he was a robot, albeit a bloody good looking one, and his capacity for empathy was limited, and therein lay the problem. So great was Jesus's creation, that Rob often attracted unwanted female attention. And hell hath no fury like a woman scorned, or so the saying goes. Only this wasn't hell, not even close, it was the People's Republic of Teesside and the women hereabouts didn't take to kindly too rejection.

The fact Rob was a droid was never hidden, but then it was never advertised either. Certainly people from his past had at one point known he wasn't human, and Rob had quickly found celebrity status, but it's true what they say, time waits for no man so when Middlesbrough FC signed Brazilian footballer Juninho in the summer of ninety-five a new demigod was born. With Rob moving from house to house and the sands of time quickly draining away, he simply fell into oblivion, a dark abyss of obscurity just like H from Steps. Whoever that might be.

Yes, Jesus was a master craftsman and you'd never guess the origins of his creation, well, not unless you got up close and personal. Some of Rob's hidden parts were stamped with the ICI logo, but then who hadn't stolen from the giant chemical company at one time or another? Even if it was just a plaggy bag in which to go sledging?

Jesus, by contrast to Rob, was a small, slender guy, who sported long, eccentric, greying hair and had a dress sense that suggested he smeared himself in glue every morning and then ran through the wardrobe. He was an only child, born to a couple of ex-hippies who conceived him one winter solstice when Stonehenge was covered deep in snow, and yet, despite his name, he found religion to be boring and false.

He had remained single for the vast majority of his life, after being unceremoniously dumped by Mary, the only woman he had ever loved. They had courted for many years and held plans of wedlocked grandeur before they eventually split after Mary announced that she was pregnant. It was a revelation that had shaken poor Jesus to the core, especially as they had agreed to wait until marriage. Immaculate conception, Mary called it. Misdirection was closer to the truth. Despite his pleas, she never once revealed the father's identity and left to live in a barn. A lovely, renovated, Grade II listed building, on the outskirts of Picton.

Jesus never recovered and sought a new direction of his own, joining the Royal Navy, where he became a decorated veteran of the Falkland Islands conflict. It was this decision to sign up to the armed forces that would play a huge part in his life later on, for it was while in the South Atlantic that his career in electronics unwittingly began. He took exception to poor manmade weapons of war when a surface to air missile he was using jammed as he tried to shoot down an incoming Mirage. Realising the immediate peril he was in, Jesus threw the launcher to the ground and ran for cover, only for the SAM to unload its lethal shell as it bounced on the ground. The result saw Private Jones shoot himself up the jacksie. The bitterness he felt never went away. Although, thankfully, the humiliation eventually did.

Returning a hero, albeit a jobless one with a limp, he vowed to right a few wrongs and set about constructing his first ever invention… the un-jamable rocket launcher. 'Broken Arrow', as he simply called it, was in some respect a huge success because it never ever did jam. But then it never operated correctly either and would often fire off spontaneously and without warning. These were events not lost on the population of Grove Hill, who turned up mob-handed one night and drove Jesus from his Keith Road home. Not because his incendiary bombs were a danger to housing or residence, far from it, but rather they attracted the attention of the boys in blue, and nobody in the area wanted that.

Forced to live in Haverton Hill after the unsavoury incident at the hands of the mob, he lasted another two weeks before 'Broken Arrow' fired its last ever round. Walking around the back of the Calor Gas site, with the armed weapon slung over his shoulder, the launcher backfired and sent an unguided round hurtling over the River Tees. It just missed the Transporter Bridge, but unfortunately slammed into the Tuxedo Royale causing her to take on water and immediately list. Luckily, she never went down due to the numerous Sainsbury's shopping trolleys propping her up, but the episode did bring to an end the party boat's days. It also prompted Jesus to move to a new abode. Holme House Prison, at Her Majesty's pleasure…

Rob threw the Star Wars duvet covers off his naked torso and swung his legs over the side of the bed. He sat for a while, allowing his central processing unit to do its daily scan for bugs. If last night's shenanigans had turned out half as bad as he was thinking, then it wouldn't be the first time he'd had to call the Norton service desk for advice on a virus. Once that was complete, he rose gingerly and shuffled, embarrassed, past Herbert without offering a second glance. He moved to the window, opening the curtains with sarcastic ceremony, a move so far removed from how he was actually feeling that it allowed him a wry smile, before finally descending the stairs to look for his charger. He knew he'd need to juice up and set about his daily chores before Jesus returned. The old boy had some form of OCD and everything had to be spotless or you'd face his wrath. And with the growing hangover Rob was carrying, that was something he could quite easily do without.

Rob needed to re-charge every forty-eight hours, which was a pain in the arse but Jesus had managed that problem amicably over the years but not without incident. The problem he found was technology; it had advanced so fast that various methods of battery boost had, over time, been utilised. In his infancy, Rob had required thirty-four AA batteries just to communicate and a car battery in order to move about. But that method had needed to change when his car battery leaked during a school science lesson. The hydrogen gas had built up quickly and found its way to the overhead projector the teacher was using. The pure hydrogen-oxygen mix ignited and burned almost invisible flames and poor Rob just sat there unwittingly heating up. For ten minutes he burned, only aware that the temperature was rising, and so, feeling rather warm, he started to strip off his clothes, much to the amusement of his adolescent classmates who wolf whistled as Rob pulled his Slazenger top over his head. Becoming irate at the growing commotion, Mr Keenan ordered the agitated youngster to sit down and behave, but Rob was having none of it.

"I'm fucking red hot, sir," shouted the cyborg, in a statement that further enraged the physics boffin, who proceeded to run at Rob and wrestle him to the ground. They entered into a crocodile death roll as Rob's now frenetic classmates formed a circle and cheered. Rob, far from happy at his teacher's show of strength, went crashing into the phosphorus store, his burning battery providing the only ignition source needed, thus ensuring the science block became no more. With half the school instantly razed to the ground, he was put on detention before later being suspended for swearing at a teacher too.

Over time, Jesus had been able to perform miracles with Rob's ageing circuits and had managed to adapt Rob's now lithium battery so that it could be powered up from the mains. So, with the turn of the century and the birth of the iPod, a sustained period of stable charging then followed. Jesus, though, had a practical mind but not much common sense and had placed Rob's charging port directly beneath the fly of his jeans. 'A practical and easy access port' was the thinking, but more problems arose when charging was required outside of the home. This was because Rob was often asked to leave the premises when he fumbled inside his fly. Life was never easy for the young cyborg.

In the early days, charging from the mains had caused Rob to shut down, the two hundred and forty volts overloading his circuits, rendering him powerless. This gave any passers-by the impression that the poor boy had been killed in a kinky game of shag the socket and caused Rob much embarrassment every time he rebooted. Jesus though, often made light of it, telling him he looked like he'd had a stroke, and the two of them would use this dark humour whenever a recharge was imminent. All was well, until Jesus arrived to pick Rob up from Sunday school with his battery flashing low. With the priest addressing the congregation on abstinence, Rob stood up to leave, much to the annoyance of the clergyman.

"You not enjoying the sermon, Robert?" asked the man of the cloth sarcastically.

"Oh yes," replied Rob, unzipping his fly. "But I need to have a little stroke." Once again, the poor boy was asked never to return.

Rob began his half-arsed attempt at tidying the house. Shuffling toward the kitchen, he first placed the dirty cups in the sink before turning his attention to the overflowing bins. But his enthusiasm for housework soon began to wane, so he parked his arse on the settee and waited for his monster hangover to rally for another counter attack. He lay there motionless, slumped on the sofa. He found if he moved his head left or right then the effect was like a herd of buffalo trampling his brain, and it was at sour times such as these that he cursed the fact he had artificial intelligence and the fact that a robot could, indeed, be hungover.

The AI technology was the brainchild of Adventure, a large company who accidentally stumbled upon its discovery while developing the video game, Your Life, the strategic life simulation video series which was, in its early years, originally designed to replace man. The idea was to create a world where machines would take over all manual labour and thus prolong human life with early retirement. The theory proved faultless, but, in practice, was flawed and the whole project crumbled when an early version of artificial intelligence was placed inside a robot and sent to work in Pripyat, a small city in the Ukraine. The droid, named simply Boris, was placed on nights with a skeleton crew of humans and its remedial shift tasks were to monitor the temperatures and pressures at the local power plant. This it did with great distinction, winning Employee of the Month four times in a row and Adventure saw the pound signs flashing before their eyes but with human/Russian interaction almost constant, it was inevitable that Boris would acquire a taste for Beluga vodka. Turning up absolutely shitfaced for work one night, he fell asleep while watching reactor four and the town of Chernobyl was never the same again. Neither was Adventure's AI project; they promptly sold it on to a company called Enron where it worked in accounts.

Being a six-foot-four inch, undetectable cyborg with chiselled good looks, Rob found he was never short of glances from the opposite sex, and as the years had gone by, his lust emotion had grown to the point where it could no longer be ignored.

Surrendering operation clean up, he crisscrossed his fingers over his torso and once again turned his thoughts to that of sex. But there was a big problem, Jesus hadn't predicted the animal that would rage within his creation and so never fitted him with a penis. An oversight that needled away at Rob on a near hourly basis.

How could Jesus, his father, build such a perfect robotic thoroughbred, incorporating human emotions through artificial intelligence and yet, miss out the very feature that gave him his gender? It was the equivalent of giving a Rottweiler no teeth. Resentment and hatred had soon grown and lust now tortured Rob's circuits to the point of insanity. Almost everywhere he looked, he felt sexual appetite as the animal within him grew but not a single thing could he do about it, partly because Jesus had been tactically clever in the building of his son. For not only had he not bestowed on Rob a penis, Jesus also embedded into Rob's mainframe computer the three laws of robotics:

1. A robot may not injure a human being or, through inaction, allow a human being to come to harm.

2. A robot must obey the orders given to it by human beings, except where such orders would conflict with the first law.

3. At no point may a robot slip a human being a quick length.

It was this third law that infuriated Rob more than any other. In fact, had it not been for laws one and two, he would have quite happily leathered Jesus years ago.

Rob was roused from his thoughts by a knock at the door.

"Forgot your key again?" he muttered, shuffling down the hall and up to the porch door to let his father in. But it wasn't Jesus who presented himself.

"Hello sir, we are here to pass on some news about Jesus, your creator," said one of two men in black suits.

"Oh aye, what's he been up to now, like?" replied Rob, folding his arms in a defensive posture.

"We wanted to let you know that he loves you very much," carried on the first man, all very matter of fact.

There was a slight pause while Rob eyed the two men before him. "You sure about that? I haven't spoken to him at all today, but I'm pretty sure he'll be pissed when he sees I haven't tidied up and he needs a new hoover."

The strange statement didn't seem to put the men off. In fact, if anything, it encouraged them further. "But you do welcome Jesus into your heart?" enquired the second man, his facial expression showing no emotion, almost as if he was reading from an autocue behind his eyes.

Rob stared at the man for a short while, not really sure what the craic was. "Ermmm, I suppose so, yeah," he confessed, before continuing to speak. "Listen, lads, I've had a bit of a rough night and I need to talk to Jesus about a particular issue I'm having, so if you know whereabouts he is?" Rob raised his eyebrows as if to emphasise he was asking a question.

"My child," cried the first man, stepping forward to comfort the huge frame in the doorway. "Jesus is everywhere. He is all over the place."

"Eh?" remarked Rob. "You mean he's shitfaced in the fuckin'

Roundel again? Have you two witnessed this? You've definitely seen Jesus?"

"Yes, we are both Witnesses, my child. We follow him everywhere. You must let Jesus enter you."

Rob removed the man's arms from his shoulders and took a few steps back. "You what? How many has he had, like? Don't tell me he's entered you two?"

"Yes, my son, at least once a day for the last fifteen years. Now, we'd like to come in to spread Jesus's love unto you in private."

Rob immediately sensed danger, but, bound by law two of the robotics code, he had to obey. His attitude shifted from that of confusion to absolute rage and it was rising up within him like a simmering volcano. This was where the conflict with artificial intelligence and those stupid laws always clashed. He started his protest about the imminent act he was sure he must perform. "Listen, guys, I'm really not into this type of thing and I'm not really allowed any close human contact," he muttered.

"Then don't think of us as humans at all, my child," said one of the Jehovah's Witnesses, "but rather messengers of God. Now, in your own time, allow us to enter you…"

CHAPTER 2

urnt out, Jesus threw down his trowel and stepped back to admire his work. Although he hated community service, he had to admit, the poppies he'd planted around the base of the Spitfire would be sure to look fabulous when in full bloom. It had taken him a full four hours of graft to complete, but he'd managed to seed the whole circumference and now he couldn't wait to see the results. A swaying sea of red that would honour Thornaby's glorious dead. Those brave few who had been stationed at the old airbase, long since gone but never forgotten. His old shrapnel war injury, which sometimes reared up, would make sure of that.

He'd taken some serious stick. Being anywhere on a Thornaby street for four hours was risking a beating, but to situate yourself smack bang in the middle of a busy roundabout while wearing a convict tag was bordering on insanity.

'Fucking knobhead,' was one of the lesser profanities he had faced. 'Peado', 'bummer' and 'doyle,' were others, but Jesus knew not to react, a lesson he'd learnt a few weeks before when he was painting the fighter's tail in camouflage colours. On that occasion, a Vauxhall Vectra had clipped the curb before entering the roundabout at speed. Jesus had gestured the need for the driver to slow down. The driver, along with his passenger, took exception to Jesus's pleas and circled around and around for the next hour, firing off pepper spray from an aerosol can.

"Ow, you! Yer long-haired bellend," they shouted. "Who you telling to fuckin' slow down?" Round and around they went, hitting Jesus with pot shots from a Taser while hanging out of the windows hurling abuse. Abuse that only stopped when the driver got a call on the radio about a road traffic accident on the A19.

With a final lap and a two fingered salute, the two police officers sped off toward the Parkway, allowing Jesus to make his escape.

Jesus looked at his watch. His day was through and just a few more of these community service sessions remained before he could call himself a completely free man.

Although he had to admit, prison had changed him, and, upon his release, his service in the community had improved Thornaby too. In the one hundred and eighty hours he had put into the town, Thornaby had managed to win Town in Bloom and had been nominated in the City of Culture category. Although the town came bottom of the pile when the results were announced, it was a feat he was immensely proud of. Especially as the only previous award the town had ever won, was the 'on Tees' recognition, an extension to its name to acquire more prestige.

Placing his tools in a bag, he took one last longing look at the Spitfire, turned on his heels and left. He crossed over the road and headed toward the town centre. Hopefully, Greggs would still be open and he could devour a steak bake before he got himself ready for quiz night in the Jolly Farmers.

He'd have to pick Rob up first of course, because Rob was shit hot at quizzes. Something that pissed off the locals who had no idea his memory stick was full of every general knowledge book ever written. Not that him and Rob ever told anyone that. The 'meat for a week' prize, donated by the local butcher and handed out to the winner, came in very handy, especially when soaking up the copious amounts of alcohol they both drank.

Jesus turned right into the new shopping complex and immediately had to dodge the usual hustle and bustle of the high street. Everywhere he looked, people were scurrying about, plotting their own agendas of shopping, eating or trying to place a bet down the bookies.

The ground he walked on was damp due to a spattering of rain and, every few metres or so, littered with chewing gum. The sky above his head offered only an overcast grey. But something different floated in the air. A familiar smell, a scent that sent nostalgic shockwaves running through his core. Like the smell of wet grass to a retired footballer, it sparked Jesus's neurons into life. He ground to a halt outside Subway and surveyed his surroundings. What was interrupting his senses? It was unmistakeable.

Could it be?

He spun theatrically on his heel and rapidly scanned the faces in his vicinity. Then he saw her. His old flame. The one who'd left him all those years ago. A woman he'd been unable to replace.

"Mary! Mary!" shouted the desperate Jesus, trying to attract the attention of the only woman he had ever loved. Crikey, she looked good with those tracksuit bottoms tucked in her socks. "Mary, wait."

But Jesus couldn't make up the ground. A queue outside the Pound Shop had swollen to three times its usual size because the shop had announced a once in a lifetime offer on Blu Tack, and the whole high street was now blocked. It was as if the shopkeeper had a huge people magnet and they were being pulled in on his store like a pisshead might be to a curry. Poor Jesus simply couldn't get through.

"'Ere, mate, there's plenty for everyone," shouted one irate veteran of bargain hunting, but Jesus just ignored her and kept on pushing and shoving, trying to break through the crowd to reach his ex.

"No, you don't understand. I need to see that woman there," cried Jesus, pointing up the road toward the fleeing Mary. He was desperate. He hadn't seen her for years and one coffee in the Pavilion café would be heaven on earth. The anguish was unbearable and Jesus felt so helpless, especially as the tide of the crowd had now pushed him into the shop doorway.

He stood on the metal detector to gain one last view of his old sweetheart, but soon noticed a sea of angry faces staring back up at him.

"If you get the latht Blu Tack, you're dead," shouted a balding guy with a lisp. A statement that confused Jesus somewhat. He stared down at the man in confusion.

"Why would I want to buy the lass Blu Tack?" asked Jesus, although he never argued the fact that Mary could kill him, she was an ex-bouncer after all. "Flowers, maybe?" offered Jesus but now it was the lispy egghead's turn to be confused.

"What you on about, you scruff?" he retorted, "I've only come here for thticky thtuff and Worthethterthire thauce."

Jesus didn't reply. He was too busy wiping the spit from his face.

When Mary had first left him, Jesus had fallen into a deep depression. He would watch romantic films of couples who get back together in the last scene, riding off into the sunset together and living happily ever after. It was a dream he had always held close to his heart in the hope that someday the same would happen to him and Mary. Yet standing amidst this volatile crowd, he saw that dream slipping away with every step Mary took away from him. He tried once more to push through the crowd but couldn't force his way out. And then it hit him. He remembered one particular scene from his favourite movie of all time. If he could pull it off, maybe he could woo Mary back into his arms, but... he'd need the support of the crowd.

Literally.

This was his defining moment, a chance to walk out of last chance saloon, but he had to act fast...

Mary was putting some serious distance between herself and the town centre. She'd heard somebody call her name and had thought it wise to leave the area as quickly as possible. Not that she found fleeing that easy, especially with a record haul of loot wedged down her tracksuit bottoms. She couldn't quite believe the Asda security guard had given chase. He'd looked at death's door when she'd rattled past him and the tin foil wrapped around her legs had rendered the security alarm useless. It was the perfect crime, or so she had thought, but things had gone very sour, very quickly. She rounded a corner and gasped for breath. She'd need about ten fags to slow her heart down from its current tommy gun rate, and, with a feeling of sheer exhaustion, she slumped with her back to the wall and lit two up. Mary hated herself for shoplifting, but she hated getting caught even more. She'd spent more time in cells than a Seventies television personality and had no desire to return anytime soon.

After ten minutes had passed, Mary deemed it safe enough to check she wasn't being followed. She allowed herself one last draw on her fag, threw it on the floor and stomped it out with her Adidas Gazelle then peered, casual as you like, around the corner.

Fuck it, thought Jesus as he leapt from the metal detector in the shop doorway and up onto the shoulders of the nearest person.

"'Ere, what's your game? Get down, you mad bastard," someone yelled.

But Jesus ignored those he now trampled on. He had to get Mary's attention before she disappeared from his life again.

"Ayas, ya clumsy twat," screamed a man in brown corduroy trousers. "What the hell are you doing? Get down, hippy."

But Jesus was committed now, he was literally climbing on the heads and shoulders of every man and woman in that packed crowd. Swinging his arms above his head, his beloved Mary was bound to see him now and, just like the scene from his favourite movie, would come running back into his arms.

But Mary had turned the corner.

She was gone.

Jesus stared in disbelief. The pain of losing her once again hit like a punch to the solar plexus, like a slap to the head or a swift kick to the plums. In fact, Jesus never thought he'd ever feel pain like this again but then suddenly realised, he was being set upon by the Thornaby casuals and they were raining in with punches and kicks at a furious rate.

The pain was unbearable. The punches and kicks kept beating down on him as he curled up in a ball to protect his bruising organs.

"Help," he cried, but his screams were drowned out by the blows from hundreds of stamping trainers and lots of laughter because somebody noticed that a man was actually wearing brown corduroy trousers.

Jesus was close to passing out and could feel himself slipping away. The adrenaline was now in full flow and he could no longer feel the blows that thumped into his body. Instead, his only thoughts were of Mary and how good she had looked in those trackies. As he drifted in and out of consciousness, he thought he heard her speak.

"Come with me, Jesus," she said.

He could feel her grabbing at his collar, trying to lift him off the floor.

"Come on, get up," she said again.

Jesus opened his eyes to see her beautiful face but instead came face to face with a bearded officer of the law.

"Come on, Jesus, get up. You're nicked," said the arresting officer, cuffing Jesus's hands behind his back. "It's another night in the cells for you."

Mary couldn't believe it. A fight had broken out right outside the Pound Shop and nobody was pursuing her.

At last she felt her luck was changing and she was overjoyed that the police scum were actually looking to arrest some other poor soul and not, as she had first thought, looking for her. She wondered who the poor beggar being dragged away by the police was as she listened intently to the voices of the baying crowd.

"Fuck off, ya crazy bastard. We all want a bargain, but we don't go climbing over everybody to get it. How many posters have you got to stick on your wall, like? Three thousand?"

The dispersing crowd laughed at that witty comment and started to drift away.

Mary made a mental note. *Next time I'm in Asda… nick Blu Tack.*

Rob stood outside the police station and waited for Jesus. He'd been there for a couple of hours and darkness had fallen.

Finally, Jesus came out.

"How come they let you out?" asked Rob, who had felt sure his father would at least have spent a night at the two-starred, police accommodation centre.

"I recognised the arresting officers through my poor swollen eyes," said Jesus, looking for sympathy. He should have known his robotic son would display no emotion. "They were the ones who harassed me on the roundabout during my community service so I managed to strike a deal."

Rob nodded in acknowledgment and the pair walked on for a little while without another word being spoken.

Finally, after a long, awkward silence, Rob turned to his father and was first to break the ice. "You did Crocodile Dundee again, didn't you?" he asked, a question that resulted in Jesus staring at the floor. "Bellend," added Rob.

CHAPTER 3

Obsessive Troy Fassbender took a last longing look at himself in the bathroom mirror and liked what he saw. His pink fluffy outfit was simply outrageous and he'd garnished the look with a white suede hat that sported a huge pink feather. Tonight he was out on the tiles and tonight he hoped to get bummed.

By day, Troy was a high-traffic nylon floor coverings engineer, designing hideous pub carpets with camp exuberance and flair. But by night, he became the North's campest man, pointing his hoop toward any male within a twenty metre radius. In his eyes, and given the right set of circumstances, all men could be turned, and he, along with his pork sword, was the very man to turn them.

Tonight Troy was attending his favourite haunt, The Sausage Cottage down in Cargo Fleet. It was Thursday, which could mean only mean one thing.

Karaoke.

And Troy's rendition of Raining Men always brought the house down.

"Mother… Mother dear, did you manage to get me any eyeliner while you were out?" cried Troy, taking his octaves up a few notches, sending his campness into orbit.

"Sorry, son, I must have dropped it," replied his mother. "The security guard gave chase and I had to leg it."

"Oh my god, how could you do this to me?" barked Troy, his arms flailing all around his head as if being attacked by a swarm of wasps. "How am I supposed to go out looking like this?" he said, pointing to his face while shouting down an empty staircase.

Troy's hissy fit was close to eruption but then it always was.

Given his large size, gaping mouth and his volatile nature, it was a miracle his mother hadn't named him Etna or Vesuvius, and as he stamped his feet on the spot right there, some might be forgiven for sounding the warning alarm, but not Mary. If Troy was her Dante's Peak then she was his Pierce Brosnan. She knew he was all wind and piss, and told him so regularly.

"Oh grow up, Troy, you big fat pudding," she said.

And with that, the eruption began.

"Aaaaarrrrrrgggggghhhhhhhhhhhh! I am not fat! It's my underactive thyroid!" he screamed, tears of anger welling up in his eyes.

"It's the fucking Parmos more like," his mother hit back, knowing it was better to be hurt by the truth than comforted with a lie.

"You… are… a… bitch!" he yelled.

"And you, my son, are a fat arse bandit. You have more tantrums than Elton John on rag week."

That was the final straw for Troy. Nobody talked about his hero like that. "You fucking cow! I'll scratch your fucking eyes out!" But the threat was empty and he knew it. Mary could, and had, kicked his arse on many occasions. With tears of frustration streaming down his face, Troy bolted down the stairs, grabbed his white feather boa and opened the door.

Before leaving, he turned to face his mother. He was about to call her a scathing, hurtful name but she'd already alluded to this. Before the words had time to leave his mouth, Mary had clenched her hands and offered him a shot at the title.

"Just one three-minute round," she offered. "Queensbury rules."

It was a familiar move designed to quieten him down and put him on his toes. And it worked. Troy saw his mother's gritted teeth, then turned and ran through the open door. Although, technically you couldn't call it running, it was more of a shuffle. But he was travelling quite fast for a lard arse.

Mary walked to the door and watched Troy heaving his way down the path to the garden gate. He really was in bad shape, he had the turning circle of the Titanic. He also seemed to be struggling with the latch.

"Troy, wait."

"Keep away from me!" screamed the camp cretin.

"Look, I'm sorry I slagged off Elton. Come back in and calm down."

But Troy wasn't having any of it. Fanning his eyes to dry them, he screamed, "No," with all the petulance of a three year old who has just been told it's bath time.

And with that Mary slowly closed the door. "Fucking knob jockey. I knew I should have called him Rambo."

"Are you just gonna sit there moping all night, or are we going to go out and have a bit of fun?" asked Rob, trying to lift the glum Jesus out of his growing depression.

Jesus didn't answer; instead he just sat in his chair holding an old photograph of Mary. He remembered fondly the day the picture was taken. They'd just been to the Lobster Road chip shop in Redcar and were walking back to the Majuba car park when Mary produced the camera.

Spinning it around so that the lens faced them both, she snapped the world's first selfie right there on the promenade. It was a lovely setting and they were happy times, although Jesus could never remember where the camera came from. Mary insisted she'd found it but then she was lucky like that, always finding things. His special little girl.

"Look, if you don't want to go to the quiz, we can try somewhere new," offered Rob, trying to distract his creator from the photograph of the thieving bitch. "There's a place we could try in Cargo Fleet. It's getting loads of good reviews."

"Cargo fucking Fleet. For fuck's sake, it's been a shit day as it is. First I had to knock a few hours off my community service, then I bump into Mary, only to be beaten up by an angry group of Blu Tack fanatics and finally, I'm arrested by those two fuckin' coppers who abused me for hours on end at the Spitfire roundabout. If that wasn't enough, I come home and find this place in a right fucking shit state. Is it really too much to ask you to tidy up and run the hoover round now and again?"

The word hoover smacked Rob's conscience like a jab to the head. He'd forgotten all about Herbert who was still tied up in a compromising position in his room.

"I've had enough, Robert, this isn't fair," went on an irate Jesus, now shifting his anger toward Rob and stressing the point by using his Sunday name. "You don't work, you don't bring in any funds and you certainly don't do anywhere near enough housework. The pots haven't been cleaned properly, the bins are full and where's that bloody hoover?"

Rob had to agree. Poor Jesus had had a bad day but it was about to get a lot worse if he discovered the state Herbert was in. Rob doubted that, given Jesus's current mood, his creator would even begin to understand.

Jesus began prowling the house, looking in the usual places in which a hoover could be placed. Under the stairs, the utility cupboard and in the garage. "For God's sake, lad, how on earth do you lose a vacuum cleaner?" asked a crimson Jesus, the bulging vein pulsating in his temple about to pop.

Alarm bells started ringing loudly in Rob's head. "I'll tidy the house top to bottom tomorrow, I promise," pleaded the desperate robot, trying to dampen down the rising tension by diverting Jesus from the hall doorway and, more importantly, the stairway to his room. "I'll clean the car too, using proper wax. I'll make a real good job of it, you'll see."

Jesus shoved Rob out of the way and began to climb the stairs.

"Dad, please, let's just go out tonight, let our hair down. You can have a sleep in tomorrow and I'll bring you breakfast in bed," offered Rob, having to think quickly on his feet. But Jesus was now firmly in rant mode as he placed his right index finger on the banister and started to climb the steps.

"This place hasn't been dusted for months. Oooh, you're one lazy bastard, Robert," said Jesus once he'd reached the top, index finger now covered in a thick layer of dust. "If your room is in as much mess… I'm warning you."

Jesus stood just two feet from the door and turned aggressively to face the cyborg. Rob had followed Jesus up the flight of stairs and had an expression of sheer terror on his face. If Jesus opened that door and saw where Herbert's hose had been placed, then Rob would probably be shut down and mothballed.

"Please, dad," he said, trying the emotional blackmail route, "let's just go out. I'll buy."

But Jesus was committed now. With his right hand already on the bedroom door handle, he turned it anti-clockwise... Rob was doomed. Other than knocking the old boy out, he was screwed. It wasn't a pretty sight in there and he was all out of excuses. With one last final attempt, he spoke.

"I know, you can wear your Crocodile Dundee hat, the one with all the teeth around the rim. You'll look magnificent in the Sausage Cottage with that," suggested Rob, as if his life depended on it. He was down on his knees, hands clasped together as if praying, praying that his words had worked.

Jesus stopped in the doorway for a few moments and considered Rob's offer. Rob was right, perhaps what he really did need was a good night out, and the offer to get dressed up as his favourite film star was a draw he could hardly refuse.

After a long pause, he turned to face his son once again. "Will you call me 'Mick' for the rest of the night?"

The words came as a wave of relief to Rob who smiled back up at his father. "No worries, mate," he said in his best Australian accent before continuing. "You can be Mick and I'll be Wally, we might even meet some lovely Sheilas."

But Jesus's eyes narrowed at the suggestion, there was only room for one Sheila in his life and that was Mary. Rob was losing him again. Now standing, he placed a protective arm around the shoulders of his father and steered him away from his bedroom door. "I hear they sell Fosters lager, mate," uttered Rob, once again in his best Australian accent. It was a wonderful recovery.

"Yeah?" said the smiling old timer, happy to be playing the role of Dundee once again. "And will it be okay if I take my favourite knife with me? The ten inch one with the personalised pouch?"

Upon hearing that request, Rob just stared at his father, not quite believing the old bastard had actually asked such a stupid question. "Take your knife?" he repeated as if to seek clarification that the old man hadn't yet gone completely insane. "It's Cargo Fleet, of course you'll need your fucking knife."

Troy Fassbender's first mood swing of the night was well and truly over. His mother, as much as he loved her, had never really understood him and he doubted she ever would, but here, in the middle of the dance floor of the Sausage Cottage he was among his own kind. Men and women of similar ilk. A place where women could be women and men could be women too, a place where nobody batted an eyelid. Well, nobody except Maddog McClane, the bouncer who worked the doors of the Cottage. He was an ugly, six-foot, six-inch monster of a man, who had the same dimensions in width as he did in height. He was the North's first solo doorman. The only guy to single-handedly crowd control a building. The only person with a say on who entered the premises and who got ejected.

And why was it that Maddog worked alone?

Because he was a complete and utter, insane maniac and no other doormen would work with him. Maddog would clip you for the slightest thing. He once knocked out an old boy from the British Legion for selling poppies, because he claimed men shouldn't carry flowers around, and one time he turned over four cars in a McDonald's car park because he burnt his lip on a hot apple pie. Yes, the shaven-headed loon was a testosterone-fuelled animal and best avoided at all costs. If he went into the toilet, then you headed for the exit. If he stood at the bar, you stood far away from it. If he had positioned himself in the cloakroom then it was best you didn't hand in your coat, nor ask for it back. But by far the most important lifesaving rules were these: never spill a drink on him, never show him false ID and never pass comment on his tie.

Soft Cell's Tainted Love poured loudly from the Cottage's speaker system and Troy was in his element. He threw his hands up and down in the air, mimicking a very camp EIO, the Middlesbrough goal celebration now cast as Holgate legend. The disco lights bore down onto his costume, sequins sparkling in the beams, catching the faces of all those around him. Troy was in the zone, transfixed only by his surroundings, totally unaware of the outside world. The only thing grabbing his attention was the next dangerous shape he was about to bust on the dance floor. But as the chorus began for the second time, Troy was spent. Never built for distance, he had all the stamina of a dead sloth. Holding his knees to catch his breath, he looked around to see if anybody was glancing at his pert buttocks. They weren't.

"Heterosexuals," he mumbled between heavy breaths.

Jesus and Rob climbed out of the taxi and offered the driver a few tips in Mathematics. "Eighteen quid from Thornaby? You robbing twat! What school did you go to? Parliament?"

But the driver had heard it all before. "Yours as it happens, Tin Head," he exclaimed, "although you clearly don't recognise me."

The driver had a venomous tone in his voice and was staring at Rob in the wing mirror, the interior light on his face adding mystique to the conversation, an effect that made Rob uneasy, sending a shiver down his electronic spine. He glanced at the driver once again, studying the man's face in greater detail. Rob certainly couldn't remember a bald, bearded bloke in his class at school. Especially one with a driving licence and he told him so. "My school, you say? You can't have been in my maths class then. I mean, I wasn't in the top set or anything, but at least I knew how to count properly." It was another cheap shot at the fare but had Jesus sniggering all the same. Rob was in good form tonight but this angry taxi driver wasn't smiling. If anything the mention of school had seemingly angered him further.

"That's because I had to take a year off from school when the science block fell on my head, didn't I? And, if I'd have had my way, you'd 'ave been turned into scrap long ago."

That grabbed Rob's attention alright. The very mention of

the science block being blown to smithereens always sat uneasy with him, partly because it was his faulty battery that had been the root cause but he'd managed to move on, so why couldn't this fellow? But the realisation soon fell into place. Rob, still staring back at the eyes in the mirror that burned into him, recognised this character now alright.

It was Little Mohammed.

The lad buried beneath the rubble for five days when the phosphorus store fell. He used to be called Big Mohammed due to early childhood development but, to be fair, the science block weighed quite a bit.

"Mo, mate. How are ya?"

No response followed because Mohammed hated Rob with a passion, and really did want to see him as scrap. These awkward vibes emitted from Mo like gamma rays and weren't too difficult for Rob to pick up on.

"So, did you pass your science exam, then?"

Rob's artificial intelligence wasn't exactly finely tuned to tact, and the mere mention of science saw Mohammed lose it. With his anger rising rapidly, he flung open his cab door and stomped to the rear of the vehicle.

Opening the car boot, he searched among the cans of food and bread he'd been asked to deliver for his next job. He was looking for the crowbar he always carried, the crowbar that would do some serious damage to an alloy cyborg. Once located, he tried to pull it free from the boot, only the curved end hooked on an Asda shopping bag and split it down the sides. Cans fell and tumbled all over the tarmac with a hefty clatter.

It was this scenario, played out on closed circuit television, that had now alerted Maddog McClane in the control room of the Sausage Cottage.

"I could have been someone," screamed Mohammed, taking a big swing at Rob who ducked to avoid the blow. "I was in all the top sets at school before the accident," Mo continued, taking another big swing that just whistled past Rob's head this time.

"To be fair, Mo, you were only in the bottom set in science

25

because the building buried you in the basement." Rob really wasn't helping himself.

"You bastard," cried Mohammed, who now had Rob cornered against the car park wall. He raised the crowbar above his head, ready to deliver the killer blow. "Taxi drivers can have dreams like anybody else, but not you. You are a machine. An imitation of life."

Rob was petrified, waiting for the inevitable. But still Mo went on, "Can a robot turn a brick into an architectural masterpiece? Can a robot offer love and understanding in times of need?" He was really going to town now. "Can a robot…" but Mohammed didn't finish, his world suddenly cast into darkness as Maddog's shadow loomed over the whole car park. Mo didn't hang about. He'd taken enough of Maddog's victims to hospital to know that this was bad news. In fact, given the science block again or a beating from Maddog, the school would win every time.

Mo began pumping his little legs as fast as he could, putting advantageous distance between himself and Goliath of the North, who was in hot pursuit.

"Next time, Tin Head… next time!" he shouted, his voice becoming more distant as he ran.

Jesus stood frozen in bewilderment. It had been a strange day to say the least. He was watching the most bizarre moment yet, as a six-foot-six mountain of fury gave chase to a midget taxi driver who clearly hated school.

Rob observed the two speed across the car park, one running to save his own life, the other trying to take it.

Jesus could only admire the taxi driver's speed. "That short arse can shift, son, there's no way the big man is gonna catch him."

He was right. Maddog, clearly not built for speed, was rapidly losing ground. In a total mismatch, similar to an elephant and a mouse, this little rodent, legs going ten to the dozen, was making haste and was sure to escape. It was a sight that caused Rob to let out a frustrated sigh. He stared at his father and shook his head. Jesus, amidst all the excitement, had somehow managed to keep his Crocodile Dundee hat on and was stood, still in character, amongst the tins of shopping on the floor.

"Hey, Mick," shouted Rob in his best Australian accent. "Take down the midget, mate."

Jesus stared down at the shopping and a grin instantly slapped on his face. The two were riding on the same wavelength and that poor mannered, irate taxi driver shouldn't be allowed to get away with it. Jesus picked up a can of beans with his left hand and tossed it up high so it landed down with a slap in his right. He glanced at Rob, tilted his hat and winked.

"Go on, Mick," shouted Rob. "Get the little bastard."

Jesus gauged the increasing distance and the trajectory he'd need for a direct hit. He closed one eye, as if looking down the barrel of a gun, then took two steps forward. With an almighty cry, he threw the can as hard as he could and it set off at breakneck speed, homing in on the midget with superb accuracy.

Jesus and Rob whooped with excitement as a direct hit looked inevitable, but with twenty metres to impact, the can started to fall drastically short, as gravity pulled the heavy food container back to earth. A look of disappointment fell onto Jesus's face, a look that quickly turned to horror, as the rampaging beast called Maddog arrived at the drop zone. With a short sharp thud, the can of baked beans smacked into the bull's bonce, sending him careering into the car park wall. Rubble and brick erupted everywhere, as the once proud wall disintegrated before their very eyes.

Rob and Jesus stared, open-mouthed, not quite sure what to do next. Was he alright? Would he need assistance? It was as if time had stood still, with the pair of them staring at the ten-foot hole that Maddog's frame had created. Jesus and Rob looked at each other.

"I say, old boy," exclaimed the inquisitive assassin, "do you think we should call an ambulance?"

But Rob didn't answer, he was too busy running probability algorithms as to whether they should escape and evade rather than worry about Maddog's health.

They stood, staring silently at the pile of obliterated bricks and mortar that used to be the car park wall and waited for the dust to settle, eyes peeled for signs of movement. It was Jesus who eventually detected the first sign of life.

"Ah, there you go. See, no harm done," he said, but the words had barely left his mouth when a terrible growling noise rumbled from the rubble, a rumble that turned into a deafening roar.

Warnings flashed in Rob's head, as his threat detection alarm flashed danger red. "We have to move," he warned his father.

But it was too late.

Maddog burst from the rubble like a cork released from a bottle of Dom Perignon and although he was some fifty yards away, you could tell he wasn't coming to offer them VIP tickets into the club.

Rob scarpered and expected his father to do the same, however his proximity alarm showed no life form within his comfort zone. Stopping, he turned to see where Jesus was.

"Dad, what the fuck are you doing?" he called back, totally bamboozled by his father's apparent kamikaze stance. Though Jesus was too focused on the rushing bull to answer.

With his head tilted to the side and a strange 'hmmmmmmmmm' noise coming from his mouth, Jesus was attempting to tame the beast with his mind powers. He extended his right arm and, with only his little pinky and index finger protruding, pointed at Maddog's forehead.

"It's not working, son," he called out in a panicked voice as Maddog closed the gap with alarming speed.

"You don't say," responded Rob, still flummoxed by his dad's stupidity.

Call it telepathy or simply common sense, they both ran through the doors and sought refuge in the safe haven of the Sausage Cottage.

Inside the Sausage Cottage, DJ Long Dong Silver was setting the pace. The Lion Sleeps Tonight was just edging to fade and the triple deck wizard was about to heat up the atmosphere further. He was a magnificent disc jockey, a real master of his craft. Wherever he played – Ibiza, Magaluf or Cargo Fleet – his party nights were legendary and this next track would have every sphincter in the room pulsating with excitement.

Inside his booth, Long Dong had control of all lighting, and every hour he pointed two beams of light into the faces of sad individuals. Nobody was allowed to be down during his set and the laser extravaganza had the locals entering fever pitch with every minute it edged closer. The rules were very simple, if the light picked you, then you had to get up and dance with your chosen partner. Oh how the punters loved it. "Oooooh, I really hope he picks me," or "Long Dong hold a torch for me," were usually heard as the clock ticked toward the start of the game. And how the DJ played to it, often turning all other lights out and ringing out the chimes of Big Ben in some form of New Year's countdown. BONG... BONG... Big Ben would sing, usually followed by screams of pleasure from the darkness of the dance floor. BONG... BONG... Another club classic began to grow...

Troy sat at the bar sipping his second Sex On The Beach cocktail. He couldn't quite believe the barren night he was having and another mini tantrum was building. He surveyed the packed room looking for a potential mate for the night, although victim was probably closer to the truth. He passed his eyes over the frenzied dance floor, but nothing caught his fancy. He thought he'd give it a few more minutes and if nothing had his anus itching, he'd do a full circuit of the room, offering his best chat up lines to any partners but, in all honesty, that was exercise he could really do without.

Long Dong Silver pushed the vinyl record gently forward, allowing the all too familiar club classic to resonate around the room. In The Navy, the pulsating dance anthem of joy, sprang from the sound system. Long Dong, encouraging his crowd to join in, switched on his laser lights to the backing track of Big Ben. Finally, with the crowd roaring their approval, he bathed a random fat bloke who was sipping cocktails at the bar and searched for somebody to partner him with. This Village People track was a gimme for any DJ, because it always had the place rocking but, to the DJ's horror, the dance floor suddenly started to empty. Every bloke in the frenetic crowd suddenly began to distance themselves from the tubster with the boa, and Long Dong Silver, for the first time in his long established career, was dying on his arse. In sheer panic, the DJ shone the second beam of light around the room looking for a partner for the plump prat. For a short while, the scene resembled that of Steve McQueen in The Great Escape, as the laser light bobbed, first one way, then another as if searching for escaping prisoners of war. Troy, of course, needed no second invitation. He wobbled down off his stool and entered the arena, ready to meet his match. With the pulsating track already halfway through, the DJ still hadn't found a match, and, as the music continued, Long Dong Silver started to sweat.

Somebody, please show yourself, if only for a spilt second, thought the master of the decks, with only one minute and seventeen seconds of this vinyl classic left to find a partner for the pink woolly mammoth, who now stood alone on the dance floor. In desperation, Long Dong threw the light to the main door. If nothing else, it would stop people fleeing the building. Agonising seconds ticked away as the bright light burned at the club exit. As the chorus started its third encore, Long Dong could see his career fading away. And to think, he'd mocked Pete Waterman for being out of touch on The Hitman and Her.

Jesus was the first to push through the club doors, shortly followed by Rob. They were hoping to find another way out of the building, because turning to face the on-rushing Maddog was not a realistic option. Their eyes narrowed due to a glaring light pointing straight at their faces, and as they tried to duck into the darkness to evade unwanted attention, the light simply followed them. They both raised their hands, struggling to see beyond the brightness. The rest of the room was in darkness except for a lone laser beam that was shining on an unknown lifeform that looked like it was dancing. Either that or it was about to have a heart attack. Whatever it was, it was in bad shape and the two new arrivals watched intrigued as this thing waved them forward. Hopefully, it would be able to show them a way out. As they approached, the blob's face shone bright red, and was surely too fat to be human? The creature, fresh from busting some seductive shapes, was sucking in lungfuls of air as it tried to gather enough strength to speak. If Rob hadn't known better, he'd have sworn that Herbert the Hoover had freed himself and was plotting revenge.

Finally, wearing a smile that suggested he'd won the lottery, the blob headed toward them. "Weeellllllll helllllloooooooo, handsome," said Troy.

"Who the fuck is that?" cried Jesus above the din.

"Who fucking cares! Keep moving," shouted Rob, shoving Jesus forward, encouraging him to look for an exit.

"Erm, excuse me, gentlemen, but I believe one of you owes me a dance. The lasers have spoken," camped up Troy, blocking the path of the fleeing couple.

"No time for dancing, I'm afraid," cried the desperate Dundee lookalike, glancing back over his shoulder for the rampaging gorilla. "But would you mind showing me your back door, please? I'm desperate."

"Oh my," said Troy with glee, "it looks like all my Christmases have come at once." He was jumping up and down on the spot, looking Jesus up and down while unbuckling his belt. "Would you like to see it here or shall we retire to somewhere a bit more private?"

"More private, please," encouraged Jesus. "If you don't hurry up then some bloke's gonna smash through those doors and give me a severe pummelling."

"What?" hissed Troy, the mere thought that somebody could steal his date infuriating him to his very core. "Quickly, follow me."

Troy set off through the club at breakneck speed with Jesus and Rob in hot pursuit.

"Can't you go any faster, wee man?" asked Rob, who was doing his best not to get this strange fat man caught beneath his feet. They skirted around the dance floor that was filling up once again and headed toward the back of the club. Once there, Troy showed them into an empty booth with a black curtain around it. He opened it wide and showed Jesus in but he wasn't expecting the big, good-looking fellow to follow.

"Oh my," said Troy, unable to contain his excitement. "Buy one, get one free," and he sat fanning himself with both hands.

"Where's the back door then?" shouted Rob, now with more urgency in his voice, peering back through the curtain. "You said you'd lead us to the back passage."

"And I will, you big hunk of love," said Troy, who was now as excited as a blind poof in a hot dog factory. "But I'm a man that needs warming up first."

"Warming up, you little cretin? There's a man charging right across the dance floor as we speak, and I'm pretty sure he's not waiter service. In fact, I'm quite positive that when he gets here, he'll give all three of us a severe fisting…"

Troy, bursting with excitement, fainted and fell off his stool.

"Now what are we gonna do?" said Rob. "He'll be here any minute."

But it was less than that, because Maddog was eating up the ground, tearing across the dance floor to deliver terrifying consequences. His eyes now firmly fixed on the bumming booths at the back of the club, he homed in on his prey like a charging rhinoceros.

"Rob, listen to me," said Jesus, talking fast like his life depended on it, "you think you're bound by the laws of robotics but in reality you're not. You have an internal override which can be activated with the flick of a switch."

"So what are you saying I can slip a human a length? What with? You've never given me a cock?"

"No, I'm not saying that at all. I'm saying you can beat this man to fuck because you're a fucking robot."

This information was a lot for Rob to take in and its

implications would provide many more questions. "Hang on, I've been growing hornier and hornier every year and taking hoovers to bed and all this time I had a manual fucking override. A switch that does what exactly?"

"Please, Rob, I'll answer your questions later. Bend over."

"What do you mean 'bend over'? What is it? Want to lose your virginity before you meet your maker?" Rob folded his arms and threw the old pervert a sour look.

"I command you to bend over and drop your wabs," said Jesus, asserting his authority, knowing Rob couldn't refuse and would have had to obey due to law two of the robotic code.

Rob slowly bent over and dropped his kecks to his knees. "I'm warning you, dad, I'm not happy about this."

But the old man knew what he was doing. He rammed a digit up the robot's arse, searching for the override switch just as Troy was coming around.

"You kinky bastards," cried the big fat lump from the floor, once again flushing with excitement. His gaze only interrupted when they were joined by a fourth person in the booth.

"Which of you three arseholes wants pummelling first?" announced Maddog, a statement that had Fat Lad on the floor passing out for the second time and saw the old man retracting his finger from the anus of the bent over gentleman. But, with his override activated, Rob could see clearly for the first time. He now knew what it was like to be free. It was a real Pinocchio moment and he announced to the now hushed club that he felt like a real boy. An announcement that didn't go down too well with the other ravers. Anything usually goes in a happy-go-lucky club such as the Sausage Cottage but that type of thing definitely did not.

Maddog drew back an arm. His famous haymaker was just seconds from delivering the bad news but Rob reacted first, sending two titanium fingers square into the eyes of the bouncer, temporarily blinding him.

"Run, you old fool," cried Rob.

Jesus needed no second invitation and the pair ran past the injured doorman.

"My eyes. The dirty bastard came in my eyes," cried the big bouncer, holding his face in pain, his words cutting through Troy like a hot knife through butter. Still curled up in a ball on the floor of the cubicle, he watched as his two hot dates, one still trying to pull up his trousers, fled the club.

As Rob and Jesus pushed through the club doors and out into the night, they saw for the second time the shopping that had been strewn over the car park by the little, yet rapid, taxi driver. As they ran past, Jesus had just enough time to reflect. It had been yet another bizarre episode in this thing he called life but why these things always seemed to happen to him, he couldn't answer. He dropped his pace to a slow jog, studying the carnage on the floor.

"Come on, dad," said Rob, "we have to get going. That lunatic will be after us again any minute."

But Jesus wasn't listening. He'd spotted several tubes of cheese and chive Pringles amongst the mess and asked his son to pass him one.

"Ah, I like your thinking, dad," said Rob who was finely tuned to his father's thought processes. "You're going to throw one at his head as soon as he reappears through those doors?" His father really did have a throw better than Crocodile Dundee himself and, in this modern day David versus Goliath scenario, Rob would fancy his father any day of the week.

"Don't be so silly, son," Jesus replied in a deadpan tone. "I'm just fucking starving." Then with the tube tucked under his arm, the old inventor broke into a jog and left the scene sharpish.

CHAPTER 4

During the quiet, peaceful hours of the night, Jesus hadn't slept well, he'd been fidgeting in his sleep. Right on the edge of consciousness, he drifted in and out of the dreamy twilight zone. He'd dreamt he was being chased by a huge, hideous, snot-blowing bull, cornered in a dark place with nowhere to run. The bull was snorting heavily, covering him with hot breath, staring through evil, vacant eyes, as if toying with its prey. Pure hatred leapt from the beast as its razor sharp horns inched closer. It gave out a huge deafening cry…

"Boooaaaaarrrrrrrrrrrrrrrrrrrrrrrrrrrrrr."

The noise was frightening. This is what ink black death looked like, the reaper forming the shape of a furious taurus. "Booooa aaaaarrrrrrrrrrrrrrrrrrrrrrrr." That noise again, that hot, furious breath. Jesus kicked out in his sleep, his bed sheets now just a sweat-soaked clump on the bedroom floor. Beads of perspiration rolled down his face.

"Boooooaaaaaaarrrrrrrrrrrrrr."

Louder and louder the noise grew, the walls vibrating with fear.

"Boooooaaaaaaarrrrrrrrr."

Again louder.

He startled awake, broken away from the clutches of his dream. He sat, bolt upright on his bed, sucking in lungfuls of air, his heart slamming against his chest like a bass drum. Of course, there was no bull, the mind can play terrible tricks especially when put through trauma. And somehow the image of a raging doorman was etched in his mind. There was, however, this loud terrible noise.

"Boooooaaaaaaaarrrrrrrrr."

At the end of the bed was Robert. He appeared to be giving

Herbert the Hoover lessons from the Kama Sutra. Seemingly freed from the three laws of robotics, his son had the hoover whirring merrily away.

"Booooaaaaaaarrrrrrrrrr."

"Robert, what the fuck are you doing?" cried a sleepy and very bewildered Jesus.

"Can I have a cock, dad?" came the memorable reply.

Troy Fassbender was also fidgeting in his sleep. He'd dreamt of wonderful mountain ranges providing a spectacular backdrop to rolling fields. There he sat peacefully next to a slow moving stream, watching salmon leap into the air as the first migrating birds of spring sang in new-budded trees.

Troy floated from his sleep and opened his eyes with a smile etched across his face. However, the mind can play terrible tricks, especially when put through trauma. And somehow the vision of beauty that was his short, yet wonderful date was etched into his mind. Now awake and yet very disappointed, Troy had no idea where he was. Worse still, he couldn't move either. His last recollection had been passing out in the Sausage Cottage, only to now find himself alone in a place he didn't know. Fear crept around him as he searched for the answer he couldn't find, the silence no longer as welcoming. Silence that was eventually broken by a deep gravelly voice, "Morning, sweetheart. Did you sleep well?"

"Mr Maddog?" cried a bewildered Troy, startled to see the huge bouncer standing over the bed to which he was tied. "What the fuck is happening?"

"Oh, nothing much, I'm just gonna cut your cock off," came the memorable reply.

Mary didn't wait for the kettle to finish before she poured the simmering water over the tea bag. She was too impatient for that. She wanted to be up and out early to seize the day. *Why?* Because autumn had arrived and the cold nights were drawing in. Clutching her Combat 18 mug, she watched from the front room window as leaves fell gently to the ground outside. She smiled at the thought of people turning their heating dials up to warm their homes. Yes, today was a grand day. This was the day, the Herald and Post told her, that Aldi would be bulking up on budget ski wear, and Mary always made a killing on cheap ski wear.

She picked up the telephone to order Troy's breakfast. "Reverse charges, please," she announced to the operator, who knew the drill by now.

Mary waited while the snotty operative woke up Parmo Pete, the local fast food restaurateur. Not that Pete minded, of course. Troy was his best customer and every morning was exactly the same. And every morning, he accepted the reverse charges without complaint.

"A-good-a-morning, Miss Fassbender. The usual?"

"Pete, why do you pretend to be Italian? You're from Linthorpe, ya thick bastard. The only resemblance to anything Italian you have is that silly curly moustache you insist on wearing. And that's only so you can look like your mother."

Mary's good mood had not lasted long.

"I'm a-sorry, Miss Fassbender. It a won't a-happen again." Parmo Pete knew better than to upset Mary, who had hospitalised his last delivery driver for turning up a minute over the promised time. The man may have escaped with only a few cuts and bruises, had he not asked for a tip. Still, you live and learn.

"Your Parmo with-a-extra garlic sauce will be there within the hour-a, Miss Fassbender."

"Fair enough, darl," responded Mary, who was ready and armed with the only joke she knew. "Do you deliver?"

Poor Pete had no other option but to laugh. "Not heard that one before, Mary," he lied and the phone went dead.

Mary climbed the stairs to look for her best tracksuit with matching football socks in which to encase her legs. She then put on her Naff Co 54 fleece jacket with special holes ripped in the thermal lining before picking up her Nokia 3310. Finally, she shouted to Troy.

"Oi, lard arse, get up!" she shouted cruelly. "I'm off out. Your breakfast's on the way." She made sure she was well clear of the stairs when she spoke. A lesson she had learnt the hard way when she was almost killed in the stampede as the camp clown fell from the top stair in excitement. But Mary heard no response, the upstairs landing remaining eerily quiet.

"Troy," she shouted... and again, "Troy!"

But still there was no answer.

Mary scaled the stairs once more and threw open Troy's bedroom door. After finally overcoming the disappointment that Troy hadn't died of a heart attack in his sleep, she wondered where he could be.

Well, the dirty little tramp, she thought. *He's finally gotten laid.*

"Don't be so silly, Robert," said the startled inventor, trying to calm his rapid heartrate back to its usual thirteen beats per minute. "A robot with a penis? It's absurd. I mean, what would you do with it?"

A silence fell as Jesus pulled the plug on Herbert's performance. He then approached the excited robot.

It was time to give 'the speech'. A speech he always knew that one day he would have to deliver. He imagined it was the same speech that Jonathan and Martha Kent had probably given to the young Clark, or one that a young carpenter had likely received after walking on water to retrieve his toy boat much to the gasps of the market goers on the way to a stoning. Yes, he'd prepared this speech alright, memorised it word for word and now was the time to climb up onto the soap box.

"Robert," he said calmly, putting both hands on the cyborg's mighty shoulders. "I created you to become something extraordinary, something fabulous, to become a global leader. The next generation of superstar. I mean, look at you... with your fibre-optic thought processes, your silent sleek mechanics, and over-exaggerated memory power. You're magnificent. Your very creation is meant to determine the course of human history. Your destiny is to eradicate all that is evil in this world. You will unite all religions and bring the globe together. People will look upon you as their king, their saviour, a beacon of hope to lead them into a new world. A world of peace for all of eternity."

But Rob wasn't listening. Instead he stood, facing the opposite way with his chin on his chest looking downward.

"Robert Jones," cried the exasperated, ex-ICI storeman, "face me when I'm talking to you. Manners maketh man."

The inventor spun the cyborg one hundred and eighty degrees as if to reinforce the point that his powerful words must be heard. But Rob was still preoccupied. With his right hand down his pants and index finger protruding through the fly in his jeans, he uttered the immortal words, "What size do you think I should I go for?"

Jesus sat back on the bed, head in his hands. His next move was critical. His army training had taught him that if you can't control a situation, then control your response. But how do you control a sexually frustrated cyborg not governed by any laws of robotics. He took in the picture before him. His boy, his sweet innocent boy had become a man. Tall, good-looking and clever. The old man had to admit, his boy would make a mighty fine swordsman, but surely it couldn't happen? He couldn't allow it. He had to bide his time, he had to control his response.

He started to speak again from a different angle. "Robert, a penis is… well, it's a tool with a purpose, there to procreate and preserve the human race. It's a thing of great importance, with much responsibility. And yet, you are not human. Yes, you have intelligence and your lustful urges are growing, but no other robot like you exists. You're unique. Alone in this world. It simply wouldn't be ethically right. I'm sorry, but I can't allow it. I'm going to have to ask you to bend over and let me reset your code."

Robert's mood dropped considerably and a silent, awkward standoff grew between the pair.

"I'm sorry," said Rob, "but I can't let you do that. My mind's made up."

The words weren't exactly a surprise to Jesus. He'd dreamt up this very scenario years ago when Rob still had that new car smell, but now, as a fully-fledged adult, things had clearly moved on.

"You treat me like an adult, yet you try and control my feelings. You design me to drink alcohol, but govern me with three laws. You ask me to defend you when threatened by rampaging testosterone-fuelled meatheads, but seek control again when not. It's always on your terms, father, but now I want change. You can't have it both ways."

Jesus sighed. Rob was absolutely correct in his words. Everything about the cyborg was premeditated. His height, his looks and even his ability to get shit-faced. He was a purpose-built soul mate for Jesus and Jesus knew it.

What the pragmatic inventor had failed to realise though, was the power of thought. By placing artificial intelligence within his creation, he'd failed to predict the outcome. How his artificial son would transform from receiving simple binary code inputs to cognitive awareness and the command of free will. As he stood there now, listening to his son, he cursed his own stupidity.

"I need to be complete," continued Rob. "Now, you can either help me fulfil my dreams or I'll go it alone. One way or another, I'll attach a bald-headed yogurt slinger to my person and finally become a man."

Jesus wasn't ready to give up the fight, just yet. Rob may have been correct in what he was saying, and Jesus may have been blinkered to the truth, but a robot walking around with a penis was just insanity.

"Then I'll hide your charger," responded the resolute Jesus. "And once you're out of juice, I'll reset your code."

The words had barely left his mouth when the mighty cyborg grasped the old scroat by the neck. It was the first time he had ever actively shown aggression toward his creator.

"Let's not get silly over this," he said, gripping the windpipe just a little tighter. "It's my time now and I'm asking you to help me. I want fulfilment, a reason to live and I want you there with me. Now, what do you say?"

As the grip relaxed, Jesus slumped back off his tiptoes. Then, with a sigh of resignation, he nodded in agreement.

CHAPTER 5

Yanking at his tethered limbs, a worried Troy Fassbender tried to move from the bed in which he lay but his arms and legs were shackled tight. He had no idea where he was, or how he had gotten there, but deduced, as he was still fully clothed and his arse wasn't ruined, it wasn't of his own accord.

The room was very dark, no light being able to penetrate the purposely drawn blackout curtains. As his eyes adjusted to the gloom, Troy could just about make out a figure that appeared to be bound to an old wooden chair, sat slumped in the corner. The man, dressed in a guard's uniform, with an appearance that Troy guessed to be middle-aged, was blind-folded and gagged.

Troy started to feel even more uneasy. Continuing to scan the room, he noted stains on the walls where pictures had once hung. There wasn't much else going on, other than a small portable television with an old Hale and Pace DVD atop.

Troy's examination of the room was interrupted when he glanced down to notice a large block of wood wedged tight between his ankles. Normally the appearance of wood between his legs was something he favoured, however this time the timber was strapped directly to each leg such that his feet protruded past the end of it.

Along the same line of sight, stood the towering, grinning frame of Maddog McClane.

"Hello, sweetheart," said Maddog in a calm, gravelly voice. "How are you finding your stay? Nice and relaxing?"

It was one of the only times in Troy's life that he was completely lost for words, as fear grabbed at his voice box and held it tight.

As they eyed up each other, Maddog let the silence hang for a while before finally starting proceedings. "We can keep things really simple, Troy. Make this nice and easy for us both and, with a bit of luck, you can be back home in time for tea. All you have to do is answer a few simple questions and you're done."

Troy remained speechless, staring back at Maddog with wide eyes of terror before breaking his stare and looking at the slumped, beaten body in the corner. It was a move that prompted Maddog to describe the other method of doing things. "Or we can do it the hard way, which won't be particularly nice for you and not something I would recommend." Maddog took a knife out of his pocket and made a cutting gesture around his groin area before slamming the blade down into the block of wood between Troy's legs. "So, which is it?"

Troy thought for a moment. Losing his tackle was an unimaginable horror but in order for Maddog to remove his penis, he would at least have to remove his trousers and hold it. Troy reasoned that if that happened then at least he could claim first base.

Luckily for Troy, Maddog interrupted his thought process by beginning the interrogation. "Where are your friends?" The big bouncer tilted his head quizically.

"My friends?" enquired Troy. "I don't have any friends."

No truer words were ever spoken. Troy really was a horrible fat bastard and nobody, not even his mother liked him.

Maddog let out a long sigh, took in a big breath and addressed the supine lump once again.

"Last night you were in the Sausage Cottage, yes?"

Troy nodded.

"And last night, while shaking your little tush, you met up with two guys. An Australian-looking chap and a tall fella who looked a bit of a handful, the type who could start trouble in an empty house. Starting to come back to you?"

Troy knew straight away who the hard man was talking about. He'd never forget those magnificent three minutes with the love of his life. Those three minutes when he almost got 'it'.

Troy was drifting off to dreamland when he was brought back down to earth with more questioning.

"Well, your friends started trouble in my club," continued Maddog. "First they assaulted a taxi driver, then me, and finally caused hundreds of pounds worth of damage to a brick wall."

Troy had no idea what the big bastard was talking about, although as the words tumbled from his mouth, the awful truth began to dawn on him. Perhaps those guys were actually looking for the back door after all and not, as Troy had first thought, his anus. It was a sombre thought, but Troy had no time to dwell on it.

"Now for your friends' little skirmish, I'm gonna give them a slap," carried on Maddog. "Nothing more than that, but they also took something very valuable from me. Something the Teesside underworld is far from happy about and I need it back. And I need it back quickly."

"What did they take?" asked Troy, gripped by the notion that the only boyfriend he had ever had was actually a rough and ready renegade.

"I'm not at liberty to say and besides, if I did tell you, I'd have to kill you," responded Maddog. "But I need it back and you are going to help me get it by telling me where I can find those two goons."

Troy had no idea where to begin, and told Maddog so over and over again. He explained how he was in the club, busting shapes on the dance floor, like Kevin Bacon before he sold mobile phones, when they burst through the main doors. Their eyes had met and they'd immediately made a play for him, falling instantly in love. Then, just like Cinderella on the stroke of midnight, they'd left without even a glass Adidas original to show for it.

Troy continued with this cock and bull story for some time, changing the spin on real events to make his tale sound better and better. With every passing hour, Maddog's temper grew and grew. He'd never heard the same story told in so many different ways and once Troy tried to get away with, "and then he said to me, 'I'll never let go, Jack'," Maddog had had enough. He marched to the foot of the bed and re-tightened the shackles, securing the block of wood to Troy's ankles.

Troy began to panic and let out an ear-piercing scream. "No, please, don't," he squealed but the irate bouncer was beyond the point of no return. He reached underneath the bed, searching for the weapon in which to attack the feet. Once he located it, he wrapped his fist around the handle and drew the torturous device above his head and in full view of Troy. He asked one more time, "Where are they?"

Troy began to cry. "Mr Maddog, I don't know, I honestly have no idea," and with that Maddog swung the feather duster to the soles of Troy's feet and started tickling ferociously. Troy was in for a rough ride. Unfortunately, not the type of rough ride he'd longed for all his life.

In the next hour, Troy managed to both piss and shit himself several times as the crazed bouncer tickled his feet without let up. Troy's cries of laughter were so loud that they pierced the ear drums of the security guard tied to the chair across the room, waking him from his comatose state. Only then did Maddog stop.

"Please, Mr Maddog, no more," cried Troy. "I don't know who or where they are."

As Maddog stared down at the stinking mess on the bed, he pondered his next move.

"Perhaps this will jog your memory," he said, before producing a tube of cheese and chive Pringle crisps in front of Troy's face. And upon seeing them, Troy broke out into another cry. Maddog allowed himself a wry smile as Troy finally cracked. "Don't worry, son," he said, "you held out longer than I thought you would but, in the end, I always knew you were holding something back. Now come on, there's no shame in crying. Why the tears?"

Troy was struggling to get the words out and sounded like a toddler straight out of a tantrum, in between the tears trying to catch his breath. "I fucking hate cheese and chive!" screamed Troy, whose stomach had never gone more than two hours without food before.

Maddog slammed the tube of crisps down hard on the table,

unwittingly causing a hairline fracture in the seal. "No, you blubbering idiot. This is what they stole from me."

It was a statement that had Troy staring in disbelief. "Eh? You mean I'm going through all of this over a tube of Pringles?"

Maddog slapped the fool. "The tube is just what we carry it in."

"Carry what in?" asked Troy, his cheeks now burning red with pain.

"I've already said, I can't tell you. It's top secret. But we've been planning this for months and it's imperative that we get that other tube back." Maddog then picked up the tube and cradled it as if to reinforce its importance.

After a small pause, Maddog spoke again. "The tubes contain a truth serum so strong, that when inhaled, it prevents that individual from lying. You can ask that person any question you like and you'll get the one hundred percent, honest answer."

"How did you get hold of it?" enquired Troy, nosey as ever.

"Greasy Thumbs, Fat Tony and me have been receiving shipments of the stuff from the Russian mafia, who disguise the serum in tubes of Pringles aboard a ship called Cirrhosis Of The River. The ship, loaded with other cargo and chemicals, docks every six weeks at the BASF plant in Seal Sands, and from there we transport it to a safe house in Westbeck Gardens via the works transport bus where a guy called Tony Green is paid one hundred quid in cash upon delivery."

"And what do you plan to do with it?" asked Troy, who was now firmly gripped by the crime drama.

"We plan to hold up the HSBC bank in Middlesbrough town centre next Thursday. We chose that day because that's when the bank's vault is replenished with hard currency. The plan is to release the gas into the room and simply ask the security guard for the access code and vault security number. That's where this chap comes in." He pointed to the figure in the corner. "The bank manager thinks he's on the sick but we've kidnapped him to return to work next Thursday."

"Why are you telling me all of this? I thought it was all 'need to know'?" asked Troy, confused at Maddog's sudden loose-tongued behaviour.

"Because I've accidently put a hole in this tube, probably when I slammed it down on the table and now I can't stop telling the truth," said Maddog, all matter of factly.

"So are you aware that I've shit myself?" asked Troy, who thought he may as well get the truth.

"Well, I detected the stench of shit during your tickling torture but couldn't be sure if it was you or Ron here. That poor fella hasn't had a toilet break in twenty odd hours," responded Maddog.

"Are you secretly thinking about seducing me while I'm tied to this bed?" asked Troy excitedly.

"No, not one bit. I've actually been thinking of how I'm going to dispose of your corpse once I'm finished with you. But I don't think I can lift you," answered Maddog.

"Why? Do you think I'm fat?" asked Troy, smiling because he knew the truth would have to come out a resounding no.

"Yes, of course I do. You're a coronary waiting to happen, you big fat lump of lard," said Maddog, annoyance apparent in his voice at all the questions.

"Are you going to kill me?"

"Maybe."

CHAPTER 6

"Right into town? That'll be one pound eighty, love," said the bus driver of the legendary route 263 to the female passenger who had just boarded his craft.

"Did you just stare at my breasts?" she asked, in an uncomfortably loud voice.

"Eh? What? No," stuttered the baffled driver. "I certainly did not." Although now she'd brought the subject up, an invisible tractor beam seemed to be dragging his eyes in that direction.

"You're doing it again, you filthy pervert," she screamed, making a big show of zipping up her coat to right under her chin. Mary then turned to face the other passengers, who by now had tuned all senses to the conflict at the front of the bus, and pretended to cry.

As always, a local hero came to her aid, berating the driver with scowls and tuts before ushering the sexually harassed lass to the back of the bus.

Never once, in all her adult life, had Mary paid a bus fare.

The journey into town was, as expected, hurried, as the poor driver sailed past several of his stops in order to lose his toxic load. As the passengers got off, he made sure he kept his head and eyes well down. When Mary finally stepped off the bus and into Middlesbrough's bus station, she turned once more and faced the distraught driver.

"'Ere you," she shouted, in her posh Picton accent. The poor fellow, fearing a harassment case was just around the corner, had no choice but to look. "No harm done," she announced, winking at him before lifting up her top to reveal a pair of bouncing breasts which she jiggled from side to side. The poor driver blushed and didn't know where to look. The same couldn't be said for an elderly gentleman who was queueing to board the bus, however.

"Corr, look at the fucking tits on that," he shouted in an excited voice from over Mary's shoulder, causing her to turn around and notice his dog collar.

"In your dreams, vicar," she said, straightening herself up before pushing past him and heading for Aldi.

Mary's route to the budget supermarket store was meticulously planned. For she had cleverly memorised the exact location of every CCTV camera in the town centre. Mary was also aware that satellites orbiting the Earth could possibly be watching her every move. So she took great care never to glance upwards, thus never offering them a clear shot at her features. Although the satellites weren't the only reason for not looking up. Last time she did, she failed to see some dog shit on the pavement and slipped a disc in the fall.

Mary's approach toward Aldi came from the westerly direction. This was intentional because the low autumn sun would be shining brightly into the eyes of the security guard as she drew near. Hopefully, she would be in there, filling her pockets, before he even realised what was happening. It was a trick she'd learnt from an old army boyfriend who had served in the Falklands war. He had told her that Argentine planes would climb above enemy formations and attack them from height by diving out of the sun's glare. The old flame had had some first-hand experience of this, when a Mirage fighter jet, dive bombed his gun position during the conflict. With bullets raining down, her ex-fella was shot in the back while single-handedly saving a whole battalion of men. Well, at least that's what he told her. She often wondered what Jesus was up to these days.

She took a deep breath and put her professional head back on. It was showtime. When she was just twenty metres from the front door, she set a timer on her watch. Mary would have exactly one minute and forty seconds to get in and out, if she wanted to make a clean and perfect get away. With the clock ticking, she upped her pace. Upon arrival, she found the automatic doors already open, held in position by the security guard who was shielding his eyes from the sun during his fag break. Once beyond him, and safely inside the store, she took a sharp left and headed straight for the 'Offer of the Week' stand. Pulling two large, neatly folded hessian Bags For Life from her pockets, she placed them in the trolley and began immediately loading them with budget ski wear. Keeping a close eye on her wrist, she threw another glance at her watch which told her she had forty seconds of time remaining. In a pre-planned move, Mary headed towards the cash counters, which were just in front of the exit, and upon drawing closer, produced a single grape from her coat pocket. She dropped the grape on the floor before acting out an over-exaggerated slip upon it. In one fluent movement, she went down, letting out a mighty cry and forcefully pushing her trolley into an old aged pensioner, who was standing conveniently in front of a well-stacked tower of plum tomatoes. With the cans tumbling everywhere and an old lady lying prone in aisle four, the checkout girls leapt from their stations to help the old dear. Mary glanced at her watch again which confirmed she had just ten seconds to go. She pulled the two loaded Bags For Life from her trolley, and counted down the seconds as she walked towards the exit door. Affording herself one final glance at the unfolding chaos she'd created, she watched as the last three seconds ticked toward twelve and smiled as the routine weekly fire alarm bell rang out a deafening two tone chime. It had all been timed so perfectly. With the security guard off to collect the muster board and nobody on the tills to monitor customers, Mary walked out of the unguarded opening and took in a large breath of rich freedom. She'd make a fortune selling this loot. All she had to do now was wait for the snow.

As soon as Maddog had left the room, Troy set about his escape plan. "Psst… Psst… Ron," he whispered, trying to get a response from the security guard in the corner. But poor old Ron had been incarcerated a lot longer than Troy, and had clearly been put through the mill.

"Ronnie, are you awake? We need to get out of here." But the words once again fell on deaf ears. The security guard had been tortured for days, for not only were his feet tickled with a feather duster, but his armpits too. Four days he'd lasted, never once revealing when the bank's vault would be replenished but finally he broke when his ribs snapped through laughing. He was a brave but broken man.

Troy wriggled about on the bed and thought he had enough movement in his arms to reach the rape alarm that he always carried in his back pocket. He'd acquired it off eBay for two hundred quid, after the description said all irresistible people should have one. The alarm, once activated, was said to produce the same decibels as Concorde on take-off, although Troy would have to take the manufacturer's word for that as, much to his annoyance, nobody had even attempted to bum him.

Troy stretched his shackles until they started biting into his wrists and strained to reach his back pocket. His fingers so near, yet so far, kept touching and probing the end of the alarm but just couldn't get the purchase to grab it. Five times he thought he had managed it, only to see the nylon casing slip from his grasp. Five times he felt like giving in, but with the bouncer's threat to kill still ringing in his ears, he had to keep trying. Finally, with a herculean effort that would probably give him a bruise in the morning, he pulled the rape alarm from his pocket. Troy couldn't believe it, this had to be the greatest thing he had ever achieved. He knew deep down that he was a loser, but for the first time in his life, he had taken control of his own destiny and it felt bloody good.

"Don't worry, Ron. I'm going to get us out of here, just hang in there. Okay, buddy?" he said in a rather accomplished, yet excited voice, before feeling for the alarm button that would have help arriving in no time. With that, he hit the switch.

Nothing. No sound.

"What? No," wailed Troy, who tried the button again, but to no avail.

"Where did you buy it?" groaned a voice from the corner.

Ron was coming round.

"eBay," replied a distraught Troy.

"And the seller, was his name Seeme Cummings by any chance?" asked Ron, wincing with pain as he spoke.

"Yes. Yes, that's him. How did you know?"

"Just a guess," answered Ron, resting his head back onto his chest.

Troy slumped back on the bed and started blubbering. All that could be heard in that dark room was the sound of his sniffling and Ron's uncomfortable groans but then suddenly, a mobile phone started ringing.

"Why can't I achieve anything great? We're going to die," wailed Troy.

Only the blubbering buffoon was cut short by the alert guard. "Shut it, you idiot. What's that noise?" And they both listened as the sound of The Communards' Don't Leave Me This Way flooded the room.

"It's my phone," shouted Troy excitedly. "Where is it?"

The phone was placed on a battered wooden chair, along with other items that a pocket may contain such as keys, money and a condom, although it's fair to say that the rubber jonny had seen far better days.

"I can't reach it," he said. "Ron, you'll have to get it."

But the bank employee had already anticipated this and was hopping and scraping his chair, as quietly as he could, toward the musical phone. Once there, Ron reached out both feet and picked up the vibrating handset with his in-step. He himself was still unable to answer it, due to his own hands being tied, so he now had to get back across to Troy and hope the pair could work together before the ringing stopped.

Ron turned, banged and scraped his chair some more, edging closer and closer to Troy's bedside. With his ribs screaming in pain, he somehow managed to lift both feet up and over the bed frame so that the mobile was neatly positioned at Troy's head. "Go on, lad, answer it," he said.

Troy stared opened-mouthed at Ron. He'd never witnessed such heroics before. Well, not since the Brookside executive producers had filmed the first lesbian kiss. He stared at Ron in awe, then in wonder and finally with love and for the first time in his life, another man reciprocated his advances.

"Answer it," repeated the blushing security guard.

Troy was first to break the loving gaze. He quickly swiped the smart phone with his nose and bent his ear to the microphone.

"Hello. Who's there?" he asked.

"Troy, it's your mother."

The captive nearly dropped the phone with happiness.

"Mother, thank God, it's you. My phone didn't recognise your number."

"No, it wouldn't. I've blocked you, you fat fuck."

"What? Why?"

But there was no time for long discussions because Ron's feet were starting to tremble.

"Where are you anyway, Troy? It's not like you to stay out all night. Finally had your sausage wallet stuffed?" Mary had such a way with words.

"Mother, shut up and listen." Another first, Troy was standing up to his mother. "I've been kidnapped and taken hostage by a huge man. He has me tied to a bed and has been torturing me. He says if I don't tell him what he wants to hear, he might execute me."

Mary couldn't believe her luck. A free bus ride, a record haul of loot and to top it all, this. Days just didn't get any better. "Troy, whatever you do, don't tell him anything," advised Mary. "Better to go out with pride than be a grass, son."

"But, mother, I need your help."

Mary was miles away with thoughts of a single, child-free life. "Troy," she said, serious.

"Yes, mother," he replied, trying to hurry the conversation along because Ron was foaming at the mouth in pain.

"Is the Madison still open on an afternoon?"

"Erm, I'm not quite sure to be honest," answered Troy

truthfully, before once again being brought back into the room by the groans of Ron.

"Okay, son, then one more question before I go." Mary felt this one needed confirming before she planned her new life. "Can I still claim your disability allowance once you die?" Mary showed absolutely no remorse in her question.

"Yes, mother," answered Troy quickly. "But I've got the book with me, in case I was asked for it. You'd need that."

"Bollocks," screamed Mary before regaining her composure. "Then any idea where you are?"

"No, mother, not a clue."

"Think, Troy. What sounds can you hear? What smells can you detect? What do the knots look like around your hands? Have they used nylon rope or tie wraps? How many left turns did you make on the way there? How many right? What vehicle did they use to transport you? Was it a diesel van?"

"Mother," interrupted Troy. "I was caught in a compromising position with a Crocodile Dundee lookalike in the bumming booths of the Sausage Cottage. The bouncer seems to have taken exception."

"Jesus?" muttered Mary.

"Oh, thanks a bunch, mother. I'm not that ugly."

"No, not you, you idiot. Anything else I need to know?"

"Yes, bring underpants."

CHAPTER 7

"**O**utrageous, I can't believe you did that, Robert," said Jesus, rubbing his neck where his son had squeezed. "Your ability to harm people may have been overridden, but you cannot and will not go around flexing your muscles like some maverick enforcement droid."

The old boy was on his soapbox now but he had a point and Rob knew it. Twenty years of increasing artificial intelligence had, if nothing else, taught him right from wrong and, possibly for the first time in his life, he felt remorseful.

"Father, I'm very sorry," said Rob, looking at the floor. "I'm disgusted in myself, I don't know what came over me. I… I… I'd never ever hurt you… ever." Robert was sitting on the sofa, looking at his palms. "These hands that you created, the mere fact I'm here, I owe you everything, my life, my existence, my being, it's all down to you. To treat you like that, like some animal…" Rob's voice trailed off to a whisper of despair and he just sat there, slumped on the couch, head bowed, unable to look his father in the eye.

The moment wasn't lost on Jesus. He wasn't even angry anymore. Seeing his son like that, a cyborg he had created from scratch was nothing short of incredible. This was as near to crying as a robot could get. Well, unless he fitted windscreen washer jets, but that conversation was best left for another time. He'd only ever seen one other depressed robot before and that was Marvin from The Hitch Hiker's Guide to the Galaxy but everyone knew he was just an arsehole.

"Robert," whispered the old man, approaching him slowly before crouching in front of him. "I'm afraid it's me who owes you the apology. I hadn't realised until now, just how humanlike you were becoming. Had I known you were capable of these emotions, this sadness, I would have helped you, my son. We could have talked through your problems, your thoughts and your hurt. I'm so short-sighted. How could I not have foreseen this? I'm such a fool."

Rob looked up. "Help me, father, I'm so confused." And with that the dam burst. The big robot was off, an explosion of human emotions poured from his artificial soul.

Jesus embraced his son, cuddling him tight, encouraging him to tell all. "Let it all out, son," he said, patting his back in a 'there there' rhythm. And Rob did just that. Over the next two hours, as the pair held each other tightly, Rob told his father of the growing feelings inside him. Empathy, love, respect, hate, anger and finally, lust. For all of Jesus's brilliance, he failed to recognise the difficulties his son would face after he'd fitted the next generation of male artificial intelligence. Mind you, after listening to his son's manic sobs for a further hour, he began to wonder if he'd actually installed the female version at that.

Jesus grabbed Rob's hefty shoulders and gave them a big shake. "Now, big lad, that's quite enough of that," he said, finally taking hold of the situation. "This is all my fault and I'm going to put it right. I'm going to help you, Robert, but you must also be prepared to help me." The inventor allowed his son to acknowledge him with a nod before carrying on. "I'll look into getting you your penis, but if we go down that avenue, then we're going to do this properly." Rob gave an inquisitive look. "I first want you to attend some counselling sessions. We need to get you in the right frame of mind. If you want to become a bona fide man, then we must open our eyes to the future. What problems you are likely to face, what backlash you may receive from the public and upon completion, what nightclubs you can and cannot frequent."

"You mean like the Bongo?" asked Robert.

"Exactly," replied Jesus. "We simply can't have you going round with all this fear and insecurities. You see, Robert, fear leads to anger. Anger leads to hate. Hate leads to suffering."

Rob nodded in agreement, he knew his father was right. Looking him in the eye, he sucked in his stomach and stuck out his chest. "I'll do it, if you think that's the right path to choose, father." A new steely grit and determination washed over him.

"Of course it's the right thing to do, son," said the inventor, already busying himself searching for the Yellow Pages. "I'll book us an appointment as soon as possible."

"Brilliant," said the cyborg, who was now thrusting his pelvis back and forth in excitement. "By the way," he said in between thrusts, "did you just quote Yoda back then?"

Jesus stopped in his tracks and faced his gyrating son. Embarrassingly he had to admit he had indeed borrowed a quote from the master Jedi. "You must think me an old fool. I've been so lonely since Mary left. Burying my head in work. And raising you alone has not been easy. Never anywhere to go, nobody to go with, I suppose television is my only release, I… I…"

Rob put a hand up to his father's face. "Whoa there, dad, I happen to like Star Wars very much and I wouldn't change you for all the tea in China. But there is one thing I'd like you to do for me."

Jesus was heartened by his son's words. The lad had come on such a long way, considering his initial memory was borrowed from a 48K ZX Spectrum. "Anything, son. Just name it."

Rob walked up to the coat stand and removed the Crocodile Dundee hat. "You see this?" he said, holding the hat toward his father.

Jesus had already anticipated what his son was thinking. "It's okay, you don't have to say any more, I realise how silly it is and I can only try to imagine how embarrassed you must be when I put it on. I promise I won't wear it ever again."

Rob stood in front of his father and let out a huge laugh. "No, dad, you're misunderstanding me, I want you to wear it. It's quiz night in the Southern Cross and I could murder a few pints."

A beaming smile as wide as the Transporter Bridge spanned Jesus's face. "Shall I take my knife," he laughed.

"It's okay, pops, if anybody starts this time, I've got your back.

I'm allowed to hit back now, remember." He wiggled his index finger in the air to remind Jesus where his finger had been.

Grinning at each other with unconditional love, Jesus placed two fists in front of his waist and waited for Rob to do the same. Drawing back the fists to their sides in unison, they both started thrusting their pelvises and laughing together. It was going to be a good night.

Mary wasted no time when she got home, she had work to do and had to move fast. She didn't really require Troy in her life, but the benefit money she received for his obesity was essential, even if all the Parmos it took to keep him that way put a sizeable dent in it. What was really intriguing her though, was the coming together of the whole story. The kidnapping of Troy was just ludicrous and the mention of a Crocodile Dundee lookalike quite fascinating, but what was really motivating her was the fact that if somebody was prepared to go to those lengths, then something big must be going down in Middlesbrough. Regardless of whether her own son was involved or not, Mary wanted in.

Hurriedly climbing the stairs, she first entered the bathroom to 'drop the kids off at the pool'. There was no benefit to getting caught short on a job. Then, mid-laying of cable, she acquired a loose bobble from the tiled floor and tied her hair back into a ponytail. Now a pound lighter, she crossed the landing toward her bedroom, affording herself a quick glance at various pictures of Troy, framed in dark mahogany on the wall. She paused briefly, studying each one in turn. Her favourite one was a snap she had taken during school sports day. It was the only time Troy hadn't come last in a race and the look on his face just before they slipped the oxygen mask on was priceless. As ruthless as Mary might be, deep down, in the fiery pit of her stomach, there was a microscopic love for her child that all mothers subconsciously develop when they give birth. Although Mary often tried to wash away that feeling with neat vodka.

She stood back from the pictures and shook her head. She hated those emotional chinks in her armour, seeing them as signs of weakness. With a sharp slap to her own face, she moved on.

Dropping to the floor at the base of her bed, she pulled a clear plastic box from under it. Whipping off the lid, she heaved the unit onto the bed and sorted through the items she'd need for the job. Rope, glass cutter, knife, crowbar, electrician's tape, hairspray and an old clock. Once that was sorted, she moved on to her attire and what was deemed appropriate for such an occasion.

She pulled out a black, figure hugging Adidas tracksuit from the wardrobe, making sure it was made of nylon so as to reduce noise. She then retrieved an old pair of Black Adidas Samba. New ones tended to squeak a bit as the black patent leather moulded itself around a warm foot. Stealth was the aim of the game tonight. Mary then taped the chrome zipper that would be rattling under her chin with electrician's tape and threw the sportswear on. Finally, she completed the look with a black Kappa snood before jumping up and down for a sound check.

Perfect.

With her kit all sorted, Mary tucked the other items into a dark blue Fila rucksack and made her way out of the door and into the cold night air. It was an hour before closing time and a further hour before she could break into the Sausage Cottage. If she got lucky, there might be some old biddies to mug along the way.

"With the final picture round over, tables three and ten are still tied for the lead," announced Tim, the quiz compere for the night. Tim had assumed his quiz questions on Baxter boilers, the trials and tribulations of Middlesbrough Football Club and the coefficient expansion of welding flux would have had the punters stumped and heading for the exits long before now, but this was not the case. Two groups had gone at it head to head, never getting a question wrong, and the man with the mic was revelling in it like Bob Holness on whizz.

The leading teams were comparably different. On one table sat Robert and Jesus, both drinking slow burners such as Carling and Fosters, on the other sat three local chaps, each as surprised as the other that they'd managed to answer any questions at all. They had started off on the Carling too, but were by now hitting the harder spirits. As the last orders bell approached, it was fair to say they weren't at their sharpest.

"So we come down to the tie-break question," shouted Tim, playing the Countdown clock music as he did so, much to the groans of the dispersing crowd who had heard enough by now. "Are you both ready? Right, here we go." Tim paused for effect. "Who started the scout movement?"

Rob scanned his history files with super efficiency but it was Jesus who came up with the answer first. "Baden Powell," he said, with a knowing grin and a chink of glasses in celebration with Rob.

"Eh? Was it fuck, man," challenged table ten. "It was head of Middlesbrough's Academy, Ron Bone."

Tim rang the bell for last orders.

Mary positioned herself in a darkened corner of the Sausage Cottage car park and waited for the bar staff to empty the used beer bottles into the dedicated bins. She'd been crouched there for a while, keeping a watchful eye on the back door, as she hid out of sight, looking for signs of movement and routine. While there, she produced the clock from her rucksack and started to break up the outer casing. Minutes later, all that remained was the mechanism with the minute hand still attached. Once content that the contraption was fitting of the task, she slipped in a new battery and set the minute hand at quarter to. Happy that the clock was ticking merrily, she then attached a small oblong piece of cardboard to the minute hand with electrician's tape and waited.

A few moments later, a couple of weary women laden with bottles, opened the back door and headed for the recycle bins. As they did so, their movement triggered the motion sensors on the car park floodlights. Most of the darkness vanished in white light. All was going to plan for Mary yet again. With the bottles now tipped into the recycle bin, the two staff members headed back inside to finish operation clean up before heading home. Now was the time for Mary to act.

With the car park still bathed in light, Mary ran from her position and stationed herself underneath the floodlight. Positioning the clock just underneath it so that the minute hand was free to slowly move in front of the motion sensor, she retreated back to her hiding hole and waited for the light to go out. The temptation to have a fag after the forty-yard dash was overpowering, but Mary knew better than to compromise her mission at such a critical stage. A burning cigarette could be seen from a mile away.

Ten more minutes passed and the staff could be heard saying their goodbyes. When all was quiet, Mary walked straight across the car park and up to the floodlight. As expected, the light never went off, due to the oblong cardboard that was attached to the minute hand slowly making its way over the sensor. All Mary had to do now was fix the clock in that position, thus rendering the light useless. She moved swiftly now, darting up to the bottom window pane of the back door, removing the glass cutters from her bag as she went. Slowly, she cut a hole big enough for her to clamber through then inched into the empty building. Once inside, she waited for her night vision to settle again.

Retrieving the can of hairspray from her bag, she gave a gentle blast of the contents into the air around her. She did this every couple of steps until the tiny mist particles detected a red beam of light from the set burglar alarm sensors. Once a person knew the direction in which the beams were pointing, it was relatively simple to avoid them. Mary carried on with this pattern, spraying and slowly stepping, until she reached the safety of the CCTV station.

Walking up to the multiscreen console, Mary fired the unit up and glanced at camera four which covered the car park. As expected it was in complete darkness, a quick rewind of the tape saw minimal activity by the glass collectors and little else. Mary grinned at her professionalism. "Ghost," she whispered to herself, before turning her attention to the main room, the one with the dance floor. Punching in yesterday's date and rough timings of when she had last seen Troy, she sat back and watched the grainy black and white show.

Mary watched the tape play back with monotonous agony, watching hundreds of people pass back and forth but seeing nothing out of the ordinary. She spent half an hour cringing, watching Troy make an absolute arse of himself on the dance floor trying to move like Patrick Swayze in Dirty Dancing, but instead resembling a wounded hippopotamus. Mary reckoned an injured hippo would receive more attention. Finally, about to give up, she watched two guys burst into the club and catch Troy's attention. A hasty dialogue had followed before they both followed Troy to the back of the club. Troy had had the sense to walk directly in front of camera two. Although if truth be known, he'd actually chosen this route as it was the shortest path of resistance to the booths.

Mary played and stopped camera two a few times, altering its sharpness while zooming in and out. When she had the best image she could get, she peered at the screen for a closer look. She had no idea who the first man was. He was tall, extremely good-looking and built like a brick shithouse. She had to admire Troy for his choice of man. But there was something familiar about the second guy. Clearly older, he was, as Troy had suggested, dressed like Crocodile Dundee. His face, however, was obscured by the rim of his hat. He was clearly a professional, always turning to see who was behind him, never looking up or at any cameras, but his gait was very familiar.

Mary altered the brightness on the screen and tried putting a light filter on but still she couldn't make out who the individual was. Frustrated, she sat back and stared at the screen. "There must be something," she whispered. Then she saw it, attached to the guy's belt was a leather sheath, protruding from underneath his leather jacket by about five inches. Black in colour with gold writing on it, it was obviously holding a weapon of some sort. Mary fiddled with the dials once more and focused all her attention on the object. Zooming in and sharpening the picture, the writing came in to focus. It simply said one word, 'Mary'.

"No fucking way," she whispered.

CHAPTER 8

"Untie the lad. Let him go," pleaded Ron, addressing an irate Maddog as soon as the bouncer entered the room. "It's clear he doesn't know anything about who those two people you're talking about are. Let him walk, he's of no use to you."

Maddog just frowned at the stupidity of the statement.

"Let him go? Let him fucking go? And then what? He runs off into the nearest cop shop and blows the whistle on the whole operation? It's not going to happen," retorted Maddog.

Ron had to admit that having only known Troy for two days, he probably wouldn't be able to keep his trap shut and Maddog was right to hold him. But the chances of Troy running anywhere, let alone to the police, were very slim. Ron wasn't about to divulge this information, though. He was starting to bond with Troy, perhaps even care for him. If he could free him, then at least something good might come out of all this mess.

"Maddog, it's me you need. I'm the one that opens the vault. Not Troy. Let him go."

But still Maddog was having none of it.

"Then at least untie him and clean him up for God's sake, the neighbours will think you have a dead body in here, such is the stench coming from his soiled trousers."

Troy could only admire Ron's bravery. There the fellow was, thinking of him, while bound to a chair himself. Troy wanted to thank him, tell him how wonderful and courageous he was, but he was too frightened.

Maddog thought for a moment. The guard made some valid points, the last thing he needed was an inquisitive neighbour knocking on the door and poking around. Not that Maddog had many visitors. Even the Grim Reaper would have to seriously think about entering Maddog's lair and, if he did, he'd probably just remove his shoes and sit quietly.

"Okay, you can both wash and freshen up," said Maddog, as if the idea was his own. "But no funny business or you'll get a slap." He slapped Ron hard across the face, as if to prove his point.

Ron rocked in his chair from the blow and Troy, fearing a similar whack, tensed up on the bed.

"No funny business, Maddog, I promise," whimpered Troy.

Maddog moved toward Troy with his knife in full show, slowly twisting the blade from side to side, allowing it to glint in the soft glow from the overhead light bulb. He was enjoying the power a little too much for his bed-ridden captive, who almost started to hyperventilate. Finally, he cut the tie wraps which were holding the frantic lad to the bed and said, "Remember what I said, now. No funny business."

Maddog moved across the room and freed Ron from his shackles too, pointing for Troy to help the man to his feet. Being stuck in that position for so long had caused the security guard considerable pain and Troy had to support Ron to prevent him from falling.

"Thank you, Troy," whispered Ron, holding onto the fatty's shoulders for support.

"Right, listen 'ere, you two, I've not got all day, and I'm not going to bed bath you both either, so this is the deal: both of you have ten minutes to get in there and tidy yourselves up. I want your clothes in this black bag for cleaning and don't be thinking of running a bath, because those things cost a fortune to heat up. That means that both of you will have to shower together and the clock is already ticking."

Troy's legs buckled as he envisaged a Cadbury's Flake in a bath tub setting. A setting in which he fed crumbly chocolate to Ron, while soft music played in the background.

The thought was interrupted by Maddog, who had let out an audible growl at their lack of progress toward the bathroom.

"Come on, Troy," said Ron, "we haven't got long."

Troy started to remove his soiled costume under the watchful eye of the big doorman with Ron following suit. Once undressed, the pair dropped their clothes into the black bin liner, as instructed, and soon found themselves standing in only their underwear.

"Hurry up, sweetheart, don't be shy," heckled the big bouncer, revelling in Troy's uncomfortable state. Troy slowly dropped his underpants and stared at the floor.

"What the fuck is that?" cried the hysterical Maddog, pointing at Troy's tackle. "It's fucking tiny and shaped like an acorn." Maddog had tears rolling down his cheeks. "What the fuck are you supposed to do with that thing?" he cried, holding his stomach as if his sides were splitting. "Shagging with that would be like throwing a sausage down a corridor, nobody would feel a thing."

Troy was beetroot red. He'd never shown his penis to anybody before and standing there under this barrage of abuse just made it shrink even further.

"Leave him alone, Maddog," said Ron, jumping to the defence of the clearly embarrassed carpet designer, he himself unable to hide the disappointment from his voice. "I think given the unfortunate circumstances we find ourselves in, Troy's member can be forgiven for hiding under those warm rolls of fat."

Troy, not sure whether this was a compliment or not, sucked in his stomach.

"Ohhhhhh! Aren't you two just the lovely little couple? Been all cosy in here, have we?" sneered Maddog, with deepening menace.

Seeing the situation worsen in front of his eyes, Ron decided to remain quiet so as not to antagonise the doorman any further. He decided he too should just strip naked. He was still aching from his previous prone seating position as he slowly removed his Calvin Klein's. With his two thumbs wedged into the waistband, he lowered them toward his knees. As he did, he revealed the largest and most magnificent porridge gun the world has ever clapped eyes on. The mutton dagger was well over twelve inches long with large bulging veins that gave off a blue hue. The helmet, a shiny deep maroon and large enough to claim its own gravitational pull, dangled on the end like a clapper from a church bell. It was the most astonishing womb brush Maddog had ever seen and his sneering smile contorted into an open jaw as he stood and stared in disbelief. He looked at Ron and then again at the monstrous vagina miner before looking back at Ron. Then he turned back to look at Troy.

"What the…? Where the fuck's he gone?" cried Maddog, panic gripping his voice as he stared at the empty space where Troy had been stood only moments before.

"Yoo-hoo, Ronnie dear," cried an obviously excited Troy. "I'm in the shower. Hurry up. The water's lovely."

Back across town, Mary made her way into a late night café not far from the infamous Club Bongo International. She sat at a table facing the door and scanned the floor plan for other exits and routes of escape. Anywhere over the border this late at night was no place for a delicate Picton lass like herself, especially one who had forgotten to pack her knuckledusters. Care was very much the order of the day. Mary ordered a strong, sweet tea and placed her phone on the table in front of her. It was time to trace the whereabouts of Troy but not before checking in on Facebook and seeing what the girls were up to. One had to prioritise at times such as these.

"Troy, you said your mother would be able to track your mobile phone signal to our exact location and get us help. Are you sure she's up to the task?"

Troy didn't hear the words, he was drifting away in a world of his own.

"Troy, for fuck's sake, my face is up here," said Ron, clearly agitated that his showering partner didn't appear to grasp the seriousness of the situation.

Troy broke away from the swaying anaconda in front of him. "What? Eh? Yes, my mother is very good at this sort of thing, she'll be here soon. And don't worry about her, when she does finally arrive, that man in there will be extremely sorry."

"Thank goodness for that," sighed Ron. "We really need to get out of here, but how will she track your signal?"

Alas, Troy was lost once again. He was transfixed, watching the soap suds slide down the shaft of Veinous Maximus.

"Troy!" barked Ron. "We've no time for this. Where is your phone?"

"In my trouser pocket. Don't worry, it's safe," reassured the transfixed Troy once again.

But on hearing the news, Ron rested his head against the cold tiles in despair. "The trousers you've just handed to Maddog, the ones he's probably washing as we speak?"

Only then did the gravity of the situation hit home.

"That's quite enough, you two. Back out here," ordered Maddog, opening the bathroom door and trying not to stare too much at Ron's kidney scraper. He threw them both a towel and a jumpsuit similar to those worn by convicts and oil workers, the ones commonly used in the offshore industry to institutionalise those on board even further. When they were both fully clothed again, he re-tied them in position. Their positions swapped this time with Troy being placed on the chair instead of the bed.

"I suppose you two benders would like some food?" asked Maddog, only for Ron to roll his eyes and wonder if the bouncer had recently read the Geneva Convention.

"Yes, please," snapped Troy, who couldn't believe his stomach had remained this quiet for so long.

"Well, don't expect me to cook. It'll have to be a takeaway."

"You're not a naked chef then, Maddog?" snorted Ron, knowing the doorman felt very inadequate now he'd met 'The General'.

Maddog nipped his shackles just a little tighter. "Like I said, takeaway."

Mary opened the app, Mobile Tracker Pro on her handset, and using Troy's mobile number, searched for his pinpoint location to flash up. She drained the last of her tea while she waited for the spinning disc of death to stop, only the disc didn't stop. After a few minutes of constant rotation, the message 'signal not found' appeared on her screen. She tried again and waited. Still nothing so she rang Troy's number but only the words, "I'm sorry the person you are trying to reach is unable to answer," echoed back at her.

"Silly fat bastard," she muttered to herself.

Mary pondered her next move and cursed herself for playing Candy Crush for the last hour. Had she not bought those extra lives, she may have reached Troy in time. "Bang goes the disability benefits," she thought.

Not one to stew on the past, Mary unzipped her blouse and put her best assets on show. Innovative as ever, she reasoned that while over the border, she may as well earn some extra cash and thumbed down the first car that came her way. To her surprise, it stopped and she leaned in through the window.

"Want any business, darling?" she said seductively, giving the young driver an eyeful of cleavage.

"Erm, no, thank you, but I wonder if you could help me? I can't find this address."

Mary could smell the fast food wafting from the van window. "And whom do you work for, darling?" she asked. If she was going to lift this naive driver's takings, she'd have to keep him talking and gain his confidence.

"Parmo Pete," answered the young driver, unable to draw his eyes from the chesticles leaning in through the window.

"Parmo Pete," exclaimed Mary. "But you're miles outside your delivery zone. What are you doing here in town?"

"Pete said Mr Fass'abender is a very special customer and that I'm not to upset his family ever," said the young lad, who was starting to stress at the time he was wasting with Hootie McBoob.

"Then you've found just the right person to help you, sweetheart," said Mary climbing into the passenger seat. "Now, what address are you looking for again?"

CHAPTER 9

Nervous Rob Jones had been awake since the crack of dawn, butterflies going round and round his stomach, like a washing machine on high spin. Jesus, whose DNA displayed traits of half-man, half-mattress, had managed his usual ten hours kip without incident. Today was an important one, the day Rob's new life would begin. The first day of the rest of his life and he was keen to start proceedings.

They both finished breakfast in the usual way, with Sky Sports News on in the background and Jesus floating the odd air biscuit over the breakfast bar in ruthless fashion. You'd be forgiven for thinking that such back door breeze wouldn't affect a finely-tuned cybernetic organism like Rob. This, however, was not the case.

Given the lad's history of being unable to detect leaking gas, Jesus had installed the very latest gas detection system inside Rob's hooter, enabling him to detect such dangerous gases as carbon monoxide and smoke, but he was also susceptible to methane. Hence his father's bottom burps often left him retching.

Jesus stood facing Robert with a beaming smile, checking over his attire with merciless precision. He wanted him looking his sharpest for the visit to the psychologists, and Jesus left nothing to chance in his quest for perfection. Once satisfied that his son was looking dapper, he reached into the fly of his boy's blue corduroy trousers and withdrew the USB power adapter from its socket. With a knowing look, they both nodded at each other with satisfaction.

"Ready?" asked the excited inventor, moving to straighten the boy's tie for the umpteenth time.

"Ready," replied the intrepid cyborg, both of them knowing that, with this new penis, they were about to boldly go where no robot had ever gone before. Well, with the possible exception of C3PO, the campest robot in the galaxy. One can only imagine the horrors R2D2 must have witnessed.

"Well, this is it, son. The start of your adulthood," said Jesus, who hadn't felt this emotional since Scott and Charlene's wedding on Neighbours.

Rob just stood in nervous silence, smiling back at his father.

The tension was only broken by the ringing of a mobile phone.

"Our cab is here," Jesus mumbled, glancing at his phone while trying to keep his croaky voice from giving his emotional state away. "Now, remember what I told you, we have to be open and honest with this psychologist. No mucking around with her."

Rob let a smile light up his face at such a thought.

"I'm serious, son. This is no time for jokes. If we are really going to get you a penis and turn you into a real human being, then I want it doing properly.

Rob replied by giving his father a reassuring embrace. "I'll be open and honest, father. I promise."

A proud smile crossed Jesus's face. His son really was ready for this. He was for all intents and purposes already a real man. "Then we should get going."

The pair headed down the hallway toward the front door with Jesus first to reach it. He paused slightly, allowing the tension to build.

"I've got a little surprise you," he announced, before cracking the door slowly to reveal a black stretch limousine parked outside.

"For me?" enquired Rob.

"For you," reiterated Jesus.

The limousine was the size of two cars and had blacked out windows, with waxed, ash black colour paint, shining brightly in the sunlight. It had the standard, chrome spoiler like in all the Hollywood films and the driver had purposely left the engine ticking over, causing the neighbourhood curtains to twitch. It was the first time such a car had ever entered Thornaby, and one could only assume it must have bulletproof windows.

"Why?" asked Rob, looking at his father in amazement.

"It's a very important day, son. I wanted to do something special, to show you how much I love you and how proud I am of you. It's a day I want you to never forget."

Rob's bottom lip started to twitch involuntarily, a moment not lost on Jesus who had been monitoring his son's impressive repertoire of emotions for some time now. However, now was not the right time to question them. Rob stepped forward to throw a large arm around his father's shoulders and together they walked toward the waiting car. Aware that eyes were still peeking upon them from behind next door's curtains, they climbed into the back and gave a trademark royalty wave from a slightly opened window. With the pair rolling in fits of laughter, the wheels began to roll.

Inside, the limousine was rather plush, with its big leather seats and plasma television, not to mention the CD player, neon strip lights, champagne bar with crystal glasses, and disco ball hanging from the ceiling. The passenger space had the option of total privacy, offered by a screen that partitioned the occupants from the driver. Strangely, the screen was in the up position as the pair entered the vehicle.

"So where can I take you two fine upstanding gentlemen on this glorious morning?" announced the driver through the intercom system.

Rob and his father looked at each other and sniggered in unison. They'd never been called fine gentlemen before. Knobheads, yes. Upstanding, definitely not.

"Baker Street, my good man. And don't spare the horses," said Jesus in the poshest accent he could muster. A command that impressed Rob, for not only was his father exceptionally good at 'outback Australian', he'd managed to master broad Teesside too.

The driver, unbeknown to the giggling duo in the back, just rolled his eyes skyward.

The limousine rolled through the streets of Middlesbrough at a snail's pace, attracting many gawps from pedestrians as it went, as well as an egg from one mucky juvenile on Parliament Road. Though, thankfully, that had sailed harmlessly wide of its target. On reaching the junction at Linthorpe Road, the driver took an unexpected right turn. Instead of heading toward their appointment in town, he was now driving in completely the opposite direction, putting distance between them and Rob's day of destiny.

"Erm, excuse me, mate, but Baker Street is that way," said Jesus, knocking on the driver's divide panel.

Only, the driver remained quiet. Instead of slowing down and correcting his route, he now accelerated at an alarming rate.

"Excuse me, pal, but you're going the wrong way," shouted Rob, agitation now growing in his voice. When the driver once again failed to respond, Rob threw his father a concerned look.

The limousine wound its way down Roman Road toward suburban Tollesby, before passing the Endeavour pub and chicaning around the Acklam hairpin. As it did so, the driver decided to ignore any speed bumps and instead jumped over them as if he was driving the General Lee itself. This bizarre behaviour resulted in the poor occupants being tossed about in confusion, like clothes in a lost property bin, only coming to rest when the vehicle handbrake-turned into the school car park, and came to an abrupt stop.

A stunned silence descended within the car.

"What the fuck is going on?" groaned Rob, who was grabbing at his dazed father to see if he was alright. But before Jesus could answer, the intercom crackled into life.

"Ironic, isn't it? Ending up here on this patch of earth. A place filled with so many memories and emotions that I could spend a millennium recounting them. Except there's one defining memory that won't leave me. It sticks in my head like a black shadow, casting darkness and sorrow on all that is good in the world and glorifying all that is wrong."

Rob and Jesus looked at each other, becoming more baffled by the second.

"Where did you say you ordered this limo from again?" asked the bemused robot of his father, while miming a loop-the-loop sign around his temple. "He's a fucking fruitcake."

The speaker interrupted once again. "Silence. I will have my say. I will have my vengeance, I won't be denied again." The confusion was increasing within the limo. "You're nothing but an alloyed freak, created by a lonely eccentric fool who should still be rotting in jail. You make me sick. Do you know what it feels like, having to watch you become successful by mere fluke? Watching whatever you touch turn to gold through no trial or tribulation? All the while, I fight this daily struggle. You... with your male model good looks, your superior height and women falling at your feet. You ruined me, Tin Head, and now you will pay."

Rob mouthed to his father once again. "Who the fuck is this guy?"

Jesus was just as clueless as his metallic son and offered a simple shrug of his shoulders in return.

The voice, more sinister this time, offered yet more clues. "You can kiss the green, green grass of home goodbye, Tin Head. Pity you don't have a mama, she'd have told you not to come. But you couldn't help yourself, which isn't unusual."

Jesus reacted first, tugging on Rob's arm in a manic eureka moment having finally guessed who the driver was. "Fuck me, son," he cried, pointing excitedly. "It's Tom fucking Jones." The pair embraced each other in wild excitement.

On hearing this, the driver became even more frustrated. "What is it with these two fuckwits?" he whispered, before jumping from the front of the vehicle, drawing his knife and heading to the passengers in the back.

"Are you sure, father?" cried Rob, watching the Welsh crooner head toward them, knife in hand. "He looks much bigger on TV, doesn't he?"

Before Jesus could reply, the back door of the limousine was flung open and it was not Tom, but a small man, no higher than a badminton racquet, that stood there.

"Actually, son, I think it might be an Ewok," said Jesus, as if he himself were Sherlock Holmes solving the latest scandal in Boro.

"You morons," blasted the assailant, becoming more agitated by their failure to recognise him. "It is I, Mohammed."

Rob and Jesus gave each other a blank look. "Who?"

"Little Mo, remember? The science block fell on my head?"

Once again the pair in the back of the limousine scratched their chins as if deep in thought. "Nope, sorry, mate," said Jesus, showing the dwarf a clean pair of palms to show they didn't have a clue.

This only proceeded to anger Mo further, and he began jabbing the knife dangerously close to the old timer. "You know, the taxi driver who ripped you off at the Sausage Cottage?" he snarled, spitting venom.

"Ooooh, that little shit," said Rob, the muddied water now crystal clear. "Why are you dressed as an Ewok, then?"

It was all Mohammed could take. Stopping just short of spontaneous combustion, he flew into a rage. He climbed further into the back of the limousine and began his offensive. Thrashing wildly with the knife, he first cut a huge hole in Jesus's Farah trousers, before whipping off half of his 80's piano tie.

"Oi, you'll have somebody's eye out with that thing," shouted Jesus, doing his best to repel the attack. But the onslaught continued, with Little Mo managing to slit Rob's trousers from groin to ankle in the most ferocious and relentless attack seen in these parts since Ian Baird single-handedly took on the entire Newcastle United defence. Cornered, scared and embracing each other, Rob and Jesus found solace in each other's arms as their imminent end drew seemingly nearer.

Mohammed, standing as only someone with his height can in the back of a limousine, raised the knife above his head. "Eenie, meenie, miney, mo," he taunted, before finally choosing to murder Jesus first. He wanted Rob to witness his father's demise, and feel the same pain he himself had once felt. Like the shower scene in Psycho, he allowed the knife to hang in the air, perilously close to the disco ball that was suspended from the car roof. As his taunting continued, so too did the friction of the blade against the disco ball fixing and the knifeman unwittingly severed the 10kg steel ball's support rope sending the shiny globe plummeting from the roof.

It landed on Mo, smacking him clean on the head. Mo, for the second time in his life, was out cold and, unfortunately for him, yet another inch shorter.

"Well, that was weird," said Rob, scrutinising the scene at his feet.

"Little man syndrome, son," replied his father and they both nodded in agreement.

"We can still make your appointment, son. We're a little late but I'm sure she'll still see us if we hurry."

"We can't go like this, dad," said Rob, looking at his shredded clothing. "We look dreadful."

Jesus was quick to disagree. "Son, I promised you that this would be a special day, and I'm not prepared to let this little incident get in the way of that. Now help me get this crazy little bastard in the boot and we'll be on our way."

"We could just pop him in the glove compartment, dad," replied Robert, causing the pair to erupt into laughter.

Penelope Stevenson was the North's leading psychologist, having served twenty-five years in her chosen profession with great distinction.

Thoroughly professional, she practised a life of exemplary virtue, not only at home, but at work too. Over the years, she had treated a number of showbiz stars from Cliff Richard to the Chuckle Brothers. It was the latter that had taught her the fine art of tennis, from me to you. It was a sport she excelled at, climbing to the dizzy heights of fifth in the British rankings having just pipped Lily Savage in the woman's rankings, an elevated position Lily was eventually stripped of when it was revealed she was actually a he.

Penelope was astute, courteous and a stickler for punctuality. Having waited for over half an hour for her next appointment to arrive, her patience was wearing thin. Finally, the office intercom burst into life. "Mrs Stevenson, your morning appointment has just arrived."

About flipping time, thought Pee, clearing her throat and

straightening her black pencil skirt before running a final check of her mousey brown hair. Once happy, she wore a false smile and beckoned her appointment to enter.

Robert Jones stuck his head around the door first, followed by Jesus. If Penelope had at first been taken aback by Rob's stunning good looks, then that image had popped quicker than bubble wrap in an ADHD clinic. As the pair now stood before her, dishevelled and mucky, with ripped, blood-stained clothing, it took all of her professionalism not to turn her nose up and ask the scruffs to leave. After all, she had once had Sir Bob Geldof on her books and that scruffy tramp had turned out alright, even if his music hadn't.

"Gentlemen, please have a seat," she offered. "Is everything okay? I mean you look, er, a little off colour."

"Oh yeah, we're fine thanks," said Jesus, before offering a form of apology. "And we're sorry for being a tad late, pet."

'Pet' was another bugbear of Penelope's. Another celebrity client of hers, Jimmy Nail, had used it continuously for two years within every sentence he'd ever made but unfortunately, he couldn't be saved. If anybody goes around muttering crocodile shoes long enough, then eventually the men in white coats will come a-knocking. As good as Stevenson was, she couldn't perform miracles.

"So, gentlemen, how can I help you?" asked Penelope, taking a seat behind her large desk and putting an end to all the pleasantries.

"Ah well, pet," started Jesus.

Penelope shivered.

"You see this case may be a little different to what you're used to."

"Mr Jones," interrupted Penelope, "I assure you, in all my time in my profession I've heard them all, and nothing, and I mean nothing, I hear in this room will faze, nor shock me. Unless you tell me you can't tell the time, in which case I will let you off for being half an hour late."

Professional or not, Penelope Stevenson was still a woman and no woman alive could resist a cheap shot remark at a down-beaten man. It would go against the laws of physics and the world might implode.

"Yes, well, ahem." Jesus cleared his throat. Not sure if that was a dig at him or a compliment, he let it ride. "This is my son and he was born with no penis."

Penelope blushed a scarlet pink colour. She had to admit she'd never heard a client say that before. Rocking slightly from the news, she managed to regain her composure. "Please, go on."

"Well you see, pet, we've had quite a traumatic week, which I think has brought out some hidden feelings in young Robert here. Feelings that I was blissfully unaware of. I've raised him on my own, you see, and he's never really had a female presence in his life. Not unless you count Anneka Rice that is, because we religiously watched Treasure Hunt for years before Channel Four pulled the plug. She was like a mother to him."

Penelope instantly regretted taking this case on. "Hidden feelings?" she questioned, struggling to decipher what the old goat was talking about.

"Nah, nowt like that, love. He likes to shag my hoover, you see."

Penelope spat her tea out.

"Only when he's horny, like, which as you can probably imagine is a bit inappropriate at times and, if I'm being totally honest, a little bit weird too…"

"Excuse me," said Penelope, shaking her head as if she'd misheard. "He likes to… ahem, make love to a hoover, you say?"

"Well, not just any hoover like. One of those Herbert ones, you know? With the face on the front. But the thing is, pet, Robert doesn't have a penis so instead what he does is…"

Penelope threw up a hand to stop the old man in his tracks. "I'm sorry, I'm getting a little lost here and, quite frankly, a little bit scared. Can we possibly start again?" she said, jotting down the word 'looney' on her notepad.

"Erm, I'll field it from here, dad, thanks," interrupted Rob, saving himself a world of embarrassment and an escape from a straitjacket or, even worse, prison. "What my father is trying to say, is that this week, he has discovered that I'm more grown up than he'd probably admit to knowing."

"Ah yes," nodded a relieved Penelope, finally on some common ground with a young man who was talking a lot more sense than his deranged father. She encouraged him to continue.

"Well, let me start at the beginning. It all began a few days ago, when I was sexually harassed by a couple of Jehovah's Witnesses."

More tea spouted from her lips and covered her blouse.

"Sexually harassed?" asked Penelope, holding the young man's gaze with a sympathetic look, while scrambling for the panic button under her desk. "You poor thing, it's quite common to feel anger after such a traumatic event. Tell me, do you blame your father perhaps, for not being there when this happened?" She'd have this one wrapped up in ten minutes, it was obvious just by looking at the parent why this young man was suffering.

"Well, I did at first because he wasn't home," answered Rob.

Penelope nodded her head.

"He was knocking some hours off his community service, you see, after being released on a firearms charge."

Penelope's eyes widened before narrowing again and scowling toward Jesus, as she underlined the word 'looney' on her pad, forcefully cementing her diagnosis with an exclamation mark.

"But it's not all his fault," explained Rob. "You see he was beaten up due to a Blu Tack sale and then wrongfully rearrested again the same day."

"Blu Tack?" asked Penelope.

"Blu Tack," said Rob, as if it were an everyday occurrence. "Anyway, on his release for wrongful arrest, we went out to celebrate…"

"Celebrate?" said Penelope, unable to comprehend why anybody would celebrate an assault from one of God's Witnesses.

"Yeah, to the Sausage Cottage. Only this dwarf taxi driver attempts to assassinate me there and then."

Penelope slumped back in her chair and pressed the panic alarm.

"Luckily though, this big bloody bouncer turns up and chases the little fella away."

"You were sexually assaulted and had an assassination attempt on your life in one day?" she asked, against the ropes for the first time in her career.

"Well, twice if you count the bouncer's threats to kill me too. You see, dad here was dressed as Crocodile Dundee and smashed him round the head with a can of beans. Most upset, he was."

"Pardon?" asked the baffled psychologist, now struggling to keep up with this most alarming of stories. "Attempted rape, threats of murder, firearms, Crocodile Dundee, Herbert the Hoover and Blu Tack. Is this some kind of joke?" Penelope was taking in big gulps of water and trying to slow her breathing.

"No, far from it," responded Jesus. "I realise it may sound silly now, but I assure you this is not something we would fabricate or joke about. On the contrary, I'm here with you today to discuss the responsibility that comes with having a penis."

"Excuse me," said the baffled Penelope, "but I think we probably have more important things to discuss with Robert than the birds and the bees, Mr Jones. Wouldn't you agree?"

"Not really, pet. As we're a little bit late."

"Half an hour late, but please go on," responded Penelope, still unable to control her natural female instinct to nag.

"Well, as we're half an hour late, we couldn't really find a decent parking space for the limousine, so I had to park on a yellow line."

"You came to this therapy session in a limousine?" The shrink was about to lose it.

"Yeah, dad got me it to celebrate getting a cock," answered Rob.

"I don't think you quite grasp the idea of celebration, but we'll leave that for another time," said the exasperated Penelope Stevenson, who was by now on the verge of seeing her professionalism vaporise into thin air.

"You see we ran into the dwarf again today. He threatened to kill us so we've got him tied up in the boot."

"You've kidnapped a dwarf?" Penelope had never heard such a fantastic tale in all her life, but was sure that, after a quick assessment, these two, or at least the author of this book, would need sectioning.

"Yeah, so what dad is trying to say, is after such a traumatic week, I broke down like a big girl and asked dad for a cock."

"What's this asking for a penis all about?" screamed the psychologist, waking her secretary from her power nap next door. "I thought you were talking theoretically. You can't just buy one off the fucking shelf, you crazy round of double-barrelled fuckwits."

For the first time in her professional career, Penelope Stevenson had used a swear word and called an actual crazy person, crazy. It was a grave error of judgement and one she was unlikely to recover from, but in all fairness, she'd never had a case like this in front of her before.

"Well, you can really," said Jesus, all matter of fact. "You can buy them off the shelf at Ann Summers for fifty quid."

Penelope's head hit the desk. She'd need some back up here for sure. In all of her illustrious career she'd never heard such tripe and, as a result, was losing her cool big time. "And just how, I'm intrigued to know, do you plan to attach a plastic penis to this brave young boy here? A boy who, in my professional opinion, should be removed from your care immediately," screamed the agitated brain boffin, clumps of her own hair in her hands, having first started pulling it out during the kidnapping phase of the story.

"With a soldering iron, I suppose," shrugged Jesus, who had the feeling the meeting wasn't quite going as planned. "But to be honest, pet, I haven't really thought that far in advance yet," he continued.

"Soldering iron? Are you completely fucking insane?" That was it, she was gone. Twenty-five years of professionalism gone down the drain in an instant.

"Well, yeah, why not? He is a robot after all," said Jesus.

Penelope Stevenson threw them out.

Ignoring the limousine parked on the double yellow line, Rob and Jesus walked side by side into Middlesbrough town centre. Neither of them spoke a word, allowing themselves time to collect their thoughts on the meeting.

It was Rob who eventually broke the ice. "I think that went quite well, dad."

Jesus could only muster a one-word reply, "Pub?"

Rob didn't need a second invitation.

CHAPTER 10

Dug in and well hidden, Mary had lain prone in her observation post all night and most of the morning, watching the address she had been given by the loose-lipped, takeaway delivery boy. She had asked him to drop her off one hundred yards from the target, telling him to stop with only his handbrake so that no lookout would be able to see car's brake lights. She also ensured that she closed the vehicle door quietly on the one click, so as to not arouse suspicion from nosey neighbours. Once out of the car, she'd signalled for the driver to carry on and deliver his fast food, but not before handing him a note. "Hide this piece of paper underneath Troy's Parmo," she instructed, before turning and silently scurrying down a tight alleyway that separated two houses.

"But, Miss Fassbender," whispered the anxious student, calling after her as quietly as he could. "The grease will soak into the paper. It'll ruin the message."

His call was in vain. Mary had gone, vanished into thin air. She'd turned ghost and was already out of earshot.

Leaping over numerous garden fences, dodging greenhouses and ducking under several washing lines, like a seasoned saboteur, she finally settled for her ideal observation post. Situated in a field opposite the delivery house, it offered elevated panoramic views, that allowed her to not only reconnoitre the enemy's position, but also afforded her a strategically beneficial view of both routes to and from the building. Having satisfied herself that nobody had followed her, she began her recce.

With Mary's message to Troy seemingly doomed to failure, Adam Baxter, the quick-thinking, fast food delivery boy, had instead hidden the note beneath the dry crisp salad that always accompanied the Teesside Parmesan. The salad, a health and safety pre-requisite, was the only way the environmental health agencies could be persuaded to allow the deep-fried, heart attack on a plate to be sold. That was to say that the owner could apply all due diligence to ensure the dish was as healthy as humanly possible. Mary, upon hearing of these heroics, would surely reward him with a hefty tip.

Mary remained silent in her hide, professional enough to keep her movements to an absolute minimum. Eyes peeled on the target house, she studied the strategic entry points that she might use when the time came. The first thing she had noticed was the front door. It was large and wooden and given the time it took the occupant to open it after Adam had arrived with the food, she had to assume it had multiple locking devices. Chains and bolts maybe, perhaps a multiple sliding key with latch. Certainly the occupant had lifted the handle up upon closing the door, suggesting the latter to be true. The door also had a spy hole, revealing that whoever was in the home, exercised much caution. With the front door a no go, she turned her attention to the windows, the next obvious entry point. They looked relatively new, with no rotten sills or mould on the putty, therefore only a small detonation charge of C4 would force an entry. An explosion was hardly in keeping with her stealth thinking, so she'd need another plan. She had to consider all options before H-hour approached. Her mantra of the seven P's had her mind working in overdrive.

"Proper planning and preparation prevents piss poor performance," Mary thought to herself, a motto that she had never forgotten. She'd first learnt of the term from her grandfather who had been drafted in to design and build the Maginot Line in France during the Second World War. The fortification was, from a strictly technical point of view, a huge success and the line itself functioned as designed. However, poor old grandad had overlooked one very important aspect, and the result was to be catastrophic. He'd failed to recognise the importance of proper planning and had manned it with French soldiers. The country fell within three weeks.

Mary continued to build the picture presented before her. She counted the cars that drove down the street, jotting down number plates of any she saw twice. She watched people go about their business, as well as various workmen starting or finishing their shifts. As for her primary target, she saw nothing. No milkman came, no postman called and nobody in that house moved a muscle.

Mary then listened out for dogs.

She heard no barking and the front lawn looked immaculate, so she gladly made the assumption that no canine was in residence. At least that was some positive news. The whole night had been one of frustration. If Mary hadn't seen the front door open, she could have been forgiven for thinking the house was empty.

Mary made one final inspection of her surroundings then decided it was time to make a move. Sixteen hours in an observation post was quite enough to build a decent picture of a place, but sadly, whoever lived there and held Troy hostage, certainly didn't like drawing attention to themselves. All she'd seen was a pair of hands, when Adam had delivered the Parmo. No watch or jewellery to note, no tattoos on show. The contact had been minimal. Whoever he was, he was good, and she'd need to be at her very best. Once ready, Mary backed out of her hole and put her plan into action…

Approaching downhill, taking the direct route, Mary headed straight for the front of the house. Leaping over the gate like Colin Jackson with a winning lottery ticket in his hand, she rushed down the path, keeping a low profile as she went. Once clear of the big bay window, she stood for a few moments, controlling her breathing and slowing her heart rate, while facing the front door. Once ready, she simply knocked and waited. As soon as the door swung open, Mary, using lightning speed, unimaginable aggression and an element of surprise, flung out her right leg and delivered a powerful blow to Maddog's plums. Down he went, hitting the floor faster than Michael Jackson's nose in a sauna. Both hands clasped around his nuts, he rolled around in the most severe of all human pains. Childbirth was a stubbed toe in comparison.

Mary stood over him like a gallant matador, pushing in and through the front door before closing it behind her again. She allowed herself a wry smile at the detailed execution of her planning and uttered her second favourite motto of the day: KISS. Keep It Simple Stupid. Then she nipped to the downstairs water closet for a piss.

With Maddog still incapacitated on the hall carpet, Mary began the audacious task of sweeping the house. Room to room she ran in search of Troy. "Lounge. Clear. Kitchen. Clear," she shouted, as she entered each room, remembering her training from the 23 Special Air Service Reserves and moving constantly and efficiently, never once presenting herself as a target. With the downstairs clear but no sign of Troy, let alone any takeaway boxes, she then ascended the stairs and, as is customary practice in the special forces, threw up a flash bang for special measure.

BOOM.

The stun grenade made a deafening noise, hopefully disorienting anybody who may have been pointing a weapon at her, while also erupting the spindles from the banister and smouldering the carpet and walls. She proceeded up the stairs two at a time.

"What was that?" cried Ron.

"Oh, that'll be mother," cried the excited Troy, jumping up and down on his chair with excitement. "I told you she'd come and rescue me."

Mary crashed through the door of bedroom one, before heading across the landing and clearing bedroom two with dashing efficiency. Rounding the bathroom door, she satisfied herself that no Tangos were of imminent threat, before focusing all her efforts on the remaining bedroom three. Troy must be in there, but with who?

The occupants would know they were under attack by now, so

any armed guards would surely have weapons trained on the door. Mary needed another entry point. Tracing steps back to bedroom two, she opened the back bedroom window and shuffled out onto the ledge. Hanging on the guttering, she shuffled sideways, hand over hand to bedroom three, before kicking back from the wall to gain an advantageous swing then crashing, Sambas first, through the window.

Much to her dismay, Troy was still alive.

"Mother, thank the Lord," he screamed, unable to hide his excitement. "I'm so glad you're here."

"Troy, I thought you'd be dead by now," she hit back, unable to hide the disappointment in her voice.

"Dead, mother? No, but I have been very brave. I've been tortured, mother. It's been a terrifying ordeal and had it not been for Ron here, I doubt I would have made it at all."

"Really?" said Mary, making a mental note to kick Ron in the head at the earliest opportunity. "But what about the note I sent you? Didn't you get it?" She was fuming and still baffled as to how Troy had survived.

"Note, mother?"

"Yes, Troy, a note. It was hidden inside your takeaway box."

"Well, I never saw it," answered Troy.

Mary's mood darkened and she stomped around the room looking for the takeaway box. Her planning had been so meticulous, so well thought out. How had he not seen it? But she answered her own question when she found the discarded box on the floor on the opposite side of the bed. Peering inside the lid, she discovered that the Parmo had, as expected, been devoured, along with the garlic sauce and chips. All that remained was the obligatory green salad. Picking up clumps of lettuce leaf with her hand, she soon unearthed what she was looking for, the note. She grasped it with furious hands and quietly read the inventory to herself. "Troy, be brave and eat these, it's for the best." Beneath the writing, attached to the letter with Sellotape, were two cyanide pills, which Mary now stared at with disgruntled disdain. Adam Baxter was now a wanted man.

"Everything okay, mother?" inquired Troy, wondering why his mother had yet to untie him from the bed.

"Yes, Troy, I'm fine," lied Mary, hiding the pills in the pockets of her tracksuit bottoms. They'd keep for some other time. "Now, what's all this about, son?"

Troy and Ron took it in turns to relay the events, while Mary sat on the edge of the bed listening intently. They told her of the truth serum hidden inside the Pringles crisps tubes, and how the Teesside underworld planned to use it to hold up the HSBC bank. They discussed how the doorman had kidnapped them and held them hostage, along with the individual roles they both were set to play. They recounted the torture techniques they had both suffered at the hands of the monstrous bouncer and how only true love had got them through it. Troy even told his mother of Ron's everlasting gob dropper, although Ron, clearly embarrassed, failed to see the relevance in that information. Mary thought the same, although found it pretty interesting nonetheless.

With the three of them still in thick conversation, nobody noticed Maddog come through the bedroom door. By the time he was upon them, it was too late. Angered by the fact his testicles hadn't re-emerged from his intestines yet and smarting because he'd been beaten up by a girl, it was obvious he wasn't there for a picnic. With his shovel-sized fist, he grabbed Mary's ponytail and dragged her from the bed to the floor.

"And who the fucking hell might you be, sweetheart," asked the huge bouncer, in not so manly a voice as he'd once had. He twisted her hair around his fist, pulling her head upwards.

Troy and Ron were powerless to help, as the two were still shackled in position, although Ron did see this as a good thing because Maddog was fuming, and not even an elephant gun would stop him now.

Maddog heaved Mary up off the floor with one hand, bringing her up to eye level. Until this point, he'd not seen the face of his swift nemesis and he wanted to look her deep in the eyes before she met her death. But those thoughts vanished once her features came into sight.

"Mary?" he said.

"Maddog?" she responded.

And with that, Maddog instantly released her. The room fell into silent disbelief, as everybody tried to make sense of the situation they found themselves in. Maddog staring at Mary, Mary staring at Troy, and Troy staring at Ron's lance of love, much to the annoyance of Ron, who spoke first.

"Can somebody please explain to me what's going on?" he asked.

"Marion and I go way back," said Mary, causing the two captives to snigger in unison at Maddog's girly name. Sniggering that didn't go unnoticed.

"If you two poofters use that name outside of these walls, I'll kill ya," said Maddog. Keen to nip his christian name in the bud, he wagged a mighty gorilla-sized finger at them to prove he wasn't joking.

"We used to be in the same gang. How long's it been, Maddog? Three? Four years?" asked Mary, thinking it best to use Maddog, rather than mention his first name again. As she remembered, nobody got away with using Marion twice and lived.

"Yeah, suppose so," said Maddog, rubbing the back of his neck in embarrassment that he'd attacked a mate.

"Hang on," interrupted Troy. "You two were in a gang. Was it the Red Hand Gang? The Sugar Hill Gang?"

"Was it the YMCA?" jumped in Ron.

"No, not that type of gang, you idiots," said Mary, with a shake of her head to Maddog at their stupidity. "We did some scaffolding in London together. We were in the gang of scaffolders who helped build the Shard in two thousand and nine."

"You were a scaffolder, mother?" asked Troy, unable to picture his eight stone mother lifting heavy tubes.

"The best," defended Maddog. "Tell me, mate," he went on, "do you still wear steel toe-capped Adidas Sambas?"

Mary simply pointed down to her current footwear and smiled.

"Explains a lot," said the big bouncer, rubbing his gonads. At which, they both started laughing.

"So, me old mucka, what's going on?" asked Mary.

"How about I brew up and explain it all downstairs?" responded the big doorman. It was an idea that suited them both. Mary hadn't had a warm drink since the evening before, and Maddog, whose testicles were yet to recover, really did need a sit down.

"Wait, aren't you going to untie us first, mother?" shouted Troy upon seeing Mary leave the room.

Mary, out of sight apart from her right arm, produced two fingers around the door and held them there until Troy got the message. Ron flashed a sympathetic look at his crestfallen co-hostage.

CHAPTER 11

Mortified, Jesus drained the last of his pint and held the glass to his lips allowing the froth to fall into his mouth. "Another?" he asked.

Rob showed his empty glass and nodded. The pair were well in the midst of an all-day session of epic proportions, having seen their promising day turn quicker than an Italian tank. Sat in the Star pub on Southfield Road, they were in that supersonic phase that all drinkers recognise, the moment your decision-making skills become scrambled with heightened confidence. The point of no return. The moment you should really go home with a takeaway in hand, but decide not to. You're a few drinks away from the stabilisers coming off and karaoke sounding like a good idea. It's also around this time that you start talking shite.

"So Kylie or Danni?" asked Rob, once Jesus had replenished the drinks.

"Danni, easy," replied Jesus instantly.

"You can't make a decision that quick, they're both quality birds, dad," responded Rob, who'd clearly pondered the question on a number of occasions.

Jesus hit back. "Kylie is probably better looking; I'll give you that. But ask yourself this, why can't she keep a fella? She must be an absolute nightmare to live with. Won't let you watch the footy or give you ten minutes peace on the crapper, I reckon. That's why they all leave her."

Rob nodded at his father's philosophy, as it all made perfect drunken sense.

"Hobnobs or Jammy Dodgers?" It was Jesus's turn to ask a question.

Rob needed time to think. Swilling his beer around his pint

glass, he stared at the mini vortex he'd created, as if the answer somehow lay in the golden fluid. After a few more moments, he'd reached his conclusion. "Jammy Dodgers," he announced, taking a few more slurps of the amber nectar before presenting his findings. "Don't get me wrong, Hobnobs are great but you get so much more with a Dodger. They're triple layered for a start and you can fit a whole one in your mouth thus not dropping any crumbs. They just pip the Hobnob, for me, because they look like breasts, so obviously good for entertainment value."

Jesus raised a glass in salute before taking another two massive gulps of Fosters.

"Okay then," said Rob. "You're stuck on a desert island, you can only take one person with you, and it can't be family. Who would you take?" It was a standard, yet intriguing question, and no doubt would take quite a bit of thought time.

"Kylie," said Jesus without delay.

"Kylie?" asked Rob. "How'd you work that out? A minute ago you said she was a nightmare to live with."

Once again Jesus had it all worked out. "Kylie is only small, right? And therefore probably fits into a size eight dress, yes?"

"So?" said Rob wearing a baffled frown.

"So I'd assume material for clothing would be scarce given the desert island location, so it would probably help to take somebody small."

Rob tilted his head slightly, as if tipping an imaginary hat.

"She probably wouldn't eat much either," continued Jesus, "so you'd have more food for yourself."

Rob nodded at his father's brilliance. "Yeah, she'd be on a diet too, no doubt. Women always are," he said, taking to the idea of Kylie as a companion.

"Besides," added Jesus, "you wouldn't have a television or toilet on the island, so she wouldn't be interrupting anything."

That comment sealed the argument for Rob.

His father was a genius.

The barman, listening to their raised drunken conversation, just rolled his eyes and pulled another beer. "Same again, gentlemen?"

"Yes please, bartender," answered the old man, getting up to go for a pee. "And give us a brandy chaser with that too."

Rob wasn't keen on that idea. "Whoa there, dad, take it easy, you're getting my cock later remember." As drunk as he was, the hairs on the back of Jesus's neck stood up as the pub fell deathly silent.

"Erm, ahem, he means cock as in cockerel," Jesus reassured his fellow punters. "We're picking it up later from the allotment." With those words out, the jukebox started up again. It was a lucky escape and they both knew it. "Best be on our way, lad," said the old timer, encouraging his boy to drink up.

Rob couldn't disagree.

The pair supped the remainder of their pints, under the watchful eye of the barman, and headed outside, slipping through the pub's big double doors toward another watering hole.

"Don't ever say that again, Robert. Not in public anyway. This is Middlesbrough. People don't look kindly on intra-family relationships. Unless it's Skinningrove where they have no choice."

"Sorry, dad, I just got a little excited, you know? So are we going for my cock?"

Jesus threw his hand over his son's mouth to silence the buffoon. "You're not quite getting this, are you, son? People here respond first and request clarification as you lie bleeding to death on the ground. We're twinned with Beirut, for fuck's sake. Their mayor comes here on his holidays. So try and keep your thoughts to yourself. To answer your question, no, not yet. I need some Dutch courage first. Two blokes wandering into Ann Summers, smack bang in the middle of town, is bordering on suicide. I'll need a few more pints. Come on, we'll try the Central."

The pair continued their shock and awe campaign against their livers, by downing more pints of lager and a few whisky chasers. Well, Jesus did, Rob didn't have a liver. Instead he had a sophisticated liquid management system, which not only controlled the levels of liquor entering his body, but vented the gas away in the form of burps. His body was programmed to react to alcohol the same way as a human does, because Jesus wanted his creation to feel liberated. He was, however, mindful enough to make sure Rob was a loveable drunk, and not a psychopathic thug after one too many.

Rob really was an exceptional work of art, masterminded by a lonely, eccentric old man, who surely should have won a Nobel Prize for his brilliance had he not spent time inside for some unfortunate mishaps.

"You shee, shon, nobody and I mean nobody..." Jesus was prodding at Rob's chest now, "could have created you from the ICI stores like I did. My boss gave me warning after written warning, but I told him... I told him, shon. This cyborg here. This bait shed sandwich toaster, is gonna be something special... and I love him, love him to bits." He caressed an equally inebriated Rob on the back of the neck as he spoke.

Jesus shouted to a group of girls who just looked on in disgust at how drunk the pair were. "I do, you know... I love him, my own flesh and blood, sat here with his dad." He reassuringly tapped his son on the leg and smiled at him. A few short seconds after, he passed out in a drunken coma on the table.

Rob drained the last of his pint and sat with a bemused but happy look on his face. His father, with head resting on a lager-soaked table looked at peace. The poor bloke had really made the effort today, but the effects had clearly taken their toll. Rob lovingly ruffled the back of Jesus's comatose head. He could never really be sure what love felt like, but if the feelings he had for his father were anything to go by, he couldn't be too far away.

Scanning the room, he passed the time by randomly watching people while his father snoozed. The guy on the fruit machine was on a poor run. He'd put a fair bit of cash in the machine and was slapping the glass as if encouraging the jackpot to drop.

Elsewhere, a group of friends had gathered around one of the multiple televisions in the pub and were watching a re-run of This Is Your Life with special guest Anne Diamond.

And some guy, who was dressed in standard rap clothing, had just put The Fresh Prince's Summertime on the ageing jukebox. It was a surreal setting after such a difficult day but Rob was content. He silently watched all these people through a drunken haze, calm and super-relaxed by the effects of the alcohol. With his father still snoring, Rob continued watching Anne Diamond, while Summertime belted out through Technics speakers, filling the room with head-nodding beats. Rob scanned the whole room. He enjoyed people watching and found humans fascinating. Once he'd given everyone the once over, he simply started again, staring at Anne with content, while continuing to listen to the words of Summertime. Anne then Summertime, Anne and then Summertime.

"Ann Summers!" he suddenly shouted. "Christ, it's ten to five, dad! Wake up, we have to go."

Rob shook his dad, trying to raise him from his drunken stupor, but he'd have had more success trying to raise the dead. Not for the first time was a bloke called Jesus in need of resurrection. Jesus was in a deep sleep, snoring loudly as if he'd inhaled a full bottle of Rohypnol. Not even a brass band would wake him now. Panicking because Ann Summers would be closing in ten minutes, the mighty cyborg heaved his paralytic father onto his shoulders and ran through the pub exit. Nothing would prevent him from purchasing a new penis today. Not a dwarf, not a jumped up psychologist, not a comatose hippy, though admittedly he'd have to get his skates on.

Through the town centre he marched, with his father slumped over his shoulder, bumping into passers-by with all the grace of a new born foal. Cries of, "Watch it," and "'Ere, you fucking doyle," could be heard from aggrieved shoppers, who'd either had to jump out of the way of the staggering man mountain or had been kicked by a rogue flailing leg of the rat-arsed vagrant. But it was the sight of a drunken six-foot-four bloke, carrying a passed-out hippy on his shoulders that really made the crowd grow.

"What's going on? Put that man down," shouted a concerned member of the public, but Rob's reasoning had deserted him around pint nine. Instead of taking the time to explain the situation, he instead turned into Ann Summers, just before they were about to shut up shop. The gasps from the crowd could be heard in Ingleby Barwick, as it was clear to them now, what was going on. A scruffy looking tramp was about to get a severe bumming and, by the looks of the poor sod, he was in no position to argue the toss.

"Poor man," they cried, "somebody call the police."

Inside the shop, the two counter assistants were equally concerned as two blokes entering the premises was unheard of, but one holding what looked like a prone corpse on his shoulder was... well, worrying...

To make matters worse, outside the store the crowd had swollen to about two hundred. A fact not lost on Sarah the shop assistant. "Erm, may I help you?" she quivered, guiding her eyes to the scene inside the shop and then to the one gathering outside.

"We'd like to purchase a rubber cock, please," slurred Robert, placing the old inventor face down on the counter, arse in the air.

"Excuse me?" exclaimed the poor girl, eyebrows raised to maximum elevation.

"A rubber penis, about this long and flesh coloured if you can," said Rob, holding his two index fingers apart to demonstrate the dimensions he was after.

Sarah looked at her co-worker for help but Rachel was just as baffled, if not scared by the scene playing out before her. An awkward silence ensued and Rob, eager to end the standoff, reached into his father's back pocket for his wallet to complete the transaction.

Outside the crowd were going mental, banging on the windows of the shop, after seeing what appeared to be Rob feeling the bottom of the poor vagrant. "Get the pervert," they chanted. "We're going to kill you."

But Rob was unperturbed. "Don't worry, girls, I'm a giver, not a taker," he reassured, trying to quell their fears of the aggression building outside the shop. Though, what he actually meant to say was, "I'm a lover and not a fighter." An easy mistake to make for a moron with fifteen pints coursing through his system.

Rachel sensibly pressed the panic button, which just happened to be linked to a monitoring station for a quick police response. A move Rob sensed wasn't good.

"Look, all we want is a rubber penis and we'll be on our way," he said, but Sarah and Rachel had run into the storeroom, as was protocol if a drunken rapist walked in with a comatose hippy on his shoulder while asking for a rubber cock.

Rob had three options. He could either wait for the police to arrive and try to explain it all away, although he didn't like this idea as he had kidnapped a dwarf earlier that morning. He could run to the back of the store and ask the shop assistants to hide him in the panic room, but his gut feeling was they'd decline this request; or… he could grab the nearest sex toy and fight his way out, but that meant facing an angry mob armed only with a drunken father and plastic phallus. If he was honest, they weren't great options, but with the police on the way, time was of the essence.

Grabbing at his father's belt, he attempted to slide him off the counter and back up onto his shoulders. Unfortunately, the belt snapped and his father's trousers fell down around his ankles, revealing a scrawny, lily white backside. For the baying crowd outside, that was it. It was all that they could take and they decided to take matters into their own hands. Storming the shop, they charged at Rob, trying to free the semi-naked man within his grasp. Rob tooled himself up with the first thing that came to hand, a mammoth two-foot-long, plastic Hampton. With the bulging veins providing him with an epic grip, he began wrapping it around the heads of the onrushing assailants. Down they went in twos and threes as the mighty six-pound phallus bopped, smacked and twatted their heads. Advancing to the door, he stepped over the prone bodies, continuing his ferocious fight for freedom. Once he was outside in the street, the advantage now lay with the mob. In the narrow aisles of the shop, the crowd could only come directly toward him, but out here in the open space, they could circle their prey and cut off his escape.

Shouting and spitting venomous battle cries, this was the calm before the storm, a brief respite before the crowd acted out its vengeance. On his shoulder, his bare-arsed father snored, unaware of the mayhem around him, his balls flapping aimlessly in the breeze, a scene that caused some women folk in the crowd to throw up, and triggered the charge to begin. From all sides, the vigilante attack came, homing in on Rob, trying to take him down with sheer weight of numbers. But Rob didn't possess the fight or flight instinct of humans, nor was he bound by laws one and three of the robotics code.

In fact, since the activation of his code override switch, he was free to injure any human he so wished, and, if the moment took him, slip them a quick length too. Lack of cock notwithstanding, of course.

With only seconds left to make a decision, he extended the newly acquired dildo to its maximum two-foot length and started rotating it rapidly like a helicopter rotor blade on take-off. Round and round he went, knocking out the onrushing crowd of people as he spun. Such was the gyratory vector he was achieving, the centrifugal force caused his father's plums to stretch to unimaginable boundaries. Dangling a good two-foot from their resting position, they too started to cut people down like a lawn mower might savage fresh grass. It was like Darth Maul's double-ended lightsaber, only this time with a plastic penis on one side and Jesus's testicles on the other. The crowd, almost beaten to death by the ring of debauched fury, lay still in less than a minute.

With bodies lying all around him, Rob began to wind down his speed till he eventually stopped. As his momentum ground to a halt, so to his father's testicles fell and slapped the cyborg on the small of his back. And on feeling the gentle tap, that low down on his back, Rob sucked in a lungful of air through his teeth, his poor father was going to be sore in the morning. Then with the sound of sirens filling the air, Rob finally made his getaway, scurrying down back alleyways and avoiding any well-lit areas until he was able to summon a cab.

"Thornaby, please, mate," he directed the driver, who upon seeing Jesus's wrinkly walnuts dangling in the rear view mirror, questioned whether a trip to James Cook Hospital would be a better option.

Rob declined. "It's alright, mate, he never uses them anyway."

The two had had yet another bizarre and ridiculous day, but the end result had worked out as planned. They'd been almost murdered, had seen a shrink, bought a penis and were home safe and sound again. All's fair in love and war, or so it would seem.

Once again Rob woke with the mother of all hangovers. His head was pounding and a moth farting at five hundred yards would have had him wincing in pain. But that was nothing to what he felt when he heard blood-curdling screams from his dad. Running to his father's aid, he flung open his bedroom door only to find he wasn't there. A quick shout and he discovered he was in the bathroom.

"Everything alright, dad?" he asked, while slowly pushing the door open to see his father sat on the throne.

Jesus was too alarmed to answer. With worry written all over his face, he just sat there on the toilet, shivering with cold. Rob tried to reassure his father that constipation at his age was quite common and patted him gently on the back as if burping a baby.

"It's not that, son. It's my balls, they're so cold, there's something wrong, I just can't feel them," he said, quivering like a shitting dog.

Rob took a quick glance between the old man's legs and quickly identified the problem. His balls were sat a couple of fathoms below the toilet water line and had shrivelled to the size of peanuts. Sucking in air through his teeth once more, Rob tried to find the reassuring words his father needed, but in all honesty he was struggling.

"I've seen worse, dad," he lied, realising that it's sometimes better to hide the truth.

"Are you sure, son?" asked the elongated inventor.

"Absolutely, just don't flush the chain until after you stand up."

CHAPTER 12

"You got something you need to tell me? What's going on, Maddog?" asked Mary, holding her tea with both hands clasped around the mug, her feet underneath her bottom on the chair. Given that Mary had just stormed the house and discovered her son bound and tied to a chair, she still managed to open proceedings in a relaxed and calm manner.

"I don't know what you mean, mate," responded Maddog, shaking his head in an exaggerated manner. "Loose lips sink ships, you know," he continued, tapping his nose.

"Don't insult me, Maddog. I take it you don't want these bad boys connecting with your family jewels again?" retorted Mary, pointing to her black leather football shoe.

Maddog winced at the thought.

"Besides, I'm already involved. You saw to that when you kidnapped my son."

"Your son? What him upstairs?" he asked, totally bemused that one of his hardest friends could spawn such a pathetic specimen. "I had no idea, mate. If anything, he got in the way. Wrong time, wrong place, but don't worry, I was never going to hurt him, my intention was to release him once this thing was over."

"Fucking release him," spat Mary with venom. "You can fuck right off."

Maddog had forgotten just how fiery his old buddy could be, but even still, he was surprised by Mary's shocking outburst. What is it they say about blood being thicker than water?

"I'm no murderer, Mary. Don't get me wrong, I've handed out a few slaps in my time but execution? Not my bag."

Mary struggled to hide her disappointment and slurped her tea in disgusted silence, although after a while she realised she still had the cyanide pills to fall back on. Continuing with her probing questions, she awaited Maddog's explanation, but the big man said nothing.

It was clear to him that Mary wouldn't give in until she had at least had some insight into what he was up to, but he also knew where this job had come from. This was no petty crime and given who his employers were, he had to stay tight-lipped.

Mary sat, frustrated at the lack of information, and drained the last of her tea, while contemplating her next move. Of course, Maddog was expecting this. He'd known Mary for a long time. They'd been very tight, within a circle of trust, but when Mary had joined the SAS Reserves they'd lost touch.

"Remember when you first joined the Regiment?" he said, causing Mary to smile in fondness at the memories. "Well, when you went away on tour, you never told me where you were going or why, and I never asked either. It's the same thing happening here, mate. It's all need to know."

"What are you talking about?" barked Mary. "I sent you a selfie from Saddam's toilet while I was taking a shite."

Maddog had lost the moral high ground after only a few moments. Not that Mary would let him off the hook that easily. She wanted buy in and she wanted it now. "Speaking of tours," she said, Maddog sensing the cunning in her voice. "Remember the stag do in Thailand?"

The hairs on the back of Maddog's neck stood on end. The stag party in question had taken place a good few years ago. Mary had been asked to be best man for a mutual friend of theirs and the resulting trip featured the usual laddish behaviours one might expect of such an event, including a hazy ending to their four-day tour, with the whole party blind drunk.

What had become clear though, was that Maddog had at some point woken up with a beautiful-looking Thai girl. As he was the only bloke to have done so, he was keen to gloat. Things did however sour pretty quickly when the pair took a shower together. The horrific screams of terror from Maddog on the realisation of his grave error was a sound like nothing ever heard before. The howls of laughter from his mates still haunted him to the present day.

"What goes on tour, stays on tour... unless?" said Mary in a devious voice.

Maddog was buggered. Checkmate.

"Look, Mary, this is big," he said, trying to gauge how much he could tell her. "It's not like the good old days. The days of blackmailing QCs into deducting a football team's three points in order to win a bet. Trust me, you'd be better off not involving yourself in this one."

"Don't involve myself?" said Mary sarcastically. "You involved me when you murdered my adorable son."

"Murdered? I haven't murdered anyone," said the bemused Maddog, wondering if Mary was a few echelons higher in the madness stakes than she used to be.

"Well, kidnapped, then," she retorted, folding her arms like a three-year-old having a tantrum. No matter how many times she said it, Troy was still alive and kicking, though God does love a trier. "Let me help you, Maddog, I really need this job."

She was soon cut short by the big bouncer. "Help me? You can help me by taking your boy home and sewing his mouth shut."

"Look, if the job's going so well, and all your little ducks are lined up in a row, why is my son tied to a chair upstairs?" pressed Mary. She'd already received half the story from the fat waste of space but wasn't about to show her hand just yet. Not with Maddog seemingly against the ropes anyway. "You don't kidnap big, stupid, fat fucks, if all things are planned properly. Come on, Maddog, stop holding back. What's Troy got that you need?"

Maddog glared at his old mate and let out a little smile, he knew he owed Mary some news. He had, after all, tickled her son till he shat himself.

The pair stared at each other in awkward silence until Mary tried again. "Who's running the show?"

"Honestly? I don't know," sighed Maddog, rubbing his weary eyes.

The big fella seemed to have the weight of the world on his shoulders and Mary hadn't seen him this stressed before.

"You don't know?" she questioned again, her eyebrows lifted.

"Honestly, I don't. It's some bloke I've never met, nor spoke to. It's sci-fi shit, man. Nothing like the good old days. It's all chemicals and mind-bending witchcraft."

"Truth serum?" interrupted Mary, thinking it best to reveal some of what she knew, given that Maddog had come this far.

It was a question that had Maddog slightly worried. The last thing he needed was a leak, but he relaxed when he realised where Mary had got that information from.

"Troy?" asked Maddog.

Mary nodded, for Maddog to respond with a knowing nod of his own.

"The truth serum is fucking wonderful," he finally announced. "Don't ask me how it works, because I don't have a fucking clue, but it bends your mind. Once subjected to it, you find yourself saying shit that you'd never dream of saying, it just comes right out."

"What, like bumming a ladyboy in Thailand?" interrupted Mary, a statement she immediately regretted, as the titters of Troy and Ron drifted down the stairs. "So give me an example, then?" said Mary, thinking it best to move the story on.

"Well, the wife divorced me after I'd inhaled some of the gas during the testing phase. I'd inadvertently told her that I'd worn a Newcastle top in Benidorm when I was pissed."

"What? The wife divorced you for wearing a barcode shirt on holiday?" asked Mary unable to comprehend such drastic action.

"It was a fair cop, Mary," said Maddog, sympathising with his ex-wife. "Given that Thai bloke again or wearing such a shit shirt, what would you take?"

Mary had to agree it was a sound argument.

"That's what I'm saying though, Mary, stuff just comes out."

Mary listened intently as Maddog told her all about the job. He took her through it all, beginning to end, and more importantly, spoke about the potential rewards. That was the bit she was interested in above all, but she was still a little sceptical about the plan. "So what, you just plan to release this chemical in the middle of the bank and what exactly?" asked Mary.

"Ask for directions, I suppose, access code to the vault, CCTV coverage, escape routes. You know the type of thing," said Maddog, as if it was all a walk in the park.

"But once the chemical wears off, you'll be a hunted man?" Mary was digesting the whole picture now, going over the complete scenario in her head.

"And that makes it different from any other robbery how?" asked Maddog. "If they catch me, and that's a big if, I won't have held up any bank because I'm not taking a weapon, so I won't be looking at an armed robbery charge. I'm just gonna talk to the manager, the security guys and the nice lady with the chained pens and they'll hand over the information for free. No aggression, no demands, no dramas."

Mary sat back in her chair trying to absorb the plan. She had to admit, the heist seemed relatively simple and almost too good to be true, and Maddog did have a point. He wasn't using any aggravating or mitigating factors during the robbery. No professional hallmarks, no gang, no detailed reconnaissance, no disguise, not even a firearm.

If he was to get caught, he'd only be looking at an eighteen-month stretch, which would be cut short to a year for good behaviour. If he managed to squirrel away enough loot from the job, then a short break away would be well worth it. It would certainly beat working the doors at the Sausage Cottage anyway. It was a no brainer.

"So... these missing tubes of serum, what you thinking?" asked Mary. She had a thirst for this job now, and the more she heard, the more she wanted in.

"Fucking unbelievable, mate. I'm due a delivery of serum by this little taxi driver. Queer egg he is, with a huge chip on his shoulder. Anyway, it's all set up and all he has to do is drive up to the Sausage Cottage and drop the stuff off at the office. Nice and simple. Only he decides to pick up a fare on the way. Two unbelievable characters. I've never seen them before in my life, a right weird pair. Anyway, they start arguing with this taxi driver and the next thing I know, the serum is lying all over the car park, in full view of everybody."

"So what did you do?" asked Mary, enjoying the banter with Maddog, just like she used to all those years back.

"Well, I wanted to give that little bastard a slap for picking up a fare, but he was like shit off a stick. You wouldn't think he could run that fast with his little legs, but bloody hell he could shift. So I'm pegging after him, when these two goons smack me on the head with a can of beans."

Mary was in fits of hysterics as Maddog continued. "I was pissed off, I can tell you, but I had to admire the cheeky buggers because I was about fifty yards away at the time. It was a cracking shot. Anyway, I wanted to give them a slap too, but they ran inside the club. They were doing some pretty filthy shit in there, all fingers and thumbs with your lad. Fucking disgusting, mate. That's when they poked me in the eyes and ran for it."

Mary had tears of laughter rolling down her face and was holding her stomach as Maddog gave a graphic demonstration of what he'd seen.

"And that's when they stole the serum?" asked Mary, once she'd regained her composure.

"Well, yeah. The CCTV confirmed that later on."

"And the job is cancelled until you get it back?" presumed Mary.

"No, far from it, there's shed loads of the stuff, but we need to identify Dumb and Dumber in case they blow the operation. It won't take a genius to realise that there's no crisps inside those tubes, and once they opened them, they'd start spouting shit. The serum will take over and they could walk into the nearest police station and tell them when and where they found it. We don't need that kind of heat, not this close to the job anyway."

Mary nodded in agreement. "You said there's loads of the stuff, but why? If the serum is as powerful as you suggest, then surely an enclosed bank wouldn't need that much of it?" asked Mary, her woman's intuition now in full flow.

"Ha ha, Mary, you never miss a trick, do you?" Maddog was laughing now and had to admit it was great having his old sidekick with him again. "The bank job is just the diversion. The big job lies elsewhere. The whole purpose of our role is to attract as much attention as possible, really go to town. We plan to have the full bells and whistles going off as we exit the bank so that a huge crowd has gathered, rubber necking and trying to get a glimpse of the action. We have to gridlock the town centre and hopefully bottleneck a few exits too."

Maddog had finally decided that Mary was to be part of the heist. He'd need her expertise, her cool head when the shit started flying and, most of all, her ability to knock people out should the need arise. But far more than any of that, it just felt great to have her around again.

"Create a crowd? But that goes against the grain of every bank robbery ever performed. Ronnie Biggs will turn in his grave," said Mary.

"Ronnie Biggs was an amateur, Mary. I told you, this is hi-tech. With a big crowd assembled, fifteen tonnes of sodium thiopental gas will be released from the top of the CNE tower and onto the unsuspecting folk below. Shortly after that, a text message will be sent to every mobile phone user whose signal can be detected this side of the Bilsdale beacon. The text will request bank details and methods of payment receipt. They'll be powerless to resist and will all reply within seconds of reading it."

Mary's jaw dropped at both the scale of the operation and the planning it must have involved. No wonder Maddog was showing uncharacteristic signs of stress. It was massive. The worst outcome would be to serve one year in jail for this unimaginable booty and that was presuming they were caught.

"My God, you'll make thousands," said Mary, once she'd got her head around what she'd just been told.

"Millions, my friend," said Maddog. "Millions. And I want you there, Mary, but I'm not sure the boss will go for it. I can't see him letting anybody in now at this late stage. What would he have to gain and how would he know you're not a plant?"

Mary threw Maddog a death stare at such a disgusting comment. And although the words had tumbled from his mouth, Maddog didn't believe them for one second.

Mary let the comment slide.

"They'll let me in, especially when they realise I have something to offer," she said.

Maddog decided to humour her. "What can you possibly offer them at this late stage that they haven't already thought of?"

"Oh! Only that I know one of the blokes that you're looking for, mate. And what's more, I know exactly how to find him."

Upstairs, Troy had managed to overhear pretty much the whole conversation between his mother and Maddog. As the plan had unfolded, Troy's eyes widened with each revelation. During every break in the conversation, he'd managed to update his fellow captive on all that he'd heard. Ron couldn't believe what he was being told, and kept asking Troy if he had heard correctly. It was an ambitious plan, but surely Maddog nor Mary would be talking so openly about it, especially with them in the house, unless it was either a decoy or they were just plain stupid.

"Did you hear when they plan to start, Troy? Do you know how or when they are going to get away? And what about us? Did you happen to hear of our fate?" Ron's questions came thick and fast and the last one seemed to unnerve Troy, whose eyes grew as big as saucers. Ron, seeing his new friend looking so scared, tried to reassure him that everything was alright, and that he was sure his mother would see him okay. But that wasn't the reason for Troy's stare. One of Ron's bollocks had slipped out of the end of his boxer shorts and had sunshine dancing off it real nice, sending Troy off into a land of erotic fantasy.

With his hands still shackled to the bed, there wasn't much Ron could do with it other than hope Troy's trance would soon subside.

CHAPTER 13

Hyped up, Rob sat anxiously in the makeshift waiting room for his father to scrub for theatre. Although cyborgs weren't supposed to feel apprehension, he was definitely troubled by what was about to happen to him. He pondered the outcome of his imminent operation and how his life would change once surgery was complete. Allowing himself a little chuckle, he remembered Jesus's reaction to the size of his new penis. It was fair to say the old boy had blown his top after realising Rob's new phallus would be two-foot long. But, after recognising the fact that he'd been absolutely shit-faced the night before, and Rob had slain a volatile crowd by swinging the sex toy around like a Scotsman might a claymore, he did eventually calm down. But that didn't make it alright.

"You can't have a two-foot cock, son," he argued. "You won't be able to wear Speedos around a pool for a start."

At that point, Rob politely reminded his father that the likelihood of the only digitally-enhanced cyborg in existence doing a few lengths of Stockton Baths was pretty slim. Once again, Jesus had been thwarted by his own argument.

"Besides, dad," Rob went on, "given the choice, would you have gone for a smaller one?"

That was the clincher because Jesus had to admit that yes, given the opportunity, he certainly wouldn't have done.

Working feverishly away, through a door connected to the waiting room, was Jesus, busy converting the dining room into an operating theatre. He didn't have to disinfect the whole room with bleach, nor did he have to wear a white coat and stethoscope, or display a name badge upon his breast, but he did anyway. Just like he'd left magazines in the kitchen/waiting room for Rob to read before the op. Not that Rob minded, he knew his father was madly eccentric, and if nothing else it showed he cared.

"Right," said Doctor Jones, finally entering the room. "The theatre staff will see you now." He was acting deadly serious, even checking a clipboard that he'd placed on the back of Rob's chair, which displayed 'nil by mouth' in big bold letters. Rob simply played along, even allowing the old inventor to place a thermometer in his mouth in an attempt to take his temperature. Jesus had wanted to stick the thermometer up the patient's arse for a more accurate reading, but Rob politely declined. The last time Jesus had entered his aluminium starfish, a huge bouncer had wanted to wage war on them.

"No, under my tongue will be just fine, dad," he insisted, without much argument from his doctor. The next thing to do, while waiting on the mercury, was the signing of a death disclaimer, something Rob did without question. Doctor or not, this man knew his way around a screwdriver and he trusted his father implicitly.

Doctor Jones removed the thermometer from his patient's mouth and studied the low reading. He then scribbled down some notes on the clipboard before listening to his own heartbeat through the stethoscope. He chose his own heart, as to try detecting a beat on his patient would have been fruitless, because Rob was a fucking robot and didn't have a heart.

Once Jesus was happy, he turned to his son. "Ready, big fella?"

"As ready as I'll ever be, doc… I mean, dad," said Rob, the pair just about keeping their emotions in check. This would be the first time since the millennium bug debacle that Rob would be intentionally shut down, that damp squib proving a massive disappointment, being surpassed only by Boro's UEFA cup final defeat in Eindhoven.

"Then let's get on with it, shall we?" said Jesus, showing his son into the room next door.

The dining room had been cleared of its usual furnishings and looked almost unrecognisable. In the centre stood a long, black table, the type a masseuse might use, and above that swung a huge, bright light. Rob knew his father must have dipped into his life savings to fund this project because from that overhead light shone an expensive, hundred-watt bulb. There was no expense spared in the Jones household it would seem, especially with a 50ml bottle of hand cleanser hung on the wall. Next to the bed was a solitary table on which rested the tools to be used during the operation. Wire cutters, mains tester, screwdriver, soldering iron and a multi-functional ammeter. Placed next to them, and taking up the remainder of the space on the table, was his new appendage.

Rob eased himself onto the table and, under the instruction of his father, lay down on his back. The room was deathly silent but for Jesus's regulated breathing. Given his aged circuits, he always feared Rob may not be the same person again. Or worse, may never start back up. Jesus had the capacity to restart the droid, no issues, but both of them were aware that adding more parts to underrated circuitry wasn't necessarily a good thing. Battery sustainability may draw down at ten times the usual rate, given the size of the new attachment, and, if so, the umbilical cords providing vital electrical life would quickly close down. What good would a flat-lining droid, with a hard-on be, if it was to short circuit? They'd never be able to get the lid on the coffin for a start, although the hymn 'He is risen' would provide a very fitting send off.

Jesus stroked his son's forehead and reassured him as best he could. "Don't worry, son, I built you from scratch, remember?" But that was a time when Jesus was a lot more alert and in the prime of his life. It was a fair assumption that Jesus wouldn't have been on a three-day bender like the one he'd just had, or, for that matter, had an attempt made on his life. That said, what worried Rob more than anything was the state of his father's trembling hands. If anything, he seemed more frightened than his patient.

"Are you scared too, dad?" asked Rob, taking one last look around the room.

"Son, my arse is twitching like a dying sparrow in the snow," he responded truthfully, with a calm angelic voice. "Now, shall I proceed?"

Rob nodded to his father and turned over on the bed to give him access to his power cells. With the access door open, Jesus reached in and located the power switch with his fingers. "Okay, here we go, three, two, one…"

Rob's viewing screen blinked, shifting from twenty-twenty vision to a single horizontal line. That line then imploded in on itself until all that remained was a single white dot which immediately began to fade. After that, Rob's world went black.

Jesus set to work on his magnificent creation, first deciding to relocate the current charging port to make way for the new appendage. He chuckled to himself at all the issues its current position had given Rob over the years, and felt a warmth at how his life would be easier from now on. That said, the job wouldn't be easy. The current lithium power cell, also crammed in Rob's abdomen, would also need to be rewired. Ideally Jesus would like to fit a larger, longer lasting power cell, but the truth was, there wasn't the room. Underneath Rob's armoured rib cage sat flash drives, conversion frames, solid state hard drives and three miles of core cable. All of which were cooled by a small temperature regulating fan, the size a regular PC might use. If all these components were crammed together, there was a real possibility Rob could melt. Both he and Rob knew, that by adding an erect, six-pound penis, that wouldn't be the only thing on heat. That was why Jesus had to take his time, thinking methodically, thinking technically and, quite frankly, thinking that this whole idea was ridiculous. But they'd been through that before.

Hours passed as Jesus worked tirelessly on his son's energy cells. Once Rob's internals were complete, he was able to concentrate solely on the appendage itself. Holding it in position with both hands, he couldn't believe the weight of the thing, as the top half of it, the bit protruding out of his grasp, rocked back and forth like the Empire State Building in a high wind, a sight that made Jesus shake his head with an accompanying whistle. He already felt sorry for the person on the receiving end of it.

As night closed in, Jesus had been at the theatre table for a solid eight hours. He was tired, sweaty and had blisters on his soft fragile hands, but he had nobly refused to quit until his son was powered back up. On and on he worked, checking terminals and transistors time and again until that was all he could see when he closed his eyes. Finally, when the old boy was about to collapse, he reached the last connection and broke for a well-earned cup of tea and chocolate biscuit.

Feeling revitalised from the sweet sugar rush, Jesus returned to the table with new determination. He gave Rob's internals one final check, comparing the drawings on the back of his fag packet to the mass of spaghetti inside the abdomen. "Seems to check out," he muttered to himself, deeming his engineering work a success before readying himself for the second phase, the punch list.

A couple of hours later and the job was finally done. Jesus stood back and admired his work. It looked phenomenal. A true thing of beauty and he was sure Rob would be over the moon when he saw the results. Jesus made one final check with the ammeter then reset Rob's transmission control protocol. All that was required then, was to switch on the power and lift his son out of his coma. With a bit of luck, they'd make the Roundell for last orders. Reaching his hand back through the access port, Jesus located the on/off switch, took a few moments to steel himself then powered him up.

Rob's penis rocketed vertically upwards, breaking through the sound barrier as it grew. It reached its pinnacle in no time at all and gave off a small sonic boom as the force broke out upon full extension. The bulging boner then cast the whole room into darkness, because upon its rise, it had torpedoed the overhead light causing the bulb to smash, something that left the lamp swinging alarmingly on its cable. Glass shattered everywhere and the unexpected event had adrenaline coursing through Jesus's veins, as he actually thought he might be bludgeoned to death. With the wires from the swinging lamp now exposed directly above Rob, Jesus tried his best to divert the vertical phallus away from danger. He wrapped both hands around the shaft and pulled with all his might, but soon gave up on that idea as the erection wouldn't move. Next he tried shouldering the six-pound beast away from the exposed electrical threat, but again he was thwarted, when the huge Hampton wouldn't budge. It was ramrod rigid, it was steadfast in its stance and Jesus was using every last sinew in his body, trying to push the penis away from those exposed wires, while all the time watching the live electrical wiring come within a whisker of contact. He puffed and he panted, gritted his teeth and groaned. Yet in spite of his brave efforts, the first inevitable connection happened, as the live electrical cables finally touched Rob's penis.

With electricity now jumping from bulb to bell-end like a spark plug in a car, Jesus had no other option than to try and shoo the swinging lamp away from the leaning tower of penis. Unfortunately, as he did so, he grabbed the shattered bulb by mistake causing electricity to shoot through his own body and form an unbreakable bond between his own hand and Robert's cock. Rob's cooling fan was the first thing to burst into life, its whirring propeller only drowned out by the chattering dentures of Jesus. The undersized fan was nobly trying to control Rob's rising core temperature, but was overwhelmed against the unstoppable power. Then there was the erection itself. It suddenly began to pulse with power, causing all the other lights in the house to dim. Rob, who was now in very serious danger of overheating, had just enough power from his start-up sequence to begin its warm-up phase, and woke for just enough moments to register the worrying scene above him.

With his visual display unit stuttering into life, he was barely able to identify his father, who shook violently, with hair stood on end while holding a firm grip on Rob's new cock. He had a pained expression, similar to the one a person may make if he'd just stood barefoot on a piece of Lego, and try as he might, Rob was unable to communicate with him. With none of his primary motor functions yet working, he had to watch helplessly as his new appendage started to glow red like a giant Swan Vesta match. Finally, with the Thornaby house's fuseboard unable to take any more, the power tripped as one last surge of electricity sought a path of least resistance. The last thing Rob saw was his father go airborne, crashing into the wall on the other side of the room before once again being plunged back into darkness, as the power was severed.

Jesus lay where he landed. He couldn't stop shaking nor prevent his teeth from chattering. He had scorch marks on the palms of his hands and his hair was still smouldering, giving off a foul burning smell. He'd been one lucky man to survive an electrocution like that. Rob's new penis had been earthed for a good twenty seconds and it was only due to its impressive size that it had been able to act as a lightning conductor, probably saving Jesus's life.

Grumbling with pain, Jesus got gingerly to his feet. He surveyed the situation before him. The room was dark, except for the glowing tip of Rob's penis which was still bolt rigid upright. The deadly light was still gently rocking from side to side, above where Rob lay still, flat and motionless on his back. Jesus checked his son for vital signs. There were none. Rob's power pack was displaying empty, and for all intents and purposes, he was gone.

The inventor knew, given the state he was in, he could do no more tonight. He'd promised his son to have him back on his feet in record time, but that was no longer going to be the case. A full analytical strip-down of every circuit would now need to be done before another switch on attempt, and that could take days or even weeks. Besides, thought Jesus, it would be best if he went to see the doctor himself. That was if he could get the key in the door, with his scorched hands shaking as badly as they were. Jesus picked up the telephone and dialled 999.

"Hello, I'd like an ambulance, ppppplease," he stuttered before proceeding to give the emergency operative all the details of his impending pickup.

"Sir, just remain calm and we'll have the emergency services with you in no time at all," said the reassuring lady on the other end of the phone.

"TTThanks aaaalot," he stammered. "I'll be outside in the

fresh air waiting for it," he said before attempting and failing three times to hang up the phone.

Jesus sat on the doorstep and attempted to smoke a cigarette while he waited for the ambulance to arrive. He sat in silence, hearing only the chatter of his teeth. In the darkness, he pondered the events of the previous twenty-four hours. His life had always been slightly weird, if not a little turbulent, but boy the last day or two had taken things to a new level. His life had no real direction and no other person he could think of acted or behaved as he did. Unique, eccentric, bizarre behaviour he liked to call it, although the locals simply called out "weirdo" when they saw him.

Jesus was pulled from his thoughts by flashing blue lights as the ambulance turned into his road and headed for his house. Once there, one of the crew jumped out and began a reassuring speech, gently easing the electrocuted boffin into the back.

"TTTThat was qqqquick," he said, his stutter no better for the cigarette break. The medic just smiled and lay Jesus down on the bed in the back.

"My name is Barry and I'm here to look after you. I'm just going to tie you down with these straps on the side of your bed to keep you secure. Our driver is new in the job you see, and isn't very good at driving ambulances," joked Barry, making sure he spoke loud enough for his new colleague in the front to hear, which he did and acknowledged by lifting up two fingers. Barry moved closer to Jesus so he could whisper in his ear. "But between you and me, his poor driving is probably due to his height and the fact he needs wooden blocks to reach the pedals." He winked with a smile, then shouted to the driver, "Righto, Mo, you can set off now."

Jesus couldn't believe his bad luck.

Little Mohammed Small was the Ambulance Service's newest member, having previously held driving jobs for both taxi and limousine firms. To his colleagues, he appeared to have a big chip on his shoulder, but given he was a fully-grown man no bigger than a tennis racket, who could blame him?

"So, Mr Jones, how's this happened, then?" asked the medic, gathering vital information from his patient en route to the hospital. "I see you're a doctor too," he went on, having read Jesus's name tag and spotted the stethoscope around his neck.

"Well, I'm not a doctor really," explained Jesus. "I'm more of an inventor. Robotics to be precise. I was performing an operation on my son, a cyborg I built many years ago when…"

The ambulance took a noticeable drop in speed, as Little Mo's ears pricked up to hear the conversation in the back.

"A cyborg you say," said Barry the cheery medic, keeping the patient talking to take their mind off their injuries and thus preventing them from slipping into shock.

Mo had heard enough and pulled the vehicle over to the side of the road, a manoeuvre not lost on Baz. "Barry, I'm ever so sorry but I think we've got a flat tyre, rear driver's side. Can you take a look?"

This was highly irregular and slightly annoying to the joke-a-minute paramedic, but ever the professional, Barry said that he would. "Back in a jiffy."

As soon as Barry was out of the back doors, Little Mo hit the gas. With wheels spinning, the ambulance took off at speed, leaving the occupant still tied to his trolley bed, though precariously close to wheeling out of the back door.

"Oh my days," shouted the excited driver above the din of the engine. "What were the chances of finding you in the back of my ambulance on my first day, eh?" He was cackling like a deranged maniac. "So you and your little droid have had a little accident, eh?" he went on. "Well, if you're in this shape after your little electrical haphazard, then I simply must see what shape Tin Head's in." Little Mo chuckled to himself at the serendipity of the moment, before making three right turns and heading back to the Thornaby house from whence they'd come.

Jesus was powerless to do anything. Still fastened to the trolley, it was all he could do to prevent himself from falling out of the ambulance. He kicked his feet, trying to widen his stance in an attempt to get some purchase on the walls of the racing vehicle.

Not that Little Mo minded if he fell out or not. On the contrary, he saw it as sport and simply ignored every speed bump or swift turn, laughing deliriously as he went.

Eventually the journey came to an abrupt end, when Little Mo, wooden blocks and all, stamped on the brakes causing the ambulance to screech to a halt outside Jesus's home. With the abrupt braking manoeuvre performed, momentum was suddenly reversed and Jesus's trolley was flung further into the bowels of the ambulance, causing all manner of medical equipment to crash on top of him, including an epidural needle that fell like a dart and wedged itself in his forehead. Not that he lay there buried for long, because Little Mo had already climbed from the driver's seat and was already pulling him out of the back of the ambulance feet first.

Ignoring the hydraulic ramp, Mo whipped the trolley out, allowing it to drop with a thud, rattling Jesus's skeleton and causing the needle in his head to quiver from side to side, a phenomenon that Jesus was unable to take his eyes off. The pain was horrendous, but the old man couldn't divert his eyes away from the swaying needle as it to-and-fro'd, first left and then right. And before he knew it, Jesus had managed to put himself into a semi-hypnotic state.

"Are you a munchkin?" he asked the angry little man pushing him on the trolley beneath many stars set against a black velvet night sky.

"No, I'm fucking not, it is I, Little Mo," responded Mo with frustration. What good was being an arch nemesis if your enemy could never remember your name?

"Then you're one of those midgets off Doctor Who then?" said Jesus, before being slapped back into reality by Mo, who took exception to the term midget, as all midgets do.

"Let's get one thing straight," said Mo, spitting venom, "the only doctor around here is you, and I don't mean because of that ridiculous outfit you're wearing. You're as real life to Doctor Frankenstein as anybody can get. In fact, I suggest we go and see your monstrous creation now." With that, he pulled the keys from the inventor's pocket before wheeling the trolley in through the front door.

Inside, Little Mo couldn't contain his glee as he saw for the first time the situation in front of him. Rob was immobile, lying completely still. Despite Mo's best efforts, he was still showing no signs of life and, for all intents and purposes was dead. Not perturbed, although a bit disappointed, Mo thought it best to make sure anyway and quickly formed a cunning plan to make sure any resurrection couldn't be performed by Jesus again. He propped up the trolley, so that Jesus could see every moment of his son's imminent demise as he dissected his nemesis bit by bit. Mo saw the tools that Jesus had been using, paying particular attention to the wire cutters. He picked them up and tossed them from hand-to-hand, hovering over the still cyborg like the grim reaper himself.

"Shall I start with the head?" he asked. "Or maybe rip out his power supply?" he questioned, a grin emblazoned across his smug face.

Jesus, now well out of his trance, watched in horror, and started crying with anguish, feeling utterly powerless to stop the horrible little man from destroying his beloved son. "Please, don't do it, I beg you."

Little Mo had been waiting for this moment for a long, long time. He was eyeing Rob's body, head to toe, looking for the ideal place in which to start his demolition project, when he eventually arrived at his mid-section. Casting his eyes horizontal and then up, Mo suddenly, for the first time, saw the massive erection Rob had going on. A penis that stood so tall that it towered above him. "You've got to be shitting me!" he said, staring at Jesus with unbelieving eyes. "You gave him a cock?" Mo shook his head at the absurdity of it all. "A cyborg with a penis. What the fuck were you thinking? It's perverse. Why?"

Jesus dropped his head and simply stared at the floor. "You wouldn't understand even if I told you," he said. "Just get on with what you came here to do." He could watch no more.

Little Mo now knew exactly where to start. He was going to

chop down the ridiculous penis, like a woodcutter would fell a mighty oak. "A breeding robot, indeed? My god, I could sell this to the papers and ridicule you for the rest of your pathetic days," he hissed. Mo stared at the bulbous tip and followed the shaft all the way down to the base. Once there, he looked for an entry point in which the wire cutters could be inserted to begin snipping. Once that was located, he placed the first of many wires between the blades and asked the beaten inventor if he had any soothing last words. Jesus had none.

The tip of Rob's penis was no longer glowing red. It had, on Jesus's journey to hospital, been given enough time to cool. As any science boffin worth his salt will tell you, energy can neither be created nor destroyed. It can however, change its form and that's exactly what was happening inside of Rob. The heat energy from Rob's once glowing member had transferred its way slowly into Rob's power pack. With the trickle charge re-energising Rob's vital start-up sequence, the colossal erection began to weaken, and when it no longer had the strength to stand up under its own weight, it gave way. Falling faster than the Boro after Christmas dinner, it plummeted, gravity pulling all six pounds of it onto the blissfully unaware head of Little Mo. Within milliseconds, Mo was out cold and yet another inch shorter.

Rob's central processing unit burst into life and after a short warm up, he found he had just enough power to allow him to sit bolt upright on the bed. He surveyed his surroundings and noticed his father tied to an ambulance stretcher, tears of joy now streaming down his face. Then Rob looked down and saw his new penis, and the little dwarf seemingly crumpled beneath it, before looking back toward his father. "Problems?"

"You could say that, yeah," replied Jesus, bursting into a huge grin. He'd really thought he was going to lose Rob, and to see him sat up and back to his normal self was a huge relief.

"You did it, then?" said the beaming robot, weighing his new anatomy with his hands and passing it from palm to palm.

Jesus just nodded, the raw emotion still choking him up.

"And what about him?" pointed Rob toward Mo.

"I'll explain later, son," said Jesus wearily.

Rob had been too lost in his own excited world to fully appreciate his father's predicament, but with growing awareness he realised that the old man looked terrible, with smouldering black hair stood on end. His hands were burnt and he also appeared to have some sort of dart sticking out of his forehead.

"Are you okay, dad?" asked the concerned robot, swinging his legs over the side of the couch to face his father.

"I will be if you would untie me so I can have a hug," responded Jesus.

Rob needed no second invitation. He leapt off the theatre table to aid his poor father. As he jumped, he forgot about the extra weight now attached to his front and it dragged him over so he fell flat on his face.

"I'm gonna need another operation, dad," cried Rob from his prone position on the floor.

"What, you mean you're hurt? Robert, are you okay?" asked the concerned inventor.

"Yes, I'm fine," giggled the mighty robot. "But now you're going to have to fit counter balances on my back."

The pair erupted with laughter.

Penelope Stevenson, still reeling from her sacking at top Middlesbrough psychologist firm, Head the Ball and Co, approached her first day as a freelance shrink with trepidation. She'd been wanting to go it alone for some time but given her wonderful company benefits, which included a fifty thousand pound a year pension and company car, she'd been unable to break from the security that the town's top firm had provided. But now at the age of fifty, with her previously, impeccable career in tatters and retirement plans blown to bits, she'd had to start all over again.

Her first advert was placed in the Herald and Post exactly seven hours after her sacking. This was done deliberately due to the power the number seven held over the superstitious. Not that Penelope believed in such claptrap, but she'd seen enough disgruntled sportsmen from the town to know that they did, none more so than the town's football team who had an uncanny knack of snatching defeat from the jaws of victory.

The Lucky Horse Shoe sports psychologists opened its doors at the Palladium shops in Middlesbrough's Grove Hill district just two days later. Penelope had managed to grab the shop in a quick-fire sale due to the ongoing regeneration of the area, and her belief that it was crammed with its own disgruntled athletes. Well, the residents could leap fences and run away pretty fast, so she thought that she'd be able to drum up enough business fairly quickly.

Penelope parked her car and approached the run-down shop. It would need a lick of paint for sure and a bit of love, care and attention, but her new project really excited her. Nothing, and specifically nobody, was going to spoil that. She had a new zest for life and enthusiasm burst from her soul. She vowed never to show the dark side of her character again. Those animals who had broken her professionalism had a lot to answer for. Every time she thought of them, her stomach tied in knots but she had to move on. How could she treat disgruntled sportsmen if she couldn't get over her own issues? She shook her head and stepped into the doorway of her new life.

"Are you Penelope Stevenson?" asked a cardboard box blocking the door.

Penelope jumped back with fright, staring at the box that now began to move. "Yes, that is I," she exclaimed in a guarded manner. Whoever was in the box was no athlete, but a potential customer all the same. The box began to shuffle and from out of the top popped a little person no bigger than a waste paper bin.

"Are you lost, little one?" asked Penelope, thinking that a small child had wandered off from its parents. On closer inspection, she saw that the person was sporting a beard, a bandage wrapped around his head and a frown that suggested he was pissed.

"Lost? Well, you might say that," responded the tiny man. "I think I have some anger issues that need addressing and I need your help. I've been waiting here most of the night."

"I'm afraid I don't deal with head injuries," said Penelope gesturing towards the man's head. "I only deal with sportsmen now."

"But I am a sportsman." Little Mo was trying hard to keep his composure. "I happened to be a very good high jumper in my day," he went on, causing Penelope to let out a laugh through her nose and make snot dangle from the end of it. The scene didn't go down well with Little Mo, who just stared at Penelope while she tried to regain her own composure and dignity.

Penelope straightened her face, wiped her nose and immediately apologised. Popping the used tissue into her handbag, she silently cursed herself for her appalling behaviour.

"How did you find me? I haven't even opened up for my first day, and yet here you are." Penelope's first customer had a bizarre, yet interesting demeanour, and she felt she could really help, if only she could keep her own gremlins in check. Those last two clients of hers had a lot to answer for.

"I bumped into a regular client of yours at KFC last night, an ex-footballer," answered Mo, all matter of fact. "Mad as a box of frogs, he was. Geordie, he was. I could barely understand a word he was saying. 'Mo, bonny lad,' he told me, 'yeev gotter goan see wor Penelope, like.' So here I am."

Penelope smiled, but alarm bells were suddenly going off in her head. If this guy was an associate of that client then she'd have to be on top of her game. That one had been the biggest challenge of her illustrious career. No more demons, no more unprofessionalism. This was serious stuff and Little Mo needed her right now. She gave him her full and undivided attention.

"So, Mo. Is it okay if I call you Mo?" she asked, bending over and peering above her glasses and down on the little fellow. "How long have you known that particular client of mine?"

"Only a few hours," he responded. "But he's somebody I really look up to."

More snot flew from Penelope's nostrils.

CHAPTER 14

"Obstacles aside, when do we get the go ahead for the job? When do we get the call?" asked Mary, who was starting to get a real thirst for this job now.

"We don't," replied Maddog. "The date and time will be sent to us via coded text message. There'll be no more contact until then, and if we so much as deviate from the plan…" Maddog tailed off into silence and wore a face that told Mary it wouldn't be the best news.

"But if there's no more contact then how do they know we'll be ready? What if something goes wrong? What if the guard escapes? What if Troy starts choking on a Parmo?" The questions came thick and fast as Mary tried to think of plausible scenarios that could ruin her big pay day. That is with the exception of Troy choking, of course, which actually made her quite excited. She made a mental note to order more fast food very soon.

"Listen, Mary, they know who we are… they know where we are… and any barriers that might lie in the way will be removed by them, one way or another. If we so much as deviate from the plan…" Maddog again became quiet, instead making a chilling slitting gesture across his throat with his fat finger. "They're watching us, Mary. The whole time. There's too much at stake to just allow a couple of ex-scaffolders to ruin it now. And I'll tell you something else, I won't need to tell them about you either because I bet they already know that you're here."

Mary leant forward in her chair to question the validity of the previous statement. "Excuse me?" she said. "I found Troy thanks to your incompetence, nothing more. I covered my tracks, as I always do. Nobody followed me here, I assure you. I was a fucking ghost out there."

Maddog stopped her in her tracks. "Spare me, will you, Mary. Do you really think you found this place through sheer accident?"

Mary recoiled at the very statement. She was ex-special forces. She moved in random patterns, never used the same sequence twice. She knew how to blend in and was absolutely sure nobody knew where she was. The only person who did know of her whereabouts was the pizza delivery boy, and he had looked scared out of his wits at the time. No, Maddog was paranoid. The size of this job must be getting to him.

Maddog could hear the cogs turning in Mary's head, and after pacing the room a few times, walked back across the room to face her. Sitting down in a big dusty chair, he waited for their eyes to meet before offering some sympathetic words. "Mary, you, me or Reggie fucking Kray have never dealt with this type of animal before. I told you, these people are top drawer. Ruthless criminals and thoroughly professional. They've got their fingers in many pies and hands in more police pockets than the Artful Dodger. I don't mind saying it, I'm in over my head, Mary, but if we stick with it, the rewards will be fantastic."

Mary sat in momentary silence taking in Maddog's words. Who were these people she was now working for? "So, what do we do now?" she asked, deciding to let it play, although it was probably his talk of reward that made her finally accept the rules of the game.

"We wait till H Hour," he said with an honest shrug of his shoulders. "Then we take the guard for a little walk to the bank."

"You make it sound so easy, but come on, what's stopping him blabbing his mouth off to the first person we meet?" Mary had only remained on the periphery of the plan up to this point, and saw only rich reward, but after Maddog's words about being watched, she was starting feeling a bit uneasy. Shit was getting serious.

Maddog laughed. "I told you, all obstacles will be removed, they've done their homework, Mary. The guard's mother is a lovely little old lady who lives in Marton Manor. Her favourite pastime is spending time with the blue rinse crew down the Mecca bingo hall and having the odd dabble on the gee gee's. She's also very accommodating to workmen, offering them copious amounts of tea while they visit to read her gas meter. How do I know this? Because I was one of those gas men."

"A gas man?" asked Mary with a raise of her eyebrows.

"Let me spell it out in layman's terms, they've been watching this guard upstairs for a while. Meticulous planning, they called it. They know his day-to-day movements off by heart, and the lives of the people he knocks around with. They've even done extensive work on his family too. They chose him due to his sexual orientation because no children makes life so much easier."

Mary nodded in agreement at such a wonderful thought.

"So, once they knew all there was to know about Ronnie, they sent a gas man round to visit Doris, his mother. He shares a nice little cup of tea with the little old dear and while she's screaming at the second favourite at Beverley, he leaves her a little present behind the meter. A remote controlled one, if you get my meaning. If Ronnie upstairs doesn't play ball, then I'm afraid the horses won't be the only ones flying over fences at speed. The beauty of it all is, it'll look like nothing more than a tragic accident."

Mary sat back in her chair trying to get her head around the whole thing. It all seemed so perfect, flawless in fact. It was a plan bordering on genius. That was until Troy turned up. How did he end up in this mess? As much as Troy gripped her shit, Mary knew deep down that he had a heart of gold. It was a weakness he had inherited from his father, all mouth and no tackle, at least that's how she saw it.

"When is it likely to be over?" she asked, wanting to know if an extended holiday abroad was needed once the job was done. If she booked early enough, she might even get extra baggage allowance with easyJet.

"By the eighth of October, I reckon. It's bank policy to send a manager round if Ronnie spends any more time on the sick after that," replied Maddog.

The date wasn't lost on Mary who gave a sarcastic smile. "The sperm donor's birthday," she said, having realised that Maddog had witnessed her silent laugh.

"What?" asked Maddog, having not heard correctly.

"The eighth of October. It's Troy's father's birthday. I'm just not sure if that's a good omen," she laughed.

Maddog just shrugged his shoulders. What was it about women and their ability to remember dates?

"So what are we going to do about Troy," she prompted again. If she was going to go away for a while, she was damned if he was going with her.

The question left Maddog totally perplexed.

"Mary, as I've said, Troy stumbled in on all of this by total accident. He was here purely to help me locate the missing truth serum and I've no doubt now that you've been brought here to clean this little mess up. How you deal with him is your business. However, now that you've told me you know who those two fucking idiots at the club are, that changes things again. It gives us a great chance of sweeping the whole mess under the table. All we need is a plan and we only have a short time left to find them."

Back in the bedroom, things had gone very quiet indeed. Troy stared at the broken figure of Ron on the bed. He had no words in which to comfort his new friend and watched helplessly as silent tears rolled down his face. Not that Troy was fairing much better in the mother stakes. The pair of them had overheard the whole conversation and realising his own mother wasn't here to help him ensured Troy wasn't exactly full of the joys of spring either.

Troy had always known his mother to be cold and callous. She could cut you down with scathing words or drop you with a swift left hook if need be. But he'd always believed that she had loved him.

He remembered fondly the days when she used to cuddle him tight and never let go. Wrapping her loving arms around him like a cotton security blanket. He'd eventually have to fight to escape her arms because she was squeezing him so tightly. Struggling for air, he'd wriggle out of her python-like grip before finally breaking to the surface in the deep end of Acklam Baths. She loved cuddling him while swimming for some strange reason. Yes, his mother had love in her somewhere. He likened her to Darth Vader. Underneath that cold exterior and forty fags a day lungs was a heart of gold. He just had to coax it out of her as Luke had once done to Anakin.

Troy's warm, wonderful thoughts were disrupted when his mother re-entered the room. He knew what was needed. He knew what to say. He may have been slow in spotting his mother's fall from grace, her descent into the underworld, but her timing was perfect nonetheless.

"Mother, I just want you to know that…" he started.

"Shut it, fat fuck," interrupted Mary, screaming in his face.

Troy, who wasn't expecting such aggression, let out a little fart of fear, a noise Mary happened to hear.

"What the fuck was that? You better not have dropped your arse near me."

Troy was now visibly shaking with fear and once again it was Ron who came to his rescue.

"I think he's just made the jump to shite speed."

Mary approached the bed where Ron lay and peered into his tear-stained face.

"Oh diddum's, you not enjoying your little sleepover?" she asked patronisingly. As the words fell from her lips, she slapped the helpless guard hard across the face. Blood splattered from his mouth and onto the bed covers.

Ron managed to keep his cool. "Well, I'd be enjoying it a bit more if you hadn't crashed through the bloody window," he started, spitting more blood out of his mouth while staring at the open window. "And as for that flash bang you used coming up the stairs, wow that was a tactful appearance. Call yourself a professional? Every person in the bloody street probably heard the commotion you made when entering this house. Windows hanging off, loud bangs and your mouth's so loud I'd be surprised if half the street haven't heard your ridiculous plan. The police are probably on the way right now."

Troy winced in anticipation of what was sure to come. Nobody spoke to his mother like that.

Crack.

Mary drove her knuckles into Ron's face causing more blood to pour from his mouth.

"Keep on talking, sweetheart," she said, "because I've got plenty more of those where that came from."

"Oh my," said Ron, spitting out a bit of cracked tooth, "you must be the brains behind the operation, slapping me about and causing cuts and bruising only days before the bank job, you really are thicker than a bowl of muesli."

Mary recoiled her fist, ready to deliver the bad news once again but was stopped by the hand of Maddog grabbing her wrist.

"He's right, Mary. We need him looking his best for the job, not walking into the bank with two black eyes. No more slapping around."

Mary walked back across the room in frustration. "The cocky shit thinks he knows everything. The job. The time. The walls in this gaff must be paper thin," she cried, looking at Maddog in the hope he'd take back control of the situation.

"Yeah, I should have figured it out really," said the big bouncer, scratching his chin in deep thought. "The heating bills have been rather high and I heard the old lady next door in bed getting banged off James Bond the other night, at least I think it was him, she kept shouting Roger Moore. It was only when I heard Troy fart while I was pegging the washing out that I remembered."

"Well thanks to her, at least you don't have to open the fucking window," replied Ron.

Mary ran at Ron, ready to deliver more blows but was once again thwarted by Maddog.

"You're losing it, Marion," said Ron. "The whole plan going up in smoke, and all because of her incompetence." But Ron's newfound courage and sarcasm were quickly cut short.

"It will be your mother that will be going up in smoke if you don't shut your trap," said Maddog, accompanying the statement with a dig to Ron's cracked ribs. "If you must hit him, Mary, do it where it'll leave no marks."

"He has got a point," said Maddog. "We've been careless. Too busy talking about the good old days and taking our eyes off the job. We have to move and sharpish. I think we should go to your place."

Mary was far from happy about that suggestion. Taking a job of this magnitude back home was against every criminal rule book ever written, although she had to admit, amongst all the excitement here, she'd screwed up big time. She'd allowed her ego to get in the way of her professionalism and providing another safe house was the least she could do.

Not that it was all bad news, by presenting herself in front of her neighbours, she'd be providing an alibi. Her cover story would be she was simply having a couple of friends round and, what's more, having Troy home again would alleviate any suspicion as to why no fast food van had been seen there this week. If nothing else, she could at least straighten her hair again, because she'd forgotten to pack her GHD straighteners for this particular job and that was a cardinal sin.

Maddog wasted no more time with the pleasantries. He produced a knife from his belt and freed both Ron and Troy. Having both been through the same ordeal, they instinctively ran to hug each other in the centre of the room. It was a hug that went on far too long for Maddog's liking. A quick, two patted backslap was more than enough for real emotionless men, so he was quick to separate the pair.

"You don't need me to tell you the score. No talking, no funny business and no trying to escape because you both know the consequences of that." He made a clicking motion with his thumb as if setting off a bomb detonator, however his two prisoners were lost, still embracing, while staring into each other's eyes.

Maddog, sensing his words had been lost on the two lovebirds, thought up another rule. "I want no bumming in the back of my car either."

CHAPTER 15

Underwhelmed, Jesus sat in the front room, feet up and sipping his third cup of tea of the morning. The shakes from the electric shock had just about worn off, although scorched scabs across both palms provided proof of the trauma he'd been through only a few hours before. Scabs that now lay hidden beneath freshly dressed, protective bandages. Given the previous day's events, one could be forgiven for allowing the old boy a well-deserved rest day but rest was the last thing on Jesus's active mind. He'd been awake for at least a couple of hours, contemplating various stages of his crazy life. His youth, his military career and his commitment to science, to name but a few. He wondered how he'd arrived at such a moment in time. His only true friend a cyborg to whom he'd just attached a two-foot phallus. The whole venture had been truly absurd and went against the grain of progressive human thinking. He knew that if this news ever leaked out, as he was sure it would, he'd have some very difficult questions to answer. Surely it would have been better using his talents for the good of the planet, he thought, rather than squander them for selfish reasons such as diminishing his loneliness. With greater vision, he could have built an army of cyborgs, which would cut down on human casualties in war zones. Or, better still, created a new breed of doctor. A quick upload of medical information and there you'd have it, a surgeon created instantly instead of taking years to train a human. Imagine the Nobel Peace Prize he might have won for eradicating human error. Yes, robots were the future alright, but Jesus hadn't capitalised when he'd had the chance. With NASA flying unmanned spacecraft to the limits of the solar system and planting robotic rovers on the surface of Mars, Jesus knew he'd missed the boat (or even shuttle, as it were). A life of fame and fortune had beckoned but, instead, here he sat in his Thornaby home, a sad and poor man.

Jesus placed the mug to his lips and drained the last of his tea. As he did so, he noticed the fading inscription printed on the side. It simply read 'Number One Dad'. It had been given to him as a father's day present by Rob a couple of years ago. Running a thumb over each of the words, he read them out softly

"Number One Dad." Jesus dropped his legs from the footstool and stared at the words again. It was like a light bulb had suddenly flicked on inside his head. Life wasn't just about money, nor was it about awards. It was about the people you surrounded yourself with, like friends and family. Okay, Jesus didn't have any of those, but he had a bloody good cyborg that treated him as such. Robert was what life was about, a person to share experiences with. A person to cherish and love till the end. If providing his son with a six-pound cock had helped to make him happy, then Jesus was fine with that.

Jesus placed the cup down on the coffee table and raced upstairs. He wanted to see his son, hoping to share the epiphany he'd just had. Bouncing up the flight of stairs, two steps at a time, he turned right on the landing and burst through the bedroom door, eager to share his thoughts on the meaning of life.

"Morning, son, I…"

Jesus was immediately stunned to silence. Lying on the bed with his kecks around his ankles, Robert was tugging furiously at his flaccid trouser snake. It was a scene that Jesus wasn't quite expecting nor ready for. He turned his head away and made a mental note to knock in future.

"It's okay, son, these things are all very natural to a boy like yourself. Don't be ashamed, we all do it and you don't have to worry. I won't tell a soul."

Jesus was still facing the other way, feeling rather awkward. He began to walk slowly to the door but never quite made it out before frantic cyborg spoke. "It doesn't work, dad," he wailed, disappointment in his voice. "It won't stand up."

Jesus scowled uncomfortably at the words he'd just heard. Masturbation was surely a private matter and something that just came naturally. He was certain that most fathers never had to give their own kids a step-by-step guide on how to tug. However, Jesus and Rob's relationship was hardly normal. In fact, it was at the complete opposite end of the spectrum to normal. It was more inscrutably weird. And so, with a big suck of air into his lungs and a slow exhale of breath, he turned around to face his son.

Rob was right with his diagnosis. His penis was in a flaccid state, hanging quite low, like a hungover boa constrictor, in spite of him doing his best to shake some life into it.

"Listen, son," Jesus coughed. "Wanking… I mean masturbating is… errr." Jesus was rubbing the back of his neck and wishing he'd stayed sulking downstairs.

"Is what?" asked the fraught droid, still pumping his knob like a person might feed bread to the ducks.

"Well, it's a natural and very normal process that all men and women go through. It happens when they're feeling a particular emotion," said Jesus, who was quite happy with his explanation and at how quickly he was taking to advanced parenting.

"I've tried everything, dad," responded Rob, ruefully, "but there's been no response at all." Having thankfully stopped his beating at this stage, he swung his legs off the bed before quickly standing up to face his father. As he did so, the pendulum motion of his new toy almost swept his father off his feet. Luckily, Jesus saw it coming.

"Hmmmm," sounded Jesus, rubbing his chin. "Have you looked at the underwear section in the Freeman's catalogue?"

Rob nodded, pointing across the room to a small pile of catalogues on the floor.

"And still nothing?" asked the inventor.

"Not even a dafty on," answered the perplexed tugger.

"What about topless darts in space or the ten minute previews on the box?" asked Jesus, raising the soft porn stakes a few notches.

But Rob just shook his head.

"This is fascinating," said Jesus, pausing for thought for a few moments, not quite sure whether to mention the names of several websites that he could recommend. The pro and cons had to be weighed up before divulging such private information. He was sure Rob would find the sites most helpful, but on the other hand, he didn't want his son to think him a pervert either. It was a tough decision to make. In the end, the old man thought it best and with cheeks flushing red. "Have you err…"

"Yes, dad," pre-empted Rob, unable to look his father in the eye, "and still no use."

Jesus saw the laptop on the bedside cabinet and made a mental noted to delete his search engine history from now on.

Jesus rubbed his tired eyes. He had worked in robotics long enough to know that prototypes didn't always work first time. In fact, if they ever did, he was truly astounded. But that didn't stop him feeling a little frustrated. He'd worked on the new attachment for hours, checking and rechecking every fixture and fitting. He'd even witnessed the thing stand up to attention, so why it wasn't working now was a mystery.

With any other project, you could just shelve it, recharge your batteries and look at it with a clear head another day, but unfortunately for Jesus, this time he couldn't. This project was his son, who had feelings and would no doubt continue to ask intelligent questions regarding the failure. Rob also had strong emotional tendencies, as witnessed a few days ago. It was no longer a case of just reprogramming algorithms, it was a case of controlling a complex mind with emotions in turmoil. Rob, Jesus knew, needed the fairy tale ending.

"Okay, son, let me take a look at it for you," he said, unbuttoning the cuffs of his shirt and rolling up his sleeves. "Pop yourself back on the bed and I'll be back in a jiffy."

Jesus left the room to fetch his tools, allowing himself time to think on what the problem might be. He knew he'd wired the components correctly. He'd witnessed with his own eyes the fantastic rise of the one-eyed monster, he just didn't want Rob to see how baffled he was by it. Rumbling around in his garage, he picked up a few token tools which might pacify his son and headed back up the stairs. He was effectively behaving like a car mechanic who looks under the bonnet during an MOT. Only this time he wasn't able to suck air in through his teeth and say… "We can't get the parts for these Japanese models."

Jesus re-entered the room and walked across to his sullen boy. "Now don't worry, son, I'm sure it's nothing to get upset about," he said reassuringly, with all the finesse of a dentist who is about to put a six-inch drill in someone's mouth. "It'll probably just be loose wiring or something."

Jesus encouraged his son to lie back on the bed and think of England. He also made sure that no overhead lighting or any other items were in striking range of the volatile trouser snake. Once bitten and all that. Pulling back the synthetic flesh covering the access port, Jesus carefully unscrewed the door and peered in. As he suspected, nothing seemed out of place or damaged and Jesus wondered if the battery power was the problem. "What battery life are you displaying?" he asked, looking up towards his son for the response.

"Sixty-seven percent," came the reply. "I recharged myself overnight, but I've exerted quite a bit of time and energy this morning, as you can imagine."

Jesus let out a long, low whistle. "Thirty three percent! That's some serious tug time," he said, before going back to his investigation. "The power source should be fine and I can't really see an issue with the wiring, son. Perhaps you just need to give it more time, you know?" Jesus was wondering if the cyborg really had the ability to be turned on sexually. More than likely, his son was getting confused with his artificial feelings, but this was no time to tell him that.

"Is there nothing you can try, dad?" asked the desperate Rob.

It was a question that put Jesus into deep thought. "I could try and plug you into the house mains again, albeit only for a very brief moment in time. The extra surge when run down to earth should at least prove the mechanics are still working properly and, if they are, we can at least eliminate that from our fault diagnosis."

Jesus left the room and returned a short while later with a simple two core cable. At one end was a standard household plug and at the other, exposed copper wire. He attached the wire to the lifting arm of Rob's penis and positioned the plug into the wall socket.

"Ready?" he said.

"Ready," answered Rob, holding onto the side of the bed.

"Then I'll count down from three, two, one."

"No wait," shouted Rob, anxiety suddenly coming over him. "What if it rises as violently as it did last time, it may come right over the top and cave my face in."

Jesus thought for a moment. The chances of that happening were practically nil, as he'd included robust shock absorbers during the engineering phase. He'd even allowed for thermal expansion, but thought it best not mention it in case Rob thought he was showing off.

"Okay, son," said Jesus softly, "if it helps you feel more at ease, why don't you lie on your stomach? If it does rise like a rocket then the mattress will absorb the force, thus preventing you from being coshed to death by your second hard-on." It was, of course, a ridiculous statement and the inventor knew it, but the suggestion seemed to settle the traumatised droid who, after briefly thinking the scenario through, did as his father suggested and flipped onto his front.

"Right, we'll try again on three, okay?"

Rob nodded in silence.

"One, two, three…"

"Wait, wait, wait," interrupted Rob, once more causing Jesus to peel his index finger from the switch. "What if the power surge shuts down my mainframe again? Two surges of electricity through my system can't be good for me, can it?" asked the apprehensive cyborg.

But once again Jesus had thought this through.

"It will only be a momentary switch on of power controlled by myself and nothing like the electrocution we both experienced last night. Besides it was me who bore the brunt of the shock, as I provided the direct route down to earth." After seeing that Rob still wasn't sure, he thought it best to reassure his son again. "Robert, I assure you that everything is going to be absolutely fine. I've got a PhD, remember."

The thought didn't instil much confidence in Rob, although he had to admit the old boy obviously knew his way around a circuit board or two.

"Look, if it makes you feel more comfortable…" Jesus left the room again, returning moments later with a pair of size eleven wellington boots. "Rubber soles," he announced, tapping them both together, before placing them on his prone son's feet.

"There, easy fix," he said, looking at Rob to see if there was anything else causing him concern. "Trust me, son, nothing is going to happen to you. You're perfectly safe."

Rob nodded his head, giving Jesus the go ahead to proceed.

He walked over to the socket and began the countdown for a third time.

"One, two, three." Jesus flicked the switch…

The electricity surged into Rob's body causing an immense erection to grow at supersonic speed. It slammed into the mattress as was the contingency plan but, as the downward thrust had nowhere to go, it instead lifted Rob into the air as if he were an Olympic pole-vaulter. His penis rose with such force that the cyborg was now flying backwards through the air, only stopping when he slammed into the MFI wardrobe on the opposite side of the room. The wardrobe, a cheap flat pack affair, shattered into a thousand pieces, sending shards of splintered wood in every foreseeable direction. Rob, who by this point was no longer airborne, then slid down the opposite wall to the floor. With shock written all over his face, he lay on his back and watched as his willy, now flaccid again, snapped down, with the crack of a whip against his thigh.

After a silent pause, Jesus appeared. "Well, I didn't see that one coming," he muttered, before pulling a splinter from Rob's arse. "But at least now we know it's not mechanical, eh?" he said, heading downstairs to put the kettle on.

CHAPTER 16

Severely corroded and an unroadworthy death trap, Maddog McClane's battered mark three Escort spluttered and banged its way through the bendy country lanes of Picton. A rusty red in colour, it sported XR3i pepper pot alloys with bald Pirelli tyres and a car sticker that said Zenith Data Systems Cup Final 1990. It was a car that could hardly be labelled as inconspicuous in a posh village such as Picton, and it certainly had a few curtains twitching as the exhaust blew clouds of blue smoke into the fresh countryside air.

"Nice to see you chose the stealth option," said Ron sarcastically, rubbing the seats with his hands.

He was soon shot down by the irate driver. "I've just about had enough of your shite," said Maddog. "All the way over here, it's been moan, moan, moan, and if I get another peep out of you, I'll bury you in that field over there and be done with it." Maddog was in a dark mood, purely down to the fact that he hated driving. Or more to the point, he wasn't very good at it. Something everybody in the car was fully aware of because they'd been covering their eyes for most of the journey. The big lummox had already run through two red lights and narrowly escaped several head on collisions but only Ron had the balls to say anything.

"It won't be difficult for the cops to find you though, will it?" said Ron, continuously poking more fun at the simmering bouncer in the driver's seat. "They'll just have to follow the trail of oil dripping from this heap of shit and you'll be done for."

It was one insult too many for Maddog who stamped on the brakes and screeched the car to a halt outside the Station pub, a noise that attracted stares from the beer-swilling farmers sitting on the benches outside. Maddog unbuckled his seatbelt and readied himself to pummel the waspy little shit, when he was suddenly pulled back at the last minute by Mary.

"Leave it, Maddog. Don't cause a scene. He'll get what's coming to him soon enough," she said, smiling at the locals and giving a little wave. In response, Picton's well-to-dos muttered something about fresh air, pollution and the chavs inside the car, until somebody recognised Mary's face and forced a wave back. "Drive on, Maddog, and slowly."

Maddog, still seething inside, knew Mary was right. They had already moved safe houses once, due to the commotion they'd caused at the last one, and the last thing they needed was another scene here, especially in a peaceful village such as Picton. Fumbling with the gear stick, he applied some revs to the accelerator and slowly released the clutch, but the car didn't move. Instead, it back-fired and stalled, sending a plume of black smoke from the exhaust blissfully into the sky. It was a bang that brought even more attention from the crowd outside the public house and the more the numbers started to swell, the more Maddog felt pressured.

"Easy, Maddog," said Mary, doing her best to calm her mate down. The big fella hated driving with a passion and once hospitalised a test examiner who had asked him to blow his horn. That was the first of his five failures.

Maddog restarted the car and Mary offered yet again another wave to the expanding crowd. When he was ready, Maddog eased the car forward, and for a while it looked like they were on their way. That was until the car started kangarooing and throwing the occupants around like rag dolls.

"For fuck's sake, man, have you even passed your test?" Ron simply wasn't going to let this one go and was actually enjoying the bouncer's discomfort.

Once again the brakes went on, and this time Maddog did get out of the car. Ripping the back door off its hinges, he reached in and grabbed the security guard by his collar. Pulling him out of the vehicle, he held him aloft by the throat, a good two-foot off the ground. The locals of the Station pub gasped in horror. Not because of Maddog's show of aggression, but rather, because they saw their neighbour Troy on the back seat, pleading for his boyfriend's life. Nobody thought they'd ever see the day the lazy fat bastard would get hooked up.

"If you're going to do it, then get on with it, man," encouraged Ron, who simply wasn't bothered if he lived or died anymore. Being told your own mother would die in an explosion if you didn't commit the world's largest heist did strange things to a man's head.

"Don't tempt me," hissed Maddog, his face only inches from Ron's. Fortunately for Ron, the threat was empty. He was key to the whole bank operation and Maddog, with the eyes of the Teesside underworld upon him, knew it. He wouldn't dare lay a finger on Ron, not yet anyway, but that's not to say he wouldn't once the job was done.

"I say, old chap, how about you put that fellow down this instant? We'll have no tomfoolery around here." A local hero had emerged from the crowd. "A big buffoon like yourself picking on the meek, it's an outrage. Perhaps you'd like to pick on somebody equally as feisty. Now come here and I'll give you a bunch of fives."

Ron wasn't expecting this and tried to discourage the stupid young fellow with a shake of his head, but with his throat gripped so tightly he found it impossible. Maddog, still holding Ron in the air with one hand, suddenly dropped him like a stone and turned to face the challenger for his crown.

Tarquin Holmes had been pushed to the front of the crowd by his wife Tabitha, who had ordered her husband to regain order and show the ruffian a thing or two about manners. However, as he'd drawn closer to the colossal beast, Tarquin was starting to have second thoughts. Troy covered his eyes and curled into a ball on the back seat while Mary climbed into the driver's seat and started the car. Ron, feeling slightly guilty for instigating this whole episode could only watch in stunned silence as brave Tarquin walked the green mile to his imminent doom.

"Get in the car, Maddog. Don't do it," shouted Mary, though it was wasted breath. Maddog had never shirked a challenge yet. All she could do was close her eyes and pray for it to be over soon. She needn't have worried…

Whack.

Maddog delivered a haymaker to the former private schoolboy that echoed with the sound of crushing flesh and bone. It was a delivery of the highest order, and one that bade Tarquin a quick good night. The poor lad would be lucky if he woke up this side of next week and even luckier if he could eat again this side of next year.

"Would anybody else care to pass comment on my driving?" asked Maddog, his mist a lava red. "No…? Good. And if any one of you jumped up, little sheep shaggers so much as utters a word of this to the law, then I'm gonna tell them all about the cannabis farm you've got in these parts." He actually had no idea if there was a cannabis farm, but he'd taken an educated guess.

This was a rural village after all, with minimal police presence. The community was made up of mostly farmers who were always bleating on the news about how skint they were, and yet never seemed to sell up. Perhaps the clincher was the fact that why else would Mary live in this shitty place like this unless there was free rock to be had?

The crowd stared down at their feet and avoided eye contact with Maddog. Not one of them was calling for the police or an ambulance, and nobody with the exception of Tabitha was rushing to the aid of Tarquin. Satisfied that all was well again, Maddog headed back to the car.

"Want me to drive?" asked Mary, pulling a spliff from her top pocket and offering it up to the big man. "It'll help settle you down."

The journey to Mary's house took another five minutes, but it was a torturously long five minutes of silence. Even Ron, who had been so brave with his mouth on the way over to Picton, now remained tight-lipped, having witnessed at first hand the frightening power of Maddog. It was therefore left to Mary to break the ice.

"How did you know about the cannabis farm, mate?" she asked, genuinely intrigued that such closely guarded secret as that could be figured out by such a thick bloke as Maddog. "I never had you down as a Miss Marple."

"Wasn't that difficult, to be honest. I've known you a long time, remember. A scaffolder living in a posh place like Picton just didn't add up. Besides, I found three kilo of it in your backpack yesterday."

The pair were still laughing as the car pulled into the driveway of an old renovated barn house just on the outskirts of the village.

Maddog whistled as he got out. "Not a bad crib, Mary," he said, impressed that his mate was doing so well. "How did you afford it?"

Mary looked round to see that Troy wasn't within earshot. "Troy's father," she whispered. "He had quite a bit of money when I first met him. He was quite famous too. But he was married and paid me to keep my mouth shut. I've never seen him since. I still get the odd payment to help with the bills like, but it's all done with a PO Box address. It's not like I can go back on a deal, is it?" She sounded as if this was an everyday child support, business transaction.

"He was rich and famous, you say?" asked Maddog, dying to hear more gossip about Mary's short life as a WAG. "So who is he, then?"

Before Mary had time to reply, Troy came trudging over.

"So what's your great plan now, mother dear?" he demanded.

Mary had to acknowledge that she'd been a bit of a shit to Troy of late, so decided against kicking him up the arse for his sharp tone.

"Take yourself inside and make sure Ron goes with you," she said, never taking her eyes off the security guard. "Then make up the spare room for our guest and put the kettle on. Ron will need all the strength he can get for when the big day arrives. Won't you, pet?" She patted Ron on the back as he walked by. He didn't even offer her a glance. He knew how to pick his battles and now wasn't the time. Slowly, he followed Troy into the house.

Mary stood outside with Maddog and took in the scenery. If this job went as well as she hoped, she wouldn't have to work again. She could live the life of luxury she'd always dreamed about.

"So what are we gonna do about those two from the club?" asked Maddog, getting his mind back on the job in hand.

"Well, I've been thinking about that actually," said Mary, with a smile on her face.

"I've seen that face before, Mary. You're up to no good." Maddog crossed his arms and waited for his mate to tell all.

"I was just wondering, why we are spending all our time and energy looking for them?" Mary threw the question out there hoping Maddog would pick it up and run with it.

"Errr, because they have the truth serum?" he answered, reminding Mary of the bleeding obvious.

"And what's so bad about that then?" she went on, encouraging Maddog to find the wavelength she was riding on.

"Because there's a small possibility that they discover the tubes of Pringles contain a drug that makes people hand over their bank account details when prompted. So they go to the local police station before we've actually committed the greatest heist in history thus ruining our lives forever?" said Maddog, eloquently. That's the way he saw it anyway.

Mary had another plan. She smiled at her mate, letting him stew for a few seconds more.

"Okay, how about this? We get them to join us down the bank on that fateful day. Have them in there with us, so that every CCTV camera in the building can place them at the scene. We crack on with the job in hand and leave via the back door as planned."

"I don't follow," responded Maddog.

"You really aren't the brightest, are you?" said Mary, making sure she was a fist swing away. "The police enter the bank and find all the suspects and money gone. So they set about with forensics, interview any witnesses and study the camera footage. It might take a day or two to recognise them, maybe even longer to locate them, but when the rozzers do eventually knock on their door, hey presto. Two ready-made criminals for the slammer. They get sent down and we ride off into the sunset."

Maddog gave Mary a silent glazed-over look, leaving her a little deflated that she had to spell out the whole, genius plan. "Maddog, providing we avoid the CCTV cameras, the police won't know what we look like. Agreed? But if we place Jesus and his new friend in front of the cameras, the police will know what they look like. You follow? So, when the police turn up at their house to question them, they are sure to find traces of the truth serum inside the Pringles tubes you claim they have." Mary stood looking at Maddog, waiting for the light bulb to turn on.

Maddog just stared blankly at her.

"Maddog…" she said finally in exasperation. "We fuckin' frame them."

Maddog took a step back as the sudden beauty of the plan eventually found its way into his brain. He'd previously been prepared to serve bird for a life of luxury upon his release but why? Mary's devious and cunning plan was so simple that it couldn't fail. Jesus and his pal had unwittingly stolen a canister of truth serum and if they could be placed in the location of the robbery at the exact time it was happening, they'd be ready made scapegoats. And guilty as charged.

"I knew bringing you into the fray was a good idea, Mary," lied Maddog, approaching his old friend to put the lips on her.

"Whoa there, big man. I like you, yeah, but not that much." Mary wasn't one for romance.

Maddog let the humiliation slide and instead gave Mary a big slap on the back, a punch that drove her forward a few paces and wishing she'd have settled for the peck on the cheek.

"So how do you intend to get them down the bank, then?" asked Maddog, hoping Mary had the answer to that one too.

"Oh, that's the easy part," she laughed, "but let's go inside and brew up first, then I'll tell you all about it."

Troy paced about his bedroom while Ron sat quietly on the end of the bed. The pair had hardly muttered a word since they arrived in Picton and poor Troy just didn't know how or even where to begin to comfort the security guard, other than offer him a cup of sweet tea, which he gladly accepted.

Troy had witnessed his mother and that horrible man laughing and cuddling from the upstairs window. They were actually enjoying the torture they were inflicting on poor Ron. How Troy wished he was man enough to teach them both a lesson, but the sad reality of it was, he just wasn't.

"Don't get any more involved, Troy," muttered Ron, who was admiring a giant Freddie Mercury poster on the wall. It had Freddie in his familiar stance, arm out aloft with clenched fist, microphone stand in his other hand. In his opinion, Freddie was the best singer the world had ever produced, and for a short minute Ron allowed himself to drift away into his memories. He remembered that very concert, the one from the poster, because he was there.

Live Aid had taken place back at the old Wembley Stadium and Ron had bagged himself tickets and found himself five foot from the front. He remembered the audacity of Bob Geldof screaming, "Give us your fucking money," swearing in front of the Queen like that as she sat on her throne watching the BBC. Only there was only one Queen in his eyes, and that was the band he'd come to see.

"He was good, wasn't he?" interrupted Troy, watching Ron staring longingly at the poster.

Ron turned to Troy and gave him a smile and a nod. "The best," was all he offered.

"I've got Andy Bell too," announced Troy moving onto another poster, "and George Michael and Boy George." He was giving Ron a running commentary of each poster that adorned his wall, from where they were taken to what inspiration they offered to him. "Take Will Young here," said Troy, curtseying with his hands clasped in excitement as he spoke. "Many said he came out too soon during his early fame and that it would ruin his career. But look at him go." Troy clapped excitedly, until Ron reminded him that the former Pop Idol singer hadn't produced a worthy song since two thousand and three.

"Okay then, what about this guy?" asked Troy, moving around the wall. "Marc Almond?"

Ron shrugged his shoulders before cracking a rubbish joke about Maddog having a soft cell.

It was a positive sign, and one that encouraged Troy to continue his running commentary. He showed Ron his whole collection, Bowie, Mika and, making the sign of the crucifix when he got to the next one in line, Stephen Gately. Finally, he came to the piece de resistance, the one that took pride of place above his bed where he slept. Elton John.

"Nah," said Ron, shaking his head in disgust, "he's not my type at all."

It was a reply that had Troy deflating faster than a balloon in a hedgehog sanctuary.

"If you don't mind me asking, how old are you, Troy?"

"The wrong side of twenty-three," he said. "And you should know by now that it's impolite to ask a lady her age."

"I'm sorry. It's just you seem to have an awful lot of posters for one so old."

Troy felt belittled and stared at the floor. "I know, but I was just trying to keep mother happy," he replied with a statement that confused Ron who gestured with his head for Troy to elaborate. "She came into possession of loads of Blu Tack a few days back but couldn't sell the stuff so I bought the posters to try and please her."

Ron looked at Troy and really felt for him. He was a nice guy with a heart of gold and didn't deserve a mother like Mary.

"Did it work?" he asked, wondering if Mary was pleased by his actions.

"Not really," said Troy, head bowed again. "She charged me twenty quid a go for a packet."

"Troy?" Ron changed the mood to one more serious. "I need to get a message to my mother but I don't have a phone."

"You can't, they'll kill her," said Troy, in a raised voice, which prompted Ron to order him to hush.

"I realise that, and I'm not prepared to jeopardise her life, but if I can just text my friend, he can get a message to her."

Troy didn't have his phone on him as Maddog had put it in the laundry back at the first safe house. He did however have an old Nokia lying about somewhere. It was an old pay as you go, thirty-three ten type that he'd replaced years ago but kept because he loved the inbuilt game, Snake.

"Does it have any battery life? Does it have a sim card?" asked Ron with urgency, waiting for Troy to turn the electronic brick on.

Troy fumbled with the phone and powered it up. The battery symbol was flashing empty and Troy gave a pained expression as he handed it over to Ron. The phone had only seconds of life left but Ron still gave it a go, more in hope than anything else. He keyed in the eleven-digit number before typing out just a one-word message, 'Bandages'. He then waited with bated breath to see if it would send before the power finally packed up and died. The message sending display illuminated the screen as Ron held up the phone, trying to encourage a better signal. It was clearly a race against time and just as he was cursing rural mobile phone masts, the phone switched off automatically in his hand.

"Did it send…? Did it send?" he asked, clearly in distress.

"I don't know, I'm sorry," said Troy sympathetically.

Ron slumped back down on the edge of bed.

Troy sat right beside his worried friend, holding his shoulders tight.

"We'll get through this, you know, we'll be alright you and me," Troy offered.

Although the words were appreciated, Ron took very little comfort from them. "I just worry about my mum, you know?"

Troy offered an understanding nod, but the reality was, he'd never once worried about his hard as nails mother in his life.

"What message did you try and get to her?" asked Troy, when he felt the moment right.

"Oh, it's just a secret code we have. A sort of password for when one of us can't really talk but is in some form of danger."

It was a reply that had Troy looking somewhat perplexed.

Ron, noticing Troy had no idea what he was talking about, elaborated. "Mum hated the idea of me working in a bank. She always thought it possible that someday I'd get caught up in some armed robbery." The irony wasn't wasted on Ron but he continued anyway. "She predicted this, I suppose, and said if I was ever unable to talk to her for fear of being overheard then all I had to do was drop a one word code into the conversation. She'd know what to do from there. That word is 'bandages'."

Troy looked at Ron with a beaming heart. It was like having his own little Jason Bourne sat in his room.

"Doesn't everyone have a secret code in their family for when their loved ones are under duress?" asked Ron, bewildered at the thought that people didn't take such precautions.

"Not in our house, they don't," responded Troy, his intrigued expression evaporating into one of sorrow. "When I send my mother a text she normally just tells me to fuck off."

With that, Ron cuddled his new best mate.

CHAPTER 17

Elf-sized Little Mo, still disgruntled by Penelope's behaviour, did an abrupt about turn and walked away. He really was running empty on self-esteem. There he was, presenting himself to a well-respected Middlesbrough shrink, and all she could do was laugh at his misfortune. He trudged off, hands deep in his pocket. As he walked, he tried to recall the good old days before the accident. A time when he was a basketball champion and, being the best player in his school, the team captain too. He used to soar through the air, as elegant as a gannet in full flight, slam-dunking the ball through the hoop and gaining another three points for his team, while that despicable Rob Jones had to watch from the side-lines. Not that Rob could even jump. His metal carcass simply weighed too much in those days. The days before aluminium alloy and eventually carbon fibres.

Mo continued to walk until his feet cried out with pain. He had no direction in which to travel, he had no plan in his mind. Penelope had been his last hope. Now, for all intents and purposes, he was a lost soul.

Penelope watched the little man walk off and cursed herself under her breath for laughing. She thought about calling him back but, seeing him so far away, thought it fruitless. That was until she realised his tiny height actually portrayed the illusion of distance, and although he'd been stomping off in a sulk for a few minutes, his little legs had only carried him twenty metres. Twenty short metres that allowed Penelope to catch up to him in a few long strides.

"Sir, wait," said Penelope, all apologetically.

Mo was past caring. He was having none of it and continued his sullen walk to nowhere.

"I'm sorry," she went on, having to keep her own strides very small in order to match the pace of her potential new customer. "I've not had the best of times myself, you see," she continued.

Mo could hear the words but showed no signs of listening.

"I too used to be good at something, just like you with your high jump. I used to be the best psychologist in the North. My client portfolio read like the Oscars invite list. I was rich, I had a reputation, I was somebody."

Mo wasn't quite sure where this was going but it was interesting all the same. A shrink pouring her heart out to a client, that was a first.

"I ate in all the best places," she continued, "and partied with all the town's big people."

The mention of big people just made Mo's head droop even more. It was a bad choice of words and Penelope knew it. She pulled him by the arm, forcing him to stop and listen. "I know what it's like to have lost something important. To hit rock bottom. But it's how we respond that counts. If we fall down seven times, then we must get up eight." Penelope was in full flow now and Little Mo was engaging. He looked up at her sincere face, eyes crying out for help. She bent forward and gently held his face. "Come back with me and let me help you, " she said gently, grabbing Mo by the hand and leading him back to her new practice.

Mo responded. He really needed her help and knew his life was only going to worsen if he didn't address his issues.

They walked back across the car park, hand in hand, Mo with a warm feeling inside at the prospect of being well, and Penelope pleased that she'd been able to prove to herself that she could be professional when it was needed, and still offer her clients expert guidance. Mo looked up at Penelope who reciprocated the glance back down to him. There was an instant connection between the pair. They both needed each other at that moment in time.

Mo was first to speak. "I don't know where to start really," he said, still gazing up at the modern angel of shrinkage.

"Then we'll start at the beginning and go from there," said Penelope, smiling down at her new customer.

"Okay then," said Little Mo, taking a big breath of air into his lungs as if banishing the demons before speaking. "It's just that I'm feeling very low at the moment."

More snot burst from Penelope's nose, but she was just able to turn away and hide her inappropriate laughter.

"Excuse me," she said, pretending that the obvious laugh was in fact the remnants of a cold she'd recently been carrying.

Mo had no other option than to give her the benefit of the doubt.

The pair entered the practice and surveyed their surroundings. There really wasn't an awful lot going for it. It was the first day of opening and Penelope had envisaged a day of setting up her office. Things like ensuring the telephone connections were working and generally establishing a clinical feel to the place. But here they were, drawn together by fate, standing in an empty old shop surrounded by cardboard boxes. It wasn't ideal but it was a start and Mo was in no place to judge. He was just pleased help had arrived at last.

Penelope shifted a few boxes and made some space in the centre of the room. She found an old plastic chair buried under the decorators' floor coverings and unfolded the collapsible couch upon which she asked Mo to lie. Finally, removing her coat, she located a pad and pen from her handbag and sat cross-legged, ready to start their first session.

"Shall we begin?" she asked.

But her first question was cut short by the sight of Mo trying to climb up on the couch. He could reach up to it no problem but couldn't manage to swing his legs up and grab some purchase. Several times he attempted, even counting up one, two, three as to gain extra swing but he just couldn't make it. It was an hilarious sight, one that had Penelope's insides jigging about, but she just managed to maintain her professionalism and stop her outburst of laughter.

"A little help, please," asked Mo, after finally giving up on reaching the summit of the couch.

Rather than make him suffer the indignity of being lifted up onto the couch, Penelope thought it best to build a little stairway from books instead, the Yellow Pages providing the base step, followed by 'Chinese Cookery with Warwick Davis' and finally 'Beaten by Wonka: My Life As An Oompa Loompa'.

Mo raced up the tower, eager to get started, shuffling along to the end so he could rest his head on the pillow provided. Penelope thought about offering him some form of safety net in case he fell off and plummeted to his death, but thought better of it, having seen how embarrassed he was after this recent failing.

Little's Mo's problem was obvious and his wounds ran deep. Penelope had already heard how he'd once been a star pupil at school, representing various teams at county level. But somehow he'd ended up here, a tiny and bitter little man with serious anger issues. It was her job, no matter how challenging it may seem, to get him back on his feet. To do that, she'd have to strip everything back, remove all the barriers and rearrange them all again, brick by brick. It usually proved a long, drawn out process, and she suspected this would be no different.

"Let's start at the beginning."

Little Mo lay on his back with his hands clasped across his stomach. He pulled in a deep breath and waited for the words to come out. They didn't.

"Take your time," said Penelope reassuringly. "You've already managed the biggest step which is asking for help. Now we'll walk side by side until the journey is complete and you can go out of here with your head held high."

As soon as that phrase came out, Little Mo flinched while Penelope silently cursed herself for such a stupid choice of words. Sure, Mo had anger issues but it was obvious they all stemmed from his height. This wasn't just little man syndrome, it ran deeper, pure resentment. He would be a tough nut to crack and Penelope knew it.

"Mo, whatever is said in this room, stays in this room, okay? Now take your time and when you're ready, tell me about school."

A long pause ensued while Mo thought about where to begin.

Finally, when he was ready to open up, he began to speak. "I loved school," he said. "I was very popular. And not just with the ladies." He smiled at Penelope and Penelope smiled back before scribbling the word 'bullshitter' on her pad.

"I used to play football and cricket for the school, and ran the odd cross country too, but basketball was my real passion. I was quite tall for my age, you see. I was well over six foot by the time I'd turned fourteen and I reckon there was still some growth left in me."

Penelope nodded, encouraging him to carry on.

"Then one day, we were all sat in our science class, I remember it like it was yesterday, as clear as that. Mr Keenan scribbling away on the board and…" Mo faded to silence.

Penelope, sensing this was an important event in the proceedings, encouraged him to continue.

He took his time, barely able to bring himself to say the name. He stammered it a few times while the rage boiled within him.

"Take your time, Mo, it's okay," said Penelope once more, sensing what she was about to hear was the potential trigger for Mo's downfall.

Minutes passed.

Penelope sat in silence, letting her client get to where he needed to be. When the words finally arrived, even she couldn't quite believe that their own fates had crossed via the same path.

"That fucking stupid bastard robot caught fire. Fought with the fucking teacher and blew up the bastard science block." There, he'd got the words out, and instantly felt better for it, however the mention of the word 'robot' had thrown the psychologist deeply.

"Robot, you say?" She'd heard the words clearly first time around, but needed more time to gather her thoughts. Could it really be that Mo's downfall mirrored her own?

"Yes, a fucking robot," said Mo, the words no longer sticking in his throat. "Five days I was trapped under that rubble. Five fucking days. It was dark and all I could do was move my right arm. The rest of me was pinned. Agony it was. The whole building had come crashing down on my head, my back had snapped, and I needed numerous operations just to be able to walk again. And all because some sad and lonely old man had built himself a fucking robot that leaked hydrogen gas everywhere. And did he, the alloyed freak, the instigator and cause of the explosion, suffer in that darkness? Of course not, he escaped unscathed, blown through the open window during the initial blast. Not a mark on him."

Penelope could hear the words but they were barely going in. She just kept thinking about the words 'robot' and 'sad lonely old man'.

"Mo, can you remember the robot's name?" she eventually asked, seeking confirmation that they both shared a common nemesis.

"His name, you ask? Can I remember his name?" Mo was coming to the boil again. "Of course I can remember his name, it's Robert fucking Jones, freak creation of Jesus Jones. The twats that ruined me."

Penelope rocked back in her chair. This was an unbelievable coincidence that had her thinking back to her own meeting with the pair. She tried to remember her own conversation, held with them before her career went up in smoke. The boy with no penis, arriving in a limousine and, of course, the attempted murder by a midget.

"It was you," she finally said, head in a spin. "You tried to murder the pair of them in the back of a limousine."

"Well, yeah, but look what they've made me become. I'm a monster and I hate them for it. I thought I was over the accident. I'd had five long years of rehab, done my physio sessions and tried to get on with my life, but at every turn my height went against me. I managed to get a well-paid job at Flamingo Land, designing the world's fastest and longest rollercoasters. I was brilliant at it and it paid well too."

"So what went wrong there, then?" asked Penelope, letting the little man spew forth his anger.

"I could never fucking ride them, that's what. Always fell below the standard height for rollercoaster usage. I could only ride the dragon coaster with the kids and how my fellow employees laughed at that." Mo was in full flow now. "In the end, I had to quit. The constant jokes and ridicule became too much. I tried other places of course, but it was always the same. If people weren't laughing at work, they were laughing in the street. In the end, more in desperation than anything else, I attempted to hold up a building society because my funds were running low."

"You turned to criminality?" asked Penelope, surprised at how far this poor man had fallen.

"Well, not quite," said Mo. "I went in to the building society armed to the teeth, ready to raid the place, but the clerk couldn't see me below the counter. For fifteen minutes I stood there trying to grab her attention before I had to walk off empty handed. I couldn't even succeed at that."

Penelope let the silence hang for a short while before sympathetically turning to Mo once again. "And I guess that must have been very embarrassing for you too?" she said, intrigued to hear more.

"Not as embarrassing as being knocked out by a two-foot penis."

Mo's statement had Penelope's eyes widening with astonishment. She genuinely felt sorry for this guy, and a little angry too. She was torn between joining forces with him and bringing an end to the hideous twosome that had almost ruined her own career, or helping this disgruntled man back on his feet. It was a classic case of revenge or reform. In the end, she decided on the latter.

"Mo," she said, her voice all soft and sincere. "I want to help you. You're obviously suffering from some form of post-traumatic stress disorder caused by the initial accident. From there, you've fallen into an obvious depression caused by many an unfortunate incident to which you are reacting through anger. The lack of sympathy you have received from various parties I find absolutely staggering and I can only sympathise with your current predicament. Luckily for you, I'm a professional psychologist and have friends in the medical profession and government claims division. I feel you have been treated very unfairly in the first instance and should be compensated. Also, I think you have grounds for an unfair dismissal claim against your former employer. However, my first priority has to be making you well again. To banish the demons that fester in your head, so that you once again can walk ttt…" Penelope quickly changed her word from tall… "You can walk with your head held hhh…" Penelope quickly changed her choice of word. "You can regain some self-respect."

These were the first kind words Little Mo had heard in a long, long time and they lifted his spirits no end. He'd known Penelope's reputation was supposed to be good, but he never dreamt in his wildest dreams that after this initial meeting, things would be looking so positive. He smiled his first real smile in a decade.

"Mohammed, I'm going to run a succession of meetings with you and we are going to get you back on your feet. Now, that will cost money but don't worry too much about that as I intend to get you that compensation and you can pay me back when that comes through. I want to see you again. Tomorrow, okay? And by then I'll have made some phone calls and hopefully have some better news for you."

Mo leapt from the couch with a zest that had long since deserted him. It was the first positive news he had heard since he'd heard the sniffer dogs bark from his hell under the rubble. Life after that had been one big struggle.

He grabbed his coat and cardboard home, and walked briskly through the door. Penelope followed and stood in the doorway, arms folded as she watched the little man leave.

The change she could see in him already made her feel warm inside. She was back alright, everybody could have a dip and she'd had hers. But now, stood in the doorway of her new practice, she felt at the helm of something big. It was a new start and she was excited. Very excited.

Little Mo turned around and waved at Penelope and she

reciprocated with warmth. He was beaming from ear to ear and shouted out the words, "Tomorrow then?"

Penelope nodded and echoed, "Tomorrow."

Just as Mo was about to head off, the biggest, ugliest, swooping seagull he'd ever seen in his life, shat on his head. It was another humiliating scene in a long line of humiliating scenes, and one that had Penelope gasping in horror.

Mo's heart sank. He stood facing the compassionate shrink with bird shit all over his face. His smile disappeared and his shoulders took on an all too familiar slump.

Penelope had to stifle a little laugh as she surveyed the shocking scene in front of her.

"Don't worry," she cried out in a high-pitched, I'm-about-to-burst-out-laughing voice, "it's supposed to be lucky."

With that, she turned around and walked back into her practice and closed the door. Once out of sight and earshot, she fell to the floor and let out the biggest belly laugh ever. Holding her stomach with her hands so her sides didn't split, she cried rivers of laughter.

Perhaps her professionalism wasn't back after all.

CHAPTER 18

"For fuck sake," cried Maddog, boredom already setting in. "Are you sure this will work?"

He was watching Mary tap the keys on her expensive laptop.

"I'm ninety-nine percent certain," replied Mary, without lifting her eyes from the screen. "The Jesus I knew loved all things gadgetry and would collect hundreds of magazines on the subject. Come to think of it, he had a stock of them higher than your own porn collection at home." Mary smiled, looking up to her blushing friend. She'd spotted the jazz mags while clearing the house in search of Troy, but had forgotten all about it till now.

Maddog, still not sure if Mary was taking the piss or not, preferred not to commit and denied the existence of his stash. The last thing he needed was his old mate ripping into him over a bit of solitary hand to gland combat.

"I don't know what you're talking about, mate," he lied.

Mary wasn't bluffing. The mouth may lie but the eyes were the window to his soul and Mary, revelling in Maddog's uncomfortable state, lifted a well-thumbed copy of Throbbing Hood from her bag. Maddog's shoulders slumped.

Mary loved to see Maddog squirm, and wasn't about to let him off the hook just yet. "Magazines, Maddog? Surely the internet is the way forward? And if you don't want people to see them, then why store them in the airing cupboard?"

"Because the internet can be monitored and the last thing I need is a nosey policeman looking into my life," squirmed Maddog, still unable to look Mary in the eye. "And the airing cupboard because it helps dry them out."

Mary dropped the magazine and ran borking to the toilet, much to the amusement of the grinning Maddog.

"Don't you worry about being monitored then, Mary?" asked Maddog, through a closed bathroom door.

"Nah, mate, my firewall is tighter than Troy's virgin little arsehole in a sandstorm. Nothing getting in there," announced Mary in between spews.

"What about your mobile, then?" he pressed.

"What around here?" Mary laughed. "You try getting a signal in Picton. You'd have more luck searching for unicorn shit."

Maddog nodded his head at Mary's technical nouse and upon hearing the toilet flush, stood back from the door to let her pass. Through teary eyes, caused by excessive barfing, she returned to the job in hand.

"Okay then, what if that expensive, shiny laptop of yours gets stolen? The information doesn't go away, you know. It remains in a ghost memory bank and the police could extract information from that."

Mary half shut the lid of the laptop to address her worried friend.

"Maddog, first of all, I never put vital information in this thing, it's simply used as a search engine. Secondly, any information I do use around social media, falls under my alias name. And thirdly, and perhaps the most importantly, this laptop isn't even mine."

Maddog threw his old mate a confused look as if to say go on?

"Let's just say I borrowed it off a lad I was sat next to on a train. He worked offshore and was travelling home from Aberdeen. By the time we reached Edinburgh he was wankered and when we rolled into Darlo, he was fast asleep. So I kindly offered to look after it for him so it wasn't stolen." Mary winked a knowing wink.

Maddog laughed and shook his head.

Troy and Ron stared at each other in disbelief at the despicable pair in front of them. How this gruesome twosome could call themselves professional was beyond them? One was a common thief, the other a serial wanker.

"Don't you two be giving it those looks," warned Maddog, pointing a fat finger in the faces of the pair. "We let you upstairs and out of our sight for half an hour and look at you both, all high and mighty in your righteous union. Yeah well, you'll both stay right under my nose from now on. This job isn't too far away now and when it's done, you'll be dealt with."

The pair didn't say anything. What was the point in antagonising the beast further? Troy did however try to catch his mother's eye to look for reassurance. He didn't get any.

"Sorry, son, but it's probably for the best. Loose lips and all that."

Troy closed his eyes and let his head drop onto the shoulder of Ron who in turn threw a protective arm around him. They both remained silent from thereon in.

Maddog grined back at Mary, who was once again buried in her laptop. "How is this going to work, then?"

Mary lifted her head to address the little gathering. "Jesus had three loves in his life," she said. "The obvious one being me."

Maddog, bowed his head as if meeting royalty.

"Well, of course, your highness."

"The other two things were electronics…"

Maddog pulled a repulsed frown.

"And Linda Kozlowski."

"Who?" enquired Maddog as confused as ever.

"Linda Kozlowski. She was an actress who starred in Crocodile Dundee. You must remember her?"

Maddog shook his head.

"I bet you would if I remind you of a certain scene where she was filling up her water bottle and is almost eaten by a crocodile, only for Crocodile Dundee himself to save the day."

With that, Maddog's neurons suddenly sparked into life. "Oh yeah, I remember that bit. She had a tiny black bather on and her arse was unbelievable," spluttered Maddog with great excitement.

"Knew you would," responded Mary, offering the universal sign for wanker.

"Touché," was all a blushing Maddog could say.

"The thing is, nobody remembers that scene for the action it displays, they just remember that woman's cellulite ridden arse," responded Mary with a hint of scorn in her voice

"Not jealous are you, pal?" said Maddog, jabbing Mary's arm just a little bit too hard.

"Not one bit," she lied.

Maddog could tell by the tone of her voice that it was best not to pursue the matter any further.

"So the guy's a bit of a geek. How does that help?" said Maddog, diverting the subject with smooth transition.

"It helps because I'm thinking of hosting an event by which old bobbly arse opens a Maplin store right here in Teesside," answered Mary, outlining the basics of the plan.

"You've lost me," said Maddog, not to the surprise of the criminal mastermind Mary.

"Look, every time Jesus looks up something in a search engine his computer stores it. For example, 'electronics'. Then whenever he logs online, his computer will share posts, right under his nose without prompt. The company pays for this, of course, and that's how social media sites make their money. Now if two of his most popular searches come up, his computer gets all excited and asks if he may know this person or event."

Maddog stared at her blankly.

Mary just rolled her eyes.

"So, if I create an event in which Linda Kozlowski arrives in Middlesbrough to open an electronics store, then the likelihood is Jesus will receive a prompt via his laptop and will be all over it."

"But we'll never get her over here to do that, not at this short notice anyway," correctly reasoned the big bouncer, to be abruptly cut short by Mary once again.

"Of course we won't, you big lummox, and we won't need to. By the time Jesus turns up, I'll present myself in front of him. Once he's spied me, we'll nab the scruffy get, lead him to the back of a waiting van and bang, he's all ours."

Maddog took a few more seconds for the penny to drop but when it did, he was in awe.

"That is genius," he said. "Beautiful, in fact. But will it work?"

"I can't see why not. Everybody has a social media account these days, and what with smart phones, it's all people can do not to check them every five minutes. No, I think this will work just fine, and once we have him in the back of the van, we'll also be holding the very person who will take the hit for our little bank job. By the time the police have finally realised, we'll be sat on South Beach soaking up the Miami sun."

"Sod that," said Maddog, excitement rising in his voice. "I'm going abroad instead."

Mary, Troy and Ron all threw each other a glance but decided in unison not to enlighten the big doorman. He really was two sandwiches short of a picnic and one had to wonder why anybody would pick this man for such an enormous job. Unfortunately, Mary's thoughts were interrupted again by the big man who once again had a serious manner about him.

"What's up, Maddog? You spotted a flaw in my perfect plan?" she asked. Her friend was displaying uncomfortable tendencies and that concerned her.

"Hmmmmm, well, sort of, yeah," he replied.

"Well, come on then, spit it out. I'm about to press send here."

Maddog was rubbing the back of his neck again and was clearly finding it hard to find the words he really wanted to say. "It's just that..."

"Yes," encouraged Mary.

"Well, what if that other fella comes along?" Maddog seemed relieved to have got the words out and yet was still a little pained.

"Well, we'll have bagged two birds for the price of one, won't we?" said Mary, unable to see what the problem was.

"Yeah but, Mary, he's a big fella you know, and there'll be two of them." Maddog had never displayed any form of weakness before. Well, that's not quite true, there was the time when he cried like a baby watching ET, but that had been years ago.

"Maddog, I've personally witnessed you single-handedly break up a riot in Blaises night club. There must have been about one hundred rioting wreckheads that day, all out of their bonces on amphetamines and booze and yet you cleared them in five minutes. What you worried about?"

Maddog couldn't put it into words, more through discomfort than anything else. The truth was nobody had ever dropped him like that big fella had. He was different, he was solid and Maddog wondered if he'd finally met his match.

"Mary, I've seen that guy in action. He's quick, he's aggressive and he must work out three times a day because he's ripped. Not an ounce of fat on him. He was like a fucking machine." He paused and let the words hang for a while but eventually blurted the words out. "Mary, I don't think I can take him."

There was a mighty gasp in the room. This was Maddog McClane, quite possibly the hardest man on the planet. His fight record was impeccable, ten thousand bouts, ten thousand wins and all by first round knockout. Yet here he stood, frightened to face just one man, just one. Mary was unsure what to say. Troy and Ron didn't say anything either and an uncomfortable silence hung for far too long. Eventually Mary, uneasy herself with Maddog's unusual showing of emotions, broke the silence.

"No problem, mate, I'll simply put limited spaces on the invite. One ticket per fan club member and to apply within. No need to worry."

"I wasn't worrying," replied Maddog aggressively.

"No, of course not," said Mary, cursing her poor choice of words though genuinely concerned at seeing her old mate this way. Perhaps it was the pressure that was getting to him and what he really needed was to get out of the game all together, finish this one last job and retire in the sun.

Maddog left the room to make a brew and Mary finalised the finer detail of her social network plan. Then with a final scan, she pressed send. All that was left to do now was wait.

CHAPTER 19

Opening his eyes, feeling refreshed, Rob disconnected his charger from its newly positioned wrist port and scanned the power bar. One hundred percent beamed back at him in neon numbering. He thought he'd only been boosting for a short while but his visual display clock, adjacent to the power bar was reading three hours more than he intended. "I must have needed it," he reasoned, sitting bolt upright in his bed.

"Dad," he cried, shocked to see his father sat on a chair, staring at his new appendage. "What on earth are you doing?"

Jesus was in work mode. He knew in his own mind the penis was attached correctly, the previous experiment had proven that, and now he wondered if the problem lay elsewhere, possibly the relay switches but first he wanted to rule out the obvious.

"Don't panic, son, I realise this looks a bit weird, but remember, I'm just trying to help." As he spoke, he tapped Rob's penis for signs of life. Rob tried to cover himself up, but Jesus was having none of it. He was holding a doctor's stethoscope around the ballbag area, listening for the mechanical grindings of tiny cogs and support bars, but it was completely dead.

"For fuck's sake, man, give over," cried Rob, before once again attempting to brush the eccentric inventor away from his waistline. "It's fucking embarrassing, and a little weird, if I'm honest."

"Exactly, son," responded Jesus, now sitting back on his chair and rubbing his chin, deep in thought. "That's what I don't understand, you've got the ability to be embarrassed, you often feel anger, often show empathy and have lust in your locker. All of these emotions run from your on board CPU and are linked

162

directly to your thought bank, which should in turn operate the appropriate systems."

"Systems?" enquired Rob, who didn't have a clue what his father was talking about.

Jesus stood up from his chair and started walking around the room. He was still deep in thought, lost in the conundrum that was the flaccid penis, and he wasn't exactly explaining himself very well. Totally immersed with the task at hand, it was quite a while before he realised his son had actually asked a question. Though once it did register, Jesus needed a few seconds to think about how Rob must be feeling. He moved his chair closer to Rob and offered a better explanation.

"When you need to recharge, you just do it, yeah?"

Rob nodded. After all, he'd just juiced himself up after a three-hour long boost.

"Exactly, I didn't do it for you, you just knew. Your CPU, linked to your memory bank, knew the consequences if you didn't. So, the feeds from that CPU operated your arms to plug in. Get it?"

It wasn't exactly Brian Cox simplicity but Jesus was just about making sense, so Rob nodded along.

"Right then, that's pre-programmed mechanics." Jesus was giving Rob a brief overview on how he worked mechanically but more importantly was giving himself a running fault diagnosis commentary trying to solve the real issue.

"Now consider, when you're at the Riverside, a corner comes over, it drops on the head of the centre half, and the keeper's stranded. How many times have you involuntarily headed an imaginary ball into the net while being in the stand? You have absolutely no bearing on the end result of the centre half's header but you still find yourself making the movements you'd expect him to make while you're sat in your seat. That's because you're lost in emotion. Whether he scores or not is irrelevant. Your CPU studies the event, it doesn't recognise a binary input, as no pre-programming has been inputted, and yet, you, a cyborg, become overridden by emotional feelings and make the movement anyway. Why?"

Brian Cox had now morphed in Stephen Hawking.

Rob had no answer and shook his head.

Jesus didn't either and that was bugging him. "That's artificial intelligence. Look, if what I'm saying is true, which I believe it to be, when you are… ahem, a little horny, whether your CPU likes it or not, your emotional override should kick in and the appendage should rise. Problem is, I have absolutely no idea why it doesn't." And, as if he'd just run into a brick wall, Jesus slumped almost exhausted back in the chair. The answer was here somewhere, he just had to keep looking.

Rob, clearly still embarrassed by being woken up in such private circumstances, knew his father well. Sure, he was a weird beard at times but he also knew he would spend all his waking hours trying to calculate why the penis wouldn't work. All that said, Rob still felt he needed to reaffirm his need for bedroom privacy.

"Dad, look, I appreciate all your help, I really do, but how would you feel if you woke up and I had a doctor's stethoscope on your weiner?"

"Well, I'd be mortified, of course," answered Jesus. Only then did he realise how his actions had more than intruded on his son's private space. "Don't worry, son, this won't happen again. I was just doing a little fault diagnosis and, as this wasn't the answer I was looking for, I can now cross it off the list. That's not a bad thing of course, it just means I'm no longer looking in the wrong place."

"What are you talking about? Cross what off the list?"

"Morning glory, of course," answered Jesus. "You know, the dawn horn." It was as simple a question as that to him, like two plus two to a five-year-old.

"Morning what?" asked Rob, confused as ever. His father wasn't making much sense at all and he was genuinely confused.

It was only then did the old inventor realise that Rob had never heard of it. As natural and often awkward as it was for any adolescent boy to deal with such a mystery as morning erection, Rob had obviously never experienced it. Never owning a penis before, how could he? It was strange, but Jesus often forgot that his son was in fact a robot. Presumably, if he'd never experienced morning glory, then there were other growing up misadventures that he'd never experienced either, like climbing a tree or twanging a female classmate's bra strap. Jesus made a mental note to list as many ideals of childhood as he could think of to teach Rob next time they were in the pub.

Jesus gave a brief overview of the workings of early morning hard-ons, but didn't spend too much time on it. That would be time wasting. If the immediate topic wasn't solving the current equation, then Jesus wasn't interested. He was a thinker, an inventor, and when a problem needed tending to, then that's where he would be. After confirming the issue didn't stand with morning glory, Jesus changed his direction of thinking. His next thought wondered around the components used. Had he bought a dodgy batch of transistors? It was the next logical step in his eyes, as he sought to find the root cause of the drooping dong through trial and error. Leaving his son to get dressed in private, he went to find his laptop.

Rob threw on some old tracksuit bottoms with plenty of bagginess at the front. One thing the new him had learnt these past few days was that tight fitting jeans were now a no-no. They hindered his movement, which was something he'd complained to Jesus about. Denim now made him walk like what he was: a robot. Jesus had chuckled at that for hours.

Rob descended the stairs and entered the kitchen to find his father brewing up. Upon noticing his son walk into the room, Jesus asked if he'd like a cup. As usual the answer was no, but it was always polite to ask. Rob could never understand the human behaviour of tea drinking. He got the beer bit okay, he enjoyed the pre-programmed release it offered, but tea was a puzzle. Humans seemed to need the stuff to wake up, or to settle their nerves after trauma. They drank it before going into battle or fed copious amounts of it to old ladies to keep them alive. It seemed like an important liquid, but to a cyborg, it was lost. It added nothing except putting a strain on his liquid management system and for those reasons he always turned it down.

The pair returned to the living room and took up residence on the dusty old couch. Jesus placed the laptop on his knee and began tapping the keys as the pair continued their discussion of Rob's trouser snake.

"No joy at all then?" enquired Jesus, who felt no need to go into detail at this early stage.

Rob shook his head.

"Nothing. It just hangs there with no pulse," he replied, his face all droopy like a kid who'd dropped an ice-cream.

"Well, don't worry, son, you're always going to get these teething problems with any major project. Do you think NASA were able to get one up at the first attempt?"

Rob thought for a moment that NASA had actually built an erect penis, but soon realised his father was actually talking about rockets.

"Suppose not," was his short sharp answer.

Jesus opened up his email account. He was looking for some Maplin correspondence which should provide a receipt of latest items purchased. From that, he hoped to discover the batch code for the transistors he'd bought and get them replaced, but he was suddenly distracted by what had appeared to be a spam email: *Come down to Maplin and meet the star of Crocodile Dundee herself, Linda Kozlowski.*

He dropped his cup and started trembling, a reaction that alerted Rob to his father's sudden change in mood.

"Dad, what is it?" he enquired, but Jesus was unable to speak. "Dad," Rob tried again, slightly concerned that a bill may have arrived from Channel X and given the game away as to how much tugging he'd given his new toy these last two days.

Jesus once again remained lost in a trance. Then with trembling finger, he eventually pointed to the screen.

"She's here," was all he could say. "Linda Kozlowski is here."

Rob turned the screen so he could see for himself. Once he had, he couldn't quite believe it either.

"Linda Kozlowski will tomorrow be opening a new section of the Maplin store in Stockton's Teesside Park. She'll be there from the hours of one till three and ready to take pictures and sign autographs for any of her wonderful fans. Why not pop along and say G'day?" re-read Rob aloud, as his father was simply too emotional to speak.

Rob recognised immediately that this was a big moment for his dad and he was genuinely happy for him. As odd as his father was, he knew this would be one of the greatest days in his empty life. Jesus had, after all, started the first UK Crocodile Dundee fan club, and although members had dwindled as time had passed by, he had righteously mailed a monthly newsletter to all that had remained. The fact that he was the only member left never seemed to bother him.

"Dad, are you okay?"

Jesus still hadn't spoken since reading the email and his breathing had become laboured.

"Dad, this is fantastic news, eh? I bet you're well chuffed."

Again Rob got no response. Jesus just sat, shaking with either excitement or shock, it was difficult to tell. Rob was very worried the old man may be about to have a stroke.

"Calm down, dad, please," he said, stroking the back of his father's shoulders and recommending the British lifesaving method of… "Let me get you a fresh cuppa."

Rob returned to the sofa with two mugs of hot tea. His father had thankfully fallen out of the trance the email had put him into, and was now full of excited chatter.

"What shall I wear? Are there any batteries in the camera? Do you think she'll sign my Crocodile Dundee hat? Shall I take my knife? Does the Talpore sell Fosters?"

They were all questions that had Rob laughing. He hadn't seen his father this excited since Joseph Job's early opener at the Millennium Stadium, and he cuddled him there and then. It was a fantastic moment. Rob slid the laptop onto his knee to re-read the email. The date and time were duly double checked and sure enough, Linda Kozlowski would be appearing within a two hour window. At the bottom of the email, in smaller print, were the words "click to accept invite". Jesus watched his son hover the cursor over the accept button but then moved it away again.

"Perhaps we should just decline the invite?" Rob teased, causing Jesus to nudge his robotic son in the arm as if to say 'you dare'.

Rob clicked accept and the pair beamed a huge smile at each other. Instantaneously, a pop up arrived on the screen confirming a secured place for the email account holder, but also stating that due to high demand, Cleveland Constabulary had asked that only invited persons could attend. This meant, the email informed them, that no guests or partners could tag along as companions.

"What...? No," cried Jesus, unable to comprehend the absurdity of the condition. "I want you there alongside me when I meet her, son."

Rob was truly wounded by the news. He couldn't care less if he met Linda or not and reasoned he probably wouldn't even recognise her if he passed her in the street, but he had wanted to watch his father's moment.

"Dad, listen, there is obviously a good reason the police have intervened here. She is a global superstar after all," began Rob. "The main thing in this serendipitous moment, is that you are invited, not only to your favourite electronic gadget store but," he drum-rolled his fingers on the coffee table, "you also get to meet the one and only Linda Kozlowski, star of your favourite movie ever."

As disappointing as it was that Rob couldn't be there, Jesus couldn't help but grin.

"Now you sit there and enjoy your tea while I go and wash and iron the appropriate attire. I'll even brush your Dundee hat so you're looking the dog's bollocks. Then, if you promise not to get upset by the fact that I can't be with you tomorrow, I'll go to the offie and buy us a crate of Australia's finest amber nectar. We'll sit back here and watch all three films back to back. What have you got to say about that?"

"Fine by me, Wally," replied Jesus, as the pair erupted with laughter.

Back in Picton, Mary, Maddog and their two captives, Ron and Troy, sat together watching an episode of Jeremy Kyle. Ron and Troy were shackled together on a snuggle chair while Maddog drifted in and out of sleep on the sofa. Mary had taken a ringside seat in front of the television and was encouraging the show's guests to stick one on poor Jeremy.

"Smarmy bastard," she would randomly shout out every time Jeremy raised his voice at one of her own.

Ron just looked on in disbelief. "Is she always like this?" he enquired in a hushed tone.

"Yep," said Troy. "She always sticks up for losers, my mother. Anybody who is up against the odds."

It was a statement that intrigued Ron. "What like Eddie the Eagle?" he whispered.

"Oh God no, she hates that man with a passion."

These were words Ron thought he'd never hear.

A bit like if somebody had told you children's television star Mr Bumble was a cage fighter. The words just didn't sit right.

"How the hell can she hate Eddie the Eagle? The man is a national treasure," Ron queried in whispered tones.

"Ah well, with good reason as it happens. Back in nineteen eighty-eight, mother had spent the last of her giro buying a flight to Calgary in Canada for the Winter Olympics. She had in tow with her two huge suitcases of budget ski wear which she hoped to sell to the eagle. The thing is, Eddie was blind as a bat, and had initially agreed to buy the whole lot when he wasn't wearing his specs. A decision he obviously regretted when he saw the poorly made clobber in the cold light of day."

"So what happened after that?" asked Ron, now firmly gripped by the Olympic scoop. "Did your mum kick off?"

"No, she didn't have to. She simply hid his glasses," answered Troy, all matter of fact.

"Hid his glasses?" asked Ron, seeking clarification that he'd heard right the first time.

"Yeah, there was no Specsavers back then. No buy one, get

one free, and his eyes were so bad that he couldn't just get another pair made up locally either."

"Then what?" asked Ron, his eyebrows at their limit.

"Well, every time Eddie descended the ramp, he was unable to see the end of it. So rather than just fall off the end, he asked if somebody could shout 'jump' to let him know when to leap. The volunteer was Mother. Still reeling that she'd wasted her flights and had no money in sales, she kept on shouting for him to jump earlier and earlier, once even making Eddie take off and land back on the ramp. The results were, of course catastrophic. Eddie became known as the biggest loser in Olympic history. Well, at least until Eric the Eel came along years later."

"Don't tell me your mother tried to sell him Speedos and had a hand in that too?" said Ron, finding the whole story hard to believe.

"No, don't be daft, you silly bugger. Poor Eric just couldn't swim."

The pair were interrupted by Mary whose laptop had received an email. She unlocked it with her unique code, *nineteen-eighty-six,* and read the message. A few moments later she let out a loud laugh.

Kicking Maddog awake from his slumber on the couch, she waited for his eyes to adjust before showing him the message. "The fish has taken the bait," she announced cheerily. "Come on, we've got planning to do."

Maddog clicked the kettle on and filled two mugs with copious amounts of coffee. If past experience was anything to go by, he knew he'd be in for a long night. He'd sat in on many of Mary's planning sessions, and knew she never left a stone unturned in her quest for perfection.

Mary left the room briefly and returned wheeling in a huge white flip chart. It was well-thumbed and confirmed Maddog's hunch that his old mate was indeed still an active wrong un. He let out a deep sigh and added another spoon of coffee to his mug. With hot water added, he passed one mug to Mary and kept the other for himself. They then clinked the drinks together. "Cheers," they said simultaneously, before Maddog returned to his seat at the table and awaited his situation report.

Mary took the floor and clicked the top off her permanent marker pen. She then addressed the chart, looking for a blank sheet. Over and over she flipped the paper, and Maddog couldn't help but notice scribblings of other jobs his mate had obviously had a hand in. He had to chuckle at some of the names. 'Operation FA' read one, before going on to mention Middlesbrough's deduction of three points. 'Operation Perm' said another, helping a Brazilian man under contract, escape his employers by going AWOL. And finally, 'Operation Canoe'.

"You've been busy, I see," laughed Maddog, as Mary continued flipping through the chart.

Mary didn't answer. She was too deep in the zone to reply. For this was her forte, this was where her strength lay and this was the reason she was involved in this job. Mary found the blank space she was looking for and set to work. Detailing the target with information such as colour, age, appearance and dress sense, before mentioning his favourite food and likely unplanned stops. Next she described the route to and from the grab. Detailing likely traffic hold-ups and the amount of traffic lights they would encounter, she also listed the exact location of CCTV cameras en route. From there, she considered the vehicle they would be using, a vehicle that must be big enough to hold three people in the back. It had to have blacked out or no windows to the rear, with restraints that must be in place as to detain the target. Tyre pressure, type of fuel and no distinct markings also made it onto the chart as Mary left nothing overlooked in planning 'Operation Dundee'.

When she had finished, she stood back and admired her work. Without giving Maddog a glance, she asked if she'd missed anything.

He slurped the dregs of his third mug of coffee and studied the plan once more. "What about weapons?" he said in a soft tone.

"We won't need them," she replied instantaneously. "But at the same time we can't rule out the possibility that he might be carrying. He's no villain, but he is a lunatic. Anybody who dresses up like he does and isn't attending a fancy dress party isn't right in the head. Therefore, once we have him, check the left hand side of his belt for a knife."

"The left?" repeated Maddog with uncertainty, unsure how Mary had arrived at this conclusion, but she had already read his thoughts.

"He's right handed," she replied. "Therefore if he was going to reach for a tool, it would be stowed away on his left side."

"Ah!" was all Maddog could reply, slightly embarrassed he'd missed the obvious.

The pair studied the plan one more time in silence. Maddog was shattered and looked around the kitchen for a clock. He wanted to know how long they had been at it.

Mary once again answered. "Four hours."

"Oh, come on, Mary, you don't even have a watch. How do you know that?"

"Because Troy has cried out for food four times. He does it on the hour, every hour whenever he's due a feed," she said, turning away from the chart and looking at Maddog. "I'd best feed the fat bastard," she growled. "And then we need to get some sleep."

CHAPTER 20

Removing a nuisance yawn from his halitosis mouth, Jesus stretched out his arms to free his body of sleep. He had woken naturally, well before his alarm and his eyes flickered rapidly open and closed, trying to adjust to the incoming daylight. In those first few seconds of alertness, he thought he was entering just another ordinary day.

But he wasn't.

He suddenly remembered. It was like somebody had slapped the stupidness out of him as he became fully aware of the day that lay ahead.

How could he have forgotten? He had a date with Linda Kozlowski. Linda fucking Kozlowski. His eyes shot wide open and he became fully alert in an instant. His heart pumping at an increased rate, he leapt from his bed like a youngster might off Jimmy Savile's lap. Throwing on an old dressing gown, not even bothering to fasten it, he descended the stairs two at a time before bursting into the kitchen with great excitement.

"Today's the day," he cried out, but Rob wasn't there.

Jesus paraded around the house looking for his son. He wasn't in the kitchen, as he normally would have been, and he wasn't anywhere upstairs either. This was most peculiar. Back downstairs again, scanning the usual haunts, Jesus noticed that the French doors were slightly open, the gentle autumn breeze swirling in the air and rocking the blinds back and forth. He approached cautiously and carefully looked out. There standing outside and cooking on the barbeque was Rob.

"What's going on?" asked Jesus, finding it a strange time and season to be lighting the barbie.

"Well, as it's a special day, I thought I'd cook you breakfast, the outback way," smiled Rob. The droid, who didn't have human sleep patterns, had been up all night decorating the garden with Australian flags. He had put pictures of Linda up on the shed and had several crates of Foster's lager chilling nicely in a paddling pool that also contained an inflatable crocodile.

Jesus simply couldn't believe it.

"You did all this for me?" he choked, with genuine emotion wobbling his voice.

"Of course," replied Rob, turning to face his father for the first time with a beaming smile, before a look of sheer terror took over his face.

"Why, Robert, whatever is the matter?" he asked, but poor Rob didn't quite know where to look, for peeping through the opening of his father's dressing gown was his erect, bulbous knob.

Jesus followed his son's line of sight down to his groin area and was suddenly overcome with much embarrassment. He stuttered and stammered through the next few sentences and was really struggling to find the words to explain.

Luckily, it was Rob who shattered the tension.

"Morning glory?" he enquired.

Jesus covered himself up and nodded.

"Thought so," replied the big robot, laughing.

It was a laugh that was infectious as Jesus realised the coincidental similarities between yesterday morning and this. Only it was Rob now staring at his tallywhacker and not the other way around.

"Sorry, son, I wasn't showing off, you know," he blurted out. The last thing Jesus wanted was to show Rob just how easy he could get an erection without even trying.

Rob was far from upset. In fact, he found the whole situation quite humorous.

"I know, dad, it's quite alright," giggled Rob, holding the cooking tongs aloft in his hand. "But it does remind me. Shall I put another shrimp on the barbie?"

With that, the pair erupted into fits of laughter again.

Mary showed Troy and Ron into the back of the parked van. There was no way these two could be left in Picton, home alone. Not this close to the operation. Especially as Mary had seen the look of love in Troy's eyes. She may well be the worst mother of all time, but she still wouldn't want Troy getting hurt. At least that's what she told herself. In reality, she didn't like the look of Ron. She thought him a bit too cocksure of himself, and knew that Troy could be easily led. She'd need to keep a closer eye on the pair from now on.

The vehicle of choice was your average white van, driven up and down the country by thousands on a daily basis. It bore no markings and brought no attention to itself. More importantly, Mary had fitted false plates to avoid the police department plate recognition system. She'd also spent the morning tinkering with the engine, giving it more soup just in case they needed it.

She was still under the bonnet when Maddog appeared outside. He was holding a bacon sandwich and a mug of tea, and was acting like today was just another day. That was good in Mary's eyes. He was relaxed and not jittery, just the way it should be. She gave him a knowing nod.

"What time we leaving?" he asked, in between mouthfuls of bacon.

"Ten minutes," responded Mary. "Everything is set, and we're good to go." She walked around the van and slid the side door shut, locking Troy and Ron inside.

"I've just enough time to drop the kids off at the pool then," said the big bruiser, placing a folded newspaper under his arm, a statement that caused Mary's face to recoil as if she'd just licked a stinging nettle.

"Well, make sure you use the air freshener when you're done," she shouted after him, but Maddog didn't say a word. Instead, he lifted his paper in the air as a form of acknowledgment and disappeared from view.

Mary, left waiting, tried to erase the image from her mind. She'd possibly need a new toilet after this.

"Listen, Troy," whispered Ron in hushed tones. "I don't think all of this is going to end well for us. Your mother and that vile man are intent on going through with this terrible plan and I fear, in the end, we'll be surplus to requirements. At the first opportunity, you've got to escape."

"I'm not escaping without you," replied Troy, shaking his head from side to side. "We'll go together."

"No, Troy," interrupted the security guard more forcefully. "If I'm out of sight for even ten minutes, they'll murder my mother, but you have nothing to lose."

"I have you to lose," said Troy, offering his only reason to remain.

It was a statement that rocked poor Ron, who up to that point had hidden his true feelings. The pair, staring in each other's eyes but with arms still shackled behind their backs, placed their heads together and revelled in the moment.

"I'm glad you think that way, Troy, because I do too, but you're only here through sheer accident. They don't need you in their plans. You have to get away," directed Ron.

Troy wouldn't hear of it and was starting to get upset.

"Troy," said Ron, "I can't do this with you here. My feelings are growing too strong. I can't lose you and mother, I wouldn't cope. That is why you have to do as I say."

"I will not leave you," shouted Troy, a little too loudly, a commotion that had Mary re-opening the van door to see what all the fuss was about.

Ron and Troy separated quickly and slumped back to the cold van floor.

"If I hear one more peep out of either of you two, or you even think of ruining this one opportunity, then I swear…" Mary didn't finish the sentence, she just made a fist with her hands and that was enough to have the pair cowering in the back. When silence was restored, she closed the door again.

Maddog returned to the scene, buttoning up his jeans. "Have I missed anything?" he enquired.

"Nothing I can't handle. Now get in, we're running late."

"Fair enough. By the way, do you know a good plumber?"

Jesus stepped clean and fresh faced out of the shower. He applied copious amounts of Lynx deodorant to his naked body and doused his shaven face with his favourite aftershave, Insignia. Next, he ran a comb through his Brylcreemed hair, ensuring its first style in more than ten years, before donning a brand new pair of designer Lonsdale underwear. Once satisfied, he gave himself a long, admiring look in the mirror, only to be interrupted by a knock on his bedroom door.

"Can I come in?" called Rob, not wanting to see his father's pecker again anytime soon.

"Yes, of course," replied Jesus, checking his fly.

Rob walked through the door holding a parcel that had been expertly wrapped.

"What's this? Jesus asked, not sure if he could take any more wonderful surprises.

"Just a little something else I've got you," announced Rob, pushing the parcel under the nose of his dad.

Jesus didn't know what to say. He was so happy for many reasons, but it was his robotic son's ability to keep surprising him that astonished him the most. He unwrapped the paper and removed the lid from the box and peered inside.

What he saw made him gasp in delight.

In the box was a brand new, crocodile-skinned waistcoat for his father. Jesus didn't know what to say. He took it in his trembling hands and gave it a closer inspection. It was a perfect match to the one that Crocodile Dundee had worn in the movie, right down to the croc markings and the brass studs on the lapel.

"You bought this for me?" he asked, gazing lovingly at his son.

"Yeah, it was supposed to be for Christmas, but I thought you'd like it now, what with Linda coming to town and all," replied Rob, beaming back at his father.

Jesus took the waistcoat with quivering hands and tried it on.

The fit was perfect and he made a few model turns in front of the mirror to get a view of all sides.

"I don't know what to say. It looks absolutely brilliant," he said, admiring his reflection. "I just hope my old hat matches these new colours, otherwise I'll need to get a new one," he joked.

"I've already thought of that," said Rob, surprising his dad yet again. "Which is why I also bought you this." He then produced the very hat Paul Hogan had worn in the movie. He'd bought the signed headwear from eBay which proved it was the one used in every one of the trilogy of films.

Jesus couldn't believe it. He had to take a moment on the bed. The hat was absolutely stunning and yet another perfect fit. He rose again, now wearing his new attire, and threw his arms around his boy.

"Thank you, Robert, thank you so much." He cuddled the big robot like he hadn't been cuddled before.

"Whoa there, dad. Now that's quite enough of that," joked Rob, grabbing his father's shoulders. "I wouldn't want you getting a hard-on again."

Jesus's face flushed crimson red, but all the same, he let out an embarrassed laugh. It had been an unfortunate incident and both had been able to laugh it off, but clearly Rob was in a teasing mood.

"Do we need to strap that thing to your leg before you meet Linda?" It was a statement that had his father gently punching him in the shoulder.

"No need to go that far, son. At my age, I count myself lucky if it even shows signs of life. Never mind having two boners in a day."

"Then you'd best save yourself for your new date, which by the way, you're running late for. Your taxi will be outside in ten minutes."

"I really wish you were coming with me, son," said Jesus, who'd love nothing more than to share the moment with his one and only friend.

"Well, I can't, and besides, I wouldn't want to upstage you

and have that old American bird drooling over me," Rob joked, before straightening his father's hat and directing him to the front door. "Now get going and I'll see you when you get back."

The white van turned slowly into the Teesside Park complex and turned right at the first roundabout. Nobody had said much on the journey over, each lost in their own thoughts. The only interruption had been a message on Maddog's mobile phone which, upon leaving Picton, had finally picked up its first signal. It was a solitary, one-word message, which upon reading, Maddog relayed to Mary. "The job is tomorrow," he said before snapping his phone shut. From that moment on, the pressure in the van turned up a few notches.

Mary eased the inconspicuous white van into a parking space at Teesside Park, positioning it so that she had full visual of both Maplin and Greggs bakery entrances. She parked there because she needed to cover the left and right approaches to the gadget store. This was to allow her to identify Jesus long before he reached the entrance, and Greggs so that she could keep Troy stocked up with pasties and therefore quiet in the back. It was this tactical planning acumen that ensured all of her operations ran like clockwork.

"Now what?" asked Maddog, fidgeting in his seat. Patience was never one of his strong points.

"Now we watch and wait," responded Mary, who was starting to think maybe she should have left everyone back in Picton and worked alone.

"What if he doesn't show?" said Maddog, gazing out of the window at nothing in particular.

"He'll show, trust me," responded Mary, working the horizon with her eyes.

A few minutes of silence followed as Maddog's attention span again waned.

"What will he be wearing then?"

"How the fuck should I know?" barked Mary, starting to get a little aggravated.

Maddog sat back in his chair and let out a huge sigh. He'd lasted only a few minutes before boredom had snuck in and was becoming a pain in the arse.

"I'm hungry," announced Troy, who could smell the scent of pastry delights wafting through Maddog's cracked window.

Mary's temper began to glow red.

"For fuck's sake," she shouted, handing Maddog a crumpled fiver. "We've only been sat here for five minutes. Go and get the first round of pasties in and I'll take first watch." It had the makings of being a very long stakeout indeed.

With Maddog gone and Troy content that food was on the way, Mary set about her reconnaissance of the area. She made mental notes of traffic and essential get-away routes. She took down notes on traffic lights, and their timings, and for zebra crossings that might cause an old pedestrian to slow them down. She detailed cars that looked out of place, looking for those with two bodies sat in the front and extra aerials on the roof. These were sure signs of undercover police, though thankfully none appeared to be in the area. Next she scanned for dogs. Any scuffle that was to take place would upset any have-a-go mutt and raise unwanted attention, so Mary needed to be sure they were animal-free.

Once satisfied with that, she turned her attention to the weather and whether it was likely to rain or not. She had previously fitted slick tyres to the van, which would provide more steering and brake traction should she need it, but now she was slightly concerned by a grey cloud that was making its way over from Stockton.

The question was: should she abort?

Mary pondered a little more, while continuing to sweep faces for familiarity. The last thing she wanted was for somebody to recognise her and place her at the scene. She studied people on their approach to the Maplin store. She studied weight, height and mannerisms. Were they walking with an excited gait? Were they laden down with bags of shopping? Was anybody acting as watchman as she herself was doing?

Mary gathered all the information and puzzled together the big picture in her head. She was happy with the current situation. Nobody had seemingly compromised her plan and even that dark cloud was shifting away on the moderate breeze. All she needed now was to confirm the target and execute the plan. It was then that Mary was interrupted by Maddog pulling open the back doors of the van.

"Fucking scruffy bastard," he cried, dropping a fully-grown man dressed as Crocodile Dundee into the back. "Weighs more than I thought."

Mary turned to the commotion in the back. With double doors open, passers-by were now getting a full showing of a man dropping an unconscious body into the back of a van where two other people were also tied up.

Mary screamed out in alarm. "Who the fuck is that, Maddog?"

"It's your fucking ex, isn't it?" shouted the exhausted bouncer, lifting up Jesus by his hair so she could identify him for herself. "And I'd appreciate it if you stopped shouting out my name in public."

Mary did a double take. It was definitely Jesus lying prone in the back of her van but she was totally confused by events.

What? How? And why? were questions that sprang to her mind, but they'd have to be answered later. People were reaching for their mobile phones as Maddog slammed the back doors shut and climbed back into the front passenger seat.

Mary gave him a stare of disbelief.

"What?" he asked. "It is the right person, isn't it?"

Mary just nodded with a baffled look on her face.

"Good, can we get going, then?" asked Maddog, in a calm and calculated voice.

Mary gunned the throttle and the big van screeched into motion. Navigating the one-way system of the retail park, she reached the A66 without hiccup or hindrance. Turning left on the main road, she then headed away from Middlesbrough town centre, keeping the van steady in the flow of traffic. It was a difficult thing to do but absolutely essential if you didn't want to present an easy target to pursuing police. After a few miles of steady speed, she was satisfied that they were in the clear.

"What the fuck has just happened, Maddog? How has he ended up here so quick?"

"Just luck, I guess," said Maddog, with a shrug.

"Luck?" responded the alarmed Mary, who never relied on luck. She preferred sticking to properly laid plans rather than luck.

"Well, I didn't realise it was him at first. I thought it was just another weirdo, buying a sausage roll in front of me. I saw the bloke, dressed like a complete twat and thought I'd give him a little slap. Down like a sack of shit he went, and I only tapped him."

Mary sat open-mouthed at the absurdity of what she was hearing.

"You hit somebody in the middle of a bakery, while on a kidnapping operation because you didn't like the clothes he was wearing?" asked Mary, seeking confirmation that Maddog was completely insane.

"Erm, yeah, but he is dressed like a twat, isn't he?" responded the big lummox.

To be fair to him, he did have a point.

"So what happened after that?" Mary thought she may as well hear the full debacle, before vowing never to work with this lunatic again.

"Well, the woman behind the counter got all arsey and refused to serve me."

"No, no, no," said the exasperated Mary. "How the fuck did you know it was him?" She was shaking her head vigorously at this dense man's brain capacity.

"I didn't recognise him at first but I saw your name on the knife sheath he was wearing and that confirmed it."

Mary turned her head to look at the poleaxed figure, still unconscious in the back. He was dressed head to toe in crocodile gear and was in fact wearing a huge knife on his belt. Mary once again shook her head at the unreal, yet incredible, situation she found herself in.

"Is he dead?" she asked. The way her day was panning out, it wouldn't surprise her.

"Nah, I only tapped him," said Maddog, rubbing his chin with embarrassment at the realisation that Mary thought him a nugget. "He'll be right. You'll see."

Mary threw him a stern, 'he better be' look, and continued driving the van in silence onto the back roads to Picton, Maddog quiet in his thoughts, and Mary furious that he'd risked it all because he didn't like somebody's clobber. She could only hope that come tomorrow, this buffoon was on better form.

They passed Crathorne Hall and navigated their way through narrow hedgerowed streets. The atmosphere in the van was still ice cold.

Maddog didn't know what all the fuss was about.

"We got our man, didn't we?"

He was shot down by Mary's icy stare.

"Oh, lighten up, Mary. Have we not made a clean getaway?"

Mary didn't see it that way. His incompetence, or, more to the point, his temper, had nearly landed them both with a jail sentence and it was taking Mary quite a bit of time to calm down.

The unconscious body at Ron's feet started to stir and he silently nudged Troy, trying to draw his attention to the fact. Up until this point, Ron had watched the full episode play out in front of him in confused silence, wondering how he'd ever been caught and held by these two morons for so long. With the body writhing and muttering on the van floor, he failed to hold his silence any longer.

"Who the fuck is this, Troy?" he blurted out.

Troy was just as equally confused.

"How do I bloody know?" he hit back angrily. He always got a little tetchy when he was hungry.

Troy kicked the long-haired man onto his back so that he could try and identify his face. He let out a stunned gasp. "I don't believe it. It's the guy I met in the Sausage Cottage a few nights ago."

"Ah right, so this is an old flame of yours, is it?" said Ron, picture fully painted, mounted and framed in his mind. "Well, isn't this just nice and cosy."

A serious cissy fit was brewing in the back of that van, one to possibly match the one simmering in the front.

"No, it's not like that," reassured Troy, who really couldn't believe the luck he was having. What were the chances of having two love interests, tied up in the back of a van? One knocked out, the other not talking. He was starting to have sympathy for Josef Fritzel. "Besides, that was all before I met you," he went on.

Ron just stared away in stubborn silence.

The atmosphere in the van was horrendous, but given the option between the back, or the front, Troy would still remain where he was.

He could sense his mother's anger. He'd been on the end of it enough times by now to realise that you shouldn't approach her or even speak to her until she'd had a good couple of hours to herself and smoked at least two packets of Embassy Regals. However, given the current critical situation, kidnappings, bank robberies, assault, and now a boyfriend that wasn't talking to him, he felt that he had no choice but to break protocol and try to communicate with his mother.

After a few big breaths as if to steady his nerves, he finally plucked up the courage to speak. "Did you get me a pasty then, mother?"

CHAPTER 21

An anxious Rob slumped on the couch in the front room and surfed through the TV channels. As was usual with late night broadcasting, there was nothing that caught his eye. With resignation, he clicked the off button and threw the remote to the other end of the sofa. He'd need something else to occupy his worried mind. He stood and walked to the big bay window that was letting in artificial light from the lampposts outside, the autumnal daylight long since disappeared. Jesus was still nowhere to be seen and the cyborg was showing his first signs of stress.

Rob had been on his own for six hours. The last he had seen of his father was when he'd climbed into the back of the waiting taxi that morning. He was cheery, almost to the point of emotional and this delay was so unlike him.

Rob had filled the time by dusting the house, giving the grass its last cut before winter and, of course, checking his trouser snake for signs of life. He had wanted this day to go down as one of the greatest in his father's life and had worked like a Trojan without stop or respite. He knew the event timings, start to finish. He knew his father would probably call in for a swift pint to unwind too, but, even so, that still meant Jesus was over three hours late, and when did the old boy fail to call?

Now either he'd managed to get off with the old American actress and was having the time of his life – a scenario that was highly unlikely in Rob's mind – or something was wrong, very wrong. Rob just couldn't put his finger on it yet.

Jesus started to pull round, the sharp pain in the back of his neck causing him to groan as he did so. His vision remained blurry, although he could tell by his surroundings that he was inside a building, somewhere warm. His vision strained for clues of his whereabouts and as the shapes formed, he knew this wasn't within the comfort of his own home. Some people were with him, two, three, maybe four figures around him. He tried to reach out to them but his hands wouldn't move. Then, his hearing returning, their voices became audible. Quietly at first and in mumbled tones, but eventually they became louder and clearer. A man's voice, although one he didn't recognise, with a female's too. A voice that sounded strangely familiar, soft, warm and gentle. And that smell, that nostalgic smell of Hai Karate. Surely it couldn't be? Please don't let this be a dream…

He flicked his eyes open and blinked some sense into his vision. Clearer and clearer the images became. He had no idea where he was or why he was there, but knew that this couldn't be a coincidence.

He took in his immediate surroundings. He was slumped on a two-seater sofa, in a room he'd never seen before. Others were with him, male figures sat opposite him on a threadbare sofa. He stared at the first man and he stared back, his face appearing sullen and in despair, almost in pain, which didn't fill Jesus with much confidence.

"Where am I?" Jesus muttered, but the first man just bowed his head, breaking eye contact to stare at the floor. Alarm bells started ringing in Jesus's head as he kept on searching the room. There sat another man, shorter and much fatter, with a dress sense that would have Gok Wan looking for a sick bucket. His hands, Jesus noted, were also bound behind his back and he looked just as confused as he himself was feeling inside. Adrenaline started to flow through Jesus's veins. As he studied the second man for a few more seconds, he knew he had seen him before. His face was somewhat familiar, but from where?

"Hey," was all the second man could offer, with a nod of the head.

An acknowledgement that proved Jesus's theory that they'd met previously.

Jesus replied with a nod of his own but the pain he felt in his neck was unbearable and offered the old man another piece of the jigsaw, the picture it painted not too pretty. Jesus continued to take in more of his surroundings. Right of the little fella was a wall partition that bore a lifesize portrait of Hitler. To that right again stood a door. A door that was ajar and presumably led into a kitchen or diner judging by the smells coming from within. Whoever had brought him here must be in there as Jesus could hear their muffled chit chat coming from inside that room. He tried to call to them, much to the disagreement of his new sofa friends. When they didn't respond, he tried to wriggle himself free.

Jesus wanted to stand, but couldn't due to the tight restraints holding him in position. Whoever had tied these knots were Boys' Brigade trained and no matter how much he wriggled, he just couldn't move. The alarm bells were growing with rapid intensity in his mind. This wasn't good.

Jesus was starting to panic.

"If this is you, Little Mo, I'm warning you," he screamed out, a statement that caused Ron and Troy to look at each other for the first time since their tiff.

Jesus received no reply and was closing in on a panic attack.

"And you're back in the room," said Penelope, clicking her fingers. She had called a halt to proceedings having just witnessed Little Mohammed's disturbed visions under hypnosis.

"Whoa," gasped Little Mo, sitting up on the couch and fighting for breath.

Penelope handed him a glass of water to calm his nerves which he had to hold with two hands because it was heavy. Penelope let him sit quietly for a bit. She handed him hankies to wipe the beads of sweat, slaloming away down his forehead. When she thought him finally ready, she spoke. "What on earth spooked you like that?"

"I'm not too sure," he replied with his usual honesty. "I've never been hypnotised before, at first I really enjoyed it. It was the calmest I have ever been in my life. It felt like I was floating on a cloud and that a huge weight had been lifted off my shoulders."

Penelope said nothing but gave a knowing nod of the head.

"I could hear your voice too. It was so calming, so soft and reassuring and with each question you asked, it was like I was able to walk through doors that had previously been locked. I'm not sure I'm explaining this properly?"

Penelope smiled before speaking. "It's called the onion effect," she said softly. "Although your analogy of locked doors works just the same. We've been removing the barriers that your subconscious doesn't want you to see. It's your inner self protecting you from what it thinks is damaging or evil. However, we must remove the outer onion layers in order to get to your inner troubles."

Penelope really was a master of her craft. Sure she'd had a wobble here and there. Who hasn't? The main thing now was she was back in the game, doing what she did best, helping people. After giving a brief explanation into the process of hypnosis, she sat quietly and let him pick his own moment to proceed.

Mo took a few more swigs of water before continuing. "I saw my childhood. Such happy memories," he smiled. "I used to play on the common close to my house with my friends. It was a tiny little greenbelt with poplar and lime trees growing on it. It had a little beck running by it too. We were a close knit bunch. Sport mad, football, cricket, hares and hounds. We used to play golf on there too, although we had to stop once the odd window went through. Sometimes we'd go catfish fishing with just buckets. We'd catch loads of them." Mo tore himself away from the memory and looked at Penelope with sadness.

Penelope caressed his hands and encouraged him to go on.

"Then I walked through another door," he went on, voice all serious this time. "Bright lights above my head, people all around with surgical masks staring down on me and the pain, the awful pain…" Mo tailed off again.

"Was this because of your accident. The school falling down?" asked Penelope, who felt she was on a voyage of discovery.

Mo had hit a critical point. The moment where the power struggle with your inner self comes into play. Penelope had seen it a thousand times. People who deny things for so long that the denial becomes reality and the truth becomes difficult to accept. She watched Mo with interest. He was a fascinating man who had lived a sad and turbulent life. Would he proceed and talk about his past now or would it come out during their next meeting? Only time and Mo had the answer to that, and Penelope was in no rush.

Seconds of silence turned into minutes. Penelope couldn't interfere at this point. She sat motionless and in silence, not wanting to offer any distraction to Mo who was wrestling his subconscious mind. It was a power struggle that only he could win. Finally, he broke.

"No, it wasn't the school," he mumbled before being washed through the final locked door in his mind on a tidal wave of tears. "It was me, all me, it's all my fault," he wailed, causing Penelope to break protocol and hold him with her strong arms.

"I had this paper round, you see? One of those rounds where you only worked one day a week. You know, for the Herald and Post? Only it was the Advertiser back then. Two hundred and seventy-five papers I had to deliver, which I did for three whole years but I broke, oh the irony when I say 'I broke'." Mo was gushing tears now, as was Penelope who was riding this traumatic tale every step of the way with him.

"Have you ever felt the weight of two hundred and seventy-five newspapers?" he asked Penelope, who was dabbing her eyes in silence.

Penelope politely offered a no.

"They're bloody heavy," he responded, wiping his nose on his sleeve like he was right back there in that adolescent moment. "My exams were coming up. I couldn't cope anymore, and that bloody paper round. Delivering those bloody newspapers that nobody wanted. That glorified junk mail that people instantly threw in the bin," he blurted out in anger. "Anyway, I'd had enough. I went round the back of Middlesbrough's Little Theatre with my papers in tow. They had those big six foot bins on wheels and nobody was ever going to know, were they? So I lifted them up and tried to throw them in the bin."

The guilt was etched all over Mo's face. Tears started streaming down each cheek again. "Only my back went." Mo clicked his fingers to demonstrate how instantly it had happened. "Right there, with two hundred and seventy-five papers above my head, leaflets tucked in too, and my back just went. Down they came, smacking me on the head with all the force of a felled tree. My back snapped like a fortune cookie in winter. I lost eleven inches there and then, and that was before my operations."

Penelope handed him another hankie before addressing her own eyes, however Mo was too far gone. Anyone who had been relieved of that much guilt and secrets after all that time would have shown the same effect, but Penelope never grew tired of the raw emotions on display.

The pair of them sat sobbing for a few minutes, Penelope trying her best to regain her composure.

"What about the school then? And Robert Jones?" she finally asked in between large sniffs. "I thought that was the cause of all your issues?"

"Well, it wasn't bloody nice, I can tell you," said Mo, before blowing his own nose into a hankie. "Stuck for five days under that rubble, with nothing but a Bunsen burner for company was horrendous. Not to mention the further back operations I needed in the aftermath. But if truth be told, it wasn't anyone's fault but my own."

Penelope stopped him there. "Now hang on a minute, young man," she said. "Hurting your back in a freak accident was one thing, but blaming yourself for the collapse of a school completely another. If anything, you are owed millions in compensation."

As she spoke, Mo shook his head from side to side.

"No, you don't understand. You see the Herald and Post had taken away my childhood. They told me as I was effectively cheating them by not delivering the papers, they owed nothing. At no point in the contract did it state we were to lift two hundred and seventy-five papers above our heads. In fact, the small print discouraged it. So I wanted to get my own back and planned to blow up the Gazette office to see how they'd like a life of no compensation. They didn't have a chemical licence, you see? So if it could be proved that the building was razed to the ground as a result of unlicensed molecules, then they'd be ruined too. So I began storing copious amounts of phosphorus in the school stockroom. I had to store it somewhere. It was just an unfortunate coincidence that Tin Head rolled in there when he did, especially when you consider he had a battery fault. It was just an accident waiting to happen."

Penelope sat dumbfounded. You just couldn't make this stuff up. She had to admit it was a terrible set of coincidences that had got Mo to where he was sitting now. But she was still a little confused.

"So why try to kill him then?"

Those words cut through Little Mo like a knife as the final door of his conscious was opened.

"That week, the school had entered a newspaper headline competition," he blubbered. "The paper in question being the Herald and Post. The winning student was to gain exclusive headline rights and have his own follow up article on the front page, the aim being to deliver a local scoop. Robert Jones created the biggest story of the decade that day. He was outed for being the big, glorious freak he was. He blew up a school, reduced it to nothing but rubble, and still made all the headlines, while I was still buried beneath it all. I'd failed in glorious defeat, while Middlesbrough basked in the glory of its first intelligent cyborg. He had found the ultimate serendipity by fighting with a teacher."

The tears stopped as the bitterness took over.

"You know they even gave him a medal for bravery? Imagine that? He had no fucking idea why the school collapsed, no fucking idea he was even on fire and yet, by fighting with a teacher, the big metal bastard grabs all my headlines…"

Penelope sat in stunned silence. Her case was done. She now knew the whole truth of this man's misfortune, and should really think of a course of rehabilitation to help him, but couldn't help find him a little psychotic.

"Do you know what his stunning competition-winning headline of the week caption read? THE APPLIANCE OF SCIENCE BURYS LITTLE MO IN DEFIANCE before his sub heading went on to say... BOMB PLOT FOILED BECAUSE THE ROBOT BOILED. Yes, in the aftermath that clever little shit even discovered my little plan and made sure I was ridiculed wherever I went after that. The subsequent inquiry was a closed book."

Penelope straightened her pencil skirt and addressed her posture. She sat for a while allowing what had just been said to digest. Whether she liked it or not, she had a duty of care to provide for Little Mo, and although he was clearly showing bitterness here, she felt there was still hope for him yet.

"Mo, I want you to come back in to see me tomorrow," she said, having finally decided the path she wanted to take with him. "I'll be in at nine o'clock sharp, so make sure you are here. I believe I can help you and I think you'll enjoy what I have in store for you. We are going to make you better."

Mary arched her neck around the door to see if her latest captive was awake. "Ah, welcome back to the land of the living," she said, before walking seductively toward Jesus, her former, gullible lover.

Jesus heard her voice before he clapped eyes on her and, as she neared, his senses went into overdrive, the smell of Hai Karate encroaching into his nostrils. There she was, this vision of pristine beauty. He tried to speak but his throat was desert dry and instead he just stared speechless at the only woman he had ever loved. She crossed her front leg in front of the other as she walked, hands on hips. Had you not known this to be Picton, you would have been forgiven for thinking it Milan, such was the catwalk momentum the queen thief was now displaying. She knew only too well the power she held over him and was enjoying every moment of it.

Jesus, mesmerised, could only watch and listen as the Adidas shell suit bottoms rubbed together making a seductive rhythm as she moved closer.

"Hello, Jay Jay," she said, in the manner of Marilyn Monroe singing to the president. "Long time no see," she smiled, before placing both hands on his knees and bending over so her nose was inches from his own. There she was, in all her glory. Blood red lipstick, painted on eyebrows and a super orange false tan that glistened under the room's sixty-watt lamp.

"Mmmmary," mumbled Jesus, his motor cortex control system scrambled by the situation he now found himself in. "Wwhere, I mean hhhoww?" Jesus had frustratingly lost all comms. They were in turmoil but given the size of the event unfolding in front of him, who could blame him?

Mary, thriving in the control she held, edged those two inches closer so that her breath could be felt on his face.

"You're still smoking Lambert and Butler, then?" muttered Jesus, always one for ridiculous statements at inappropriate times.

Mary knew him too well and planted those big painted lips on his, ensuring no more words sprang from his mouth.

Jesus fell into a deep trance and as Mary retreated ever so slowly, his head remained where it was, eyes still closed and basking in the moment.

Mary watched him with glee.

"I need you, Jay Jay. You don't know how much yet, but I do."

Jesus still hadn't come out of his trance, but could hear the words perfectly, his heartrate picking up to a whopping thirty-five beats per minute.

"I'm on the verge of greatness, Jay. Tomorrow I will have finally reached my goal. I've waited a long time for this, and I need you there with me. You took some finding, let me tell you, but it'll all be worth the trouble."

Jesus finally opened his eyes.

"What's happening, Mary?" he asked. It was a question he really needed answering, given that he was reunited with his old flame, while tied and bound on a sofa with two other blokes, in a house he'd never been to before.

"Well, Jay Jay," she said once again, stroking his hair, with both legs now straddled across his lap. She resembled a preying mantis about to devour her mate. But her seductive dance was soon halted by the man on which she now sat.

"Hehe! Who'd have thought, eh?" said Jesus. "Two boners in one day." His inappropriate Tourette's mechanism was back to its brilliant best.

It was an outburst that confused Mary, who initially thought her former lover was perhaps going a little senile, but she eventually twigged when she felt the growing lump under her thigh. A lump that caused her to vomit in her mouth.

"Wait till I tell, Robert," he went on excitedly. "He'll never believe it."

"Robert?" enquired Mary, after swallowing the diced carrots once more. "Is he your tall friend? The big good-looking one with all the muscles?" she enquired, a question that diverted Jesus from his current childish predicament.

"My friend?" laughed Jesus. "He's my son."

The words tumbled from his mouth and slapped Mary hard across the face. She had never even considered the fact that her once beloved would meet somebody else, let alone have a child with them. The revelation rocked Mary to the core, although you wouldn't have known it given her cool demeanour. Sure, she was hurt by the news. Why wouldn't she be? Jesus had never once touched her that way, always preferring to wait till they were married, yet he swore she was the only woman for him. Had he really found somebody to better her? She simply had to find out.

"So you moved on then, Jay Jay?" she said, stroking his long greasy hair. "Found yourself somebody else and remarried?" She was pondering how long he must have waited, trying to control her growing jealousy as she spoke.

"Oh, I never remarried, Mary. There is just Robert and me in my life. We live together in a cosy little house in Thornaby…"

Those words were like music to Mary's ears. She had been right all along, and knew no woman could better her. She was a million dollars in his eyes and her self-esteem was quickly restored.

Mary held him tightly by both shoulders and shook him till she once again had his full attention.

"Jay Jay," she said, placing a pillow under her bottom before sitting back down on his lap. She looked him coquettishly in the eyes and bit her bottom lip. Once her eyes had stopped watering and the pain had subsided, she whispered in his ear. "Let me enlighten you as to why you are here."

He was all ears now.

"I've been saving quite a bit of money these last few years. A nice little nest egg for when I retire. But the bank won't let me have it." She was wrapping her hair around her index finger as she spoke. "They say it's a joint account and that my partner must be there too. Apparently that silly bank manager is a stickler for the rules and he's been terribly unkind to me."

Troy and Ron watched the whole ridiculous episode unfold right in front of their eyes. They knew Mary was playing the old fool, but Ron knew not to say anything, not yet anyway. He even had to kick Troy and shake his head when he thought he was about to warn the lanky scruff.

They had to bide their time, especially with Maddog in the next room. Instead they let it play on, in cringe-worthy silence. It was drama worse than Eldorado and that was saying something.

"I started saving for us," Mary continued, after being interrupted by the sight of Ron kicking her son, a stern look proving enough to turn him to stone. "I wanted us to be together, live in luxury on a paradise island like we always dreamed we would."

It looked like, for all the world, Jesus was taking the bait. He sat there listening to his former lover.

He'd longed to hear these words for so long but now things weren't quite the same.

He sat there aghast as Mary straddled him. Aghast because he couldn't believe how much weight she'd put on over the years and was really fighting to keep his Tourette's in check.

"So why am I tied like this, Mary?" he said, snapping out of the trance she held over him. "And who the fuck smacked me around the back of the head?"

"That'd be me," said Maddog, his mere presence causing Jesus to fart and, in turn, Mary to vacate his knee.

"Jesus, I want you to meet Maddog McClane. I suppose you remember him from the Sausage Cottage?"

"Fuck," was the only word that sprang to the captive's mind.

Maddog dwarfed the frame of the door in which he stood and looked even more frightening in the light. He wore a menacing smile that emitted danger signals to all in the room. A smile that had Ron and Troy cowering under his mass shadow.

"You are tied up like this, because I have been searching for you for such a long time," said Mary. "I eventually tracked you down via a taxi driver who dropped you off at the Sausage Cottage. A driver you upset somehow."

"Now wait a minute," interrupted Jesus, "that's not quite what happened."

Mary ignored the interruption and continued with her version of events. "My friend here," she continued, pointing to Maddog, "knew I was looking for you and when he saw you arguing with said taxi driver, he tried to help. Only you assaulted him and whacked him on the back of the head as your assailant ran away."

That much was true and Jesus had to accept that with a nod of the head.

"So when Maddog came back into the club to try to clear the air and reunite you and I, your son assaulted him too." She was now standing close to Jesus again, the foul smell having thankfully gone.

Maddog folded his arms and basked in the injustice of it all.

"So we had to tie you up in case you became violent again." Mary hid her face in her hands as if crying.

Ron and Troy just looked at each other and rolled their eyes. It was a ridiculous statement to make, given the huge creature who terrorised pub doorways for a living, and was in fact, planet Earth's bare-knuckle champion, even more so as this old man was probably eleven stone wringing wet.

However, Jesus bought it, and begged Mary not to be upset. With his face now full of remorse, he started to apologise for his actions.

"I'm sorry, I didn't realise you were just trying to help, Maddog."
Maddog nodded.

"And Mary, I'm sorry too," continued Jesus. "All this time you have been looking for me and I've treated you like this. You must think me a violent fool?"

Mary still had her hands covering her face as if in floods of tears. She sniffed a few times and rubbed her eyes red before turning back to Jesus. "I need to keep you tied like this until I can trust you again," she said.

Jesus nodded in agreement. "Of course, anything."

"And I need you to help me get my money from the bank tomorrow," she said.

Jesus nodded again. He was smitten once again and acting like a soppy, loved up teenager. Mary could have demanded anything at that moment in time and he wouldn't have said no. "One more thing," she said, voice becoming all serious once again. "I need you to invite your son to meet us at the bank, at midday."

"Robert? Why?" asked Jesus, bamboozled as to why his boy needed to be there, but comforted to know that the lad would finally get to meet Mary, the girl he'd spoken so lovingly about over the years.

"Because I'd like him to meet my own son." Mary gestured in the direction of Troy.

"That's your son?" asked Jesus.

It was only then did Mary realise the devastating effects the words would have on Jesus, who stared blankly at her, then at Troy and then at Mary once again. Jesus's stomach was doing somersaults. He'd agonised daily over the identity of the biological father since she'd walked away. "That's the reason you left me, you were pregnant and wouldn't reveal who the father was. You said I wouldn't understand."

All of this was new to Troy, who had, up until this point, no idea the man he had nearly rattled in the Sausage Cottage had once been a partner of his mother.

"Jesus, just leave it. Now is not the time," said Mary, genuinely gutted at her slip of the tongue.

"Not the time? When is the fucking time, Mary? When? It's been fucking years since you walked out on me. Never once saying sorry. At least have the common decency to enlighten me and tell me who the boy's father is?"

"Oh, I can answer that for you quite easily," said Troy, causing Jesus to give him his full and undivided attention. "It's…"

Mary slapped a fair sized chunk of duct tape over Troy's mouth, shutting him up instantly. She then ordered Maddog to remove him from the room.

Jesus was deflated. He was so close to hearing the truth, only to be thwarted once again by his ex-lover.

"Why have you got me tied up, Mary? Who is that man there?" he asked, nodding to Ron, the kidnapped security guard. "Why is your son gagged and bound? Why is that ghastly man in your home?" He was ranting now. And the questions kept coming. "Why, why, why?"

Mary started to lose her cool. She was no longer the temptress. She was a horrid and devious excuse for a human being and she knew it. One more job, she promised herself. One more big job and she'd be out of this terrible game. Her head began to spin with all the questions aimed at her. She knew she owed Jesus something, but the more he went on, the more she hated herself.

"Shut up, just shut up," she screamed in Jesus's face, finally breaking under interrogation. "You wouldn't understand if I told you right now, but I will reveal all tomorrow, my darling."

"Oh, for God's sake," cried Ron, who'd seen enough of this whole debacle to last a lifetime. "She's planning to fr…" but his words were cut short by another, ample amount of duct tape strategically placed over his mouth.

"What was that, Mary?" asked Jesus. "What was he about to tell me?"

"He was about to say that I was planning to free you," said Mary. Any sharper and she'd cut herself. "But your outburst has caused me much upset." Mary then placed duct tape over the lipstick-smeared lips of Jesus himself. She rifled in Jesus's pockets and pulled out his mobile phone. Typical of him, it was an old pay as you go affair that was surprisingly locked and required a four-digit password. She stared at the screen and then back at Jesus who, despite his current dilemma still had loved up puppy dog eyes staring back at her. She then keyed in the word, M-A-R-Y.

The phone lit up. She offered him a warm smile but he knew he'd let himself down with such a pathetic password.

Mary scrolled through his three contacts, an act that took only seconds and found the name she was after: D for doctors, R for Robert, M for Maplin.

She waved the phone around until a single bar of signal appeared then, trying not to move a muscle, she sent the impressive Robert Jones a text that simply read: 'Staying with an old friend, meet me at the HSBC bank in Middlesbrough town centre tomorrow at noon. She'd really like to meet you x'. Then she turned the phone off. One more day, she promised herself, then I'm getting out for good.

Robert was watching a ten minute freeview channel that was breathing absolutely zero life into his knob, when his phone bleeped. He opened it up and read the message from his father. The lucky bastard, he thought while tapping his lifeless cock. Hope he's having more luck than I am.

CHAPTER 22

Penetrating rays of dawn sunlight struggled to burn through Teesside's industrial fog as another autumnal morning in Middlesbrough started like thousands before it. The early morning sun rose above the buildings, bathing the swept streets below, its low elevation casting shadows from the town's once mighty industrial heritage like ghosts. Shopkeepers began their groundhog day routine of setting up shop, and wafts of freshly baked bread and pastries travelled out into the cold air, hooking those who'd skipped breakfast by the nose, as if they'd starred in the Bisto gravy advert themselves.

With shopkeepers ready and waiting to start their daily business, so too did the shoppers themselves turn out to spend their hard-earned cash. What an awesome spectacle it was. Mothers, fathers, brothers and sisters, along with numerous friends and colleagues, all treading the moist ground whose dew was resisting the temptation to evaporate in average seasonal temperatures. The bankers, the homeless, the councillors and the average joe, the town was going about its busy humdrum, with rushed employees colliding with busy mums pushing collapsible buggies from Watts and Sons, the long and sustained child ferrying service company from Parliament Road.

"Beautiful, isn't it?" said Maddog, in a manner not befitting of him. Mary knew exactly what he was talking about as they both watched the controlled chaos from their vantage point of the Cleveland Centre roof. It was ten o'clock in the morning, and the busiest day of the banking week. It was the day when wages were paid into banks and benefits were handed out to the masses. It was the day that retailers deposited their week's worth of takings into bank accounts and punters exchanged the fruits of their labour for hard currency, ready for the weekend boom.

Maddog nudged Mary and nodded in the direction of the bank. A white, G4S van had pulled up outside and was depositing more readies into the safe. This was shortly followed by another and then another, their timetables randomly set to confuse anybody watching but that didn't matter here. As long as that cash poured into the bank, then Maddog would be happy.

Perched on top of the Cleveland Centre roof, they were able to watch their plan come together over a good few hours, the early start being at the request of Mary who, as professional as ever, wished to recce all possibilities. Occasionally, they checked on their three companions, all tied and gagged in the back of the innocuous white van, but more often than not they stood with elbows on the car park wall, watching the crowd swell below.

"Another tab?" offered Maddog.

Mary took one without a word being spoken. Lighting cigarettes while manning an observation post was strictly against protocol, but Maddog had been right. This job was way above anything she had ever been involved in before and the nerves were starting to bite. Besides, smoking in broad daylight would hardly raise suspicion.

Mary drew in a lungful of smoke and blew it out slowly. As the blue smoke twisted and rolled out over the shoppers below before disappearing into thin air, she hoped that she could do the same when the time came. Taking in another drag, she looked up toward the CNE tower. The hulk of the town centre skyline looked quiet and still. It was hard to believe that in just a few hours time an explosion to match the lighting of the Olefins flare, would eject from its summit, spewing a non-lethal truth serum onto the unsuspecting folk below.

Whoever in their right mind had come up with such a genius plan? Mary wondered, although she knew she'd never find out. She set herself a mental note to turn her phone off when the time came. What good was being involved in a heist such as this, if she simply handed over her bank details? She continued to look skywards, watching white fluffy clouds pass over the tower. Her mind was racing. Clearly the person running the show had to be somebody who worked in there to pull off a stunt like this. How else would you get access to the roof? Unless of course, the godfather of Teesside had another insider, that was more than likely the case, after all, if they had gone to the trouble of contacting the captains of cargo ships in Seal Sands, then it was hardly beyond the realms of possibility that somebody with keys to that roof was involved too. Mary pondered just how deep this rabbit hole went?

"You're quiet," said Maddog, noticing his old friend deep in thought.

Mary muttered something inaudible and broke her gaze from the tower block.

"Do you think he'll turn up?" she asked, eyes now focused back on the bank.

"Would you?" offered Maddog in response.

"I can't see why not," replied Mary. "He received the text, he's no reason to suspect anything is wrong, has he?"

Maddog took another long drag from his cigarette before turning to Mary once again. "It doesn't really matter now, does it? If he comes or doesn't, the job still goes ahead. We've still got old Jesus there and once the police suspect him, they'll find the truth serum he's unwittingly held for some time. Now if you consider he's on release, then the old fool is looking at a ten stretch by any jury standard."

"And us?" asked Mary, a seed of doubt growing in her stomach.

"Robbery without a weapon, offering the police information on Jesus over there. Three years max, a year and a half with good behaviour. I could do that standing on my head. We come out, we lie low and we receive our big fat lump sum for the inconvenience. That is if we get caught. I've not told you the half of it yet and I know you're gonna love our escape and evasion technique. It's genius."

"There's more?" asked Mary, aggrieved she was just finding this out now.

"I'm not as daft as you think, Mary. I'll get you out. You can trust me on that score. But I'm still not going to Miami Beach. I'm definitely going abroad."

Mary started to get a sinking feeling. The plan was starting to wobble and it made her feel uncomfortable, but like it or not, she'd asked to be there and had lodged herself right in the middle of it. The only thing left to do now was wait till zero hour.

Way across town and de-burdened by his last psychologist meeting, Little Mo had leapt from his bed with new enthusiasm and zest. For the first time in a long time, he saw the world for what it was, a beautiful gift, and life was the overwhelming prize. Birds in song he could suddenly hear, the sun's warmth he could actually feel. A dark shroud had been lifted off him and Penelope Stevenson had been the person who removed it.

Mo had showered, eaten breakfast and left the house by nine o'clock. He headed straight for the Palladium shops, choosing to walk rather than take public transport. He had wanted to see life, feel it and breathe it. He wanted to meet people on their way to work and exchange pleasantries. It truly was great to be alive.

After fifteen minutes of brisk power walking, it came to Mo's attention that he had in fact hardly gone anywhere, he was built for speed, not distance. The fact he'd been called a midget on three separate occasions, by rude passers-by, didn't help either. So not wanting to be late for his cherished appointment with Penelope, he hailed the next available cab.

Mo sat in the front passenger seat and buckled his belt. The driver, a rough-looking, bald-headed hulk of a man, simply stared at him and waited for direction. Unperturbed, Mo smiled and gave him the address. He stared out of the window, watching the treetops and streetlights go by. It was a rather boring journey but that's all Mo could see out of the window as he didn't have a box to sit on. Once again, he fought the urge to moan about it. Penelope had taken this broken, down-beaten man and shown him that no matter how bad things may seem, you are who you are and what you are is beautiful. Her philosophy was pretty simple. Can you change the situation? Yes, then worry about it. No, then don't worry about it. They were words that had etched in Little Mo's brain. With every passing negative situation or comment, they sprang to the front of his mind. To this end, he worried no more about anything he couldn't control.

How much I owe that woman, he thought. If only I'd had the courage to seek help earlier.

The taxi pulled into the Palladium car park and Mo paid the fare. He even tipped the driver who had stared at him so rudely for most of the journey. It was an action that caused the embarrassed driver to utter his first words of the journey.

"Want me to lower the ramp so you can climb off?"

Mo flatly refused.

"No, thank you, my good man, and you have yourself a wonderful day now." Mo jumped down from the cab and prepared to close the heavy door with his back.

"Please yourself, you little shit," replied the driver.

It was a comment that planted doubt in the mind of Mo, who was wondering if he could keep up with all these niceties for no return.

All he felt in this moment in time was anger, and he could easily have been tempted to murder the driver. That was rage that soon vanished though, when he heard the smooth, velvet voice of Penelope Stevenson.

"Nobody said it would be easy, Mo." She had been standing in the doorway of her clinic watching the event unfold.

Her voice had instantly diminished any growing self-doubt that Mo was harbouring, as he walked briskly toward her with a wave and a smile.

"Hi," he offered.

Penelope responded with a merry, "Morning soldier."

Given Mo's tiny height, it was impossible for even the most professional of shrinks to not treat him as a child from time to time.

Not that Mo minded. Secretly he loved it.

"Well, here I am. Bang on time," he said, before asking her if he should lie on the couch again.

Penelope had other ideas. Fastening her coat up to all but the top button, she locked her office behind her and offered down her hand to Mo.

"Come with me, I've got something to show you," she said, leaving an intrigued Little Mo to wonder what this brilliant person had up her sleeve now.

His question was short-lived, as a snotty, well-used tissue, full of germs, fell from Penelope's coat sleeve and landed on his head.

"Oh, Mo, I'm ever so sorry," she said, plucking the rag off his bonce with index finger and thumb. "I've had a terrible cold and was keeping it there for an emergency," she went on, utterly devastated by what had just happened.

Yet Mo quickly got over it. Looking up, staring deep into her warm eyes, he muttered, "Happens all the time, but if you can't control the situation, don't worry about it, right?"

It was a statement that almost had Penelope in tears.

"Come here," she said, proud as punch, and she gave him a quick squeeze. As far as professional and patient relationships went, this was strictly taboo but Penelope couldn't resist. As much as she had helped him in his hour of need, he had also rescued her, and they were rising from the ashes together.

They walked for a short while through the Palladium car park, before Penelope stopped and said, "It might be easier if I carried you."

Mo winced but her suggestion made sense. "Okay," he huffed.

A short while later, they eased to a halt. "So, what do you think?" said Penelope, putting down the slightly bemused Mo.

"I think it's an ice-cream van," responded Mo, stating the obvious.

"It is," laughed Penelope out loud, before producing a set of keys from her coat pocket and handing them over. "And it's all yours," she said in between giggles.

Mo looked at Penelope, then the keys and finally at the bright coloured ice-cream van before him.

"I thought it was me that needed the shrink, Penelope, not you," said Mo, as he studied the poster of the van's wide array of iced treats that was stuck on the window.

Penelope knelt down. She looked at him with a serious face and once she was sure she had his full, undivided attention, she spoke. "Mo, your deep depression has been brought about by your accident, and that's all it was, an accident," she began. "What followed was a series of incredibly unfortunate events that left you a little person. Incredibly unfortunate events," she repeated to reinforce her point. "None of this is your fault, and yet, you've hidden a self-loathing for decades, something which has left you selfish and bitter."

Mo broke eye contact, because the words cut deep. He knew what she was saying was true.

"As time went by and the uneducated mocked you, your bitterness turned sour. That's when the real trouble began." Penelope was in the zone now. She was talking slowly and with purpose, dissecting Mo's unlucky past with perfect precision. "I've seen the change in you, Mohammed. You've got good in you. You just require a positive mental attitude and people to like you. And what better way than this?"

Mo had to agree with everything that Penelope had said but was still as confused as a chameleon in a bag of Skittles.

"Don't you get it, Mo?" asked Penelope, excitement in her voice. "This is perfect for you. Everywhere you go, people will be pleased to see you, and they'll look forward to you turning up. People will run after you with excitement as you make your way down their street. Have you ever seen anybody be angry at an ice-cream man before?"

"Well, there was this one time when my old neighbour Gibbo had been on a week of nights," replied Mo but Penelope cut him off before his negativity could raise its ugly head.

"You want to know what else is good about this?" she asked.

"What?" replied Mo.

"Get in and I'll show you," she said, giving Mo a little shove of encouragement.

She remained near the serving hatch and waited till he appeared at the window.

"What?" asked Mo, looking down onto Penelope's face. But Penelope stood smiling quietly, waiting for the penny to drop. It didn't take long.

"I'm looking down on you," said Mo, causing Penelope to giggle. "I'm looking down on you," he repeated.

Penelope nodded her head vigorously with a beaming smile.

As Mo took in the view, three infants ran over to the van holding a fist full of coins each.

"Two ninety nines and a Funny Feet please, mister," they cried with excitement, their faces lighting up with glee at the sight of Mo in his van.

Mo looked over to Penelope for encouragement, but she didn't need to say anything. Instead she took a few steps back so the children could be served.

As Mo curled the frozen treat around the top of the cone, he asked if the kids had any good jokes to tell. "The best one gets their ice-cream for free," he announced and how the children responded. As each shouted out in turn, Mo let out huge belly laughs and soon the small gathering around the van was in hysterics.

Penelope couldn't help but laugh out loud with them.

With nobody able to see Mohammed's real height, nobody mocking him and everybody seemingly his friend, Penelope thought that she would slip quietly away but Mo soon called her back.

"Excuse me, little lady," he shouted. It was the first time in his life he had called somebody else little. "I thought as a shrink you might be needing one of these," and he held out an ice lolly at arm's length.

Penelope walked back up to the van and took the iced treat in her hands.

"It's a screwball," said Mo, laughter bellowing out of him.

The joke wasn't lost on Penelope who also cried with laughter. She took in a spoonful and nodded her satisfaction. She loved the sight of Mo being so happy and doubted he'd laughed this way in a long time, but she also felt quite sad, because she knew her work with Mo was done.

"Right kids, I'm off," shouted Mo, much to the groans of the crowd. "Now everybody stand back, away from my van so nobody gets crushed."

All the kids did as they were told, such was the respect for their new favourite ice-cream man.

"See you all tomorrow, kids. I'm off into town to hear more jokes," he said, before jumping into the driver's seat and gunning the engine. He adjusted the mirrors and drove to the car park exit where he suddenly stopped. He looked back across to Penelope who was watching from the doorway of her practice.

"Thank you," he mouthed.

"No, thank you," she mouthed back in reply.

They both held a knowing gaze for a few more seconds, tears of happiness welling up in their eyes.

Mo cleared his throat and prepared for his new life. He put the van into first gear and began his journey into town. As he was driving, he saw a button that said 'music' and so desperate to hear which children's favourite his van played, he pressed it with great excitement. Disney's It's A Small World After All sprang from the speakers.

Rob stirred from his trickle-charged sleep and discarded the charger from its port. He lay on his back for a while, listening to the magnificent sound of nothing. The silence was deafening. He stared up to the ceiling, focusing on nothing in particular, and wondered why he felt a longing in the pit of his stomach. It was a new sensation he hadn't felt before. A feeling he couldn't quite explain. All he knew was that he wasn't happy when Jesus wasn't around. The loneliness emotion, it would seem, had finally found a home in the droid's artificial intelligence memory bank.

He sat up on the edge of his bed and gathered his thoughts. Things were definitely changing within him. He could sense new things every day. Seeing his father happy made him warm inside.

Seeing a child cry made him upset and dull. Any responsibility he showed gave him great satisfaction and left him feeling proud. When he saw an act of unkindness, he felt quite edgy and abrupt, almost angry and yet he was never programmed that way. Yes, things were changing alright, and he had no idea why.

He stared down at his flaccid penis for a few minutes and wondered if there was any glory to be had that morning. There wasn't. In fact, just like every morning since he'd had the appendage fitted, the penis remained its sick, droopy self, hanging loosely downward like a dead corn snake.

He stood up slowly and threw on his old dressing gown. Shuffling over to the smashed wardrobe on his bedroom floor, he wondered what he should wear. It wasn't every day his father wanted to introduce him to a lady friend. In fact, that scenario had never once presented itself, as the old boy had, at one time in his life, agreed to remain celibate since that evil Mary had departed. Rob was pleased his father was finally able to move on. But what to wear?

Normally under these circumstances, Jesus would be on hand to offer sound advice, offering human takes on the small things that really mattered to them, such as "Don't talk with your mouth full". It was a phrase that used to confuse Rob no end.

"Why not?" he used to argue. After all, his mouth was capable of eating lots of food and talking at the same time, but seemingly it wasn't in keeping with etiquette according to his father.

"Manners maketh man," his father used to say.

It was only after years of studying human behaviour did Rob finally start to understand. Humans didn't operate under any code and they didn't often stick to patterns. They laughed when things weren't funny or cried when things weren't sad. They would risk life and limb to save a drowning dog and yet walk past a homeless man without so much as a glance. If Rob once thought his circuitry complex, then he certainly wasn't prepared for how complicated humans could be.

He pulled his best suit from the wrecked wardrobe and dusted off the wooden shavings from the leather bag that protected it.

A suit would be ideal, he thought, hoping to make a good first impression for the sake of his father. He'd been given the expensive attire for his birthday. A gift from Jesus for his record twenty-five A+ GCSE results, a record that still stands on Teesside to this day. They'd gone to the designer store in Middlesbrough and his father had ordered the most expensive service that they offered. It was the full tailor-made job because Jesus was not only immensely proud of his son, but figured he would never grow beyond his already large frame. With that reasoning, the suit should have lasted a lifetime and beyond, but that theory was being severely put to the test because now, Rob couldn't even get the trousers on. In layman's terms, if he ever had to be measured up for a suit ever again, there wouldn't be a need to ask, 'what side does sir dress?'

He searched the cupboard once more, pulling out various clothes and trying them on. But every item he tried was the same, thirty-four-inch waist with extra-long leg. These were the measurements he'd carried right the way through nursery school to college. It was only now, for the first time in his life, that he had a problem.

With his trouser-legged items a no go and his wardrobe itinerary exhausted, Rob began to worry. The last text he had received from his father simply stated to meet him at the HSBC bank at noon and a quick glance at the time left him with hardly enough time to go shopping. He'd have to find something else to wear but what?

He moved into his father's room and opened his wardrobe doors. Jesus was smaller, of course, and a lot thinner than his son. So ordinary clothing was clearly out, but Rob wasn't looking for ordinary clothing. He had remembered one item that was offered to his father upon being injured in the Falklands War. The medic who was treating his father's buttock injuries, was attached to the Scots Guards, and needing to gain access to his father's ring piece to treat his shrapnel wounds, had presented him with a kilt. If Rob could find that, then that would be problem solved. He rummaged through the drawers and then checked the items dangling on coat hangers. When that failed, he tried the drawers in the divan upon which his father slept, however he soon wished he hadn't.

Sure the kilt was there, decked out in McDonald clan tartan and Skean Dhu, but something far more disturbing lay next to it. A black and white photograph of his father standing above a large air vent, wearing said kilt. Not only that, but he appeared to be wearing a blonde wig, stuffed bra and had painted on a beauty spot too. The photograph showed his hands pushing down on the kilt hoping to hide his modesty as the tartan edges rose in the wind and his father was wearing an ecstatic face. It was a truly terrible sight for any son to witness.

As he sat perplexed, staring at the picture, a new emotion quickly rose within him, despair, and Rob dashed off to the toilet to be sick.

The toilet visit lasted only a few minutes, as Rob tried and failed to delete his recent places folder. It took him three attempts to step into the kilt, but every time he did so, his body involuntarily shuddered at the graphic photograph now etched in his mind. His father dressed as a Scottish Marilyn Monroe was the most horrendous thing he had ever seen. As he stepped into the kilt for the fourth time of asking, Rob decided to keep his mind busy and try to forget the whole episode.

He pulled the kilt up to his waist and fastened it tight. Next he threw on a top hat and a casual Ellesse top, before finishing the look with a pair of green wellington boots. One look in the large wall mirror told him he looked like an idiot, but what else could he do? He was almost out of time.

It had been a strange request indeed to meet in a bank, but then wherever Jesus was concerned, strange was an everyday occurrence.

Surely, he hadn't been with Linda Kozlowski all night, Rob thought, although he couldn't rule it out. His rational reasoning had the odds stacked in his favour. He had, after all, met the American beauty that afternoon. But his artificial intelligence said "no way". He loved his father dearly, like any son should, but no amount of persuasion or reasoning could place them together. His dad was an ugly, strange bastard who dressed up in women's clothes after all.

I guess there's only one way to find out, he thought, picking up the phone and dialling a few short numbers. "Hi, can I have a taxi please," he said, before pausing a few seconds. "The HSBC bank in Middlesbrough town centre," he went on, before finally, "Fifteen minutes, that's great, the name... Monroe, I mean Jones, it's Jones, for fuck's sake."

Was the curse of the kilt catching?

CHAPTER 23

An annoyed Mary Fassbender pointed an angry finger at the trio of captives and let the words fly so that everyone who heard them knew they carried bad intentions.

"So this is how it's going to play, you slimy fuckers," she said, addressing the three frightened occupants in the back of the parked van. "Anytime now, that son of yours is going to walk into the HSBC bank, and when he does he'll be expecting to find us. So the last thing we want to do is let him down, isn't it?"

Jesus didn't look at her.

"He'll be expecting happy faces too," she went on, noting Jesus's lack of enthusiasm, "so you'd better start wiping that miserable look off your ugly face."

Again, he offered her no acknowledgement.

"You two," she said, diverting her attention to Ron, the main man of the operation, and, of course, her own son, Troy. "You two lovebirds are key. If you play this thing right, then in a few hours' time, you can tickle each other's prostates to your hearts' content. But until then, your arses belong to me."

Ron gulped at the thought but Troy was quite happy to experiment.

"When Rob finally turns up," Mary continued, ignoring the glint in Troy's eyes, "we're all going to take a nice stroll. We will descend the car park ramp and have a nice, friendly, little reunion. But don't you worry, Maddog and I will be the ones dealing with the pleasantries, and if any of you so much as utter one word to anyone between now and then, you'll get this."

With that, Mary pulled a handheld taser from her overcoat pocket and jabbed it under the armpit of the shackled Jesus. Pressing the button, she sent a sustained electric shock into his torso and watched as his body contorted and went into spasm.

Jesus slumped to the floor of the van, his muffled cries of anguish going unheard due to duct tape still covering his mouth.

Ron and Troy looked on wide-eyed. Up until now, apart from an odd slap here and there, and copious amounts of verbal abuse, Mary had been surprisingly calm, but this was new territory, the use of force a game changer. Any thoughts they had harboured about raising the alarm, or even making a run for it, evaporated in that moment. Although thoughts of that ilk probably evaporated earlier in Troy's mind when the word "run" got a mention.

"Anybody else want a little go? The batteries are brand new," asked Mary, taunting those yet to feel the power of her stun gun.

Not surprisingly, there were no takers. Mary closed the door of the van and walked the short distance back to Maddog.

"How they getting on?" he asked, never once lifting his eyes up from the binoculars he was using.

"Oh, they won't be causing us any trouble, I assure you," she responded.

Maddog didn't ask her to clarify because he could probably already guess.

"Anything?" asked Mary, changing the subject to more pressing matters.

"Not yet, but he can't be far away. That's assuming he does actually turn up, of course," said Maddog.

Before Mary could respond, she was interrupted.

"Hello, what have we here?" Maddog had been covering as many approaches to the bank as possible. Perched on the roof with binoculars firmly attached to his eyes, he was scanning anything and anyone that moved. Pedestrians walking to the bank's main entrance were a given, but knowing that the target would arrive from Thornaby, he guessed it would either be by bus, in which case he'd arrive in the direction of the bus station, or by taxi, and therefore via the A66 turnoff. It was the latter approach that now grabbed his attention.

"What have you got?" asked Mary, straining her naked eyes down the road, but unable to make anything out.

"A taxi with a single, white male passenger," he said. "It's just pulled over at the bus stops, adjacent to the town hall. Whoever they are, they're tall." Maddog initially thought that this was his man. However, doubts soon arose when the passenger alighted the vehicle. Adjusting the focus on his binoculars, he screwed his eyes up for a better view. It definitely looked like him, good-looking, big muscles and a right handful, but it surely couldn't be? Maddog turned to Mary with confusion written on his face. "I think I've identified him, mate, but I need a second opinion."

"A second opinion?" snorted Mary at Maddog's target recognition incompetence. "Your lamps going, old boy?" she teased. "How difficult can it be? He's six-foot-four, weighs eighteen stone, is a walking brick shithouse and can cause trouble in an empty fucking house? Is it him or isn't it?"

"Well, that's just it, Mary, I'm not sure because this guy appears to be wearing a skirt."

Mary shoved Maddog out of the way and snatched the binoculars from his grasp. She adjusted the focus until clear vision was restored and looked to see this man for herself. Sure enough there he was, a huge unit of a guy wearing a kilt with green wellington boots.

The audacity of it, thought Mary, a grown man wearing a skirt in Middlesbrough town centre. He was either feeling suicidal or thought himself large enough to fend off multiple attacks. As this man clearly fell into the latter category, she thought it best if they err on the side of caution.

"Why is he wearing a kilt, if he isn't even Scottish?" asked Mary.

'Don't know. Maybe he's going to a wedding?" responded Maddog, as confused as ever.

"In fucking wellies?" reasoned Mary, becoming exasperated by the whole situation.

"Well, it does rain quite a bit in Scotland," countered Maddog.

"Either way, I think we need clarification on this one, mate," she said, heading straight back over to the van.

Mary flung open the door with force to address Jesus, who had recovered from his earlier shock, but was still cowering as Mary leaned into toward him. She grabbed at the duct tape covering his mouth and ripped it off in one fell swoop.

"Ayyyasssssss," shouted the distressed inventor, his thin moustache ripped from his upper lip and firmly attached to the tape in Mary's hand. It was an action that even had Maddog McClane wincing.

"Shut up and listen, you little, scrawny fuck," pointed Mary, drawing the Taser from her pocket again to prove she meant business.

The sight of the stun gun worked, with neither Jesus nor anybody else muttering another syllable.

Jesus stared up at her, water spilling from his eyes.

"Your son, is he Scottish?" she asked urgently.

It was a curveball of a question that Jesus hadn't expected, and it took him longer than usual to answer.

"Well?" demanded Mary, shoving the stun gun forward.

"No," cried Jesus in a panic. "He's not Scottish. Though he did watch Braveheart once. Walked out halfway through though, it was way too fanciful. He's a stickler for historical accuracy." He was still confused by the question.

"But he is good-looking? Tall? Built like an outhouse and leans slightly forward when he walks?" continued Mary, the questions coming a little too thick and fast for somebody still recovering from fifty thousand volts.

Leans slightly forward when he walks? thought Jesus. Whatever is she talking about?

Until he remembered Rob hadn't been fitted with counterbalances yet and a warm smile almost broke out across his face. "Yes, Robert is tall and very good-looking, as you describe. He also has a well-toned torso with bulging muscles and does indeed lean slightly forward when he walks, due to his extra-large penis," replied Jesus.

A statement which caused Troy to faint temporarily, something Ron was far from happy about.

Mary looked at Maddog, but the big fella just shrugged his shoulders, unsure of which way to call it.

Rolling her eyes, Mary turned back to Jesus. "Does your son own a kilt?"

The words had hardly left her lips before Jesus felt the full ramification of what she had just said. His head dropped as if pulled by a lead weight and he let out a loud cry.

"Well, is it him or isn't it?" she demanded, shoving the Taser forward once more.

"Please do," demanded Jesus, egging her on to zap him in the side once more. "It'll be better than facing him now," he cried. "The big bastard's been in my private weekend drawer."

Now it was Mary's turn to be confused. But nonetheless, they'd just positively identified their target. Now the job could begin for real. It was show time.

Maddog grabbed Jesus by the collar and physically removed him from the van with ease. Then grasping Troy and Ron in each hand, he dragged them out too.

They were all untied and made to look presentable before being offered some final friendly advice. "Utter one word and you die," they were told. Maddog's calm and calculated voice left them under no illusion that he meant business. Without another word being said, they were pushed forward, Maddog's hands in their backs, toward the car park ramp.

The small gang descended the car park exit and turned right toward the now closed Walkabout bar. Jesus felt a little flutter of sadness in his stomach. Where would he get some authentic Australian tucker from now? he thought to himself, but refrained from raising this question when he was shoved in the back by Mary, who had the Taser protruding from her coat pocket.

At the crossroads, they waited for the lights to go green, all very normal, like a pack of polite school children on an outing, before jumping across the road, diagonally when the green man said they could. Maddog offered Mary a quick glance that she took as 'no turning back now'. And she reciprocated with a nod of her own, then the five entered the building.

Mayhem was just seconds away.

Inside the bank, people seemed to be in various states of financial engrossment. Some people simply stood and waited their turn, while others were being offered coffee from greedy bankers, buttering them up for their custom. There were about thirty or so customers on the ground floor alone, most of whom stood at the ATM machines situated by the front door. Assumedly they saw this as the safer option rather than being stood exposed outside.

It was Rob who spotted his father first. He'd been watching the door for his arrival and was quite surprised when he turned up with four other people. Crossing the room to greet them, he soon slowed his step when he saw his father's face. It wasn't one of happiness as he'd been expecting, and knowing him like he did, he knew something was clearly wrong. He scanned the faces of his father's company. The first one was a guy he didn't recognise, nor knew from his father's past. He didn't appear to be very threatening and had a face as glum as his dad's. The second person was short and fat and did have a face that he recognised. Sifting through his face recognition files, he soon pieced together where he knew him from. It was that little weird fellow from the Sausage Cottage a few nights ago. Things weren't adding up. The next guy to receive a quick scan compounded Robert's fear. He was the big doorman who wanted to kill them both, again at the Cottage. This interesting lead led to Rob's danger proximity senses flicking to a state of readiness. A few short seconds later, they flicked onto red alert. Scanning the face of the final pack member, he clocked the face of Mary Fassbender. He knew there and then that his father was in deep trouble.

"Look who we have here," said Mary, goading Rob as their eyes finally met. "It's Teesside's version of William fucking Wallace."

"What's going on, dad?" asked a concerned Rob, ignoring the scruffy tramp Mary. "Everything alright?"

Jesus had a look of sheer terror in his eyes. He wanted to look up and warn his son of the imminent danger, but felt embarrassed because the lad was wearing his Sunday Tartan.

Rob, having never seen his father in so much distress rushed forward to help.

"Not so fast, sunshine," said Mary, giving Rob just enough time to see the Taser attached to his father's side, much to the relief of Maddog who had taken up refuge behind her. "We'll do this our way, if you don't mind."

On seeing his father's predicament, Rob slid to a halt. He had no other option but to bide his time.

"Ronald, you're back?" said the excited voice of the on-shift security guard. It was an unexpected twist that nobody had anticipated, but Mary let it play.

Tony was one of the most experienced guards at the bank and had worked alongside Ron for many years. He approached his work colleague with his hand held out and asked how he was feeling. Seconds later, he wished he hadn't as Maddog delivered an earth shattering right hander that sent the now comatose guard skidding back across the floor from whence he came.

With gasps of horror from customers and staff, Mary could think of no better time to start the party. "Everybody get down on the floor, this is a fucking stick up!"

"A fucking stick up?" asked Maddog, shaking his head in disbelief.

"Sorry, I've always wanted to say that," shrugged Mary, before cracking two, high pressure gas canisters and throwing them across the floor.

Maddog followed suit, rolling two more truth serum canisters in the opposite directions. Gas billowed out at a rapid rate, hissing and spluttering itself into all four corners of the bank.

Mary, following the plan with military precision, ran to the entrance, opened the door and screamed, "The bank is being robbed," before going back inside and securing the exit shut. With phase one complete, she then smashed the fire alarm for good measure, leaving the people outside of the building in no doubt that something was very wrong at the bank.

Pandemonium ensued, as panicking employees and customers ran back and forth trying to escape the assailants in front of them. It was a scene that had Maddog psychotically smiling amongst the chaos as he knew what he had to do to silence them. With gas filling the room nicely, Maddog knelt down on one knee and produced two full-face gas masks from his rucksack. He placed one immediately over his head, so that the fine filter would stop the gaseous fumes, and threw the other one toward Mary.

He then walked toward the remaining screaming hostages, before punching them quiet one by one. It was a heavily one-sided affair with Maddog outnumbered by fifteen to one, but nobody could argue with the result. With the sound of jaws broken and an increasing body count that would have put Rambo to shame, the screaming finally stopped. All that could be heard in the room was the drone of the fire alarm and hissing of venting gas.

Mary walked over to the glass entrance doors and peered out. As suspected, a fair sized crowd had already started to gather as social media went into overdrive. Many a folk were stood rubber necking, trying to get the best possible view as to what was happening in the bank, while others were filming the scene on mobile phones. As a result, the media coverage they were attracting was phenomenal. Sirens could be heard, as emergency service vehicles rushed to the scene, having received numerous calls of distress and, as was always the case, the low-life news crews had begun to arrive, and were already setting up their cameras and equipment. They'd be ready to 'go live' very soon. Mary smiled as she watched reporters holding microphones jostling for position.

"What's the sit-rep, Mary?" asked Maddog, wanting to know if the operation was being executed to perfection.

"Everything is going just as we planned," shouted Mary above the din, offering Maddog a thumbs up at the same time. "There's a decent sized crowd gathering right outside, and it seems to be growing by the minute."

"Perfect," replied Maddog, whose eyes were still firmly glued to Rob, "then we'd best move on to phase two."

Maddog and Rob were in the midst of a standoff, growling at each other prior to battle. It was sure to be a fight of epic proportion.

The pair were rotating around in a small circle, eyeing each other up while looking for weaknesses, looking for the right time to attack, but in this early stage of the contest, it was Maddog who held the advantage.

"Try anything funny, lad, and the old man gets it," he said, as the cold blade of a knife pressed against Jesus's throat.

"Listen to what he's saying, son," said the frightened hippy in a quivering voice. "I've been with them only a short while and believe me, they are ruthless. Get yourself out of here while you still can."

"I'm going nowhere, father," Rob reassured. "And you," he said, pointing a lethal titanium finger at Maddog's face. "If you so much as damage one strand of hair on that man's head…"

"Settle down, lad," responded Maddog, not put off by Rob's newfound aggression. "This is my party so I'll be host. Now if you play your cards right, maybe you'll get to walk out of here holding your daddy's hand. How does that sound?"

Rob didn't respond. He just continued his stare off with the bouncer.

"Brave lad, isn't he?" said Maddog to Jesus, who by now had swallowed enough truth serum to cleanse Parliament of lies.

"You'd think so, wouldn't you? But to be perfectly honest, he's quite a placid boy who hates violence, and do you know, he's never had a fight in his life," replied Jesus, baffled by his own unhelpful comments because he was hoping to keep up the charade that Rob was in fact a hard man.

"Hates violence?" repeated Maddog, not sure if he'd heard right. "This bloke challenging me here, hates violence? This man who attacked me in my own club hates fighting. Do my ears deceive me?" There was sarcasm in his voice now. He was beginning to enjoy himself.

"To be fair, he didn't attack you, he was simply acting in self-defence and even then, that was only because I'd just disarmed his robotics code, lodged up his anus," said Jesus, who then threw his son a startled look before slapping his forehead in frustration and cursing his loose-lipped mouth. "Sorry, son," he said, with a grimace.

Maddog and Mary looked at each other.

"Do you have any idea what he's talking about?" he asked her.

"Not a clue, mate, although he was always a strange one was Jesus."

Maddog then turned to Rob himself. "What's all this finger up your hoop business then, big lad?"

"Haven't a clue, the old boy's been acting quite peculiar of late, and often mumbles loads of old rubbish. I really wouldn't pay much attention to what he's saying." Rob really wasn't making a good job of hiding the truth.

Maddog's eyes narrowed. "What's this robotics code, then? Why's he talking about that?"

"I've told you, he talks shite," said Rob again.

Maddog tilted his head slightly to the side and studied the man in front of him. There was something different about him but he just couldn't put his finger on it. He'd been stood in the gas cloud long enough for it to take effect and so he should be telling the truth and yet, he didn't appear to be at all.

"How tall are you in feet and inches?" Maddog asked, waiting for the accurate truth.

"What the fuck's that got to do with anything?" reacted Rob, still unaware that the gas hissing all around him was truth serum. Not that it mattered to cyborgs as it only affected humans.

"Why isn't it working, Mary?" asked Maddog.

It was Jesus who volunteered the answer. "Because he's a fucking robot." Again Jesus felt like punching himself in the face as the awful truth spilled from his mouth.

"You built a robot to protect you?" asked Mary, who knew Jesus's past better than anyone. She knew electronics to be his forte so it wasn't beyond the realms of possibility.

"To protect me?" laughed Jesus. "I didn't build him for protection, I built him for company. I wanted somebody in my life who would be loyal, somebody who wouldn't just get up and walk away." Jesus paused, throwing her a dirty look.

"For Christ's sake, dad, shut it," pleaded Rob, but once Jesus had been asked a question, he was powerless to remain schtum.

"So what's this code all about, then?" asked Maddog, intrigued to learn more about his tall, alloyed nemesis, happy to learn that his one and only defeat to another man, would now be chalked off the record. It was a question that neither Jesus nor Rob wanted to answer. Rob shook his head, telling his father to remain silent, but no matter how hard he tried, the damaging words flew from Jesus's mouth like a flock of bats from a cave.

"Robert is, or should I say, was, governed by the three laws of robotics."

"Being?" asked Maddog impatiently, time still of the essence.

"Being that a robot may not injure a human being or, through inaction, allow a human being to come to harm."

Rob shook his head.

"A robot must obey orders given to it by human beings except where such orders conflict with the first law."

"He doesn't know what he is saying," cried Rob.

"And finally, at no point may a robot slip a human a quick length." Jesus buried his head after he answered the question for he knew the ramifications of his words.

"Well, isn't that interesting?" asked Maddog.

"More weird, if you ask me," said Mary, making reference to law three. But then Jesus was as odd as they came.

"And this override is lodged up his arse, is it?" laughed Maddog hysterically.

Rob just closed his eyes and couldn't believe what was happening.

"Okay then, this is how it's going to play," said Maddog. To reaffirm his authority and to show the frivolity was over, he nicked the face of Jesus with his knife. "You're going to bend over and let one of these flick your switch," he continued, pointing to Ron and Troy. "Don't worry, I'm sure they'll be gentle. They're going to make you nice and safe to be around. Keep you under control so to speak. Because if you don't, then I'm going to cut your dad's head off." Maddog drew the blade once again across the skin of Jesus and drew more blood.

Rob, fresh out of options, had no other option but to agree.

"I'm sorry, dad," he muttered, his words cutting deep.

Jesus knew this was all his own doing. Guilt was etched in his eyes as he watched his son bend over and lift his kilt.

"Go on then, my little bum chums, finger away," encouraged Maddog, with a stupid grin on his face.

Troy didn't need telling twice and raced forward with excitement. Troy hadn't gone more than a few feet when he was abruptly dragged backwards by Ron.

"Can't you see what's happening here?" asked Ron to the shameless Troy, who in his eagerness to get some action, had failed to see the hope that Robert the robot carried with him. As usual it was Ron, his intelligent best friend, who highlighted this for him.

"This isn't a game, Troy, this man is our last hope."

Troy paused for thought and true to Ron's words, saw things in a different light. With Rob's safety override back in place, then their plan to foil the biggest bank robbery in Middlesbrough was doomed. A free Rob was the only person who could defeat a violent hulk such as Maddog, but a robot governed by a set of laws in which he must obey human commands could make him an adversary. A weapon for evil rather than against it. Troy listened to his boyfriend's words and wondered if he'd ever be as clever as Ron. He had the ability to see the bigger picture, to be able to think outside the box and Troy was in awe of him. He watched Ron walk sympathetically toward the bending robot. He studied how Ron behaved, how he presented himself in these difficult situations. He really was a champion of the people.

"Thank fuck for that," thought Ron, who for a short while had thought he was about to miss out on fisting the hunky Rob. He'd had to think on his feet, but luckily the thick bastard had fallen for it.

With the deed done and all hope of rescue seemingly lost, the three hostages stood in silence and watched Robert rise slowly to face Maddog once again.

"Clap your hands," ordered Maddog.

Rob instantly began to clap.

"Now do the E… I… O," he ordered again with great amusement and Rob, feeling totally humiliated, began thrusting his hands in the air, while jigging from side to side as if Boro had just scored a goal at Wembley.

"Oh my, well, isn't this just perfect," laughed Maddog.

Jesus shouted enough was enough. "Robert, stop right there."

Rob did as he was told.

"I can't believe you'd stoop so low as to build a robot to replace me. I knew you were strange, Jay Jay, but come on?" said Mary, who was walking in circles around Rob giving him a close examination.

"Me? Strange? You were the one who got up and left one day without word or warning," retorted the seething Jesus. "What happened, did you get cold feet? Were you too spineless to commit to our perfect life together?"

Mary stepped forward and got right into his face. She ripped off her mask so that he could see how angry she really was, as years of pent up frustration came to the boil.

Maddog tried to stop her, but it was too late, truth serum was now making its way into her bloodstream and before she even had time to realise it, she was spouting the awful truth. Jabbing a finger into her ex-lover's breast bone, she started.

"If I told you the real reason I left, then you'd be a broken man. I've kept my distance to protect you. Kept my silence so that you wouldn't find out the truth." She was really spitting now. "How dare you say I wasn't committed? I wanted to stay with you for the rest of my life. I would have probably still been with you today if you hadn't booked that stupid weekend in London. I told you I didn't want to go, but would you listen? No, you dragged us there so it was all your fault."

"London?" asked Jesus, confused by the mixed signals he was receiving. The revelation that Mary had loved him and had wanted to stay with him made him happy inside, but to hear her criticise that London weekend, a weekend that was one of the greatest nights of his life was baffling.

"Don't blame a romantic weekend away for leaving me. You walked out on me because you fell fucking pregnant. Then you just vanish, walked away and not even a sorry to say for it."

Maddog stared at his watch and Troy, Ron and Rob all stared at their shoes in awkward silence as the argument rumbled on.

"So come on, Mary, put me out of my misery. What was so bad about our fantastic weekend in London that you had to leave me? We ate, we danced and we drank. I even managed to get hold of two VIP tickets to the Crocodile Dundee premiere and watched you walk up the red carpet with the stars. So what, Mary? What?"

"He was conceived, that's what," shouted Mary, pointing to Troy. She couldn't believe she'd just said those words. After all these years of keeping that a secret, she suddenly blurted it out just like that. She covered her mouth and felt for the first time that her mask wasn't on. The realisation of sudden doom washed over her. She really didn't want to hurt Jesus that way, but could probably guess what his next question would be.

"He was conceived that very night?" replied Jesus, pointing at the portly blue-eyed kid. "But how? We never, did we?"

"No, we didn't," interrupted Mary once again. "Because you always insisted that we marry first. But a girl has needs, you know."

"So if it's not me, then who is it?" asked Jesus, now being as good a time as any to finally hear Mary tell the truth.

Mary held her mouth closed, trying to stop the words coming out.

"Come on, Mary, don't be shy. Who is this man who stole your heart on our romantic weekend. Let's hear it. What did he have that I didn't, eh?"

Mary slapped a second hand over her mouth, hoping to prevent the truth from coming out.

"You can't keep the truth to yourself here, Mary, and I've waited long enough to know. One minute we're in London, mixing it with celebrities on red carpets at grand film premieres, and the next you're pregnant, seemingly swept off your feet by some modern day Casanova. So, who was it?"

With every question thrown at her, the truth serum pressed her neurons in the frontal lobe for an answer. That's how the gas worked. It took control of that side of the brain that controlled speech and pushed words down to your voice box with such pressure that it was impossible to prevent them popping out. When it all became too much, Mary had to let go... "PPPPaaaauulllll HHHoogannnnnn," she stuttered.

"Who?" asked Jesus, genuinely unsure of who she had just named.

"Paul fucking Hogan," she screamed, the relief washing over her as the secret finally came out.

Jesus stood and stared at her in disbelief. The name Paul Hogan had entered his head, but his love of the Australian actor refused to believe it.

Everybody else just stood in silence and watched as Jesus rocked back and forth. Even Maddog, the most heartless man on the planet, felt for him, particularly as Jesus was dressed like a twat, in Crocodile Dundee clothing.

"Fucking hell, Mary," said Maddog, trying to break the awkward silence. "Why don't you just cut his heart out?"

Robert rushed forward to catch his falling father. Hearing the news had even rocked Robert to the core, so he could only imagine how his father must be feeling.

"Speak to me, dad," he said, slapping the old boy around the chops. "Dad, say something."

Jesus appeared to have fallen into a deep state of shock. He was suddenly incapable of saying anything. Overcome with raw trauma, the truth hit him so hard that even a fresh canister of serum would have been rendered useless. Such was the state he was in.

With Jesus incapacitated in the arms of his son and the others stood there in silence, it was left to Mary to put the operation back on track and get things moving again. She walked back over to the door and surveyed the crowd. Thousands of people were gathered out there now. So far, nobody had attempted a counter-terrorism attack, but it must be imminent, considering the large police presence gathered only a few metres away. Mary had to buy a little more time. She opened up her rucksack and pulled out a flash bang. Pulling the pin, she allowed a few seconds for the timing fuse to burn before tossing the grenade outside into the street. Flashes from cameras and phones began instantaneously, followed shortly by screams from the crowd who saw the device for what it was, a weapon of terror. Suddenly a large explosion erupted and filled the air, smoke began billowing from the ruptured container and many windows smashed, showering the crowd in shards of broken glass. Everyone to a man had either ducked for cover or retreated many yards. With such a show of force from inside the bank, the police would have to rethink their plan.

"How long have we got, Mary?" asked Maddog, finally getting his shit together.

"Less than an hour. They know we are serious now, but don't yet know what we want," she replied. "I think we need to establish some communication lines though. It'll keep them away for longer if they think we'll negotiate." Mary was in full flow now.

"You can walk out there if you want, Mary, but I'm not risking it. Not this close to wealth," said Maddog.

"Me neither and nor do I intend to, but I think we should send somebody," she replied, looking around the room at her options. Her options weren't great. The bank was littered with the bodies of people that Maddog had knocked out during his frenzied attack, and she didn't like the thought of sending Troy out into the open. The guard was an obvious no, as he was required to access the vault, and Jesus still hadn't moved since finding out Paul Hogan had showed her his digeridoo. That just left the robot.

"You," she said, kicking Rob in the leg. "Get up."

Rob rose to his feet.

"You must do everything as ordered by a human, eh?" she said smugly.

Robert didn't answer and didn't like what was coming.

"You are to go out there and slow the police down," she said, pointing to the main doors of the bank and the ensuing chaos outside. "You're going to tell them that if they remain outside of the building, then nobody will get hurt and that you'll be back in touch very shortly with a list of demands. Then you walk straight back in here, back to us, nice and simple. You got that?"

Rob gave a defeated nod.

"I love your thinking, Mary, not only does that buy us more time to complete the job and escape, but by showing his face outside, it also puts him firmly in the frame. When they eventually raid their home looking for more evidence, they'll find traces of truth serum that they stole from me. They'll be looking at ten years at least," sang Maddog, happy that the already brilliant plan was seemingly getting better by the minute.

Rob threw his father one more look before setting off as instructed, but Jesus, oblivious to his surroundings, didn't respond. Mary could quite possibly have ruined the man's life forever.

Approaching the door, Robert kept his movements slow and deliberate, making sure that both hands were on show to demonstrate he was unarmed. Stepping into the street, the whole crowd seemed to quieten down and focus solely on him, while the police, weapons drawn, zeroed in on his chest.

"I've come out here to tell you to be patient," began Rob, cameras flashing and film rolling as he spoke. "If everybody remains calm, then nobody will get hurt. I have a series of demands that I will present to you sometime within the next hour." He then turned on his heel and walked back inside.

Five minutes later, Detective Inspector Appleton, surrounded by his SWAT team reviewed the video.

"He's definitely carrying, boss," said one eagle-eyed policeman, pointing to the bulge protruding through the kilt between his legs.

"I'm no weapons expert, but that looks like an AK47 to me,"

said another, as all officers viewed different angles of the captured film, trying to determine what sort of force they could expect if they stormed the building.

"It's too large for a Kalashnikov," said one old timer. "I mean look at the barrel on that thing. It's got to be a bazooka, surely?"

The team were huddled over a squad car bonnet, formulating their next move when the youngest officer on the force ran over to the car and planted a laptop down in the middle of the group.

"Sir, you need to take a look at this," he said. "It's CCTV taken in the town a few days back."

As the gaggle of policemen gathered around the screen, the out of breath runner pressed play and waited for the grainy footage to begin. Eyes now peeled on the monitor, the group of law enforcers watched as a large gentleman, of similar build to the one in the bank, attacked a baying crowd with an old man on his shoulders outside of Ann Summers. In a ruthless attack, and against terrible odds, this man had felled the angry mob of about two hundred at will.

For the police huddled around the screen, it was a terrifying show of strength. It was aggression that brought gasps from them all. The young officer then zoomed in on the large man's face.

"This is the best picture we can get of the man attacking the crowd a few days back," he said, before popping another picture up onto the screen next to it. "And this is a picture of the man who has just gone back into that bank."

There were more sharp intakes of breath from the officers as it became apparent they were dealing with the same man. He was obviously capable of dominating a huge angry crowd of people and yet had appeared so calm outside the bank only a few moments ago.

"Do we know who he is yet?" asked Appleton, trying to disguise the concern in his voice.

"No, not yet, but we do believe he may be a paranoid schizophrenic given the evidence presented before us," said the young officer, eager to please his boss.

230

"Then we only have one hour in which to prepare, and I'm going to need extra help."

"You want me to call the army, boss? You know, leave it to the professionals?" asked one sensible officer not far away from retirement.

But Appleton wasn't keen. Besides, it wouldn't look good in front of this crowd if they thought the police couldn't handle one lone rogue.

"Army? No, that won't be required, but I'd like professional help all the same, especially during what's sure to be difficult negotiations," said Appleton to his men. It was important he remained steadfast for them if not himself. "Somebody get me Penelope Stevenson."

An awkward silence fell amongst the gathered policemen.

"Er, sir, Penelope isn't in a good place right now. She's had a bit of a crisis of confidence and was relieved of her duties not so long back," said one brave policeman, who knew Appleton's feelings for Penelope.

"What? Don't be absurd. She's forgotten more about human behaviour than you lot will ever know. I won't hear of such nonsense."

"But, sir?" interrupted the young police officer again. "The latest reports are she's off her rocker after having some form of mental breakdown."

Appleton refused to accept it. He'd worked alongside Penelope many times in the past and knew she always delivered. If he was in any form of crisis, then it was her name he placed first on the team sheet.

"Get onto the mayor and get me Penelope Stevenson," he repeated, his voice much slower and precise this time to drive the point across.

The young police officer rolled his eyes and did as he was instructed.

CHAPTER 24

Resistance to the truth serum was futile but even so, the scene back inside the bank was a morbid one. Rob, back at his father's side, was trying to bring him out of his hypnotic state, while Troy and Ron continued their lovers tiff, the hornets' nest shaken seemingly further following Ron's fingering of the mighty cyborg's rectum.

Mary and Maddog looked on in disbelief.

"Now, listen here you bunch of pathetic vermin," said Maddog, fully aware that the show must go on. "We've got a job to see through and we're going to finish it right now. You," he shouted, pointing at Rob, "pick that silly old bastard off the floor. And you two," he barked, now pointing at Ron and Troy, "if you don't stop your bickering, then I'm going to put my boot up both your arses so you can compare fucking notes. Got it?"

"Yes, I understand perfectly well, thank you," said Ron, the truth serum now firmly running through his system. "And you won't get another peep out of me, although I'd be careful with what punishment you offer this tubby virgin here, because he would probably enjoy it," he added.

Troy was furious at such a cheap dig, finding it totally uncalled for.

"Yes, I would enjoy it," he shouted, before screwing his face up in confusion. "Very much in fact," he added, although it wasn't the statement he was looking for. He'd planned to respond to Ron's quip with a resounding, "No, I wouldn't and I'm not even fat," but the truth serum simply wouldn't allow it. "I am a big fat virgin and the only sex I have ever had is from a pokey bum wank," Troy shouted out with rage. But again he was totally confused by his own honesty.

So was Mary. "I think you should stop talking now, Troy," she said.

Maddog echoed her sentiments. "I'd listen to your mother's advice if I were you, fatso."

Troy's temper now bubbled away. He was furious at the current situation he found himself in, yet confused by what was happening to him. He was a profound liar, a bloody expert and yet here, words tumbled from his mouth that he had no control over. It only angered him further.

"I am not skinny," he shouted out in Maddog's direction.

"You don't fucking say," said the big bouncer. "Now if you don't mind, we've wasted enough time as it is."

Rob lifted his father off the floor. With little effort, he swung poor Jesus round onto his big shoulders and waited to see what came next. He didn't have to wait long. Marching up to Ron, Maddog grabbed him by the back of the collar and dragged him toward a heavy door situated to the rear of the bank.

"What's the code?" he asked, and as much as Ron tried to resist, he couldn't help but spit out the six figured sequence that would allow them access to the bank's vault.

"Eight, three, four, nine, two, and five," he announced. Sure enough, a green LED lit up on the digital display to say that access was granted.

"Now before we go in, are we likely to encounter any armed guards?" asked Maddog, a question that had Ron shaking his head before answering.

"No, the Health And Safety Executive removed them all after the Christmas piss up got a little out of hand one year," answered Ron.

"So they did used to have live ammunition at the bank at some point, yeah?" probed Maddog again, knowing detail was everything on a job like this.

"Live? No, we only ever stocked Nerf guns, but they were eventually banned after Jacob shot Wendy in the eye during some slap dash tomfoolery. Got suspended he did. Poor fellow."

Maddog stared down at Ron wondering if he was taking the

piss, however it turned out he was telling the truth when Ron pointed to a cardboard box hidden beneath his manager's empty desk, filled with loads of the colourful plastic toy guns.

"Gun amnesty," announced Ron with genuine disappointment. Maddog just shook his head.

Ron pushed through the now unlocked door, with the others following close behind. Mary, ever the professional, took up the position of tail end Charlie and monitored the rear.

The game was now afoot.

They walked down a tight, dimly lit corridor and descended some steep steps, the bottom of which opened up to form some sort of basement. Yet again there was a corridor running right through the middle of it, only this time there were doors leading off into more office space, doors that still held hidden bank staff. Maddog took great delight in ordering his advance party to halt while he cleared out these stragglers.

"Clear," he would shout, closing each door behind him as he exited the room. The sickening sound of fist against flesh left the others in no doubt that nobody was going to spoil his big day by raising the alarm. The group descended yet more steps, twisting through many more yards of featureless corridor and down further into the bowels of the bank. In some places, light bulbs had blown and had failed to be replaced, and on some of the damp, unloved corners of walls, mould had begun to grow.

Concern was etched across Mary's face. The cash surely wouldn't be kept this deep, she wondered. It just wouldn't make sense. Besides, surely only Hades himself would work this deep underground in a depressing place such as this?

"I'm pretty sure the money won't be down this way, Maddog. Are you sure you've got this right? I saw a doorway back on the bank floor which stated secure room. I think we need to go back there if you want to find the cash."

Maddog's laughter echoed off the barren walls. "Money, Mary? Whoever mentioned money?"

Mary was alarmingly lost. The whole operation in her mind was to cause a massive crowd outside, secure the loot and make good their escape. Had she become confused somewhere in reading the script?

"Then what's the score, mate?" she said, stopping in the deep corridors beneath the packed Middlesbrough streets above.

Maddog sensed it safe to remove his gas mask. The truth serum hadn't made it this far down, so he was unlikely to be affected.

"We're here for the gold, Mary."

"Gold?" Mary responded inquisitively. That subject always aroused her greedy mind.

"Middlesbrough has the biggest gold reserves in the UK," Maddog said, delivering the astonishing news with a warm smile. "While those police are twiddling their thumbs, waiting to hear our demands, we are going to sneak it out the back and escape to that life of luxury you always wished for."

"Bullshit, you've been led down the garden path," she said. "Middlesbrough was voted one of the worst places to live in England. It's got the highest crime rate in the North and is in the top two percent for poverty and the unemployed. Gold reserves, my arse."

"Ha ha, exactly my thoughts, Mary, but you're wrong about the unemployment figure. It's actually in the top one percent. But who's counting, right?"

Mary shrugged her shoulders at the pointless statistic and encouraged Maddog to start talking and fast. He had seen that look in her eyes before though, and not wanting another swollen pair of testicles, addressed her face on and laid all his cards on the table.

"What if I told you that this town's awful reputation was man-made? Dragged deep into despair purposely by those wonderful people we all call politicians."

"What are you talking about, Maddog?" said Mary, frustration growing.

"It's deception, Mary. The once thriving town and its residents have been hoodwinked by Parliament. A fabricated, hard luck story to get them thinking that this once industrial giant is finished. But the reality is far different. The government offered all the big companies a deal they couldn't refuse. A nest egg, if you will, for shutting down most of the industry around here. Have you never wondered why they never stepped in when Nylon Intermediates was shut down, or why British Steel died without so much as a fight? It was to create an illusion. One so far removed from reality that nobody would be roused by suspicion. Only somebody was, Mary, and now here we are, ready to reap those rewards."

"This makes absolutely no sense. Middlesbrough and its surrounding areas were truly run into the ground. The people here live tough lives and grind out a living by any means possible. If that means turning to crime, then so be it. Kids need to be fed and mortgages paid for. It would be a major atrocity if this story was even half true." Mary was on her soapbox of injustice now, but to be fair, she had lived one of those tough lives herself, still did, and crime had been a massive part in it.

"Oh it's true, Mary," insisted Maddog, pushing Ron forward so that Mary could hear him clearly. With the powerful truth serum, still coursing through his veins, it would be impossible to resist. "Go on then, tell her."

Ron tried to lie. He wanted to tell Mary that what Maddog was saying was absurd and that the only thing in her future was a prison cell. But the words wouldn't appear. Tears began to sting his eyes as the small entourage looked toward him in shock. Even Jesus, still slumped on his boy's shoulders, turned his head toward the security guard on hearing the news of gold. All but Maddog were open mouthed with revelation.

Finally, he spoke.

"Yes, it's true." Ron's head rocked backward with anguish. For years he had protected this secret and with those first few words now out in the open a stinging truth followed. "Middlesbrough is on a par with London and Aberdeen in terms of monetary value. Although the currency here isn't from greedy bankers or from crude oil. Beneath this bank, over half a mile down through these descending corridors is Europe's single largest gold deposit. Over four billion pounds worth of gold bullion stored inside a secure, safe complex. Putting that simply, this is England's Fort Knox."

Mary stood, wide-eyed and in silence, elation and anger washing over her simultaneously. She wanted to believe the story, she really did, but was struggling to come to terms with the size of the job in which she now found herself. Sure she'd invited herself in, that was her own fault, but the planning for such an audacious raid was astounding. Had she known, would she have still proceeded? This wasn't just a few years in jail any more. If caught, she was looking at a life sentence. This made Ronnie Biggs's great train robbery look like taking candy from a baby. On top of all of that, she was still pissed off that the Infant Hercules had been made to suffer at the hands of the fat cats at Number Ten.

"Why Middlesbrough?" she asked. "Why go to the trouble of creating an illusion when London could easily have managed it?" She needed to hear the full story now, not just for her own peace of mind, but because she felt the town had been dealt a cruel blow.

"Who would look for a king's ransom amongst paupers, Mary? It's just like the Great Egyptian Pyramid where the king and queen's chambers were littered with gold. With the apparent symbol of wealth already presented to the discoverers, nobody bothered to check what lay underneath. Well, not for a few hundred years anyway. It's the same in today's ever increasingly violent world. A place where terrorism reigns and cyber attacks are aplenty. What better way to hide your country's wealth than in good old shiny bullion and in a place where nobody thinks to look? It's misdirection, Mary," said Maddog, with a rub of his hands.

"Misdirection?" asked Mary. "Britain has a national debt that runs into billions, we have no wealth."

But Maddog laughed out loud once again.

"That's not true either. If you go around showing off your valuables to your neighbours, then you're going to be resented, right? Same goes here. Tell them you're skint, and nobody bothers to check. It's all smoke and mirrors really," said Maddog, now looking at his watch. "Now if you've finished with the questioning… we've still got quite a bit to get through."

Maddog grabbed Ron's collar once more and pushed him forward, further into the depths of the bank. The rest followed in stunned silence, marching deeper down into a seemingly endless chasm.

Eventually, they arrived at a large, metallic security door that looked like it hadn't been open in years, although it had been fitted with a modern, voice recognition system that allowed entry, so it must have been visited in the not so distant past.

This door was known to only a chosen few, all of whom had signed the Official Secrets Act to hide its existence. Poor Ron, one of the bank's senior and longest serving guardsman, just happened to be one of those people. The door asked a series of questions which had pre-recorded answers. If, for whatever reason, you were at the door and under duress, then you simply provided an alternative answer, an incorrect answer that would go undetected to those wishing to gain unlicensed access.

On processing this response, the door would still open, thus protecting the bank's employees, but would also silently alert MI5 of a possible security breach. The only problem with such sophisticated technology such as this was it never took into account that the person answering the question may be full of truth serum.

"Please state your code name and access level," asked the door, much to the annoyance of Ron who wanted to lie but couldn't.

"Code name phoenix, access level black," he answered.

Troy sniggered in the background. "Phoenix."

"Password and security clearance number," it asked.

Once more, Ron couldn't help but give the correct answer.

"Condor blue ray, five one five eight three."

Troy sniggered again, much to the annoyance of Maddog who had already warned him back in the bank. Troy clammed up when he saw the big man staring at him.

The door processed the answers given and once accepted, raised a small panel at head height. Once the cover was lifted, Ron put his eye to it and a retina scan was carried out to prove authenticity. The scan accepted, the door clicked and banged, as locks were removed. It then slid open automatically. Five seconds later, they all stepped forward into the vault.

Penelope Stevenson was sitting on a barstool in the plush Treebridge Hotel, basking in the glory of her return, when her mobile phone rang. She'd been holding court with Middlesbrough's well to dos, back amongst the elite, back to where she belonged, when the phone interrupted her latest witty anecdote. Placing her fifth sparkling wine on the bar, she reached into her handbag and grabbed her mobile firmly with one hand, her face lighting up with self-importance as she realised who it was.

"Excuse me, ladies and gentlemen," she said, feigning disappointment while holding her phone up for crowd to see. "But the Mayor is on the phone and I should really take this."

Penelope walked outside slowly, listening to the mutterings of approval behind her. "The Mayor, fancy that," said one anonymous person from the crowd, while another simply clapped in astonishment. Yes, Penelope, like a modern day Lazarus, had risen back from the dead.

"Raymond, how nice of you to call. To what do I owe the pleasure?" she asked, trying to sound posh through her alcoholic haze.

"Penelope, so glad I've managed to reach you, we have a situation in the town that requires your urgent attention," said the Mayor, concern in his voice.

"The town? What is it?" she asked, eager to find out more.

"It's a human settlement that's larger than a village but smaller than a city, Penelope, but that's not really important right now."

Penelope rolled her eyes skywards and let the comment slide.

"We need you to rendezvous with DI Appleton outside the HSBC bank in town immediately," he went on, before scrambling a squad car to pick her up at her current destination. "Hurry now, Penelope, things are turning quite sour."

And just like that, the phone went dead.

Penelope pulled the phone away from her ear and wondered what on earth was going on. She'd only received phone calls from the Mayor on two previous occasions. One, when she was asked to provide a detailed psychiatric report and act as negotiator during an armed hostage situation and the other was when he invited her over to his house to play Twister. Both times Penelope had walked away victorious, both times the Mayor had managed to get pissed and soil his pants.

As Penelope waited to be picked up, the air outside soon began to mix dangerously with the alcohol already in her system. As those from her entourage ventured outside to see their heroine, all smoking on their large Cuban cigars, it was clear to all that she was quite pissed. What's more, the wind had got up and her hair had become unkempt and dishevelled.

"Everything okay, Pee?" asked Marjorie, chairperson of the Nunthorpe Women's Institute.

"Yeshh, yeshh jush fine thanksh," slurred Penelope. "It's jush the Mayor who's having a little storm in a tea cup. Nothing that can't be sorted quickly." She was rocking visibly from side to side.

"Good for you, Pee," said Marjorie, necking a double Bourbon and taking another heavy drag from her cigar. "I'll keep your seat warm for you, sweetie."

The pair were interrupted by the sound of tyres rolling over the car park gravel, as a big, unmarked Jaguar pulled up outside the hotel. Marjorie offered a drunken military salute, while Penelope offered her face to the driver's side window.

"Miss Stevenson?" asked the serious driver.

"Yesh, that is I," she replied, the smell of booze on her breath causing both the passenger and driver to look at each other in unison.

"You'd best climb in, Ma'am. DI Appleton is expecting you."

The car sped out of the car park and turned left toward the town centre. The driver, who had a suspicion that Penelope may be drunk, had his eyes on her and couldn't believe the fall from grace he was witnessing.

Sure, he'd heard of her demise, who hadn't in the force? But seeing her in this state was hard to believe.

"Is everything okay, Ma'am?" he asked, but Penelope didn't respond, instead she appeared to have fallen asleep, her head resting against the window and loud snoring being heard above the roar of the engine.

The driver called it in.

"What do you mean, she may need a coffee?" screamed Appleton. "Don't be so ridiculous, man, just get her over here right now and I'll be the judge of whether she's fit for service or not." He was clearly in no mood for mundane particulars, especially with a six-foot-four inch lunatic holding up a bank in his town.

A few minutes later, the big Jaguar screeched to a halt beside the temporary field operation desk and DI Appleton approached. The driver once again tried to put his boss in the picture, but was once again brushed aside in Appleton's haste to get the job done.

"Penelope," he shouted above the din of the crowd, his voice startling the professional psychologist awake.

"Morning," she said, in drunken confusion. "Is there any chance of a brew? I've got a mouth like Ghandi's flip flop."

"Not now, Penelope, let me give you the full sit-rep on what's happening here. Then we'll sort the coffee out. Follow me."

Penelope unbuckled her seatbelt and climbed from the back of the car. As she did, her skirt was blown up by the wind, and blew right over her head, much to the amusement of the huge gathered crowd who all cheered at the sight of her Bridget Jones belly pants.

"Oh fuck off," she shouted, sticking two fingers in the air, an explosion of anger that had Appleton and his colleagues turning around and witnessing the shocking scene.

"Is everything okay?" he asked, concern etched over his face.

"Yes, absolutely fine. Bloody wind caught me skirt and displayed me knickers, that's all," she responded. "So what is it you want me to do?"

"Penelope, approximately two hours ago, a gang of people entered the HSBC bank, just over there. They have already used substantial force, as we can see by the many bodies lying on the floor just beyond the entrance, although we don't believe they've killed anybody yet. We're just formulating our response and awaiting to hear their demands, but these haven't yet been received."

"So this is a hostage situation?" asked Penelope, both hands resting on the police table for support.

"We're not sure. CCTV shows the group of people walking into the bank as calm as you like but since then only one of them has been back outside to communicate with us."

"Did you give him a coffee?" she asked Appleton accusingly, her mouth now foaming with dehydration.

"What? Eh? No?" retorted the confused DI. "Why would I do that?" He was now guessing correctly that rumours about his former colleague may just be true after all. "Are you alright, Penelope? You look a bit… tired." It was the best he could come up with given what he really wanted to say.

"Yesh, I'm fine. It's jusht been a long day, that's all," she slurred. "What else have you got?"

Appleton paused for a brief second, not knowing whether to proceed.

Penelope clearly wasn't on top of her game, but after he'd failed to heed the warning of his colleagues about her recent performances, he didn't wish to be a laughing stock in front of his men. With absolutely everything to lose, he carried on.

"Well, what we've been able to determine so far is that, whoever this fellow is, he's done it before. Here he is, stood outside the bank not long ago," he said, dropping a photograph of Rob in front of Penelope. "And here he is again, just a few days ago, with another member of his gang," he continued, throwing a second picture in front of her, showing Rob with Jesus on his shoulders outside Ann Summers.

"I don't believe it," whispered Penelope, a reaction Appleton wasn't expecting.

"You know these two men?" he asked.

"Yeah, you could say that," said Penelope, colour draining

from her cheeks. "They're ex-patients of mine. These two nearly ruined me."

Nearly? thought Appleton, staring at the dishevelled, drunken shrink before him.

"They nearly ruined Little Mo too," she said with her hand resting on her forehead as if to keep a headache at bay. "But I managed to save him from their evil clutches."

"Who is Little Mo? Come on, Penelope, you're not making much sense."

"Little Mo is an ice-cream man," growled Penelope, totally baffling the on-scene commander.

"Ice-cream man, Penelope?"

"Yes, are you bloody deaf? An ice-cream man," she shouted in annoyance. "But he didn't always have that job. He used to be a paper boy, only several hundred papers fell on top of him, so he had to quit."

DI Appleton looked to his colleagues for help, several of whom were miming the international symbol for drinking behind her back, as others suggested she had a screw loose too.

"That man there," stammered Penelope, pointing her slim, bony fingers at Rob in the photo. "He caught fire once, and his school collapsed as a result."

"Okay, that's enough, Penelope. Can somebody take her home, please?" Appleton would have to take the hit for calling on Penelope. His colleagues were right, she was a raving looney.

"Don't you patronise me," she slurred, freeing her arm from the DI's grasp. "I'm telling you the truth. Hic! You see that scruffy bastard in that photo too?" she said pointing at a guy dressed as Crocodile Dundee. "His name is Jesus."

"Right, take her away," said Appleton, who had heard enough by now.

"Are you even listening to me?" screamed Penelope, as two police officers started to drag her to a waiting ambulance. "The big fucker didn't have a cock either," she shouted, "so Jesus had to build him one."

That was all Appleton could take. "Penelope Stevenson, don't make me do it. Shut your mouth, I'm warning you."

"But he's a fucking robot," she screamed out in pure frustration.

With those words echoing all around, DI Appleton had no other choice. With his fingers rubbing the bridge of his nose and the sniggers of his colleagues ringing in his ears, he had no other option than to arrest his former friend and detain her under the Mental Health Act. He took absolutely no pleasure from this, but her appearance and ranting behaviour spoke for themselves. He watched the ambulance crew tie Penelope down on the bed and inject her in her arse cheek to quieten her down. A tiny tear of sadness rolled down his face as the ambulance drove away.

CHAPTER 25

Mary, gobsmacked that not a single soul, except for themselves, were standing beside the biggest gold reserve this side of the Atlantic, asked, "Right, come on then, where is everyone?"

"It's never manned," said Ron, without prompt, the truth serum as potent as ever.

"Not manned?" repeated Mary, unable to comprehend such an idiotic idea as to leave billions of pounds worth of bullion unattended in Middlesbrough.

"That's right," answered Ron again, frustrated that he couldn't stop telling the truth. "Who's going to steal it if they don't know it exists? The idea is brilliantly simple. Cunning in fact. The UK's government has played an absolute blinder. They purposely set about crumbling a once thriving industrial town, letting it dwindle into ruin. With an incredible feat of imagination, they even ran a sustained negative press campaign against the place, subtle at first because changes needed to be made slowly, so as not to cause a revolt. They started with the demise of industry, then topped up the negativity by allowing the southern press to mock the Boro's multi-million-pound superstar footballers, and finally paid a popular television company thousands of pounds to label it the worst place to live in England. All to provide a top secret money pit and secure a better future for Great Britain, in the least likely of places. This was a modern day Hiroshima, a place that took the hit to secure a better world."

Mary looked on in disbelief, and she wasn't alone. All five members of the group were staring at Ron, as the surreal truth fell from his lips. The town, their town, had purposely adopted a cruel persona to secure the greatest hiding place on Earth and why? So the UK's banking wealth could be hidden in a place where nobody would dare to look. How do you keep such a massive secret quiet? By telling no one, of course. Only a chosen few knew of this vault's existence, and those that did were paid handsomely to keep it that way. It was the simplest form of deception there was.

Maddog let out a long, loud whistle which echoed around the great expanse of the underground treasure trove, reaching out and reverberating off the bare concrete walls and floor. Overhead strip lights hummed gently and only the sound of their footsteps against the bare floor broke the eerie silence.

The group walked over to a dark metal cage that stood alone in the middle of the huge expanse. It was floor to ceiling in height and locked only by a simple multi-hasp security system, similar to what a teen might lock a bicycle up with. The lock, which required a four-digit combination, was now all that stood between them and a multitude of wealth beyond their wildest dreams.

"You've got to be kidding," said Mary, holding the lock in her hand.

Maddog could only agree that for a lock to provide security for such an important job, it was rather a flimsy affair.

"KISS," whispered Maddog, before both he and Mary replied in unison. "Keep It Simple Stupid."

Ron offered no resistance when asked for the code, and upon receiving the information, Maddog spun the dials of the lock to reveal the correct combination. With a gentle tug of the lock, it sprang open in his hands. He opened the cage and stood before the loot. A jaw dropping eighty billion pounds worth of solid gold, shining bright before him.

"We've done it, Mary. We've only gone and bloody done it," he said, watching Mary's face light up as she entered the open cage. Holding one solitary gold bar each, they both tossed it from hand to hand as if to feel its purity in weight. As they did, Mary had an awful sinking feeling in the pit of her stomach.

"Maddog, we'll never be able to shift this lot. How are we going to carry it? It weighs an absolute tonne."

Maddog smiled and put his gold bar down gently.

"Thirty-eight tonnes actually, but who's counting, eh?" he laughed before slapping his eight stone mate a little too hard on the back. "But don't worry, Mary. They've thought of that too." He reached up to a tall shelf within the cage and handed her a pair of black overalls with matching cap, both of which had the words 'UTB International' emblazoned on the front.

Mary's eyes narrowed with confusion. "I don't understand," she said, watching Maddog squeeze into his own pair of snugly fitting overalls.

"You will in a minute, Mary. Just have a bit of patience." He zipped up his overalls to under his neck and offered a "ta-dar" noise.

Mary stared at him in dumb silence causing Maddog to tut at her unwillingness to play. He tapped the top pockets of his newly fitted overalls and then reached round and patted the arse ones too. Finally, he fished into the side pouches and found exactly what he was looking for, a single vehicle key on a blue plastic key fob.

"Happy days," he announced, before shaking the key in front of Mary's face. Still she returned a dazed look, much to Maddog's disappointment. "Keep an eye on this lot, Mary, I'll be back in a jiffy."

Maddog strode back out of the cage and across the vast expanse of the vault. He whistled as he walked. He could easily be mistaken for a man out for a morning stroll rather than a bloke who was about to commit the biggest bank robbery the world had ever seen. Only now, did Mary begin to understand the planning that must have gone into this particular job. She watched Maddog disappear into the dark shadows across the vault.

Could they really get away with this? Surely the police would have the place locked down by now? But Mary's train of thought was soon derailed by the sound of an engine starting and then by the beep beep beep of a vehicle reversing. She stared across into the darkness to where the noise was coming from, and watched in amazement as a huge articulated lorry emerged from the shadows. It was massive and Mary couldn't fathom how she'd failed to see it parked there, but then again, her greedy eyes had been glued to the gold for most of the time.

Maddog steered the huge beast to a nice stop, coming to rest only metres from the cage entrance. With the sound of the airbrakes blowing off, he descended from the cabin and re-joined the group.

"I thought this may save your back from all that heavy lifting," he laughed, but the arrival of the big truck only prompted more questions.

"Who the fuck parked that in here and, more to the point, how?" enquired Mary, clearly uncomfortable with being kept in the dark. She didn't like the fact that this whole operation had been meticulously planned without her knowledge, yet here she was, the guinea pig seeing the job through.

"Oh for fuck's sake, Mary, what's with all the questions?" responded the ever-increasingly frustrated, but soon to be millionaire, ex-doorman. "You explain it to her, Ron."

Once again, the security guard was unable to resist, much to the amusement of Maddog who stood grinning with his arms folded.

"The bank's vault was created to be evacuated quickly for obvious reasons. There is enough room down here for three hundred or more of these lorries. Although I wouldn't recommend standing here with all those emissions, or you'll end up looking like him." Ron pointed to Jesus who still had a pained expression on his face caused by his ultimate betrayal by Mick Dundee. "They come in via the Seal Sands road, in a secure tunnel that begins five miles away. The tunnel, again known only to a few, descends underground at a leisurely gradient, before passing under the Tees to here. If you've ever wondered why so much money is spent keeping the Transporter Bridge operating, then now you know. The government don't want some smart alec building a Tyne Tunnel here. Not if they could accidently run into this place. So they happily keep the only car transporting bridge open by throwing petty cash at it. Simple when you think about it."

Ron hated himself for telling the Government's secrets but couldn't lie, even if he wanted to.

Once again, Mary was overwhelmed by the scale of deception in her beloved town. "It makes you think, doesn't it? If this is what they've done to a town like Middlesbrough, you have to wonder what they are hiding in other places like Sunderland or Newcastle."

"Eh?" said Ron and Maddog together.

This prompted Mary to further explain. "Well, look at the people up there, acting all weird, like a bunch of inbred zombies."

"There's nothing hidden up there. They're just a stupid bunch of deluded Geordies and Mackems," said Ron, quite irate at Mary, but perhaps that was just the effects of the serum.

"Ah right, my mistake," she said. "Presumably, we just load up the van and drive out of here via an underground secret tunnel to where exactly?"

"France," replied Maddog. "We've been told to hide up in a rural village, where a chateau overlooks the railway station. The actual destination will be sent once we're on our way. Speaking of which…" Maddog tapped his watch again. "We really should be getting on." As he spoke, he ushered Mary toward the cage in order to start the loading process.

"What are these overalls for and what are we going to do about them?" asked Mary, quietly impressed that the big lummox had managed to keep all this to himself, let alone know what a chateau was.

"I was wondering when you'd ask that," said Maddog with a wink, before moving to the back of the vehicle. "I'm afraid it's the end of the line for our wee party. Once they've helped us load the wagon, they're done. Collateral damage, and by that I mean, we slot them."

Troy glanced at his mother for support but she just shrugged her shoulders and egged on Maddog to continue.

"Then we head to France. Now obviously this means we're going to have to cross the channel, and as you know, our friends on border control will quite possibly want to snoop in the back of this baby." Maddog tapped the wagon. "So we have to hide the bullion somewhere right?"

Mary nodded with agreement.

"Now this is the cute bit," said Maddog with a proud smile on his face. "We are going to hide these gold bars in little plastic, cylindrical containers, loaded in the back. To the untrained eye, it'll just look like we are transporting British trade overseas. We'll help complete the charade by dressing like company employees. That's why you're wearing those overalls. From now on, we work for UTB International and we are delivering these guys all the way over to France." With that, Maddog threw open the big double doors of the truck to reveal exactly where the gold bars would be hidden.

The group, with the exception of Jesus who was still yet to speak, were all stood at the back of the lorry when the cargo was revealed. Staring down upon them, were not just one or two, but hundreds and hundreds of seductive eyes, all belonging to Herbert the Hoover. All with that cheeky, come hither grin.

In that microsecond, a ripping, almost violent, tearing sound could be heard as Rob's mammoth penis tore through his underwear and burst into life.

It rose from under his kilt like the Loch Ness Monster, like a caber freshly tossed by a hardened Glaswegian, and slammed into the jaw of Maddog before the big bouncer had time to react. Down he fell, knocked unconscious by a furious Robocock, much to the delight of Rob himself, who spun around quickly to show his father that he was no longer impotent.

"Look, dad, it works," said Rob, rotating with great velocity. From a distance, he resembled Babe Ruth, the famous baseball player, swinging his bat to hit another home run.

And as he spun, his rock hard penis connected with Mary's temple, knocking her out cold too, poleaxed by the swinging todger.

"You've done it, son," cried Jesus, his sulky spell seemingly broken.

"I know," shouted Rob triumphantly, holding his arms aloft.

"No, not that, yer daft bastard. You've stopped the heist. You're a hero, son," said Jesus proudly.

"Oh right, I thought you meant…"

"No, son… although I am pleased about that too."

Rob stared down at the floor, his hands behind his back and twisted from side to side with embarrassment. His blushing emotion was in full operational mode, although the swinging motion had Troy diving out of the way in case he was knocked out too.

"Quick everyone, help me put them inside this cage and lock the door," shouted Jesus, realising that the slumped pair might wake up at any moment.

Troy and Rob both grabbed a prone body each and started dragging the criminal masterminds toward the cage, but Ron had other ideas.

"You deal with that and I'll stop the explosion," he shouted, before turning to run through a secret exit that only employees knew existed.

"Ron, wait. What are you doing?" asked Troy. "Let the police deal with it."

But Ron was having none of it. "There's only a few minutes to spare, Troy," he said, skidding to a halt. "By the time I've explained to them, it'll probably be too late."

"But you don't know where the bomb is?" reasoned Troy, walking toward his newfound lover.

The pair faced each other, and Ron caressed a soft palm against Troy's chubby cheek.

"Troy," he said softly, "when I was held in that house, I was so lonely, so scared of what would happen to me, what would happen to mum. But then you arrived, like a gift from God and saved me. If it hadn't been for you, I wouldn't have dealt with this ordeal. But remember when they were talking so loudly that we could make out what they were saying? Well, I heard the words clearly. The bomb is situated on top of the CNE tower and I think I can reach it in time. I have to at least try." Tears were welling up in both sets of eyes as he spoke. "You stay here and help Rob and Jesus, and I'll try to stop that bomb."

These were the bravest words that Troy had ever heard, and he embraced Ron in a tight grip, not wanting to let him go. They kissed ever so quickly and Troy thought his heart would burst from his chest. Reluctantly, he let Ron go and returned to the cage.

"Where's Ron gone, lad?" asked Jesus, on seeing the security guard disappear through a side door.

"He's gone to stop the diffusion bomb that's due to go off very shortly, above the crowd outside," said Troy, although the whole ambitious plan was somewhat lost on the carpet designer.

"You can't let him go on his own, Troy, he might be blown to smithereens," said Jesus, a statement that had Troy gasping in horror.

"I never even thought of that, I'm so stupid."

"It's not too late, Troy, go after him. There's nothing more you can do here now," encouraged Jesus, snapping the lock closed on the cage that held Maddog and Mary. "He needs your help."

Troy needed no second invitation and ran toward the door that Ron had exited through. The word 'ran' was used quite lightly though, as he had to stop three times just to catch his breath. If Ron was going to be blown to bits, then Troy was going to be at his side when it happened. He'd found true love at last.

CHAPTER 26

Oath set in stone and a promise to be at his lover's side, Troy Fassbender, freshly topped up with testosterone and vigour, disappeared through the side door in slow pursuit of Ron. This route, he found, took him away from the front of the building and, more importantly, avoided the waiting police, who remarkably were only just beginning to enter the building in a bungled rescue attempt of the hostages. Though in retrospect, the timing of this was brilliant for Troy, because as he emerged, albeit out of breath on to the main street, all eyes were focused on the police counter attack, allowing him to slip unnoticed into the rubbernecking crowd.

Troy grabbed his bearings, which was relatively easy to do, considering that the CNE tower stood at a punishing two hundred and thirty-two feet high, and was Middlesbrough's tallest building. To shatter any lasting hope that Troy wouldn't have to scale such heights, the building also had CNE written on the side in big bright lettering. With another gulp of air, he took off in that direction.

Troy weaved in and out of the packed crowd, some of whom had taken to sitting on each other's shoulders for better views of the bank. The large building loomed in the distance, a whopping fifty metres away. Troy stopped and looked up at a burly gentleman standing on top of a bus shelter.

"Seen any taxis?" he asked, but the man just ignored him.

With most of his energy spent, Troy finally reached the front door and rested with his hands on both knees. He stared up at the immense climb he was about to undertake. His lungs were at bursting point and one alert passer-by asked if he needed an ambulance.

"No, it's okay, I've just ran all the way from the bank over the road," he said in between breaths. "I'll be alright in a minute."

A minute was a bit optimistic though, as he usually needed half an hour recovery time if he even took a dump, never mind run the marathon as he just had. But dawdle he could not, not if Ron needed him. With new grit and determination that only newfound love could provide, Troy pushed on and into the building.

Once in the reception area, Troy went unchallenged, with even the office security guards looking over at the chaos happening outside. That suited Troy, because his track record with security guards was awesome, and he could do without having to explain to them that he was already with somebody. He'd hate to be the bearer of bad news.

He spotted a sign which read 'stairway'. It was just across the foyer and through a set of blue fire doors. Troy pushed on through and found himself staring at a site map. First floor, telesales. Second floor, secretary of state and on and on it went. All the way up to nineteen, where veterans of the Vietnam War ran a global charity for stuck records.

Troy felt a hot flush coming on and let out a cry as if he'd been kicked in the knackers. "NNNNNNineteen?" he shouted, his face a picture of agony as he tried to comprehend the climb he was facing.

"That's the spirit, lad," said one passing war veteran from that very floor, though Troy had no idea what the old boot was on about.

They say the journey of a thousand miles begins with a single step. Well, Troy Fassbender had just begun his very own mammoth quest, an ascent to greatness. On and on he climbed, lungs bursting with pain, calves weak with lactic acid and knees screaming in agony and yet he never stopped moving. He had to get to Ron, had to somehow help him defuse that bomb. He just hoped his burning lungs would hold out.

After what seemed like an age and weary from battle, Troy reached a water fountain from which flowed delicious cool water. It was situated on the mezzanine level between the basement and floor one and Troy was absolutely knackered. With glugs of fluid taken on board, an amount of which would make a camel proud, Troy continued with his climb to level one. It was going to take everything he had.

The sound of the ice-cream van's chime filled the streets and instantly put a smile on the faces of everyone it passed. Pensioners waved, dogs wagged their tails and children ran after Little Mo in order to taste his wares. Sometimes Mo pretended he couldn't see the chasing little scamps and drove on a little further on purpose. He was always amazed at how they never gave up. It seemed a child, with a fist full of copper, would run through hell and high water for a ninety-nine. Nature's way of keeping them slim, like a bee who must work for the pollen. It could make you philosophical being an ice-cream man and Mo was absolutely loving it. For the first time in a long while, he was seeing the world for what it was, beautiful. He had so much to live for.

Mo swung a right and headed for the town centre. There he noticed a huge assembled crowd gathered next to the impressive Victorian town hall. There were thousands of people gathered. Mo hadn't seen a crowd this big, gathered outside the Town Hall since Bruce Rioch's boys won back to back promotions straight from liquidation. Although, he seemed to remember the celebrations hadn't lasted long as the Boro were relegated the season after. Best strike while the iron's hot, he thought, and clicked his chime on extra loud. The music blasted out from grey plastic speakers and Mo gleefully bobbed his head to the rhythm. He never got sick of that music, and doubted that he ever would.

As he neared, he saw the faces of concern on the people in the crowd disappear as they saw the mobile frozen treat man arrive.

If only President Bush had driven one of these down the main streets of Baghdad and up to the palace, thought Mo. The world would be a much more peaceful place to live in.

With the crowd swelling and Mo unable to move his van any further, he applied the handbrake and sat with the engine ticking over, by the side of the road, directly outside the CNE tower.

Lots of hands, all full of money, reached toward him, through his van window and faces beamed back at him as he passed ice-cream after ice-cream back to the masses. It wasn't quite bread and fish, but feeding the five thousand was certainly the challenge.

If only Penelope could see him now.

Troy reached the nineteenth floor a triumphant man, although that hadn't lasted long when he realised the rooftop he was actually seeking was another floor up from the one he was standing on. He made sure he grumbled every step of the way. Once he arrived, he was presented with two options, one, lie down and go to sleep, it was all the strength he had left to do, or two, walk through another fire door marked 'Rooftop' and stand side by side with Ron.

At this point, Troy wasn't bothered what the outcome was. He was so pissed off that he'd climbed all this way, only to hear an ice-cream van outside far below. He flipped a coin and let the gods decide. "Tails… bollocks."

Troy staggered back to his feet and pushed through the door and, after momentarily allowing his eyes to readjust to the bright sunlight, finally clapped eyes on brave Ron. The climb had been worth it after all.

"Troy, what are you doing here?" asked Ron, spinning around quickly when he mistook Troy's heavy breathing for that of a moose with asthma.

"I couldn't leave you to do this alone, not up here, not like this. What if something were to go wrong and I never set eyes on you again?"

"But, Troy, I told you specifically to stay where you were. Look at you, you're exhausted," said Ron, holding Troy at arm's length to see if he was alright.

"Don't tell me you weren't a bit out of breath climbing all those stairs. There must be over a thousand," puffed Troy with genuine reason to be tired.

"Climb? Why didn't you just take the lift?" asked Ron, a statement that caused Troy to spew on his shoes.

"Is there a problem?" asked a man with a clear, silky voice from somewhere behind Troy.

"Maybe," answered Ron, never once taking his eyes off or removing his grip from Troy.

"I thought there might be, especially when I received your 'bandages' message."

Ron simply nodded to confirm he understood.

"I told you not to come here, Troy, I practically begged. But no, you had to, didn't you?" There was genuine concern in Ron's voice now.

"But I wanted to help you," answered Troy, his eyes all swollen and puffy as the raw emotion of the situation gravitated towards its conclusion.

"Can't you see what you've done, don't you realise what's going to happen now? Oh, Troy, the plan was so perfect. Faultless, in fact. Years of planning, years of putting myself in a monotonous nine to five world, just so one day I could pull off the world's greatest heist and live like a king." Ron ran his fingers through his hair, trying to find an answer that wasn't there.

"I don't understand," said Troy, blinded by deceit and stupidity.

"What he's a trying to say," said the voice, much closer this time, and placing a hand on Troy's slumped shoulder, "is that you weren't part of our plan. Good a morning, son."

"Morning, dad," responded Ron.

Troy looked up and saw the face of fast food legend, Parmo Pete, and although he wasn't dressed in his white chef coat with blue chequered pants, there was no mistaking that terrible curly moustache, or that fake Italian accent.

Ron stepped aside so his father could address Troy. Pete's aura of celebrity was so big, that it almost rendered Troy speechless and his natural instinct was to step away like a star struck teenager, putting distance between him and the famous face of the Parmo King.

But with every backward step he took, Parmo Pete narrowed the gap with his own step forward, and soon Troy found himself with nowhere left to go, the back of his legs catching the narrow wall on the edge of the tower roof. He gulped as Parmo Pete finally closed the gap.

"You," he prodded at Troy's chest, "are a proving to be a quite a troublesome young man."

Troy was unable to answer. He was too busy looking at what Pete held in his hand to speak.

"But I wonder, can you be a trusted?" Parmo Pete turned toward Ron for advice, but he in turn could only glance away.

Ron knew how close he'd come to screwing the whole operation up, and deep down he also knew the outcome of this rooftop meeting. He should never have gotten too close to Troy. Sure he liked him, but playing him along the way he did was just unprofessional. The fact was, it was a total freak accident that Troy was stood on that rooftop now. He was never once part of the planning.

Ron turning his head away was all the evidence that Parmo Pete needed. He had after all, received a distress signal from Ron, who must have known this ending was possible. He then turned back to Troy.

"You look tired. Here, sit on the wall and have a rest," said Pete, patting the top of the wall with his right hand, showing warm affection toward the shell-shocked Troy.

Troy did as instructed, more out of respect for what Pete was holding in his left hand than anything else.

"Here, I made this for you," said Pete, reaching out his hand and presenting a deliciously hot twelve inch, Chicken Parmesan.

Troy's senses went into overdrive. His eyes lit up as big as saucers, and his mouth started salivating like a George Foreman grill.

Pete didn't hand it over straight away, instead he swung it to and fro, like a hypnotist might a gold watch. Back and forth it went, as did Troy's eyes which were firmly glued to the heart attack in a box treat.

For a few minutes, Pete toyed with his prey, until finally he was beaten by the time. Becoming bored with the cat and mouse game, he tossed the Parmo high into the air, with just enough trajectory so that it would sail just out of Troy's grasp.

Troy watched as the box, now airborne, passed straight over his head and headed out over the rooftop wall. It spun, head over tail and seemed to hang in the air as if taunting him, but nothing ever came between him and his food. He leaned out backwards over the wall and flung out an outstretched arm. He was right on the limit of his balance, at the crossroads of life and death itself, any further and he would topple, any less and the Parmo would evade his clutches.

Ron could only watch on helplessly as the Parmo in a box bounced around on Troy's fumbling fingers. It hit him on the hand several times as he fought the evil clutches of gravity. He juggled with it for several seconds, sometimes hitting it back up toward the sky, willing it to fall a little closer. It was a great battle, played out in slow motion.

Parmo Pete with the wry smile, Ron with a look of sheer horror, but it would be Troy who wore the victorious smile as the succulent Chicken Parmo with extra béchamel sauce, tumbled again, finally coming to rest in his clutched hand. It was the second best thing Troy had ever achieved in his life, but he had underestimated its weight. It was an extra-large Parmo, meant for sharing, and the extra hundred grams of cheddar cheese was all it took for the gravitational pendulum to swing. Still clutching the box in his hand, the extra load dragged Troy off the wall and he plummeted toward the onrushing ground, twenty floors below.

Parked directly outside the Central North East tower, Little Mo, the ice-cream man, had just had the best day of his life. Everybody he'd encountered had been so friendly, so loving, and what's more, nobody had said a single bad word about his height. He sat perched in his little serving hatch and pulled himself an ice-cream, and as he licked it, he thought back to how quickly his life had turned around. How that wonderful person Penelope Stevenson had helped him crawl out of the blackness? He thought long and hard about the dark place his mind used to take him and about what bright future his life may hold now. Fortune favours the brave, or so they say. Well Mo was certainly going to be that from now on. No more negative thoughts from him, no more being in the doldrums, all that had ever achieved was more bad luck and he'd had enough of that to last two lifetimes. Mo smiled as he recalled how things would often hit him on the head whenever he felt down. That was his case in point here. As long as he had blue sky thinking, nothing would ever hit him on the head again. And as if to prove that point, he looked up to the clear autumn sky above and saluted it with his ninety-nine ice-cream.

Troy hit terminal velocity around the tenth floor and, with an imminent sense of doom, shoved that extra-large bite of Parmo in his mouth. No way was he dying on an empty stomach.

Seconds later, he crashed through the roof of a parked ice-cream van and pulverised the head of the poor guy inside. Whoever said eating fatty food was bad for you, had proven their point, as both unfortunate souls died instantly. Confusion reigned in Middlesbrough town centre as the police not only had to contend with a bank robbery, but also two unidentified dead bodies.

The crowd, appalled by the shocking scenes that lay before them, grew in morbid fascination as each fought with one another to get video footage of the carnage.

With seemingly no space left for even standing in, an explosion ripped the sky.

BOOOOOOOM.

Everybody who was there that day looked skywards as the noise from an unknown location echoed in and around the town centre buildings. The crowd cooed and sighed as rumours started in the first milliseconds as to what could have caused such a blast. With every word uttered and every breath inhaled, truth serum was silently working itself into every pore and, with every passing moment, the makings of a riot grew nearer.

"What was that?" was the most common question asked, but that was soon followed by other, not so obvious questions. As is common with truth serum, these questions were answered with blunt honesty.

Not everybody wants to hear the truth, not when it involves lies and deceit or robbery and gluttony. But that's what was happening now. The more the crowd didn't want to hear, the angrier they became and soon the fighting started and the police were completely overrun.

"Beautiful, isn't it, son?" said Pete, looking down at the chaos unfolding below.

"It certainly is, dad," replied Ron, opening the phone he had kept from Troy's Picton house. "Even more beautiful when they trace this text back to a dead man's home."

Pete ruffled his son's hair, although Ron would never be able to return the favour. Nobody was allowed to touch his dad's greasy Italian hair, not even Fabrizio Ravanelli, the Italian goal getter, who used to lift his shirt over his head to prove he never ate Parmos. It wasn't just the locals who learned of their ability to destroy abdominal six packs.

With a global text message sent to everybody in the carnage below, it wasn't long before the first replies came in. Bank details and money transfers suddenly began to fill an offshore bank account. The two crafty criminals, on top of the CNE tower, were seemingly the richest men in England as they plotted their retreat in earnest.

About two hundred metres away, Rob and Jesus were preparing to hand themselves over to the police. There was no doubting they'd spend a few days in police custody, especially given Jesus's previous history of firearms, but the truth was they were totally innocent of any wrongdoing. Their faith in the justice system would surely be tested, but given that they could explain the complicated story that had unfolded around them, and the fact that they had the real culprits locked in a cage, they guessed a slapped wrist would be the worst outcome they'd face and maybe two hundred Actual Bodily Harm charges.

That assumption was to prove absolutely correct.

Two days later, both Rob and Jesus walked from Middlesbrough police station, arm in arm together as free men.

"Well, that was a strange set of circumstances, wasn't it, son?" said Jesus, noticing Rob hadn't said anything since being freed.

Rob nodded quietly in agreement.

Jesus ground to a halt outside the Bongo and faced his son.

"What is it, son? What's troubling you?" he said, compassion in his voice. It had, after all, been a traumatic few days. But at least Jesus was used to jail. He'd never even considered the impact on his poor adolescent robot, who was struggling to come to terms with his new, uncharted emotions.

"Oh nothing, dad. It'll wait," said Rob, but Jesus wasn't prepared to let the emotions fester. From now on, he'd be a better father and listen to the troubles of his son, regardless of the time and place.

"Son, I don't want you bottling up anything anymore, you understand?"

Rob nodded that he did.

"If you have anything on your mind, anything at all, you must tell me, okay?"

"Well, I didn't want to say anything, especially this soon after what's just happened," said Rob, "but now that you've asked… I was wondering if I could have a big set of hairy balls. I've seen a nice pair of size four Mitre Deltas in Jack Hatfield's."

Jesus stared at Rob in horror. "Oh, fuck off, son."

35223666R00164

Printed in Poland
by Amazon Fulfillment
Poland Sp. z o.o., Wrocław